THE POLICEWOMEN'S BUREAU

A NOVEL

THE
POLICEWOMEN'S
BUREAU

A NOVEL

EDWARD CONLON

ARCADE PUBLISHING • New York

JUN 2 7 2019

First Edition

This is a work of fiction. Names, characters, places, and incidents are either the products of the author's imagination or used fictitiously.

Arcade Publishing books may be purchased in bulk at special discounts for sales promotion, corporate gifts, fund-raising, or educational purposes. Special editions can also be created to specifications. For details, contact the Special Sales Department, Arcade Publishing, 307 West 36th Street, 11th Floor, New York, NY 10018 or arcade@skyhorsepublishing.com.

Arcade Publishing® is a registered trademark of Skyhorse Publishing, Inc.®, a Delaware corporation.

Visit our website at www.arcadepub.com.

10 9 8 7 6 5 4 3 2 1

Library of Congress Cataloging-in-Publication Data

Names: Conlon, Edward, 1965- author.
Title: The policewoman's bureau: a novel / Edward Conlon.
Description: First Edition. | New York: Arcade Publishing, [2018] | Includes
    bibliographical references and index.
Identifiers: LCCN 2018059388 (print) | LCCN 2018061582 (ebook) | ISBN
    9781948924085 (ebook) | ISBN 9781948924078 (hardback)
Subjects: LCSH: Detectives—New York (State)—New York—Fiction. |
    Criminal investigation—New York (State)—New York—Fiction. | New York
    (N.Y.)—Fiction. | BISAC: FICTION / Biographical. | FICTION / Crime.
Classification: LCC PS3603.O5413 (ebook) | LCC PS3603.O5413 P65 2018 (print)
    | DDC 813/.6—dc23
LC record available at https://lccn.loc.gov/2018059388

Jacket design by Brian Peterson
Jacket photograph: iStockphoto

Printed in the United States of America

For my nieces—

Elizabeth Conlon
Delia Conlon
Anna Conlon
Eleanor Conlon
Caroline Conlon
Lauren Pacicco
Annabella Timpanaro
Maryjane Timpanaro
Grace Conefrey

AUTHOR'S NOTE

*T*he Policewomen's Bureau is a work of fiction based on the life of my late friend, Marie Cirile-Spagnuolo, and was written with her permission and cooperation. I was drawn to her story through her memoir, *Detective Marie Cirile*, and decided to adapt it as a novel over the course of our long talks. Both of us were detectives in the NYPD, though in different eras. Marie was appointed in 1957, and she was at my retirement party in 2011, three months before she died. The affinities between us were peculiar and deep. She'd lived a few blocks away from where I grew up, in Yonkers, and our families attended Mass at the same parish. Her husband, Sid, retired from the 44th Precinct, in the South Bronx, where I was a detective, and cops I worked with remembered him.

The first question most readers will ask is "How much of it is true?" The short answer: Most of it, and the worst of it. It was hard for me to make sense of what she went through. Though we had much in common, Marie was an outsider and a trailblazer, an Italian in an Irish police department, and a woman in a man's world. The indignities she suffered, on the job and off, were experiences I could only imagine. And so, I decided to relate them with as little imagination as possible, relying on her versions of events and her emotional reactions to them. Whether this loyalty to the facts, or to my friend, represents a disloyalty to the reader, I can't say. But I do know that she wasn't crazy for believing and behaving as she did.

At the same time, when Marie and I talked about this book, I told her I wanted the freedom to invent anything that might improve the story. She told me, "Go for it, kiddo." I went for it.

Despite the title, this isn't a "cop book." It isn't a thriller or a whodunit. Though Marie saw more than her share of action, and solved more than her share of cases, no crime is as important as the character, how she changed in the changing times. How Marie became herself is the only mystery that matters, and this novel doesn't solve it.

"'I could tell you my adventures—beginning from this morning,' said Alice a little timidly: 'but it's no use going back to yesterday, because I was a different person then.'

'Explain all that,' said the Mock Turtle.

'No, no! The adventures first,' said the Gryphon in an impatient tone: 'explanations take such a dreadful time.'"

—Lewis Carroll,
Alice's Adventures in Wonderland

PROLOGUE

Six women sat on a row of metal folding chairs backed up against a wall. All in their twenties, dark-haired, in bulky black sweaters, dark blue skirts extending below the knee. All white, against a white wall. None too tall or short, too fat or thin. All alike, or enough alike, at least to a stranger. That was the way these things were done. A man watched the women through mirrored glass from a dim and narrow hallway. Another man stood beside him, watching him watch. The second waited for the first to say something. When nothing was said, he asked, "See anyone you like?"

"I don't—it was quick," the first man said. He sounded less uncertain than unimpressed. "The sweaters make them—she looked much nicer. Little black dress."

There was another woman with the men, standing behind the one who asked the question. *See anyone you like?* She wouldn't have put it that way. She knew what he meant, but the other man didn't seem to, and the point was to make him understand. She considered saying something, then decided against it. She was an inspector, the commanding officer of the Policewomen's Bureau. It was the detective's case, but it was one of her girls who had made it, and she had called in more of them to see it through.

"Not like-like," said the detective, with a hint of strained patience. He was an Irishman with cold blue eyes, gray hair in a crew cut, a Brooklyn accent that rubbed like a dull razor. "Take your time. Look at the faces, not the sweaters. They're all wearing the same thing, so you see what's different about 'em."

"Is she there? She's one of them?"

"That's for you to say."

"They all look so frumpy."

"It's not a beauty pageant," the inspector said. "You're supposed to pick out the lady who stole your wallet, if you recognize her. Did she say anything to you?"

"We were at the bar at the Carlyle," said the man. He was from out of town, a vice president of something, visiting for a convention. Midwestern, tall and thick and fair. "I bump into her, and she says, 'Careful, big fella! It's not rush hour!'"

The man hadn't known he'd been pickpocketed. A female undercover had been observing from the bar, high-signing her backup after the slick-fingered missy caromed into a stockbroker, spilling her gin fizz on his pinstriped lapels. His billfold had been tossed aside before she was cuffed, but the Midwesterner's wallet was in her purse. They had two cases—two half-cases, one without evidence, the other without a witness, at least so far.

The detective leaned in to a microphone. "Number One, would you please stand up, take a step forward, and say, 'Careful, big fella! It's not rush hour!'"

On the other side of the glass, the woman in the first seat did as instructed, moving slowly—reluctantly, it seemed—and speaking in a list-less monotone. "Careful, big fella. It's not rush hour. "

The Midwesterner made a face of uncertain disapproval, as if smelling milk that was about to go sour. Again, the detective called into the micro-phone. "All right, Number One, sit down. Number Two, same thing."

The second rose, trembling. Her arms were rigid, her fingers splayed wide. She could have been standing at the edge of a gangplank. Her mouth gaped like a goldfish, but no words emerged. The inspector wondered how guilty she'd look if she'd actually done anything wrong. The detective urged her on. "Come on, now."

When the third woman leaned over to tug her hem, she jumped up and screeched, "Watch out for the train!"

"No, not her, poor kid," said the man. "Not the first one, either."

"Okay, Number Three. Take your time, and speak up. Number Three?"

The third woman didn't suffer from stage fright. If anything, she seemed too eager for the spotlight. She put a hand on her hip, tossed her head back, and nearly sang, "Get out of my way, big guy, I'm late for the train!"

The detective corrected her, "'Be careful, big fella! It's not rush hour!'"

The woman seemed cross. "Isn't that what I said?"

The man leaned over to the detective. "No, it's not her."

"If you want," the third woman said, "I can do it again. I can—"

"Nuh-uh," said the Midwesterner. "Too—I dunno. I bet her husband has his hands full with her, though. Is she married?"

"That's enough, that's fine," the detective said, rather abruptly. "Number Four? Again, the line is, 'Be careful, big fella! It's not rush hour!'"

The inspector wasn't pleased. Yes, a lineup had to follow a script as old as vaudeville, but none of the assembled understood their parts. The Midwesterner could have been picking out pastries at a bakery counter, and the women were like a motley lot of schoolgirls drummed into auditioning for a school play. The first sullen as a delinquent, the second scared silly, the third believing she was already a star. Would it get worse? Not better, anyway: Number Four rose from her seat as if she were in the fourth grade at St. Rose of Lima and Sister John Margaret had chosen her to lead the Pledge of Allegiance, loud and clear: "Be Careful! Big Fella! It is not rush hour!"

The inspector didn't disagree with the review: "Eh."

And then Number Five rose and stepped forward. There was an ease in her voice, sexy in its offhand confidence, and she delivered the line as if no one had said it before, unforced and unfussy: "Be careful, big fella! It's not rush hour!"

The man bellowed his approval, "That's her! That's definitely her!"

The detective looked at the inspector and winced. He turned to the man. "Why don't you wait for the last one, we're not finished—"

"That's her! I'd know her anywhere!"

"Hang on, just wait—"

"We're finished, Detective," the inspector said. She spoke into the microphone. "Thank you, ladies. That's all."

As the six women began to take off their sweaters, the man paid even closer attention. Vaudeville had become burlesque. His eyes were still on them when he asked the detective, "That's her, right? The one who robbed me?"

He took out a handkerchief to mop his brow and didn't wait for a reply. "It took me a minute. I've never had anything to do with cops before— Don't get me wrong, I have nothing but the highest regard—but once I saw her, I just knew. I'd never forget—"

The case had been lost, mostly. Two felonies would become a misdemeanor—Grand Larceny in the Third Degree cut down to Criminal Possession of Stolen Property in the Fifth—and then discounted again to next to nothing when the judge heard the case. The women pulled off their sweaters as if they were lice-ridden. Were they? The inspector made a mental note to inquire. The Midwesterner gasped as the differences between the women were revealed. One through Five were positively parochial, in white cotton blouses and crossover ties, navy blue wool skirts. Number Six had a figure like an hourglass, and it was sheathed a blue-black cocktail dress. She looked as if she should be sipping gin fizzes at the Carlyle, which is what she'd been doing a few hours before.

The man shouted, "I wanna change my answer! It's Number Six! Shit, now I see it. Pardon my French! Who are—what are the other ones? Meter maids?"

"They're policewomen," the inspector said.

"Really? Seriously? What do they do?"

"Not nearly enough."

Four policewomen picked up their sweaters and began to leave. Number Five took out handcuffs from a pouch on her belt and beckoned Number Six to cross her wrists behind her back. *Click-click.* It was done correctly, the inspector observed, but the commanding presence was gone; the policewoman seemed smaller, vaguer, a little timid, as if she were asking a favor of the woman instead of taking custody of her. The shift was interesting, and all the more impressive to think of her as a shy girl who had risen to the occasion. One of the new ones. Marie? Yes, that was her name. She could blend in or stand out. She knew how she needed to be seen.

"Still, that Number Five, she's got something," the Midwesterner said, turning to leave.

"I think you're right," the inspector replied.

ONE

A DOUBLE LIFE

1 YOU HAVE YOUR UPS AND DOWNS

Today, tomorrow, next week, we'll pose as hostesses, society girls, models. Anything and everything the department asks us to be. There are two hundred and forty-nine of us in the department. We carry two things in common wherever we go: a shield—called a "potsie"—and a .32 revolver. We're New York's finest. We're policewomen.

—Beverly Garland as Patricia "Casey" Jones
Pilot episode of *Decoy*

JUNE 12, 1958
2330 HOURS

Policewoman Marie Carrara had a feeling something meaningful had happened, but she'd be damned if she knew what it was. The ID procedure in which she had just taken part was an age-old ritual of the law, solemn as a sacrament, but the whack-a-mole chorus line reminded her of a vaudeville gag. Marie didn't know what to make of it, or of the girl marching down the stairs in her handcuffs, two steps ahead. She'd first seen the café society stowaway an hour before, when she'd been called for the lineup. Now she had to while away a weary night with her, filling in for the station-house matron whose kid had tonsillitis. Still, Marie was giddy, and she struggled to not let it show. *Careful, big fella!* She was better by far than the other policewomen. Whatever was happening on the other side of the mirrored glass stopped cold when she stood up and spoke. That was a good thing, wasn't it? For a few seconds, she felt so wonderfully different that it was as if she'd tried on eyeglasses for the first time, or shoes that fit.

When they reached the bottom of the stairs, the girl stopped and turned with a shy half-smile. "How did it go?"

3

"I dunno," Marie replied. "But the detective sounded disappointed. That's good for you, I guess."

It was as if they were friendly rivals, auditioning for the same part. Could it be that this was the first lineup for both of them? The girl wasn't much younger than Marie—twenty-five?—but she was top-heavy like a pinup taped to a GI's locker, and her frock must have cost more than the eighty-six bucks Marie took home for her week's pay.

"Does that mean I'm getting out?"

"I wish I could tell you," said Marie. No one had explained anything to her. She was new at this, and she didn't know whether to believe the older policewomen who told her to pretend to be terrifying to prisoners or the ones who told her to pretend to be chummy. Like nice nuns and mean nuns, and both orders discouraged chitchat until it was safe to talk. The stair landing led to the precinct lobby, and the grim little hallway with the female cells was less than ten steps away. Two cops staggered in, on either side of a slobbering giant in a shredded, blood-soaked T-shirt. The giant howled, *"We were on the same bowling team!"*

Marie nudged the girl forward. The hall with the cells had one working yellow bulb out of the three in the cobwebbed ceiling, and it reeked of bleach and pee. Gray-green paint flaked from dank walls. Marie guided her prisoner into the cell, uncuffed her, shut and locked the door. *Clang, click.* Inside were a cot, a sink, a toilet. The girl looked like an orphan when she pressed her face against the bars. "Are they letting me go?"

"I don't know. I don't know what you're charged with," Marie said. Now that they were settled, the kooky, kicky feeling came back. She'd *done* something tonight, whatever it was. She'd never arrested anyone before, but she tried not to let it show. She was familiar with the theory if not the practice. "What did the officer tell you?"

The girl's expression darkened. "They say I took a guy's wallet."

"Well, he didn't pick you out, so that's good," Marie replied, her tone measured. She sat in the rickety metal chair that would be her post until dawn. "Did you have the wallet when they arrested you?"

"I found it at the bar," she grumbled, though she didn't seem to believe it herself. "I was on my way to the lost and found—I don't even know why they stopped me."

"Huh."

The girl had receded into the gloom. Marie felt as if she were advising a lovelorn caller on her radio show.

"That lady at the bar, she was eyeballing me," the girl mused. Her voice lowered then, her tone hardening. "I took her for a dyke."

Marie didn't care for that kind of talk, but the suggestion that a female undercover might have taken part in the caper thrilled her. She pictured a lady agent in an off-the-shoulder evening gown, a transmitter concealed amid the diamonds of her necklace. At a gala in the ballroom of the Plaza Hotel, maybe; maybe there were Russian spies. A clarinet began to croon the opening bars of "Begin the Beguine"—

"Do the cops have gals like you doing sneaky shit like that?"

Marie was so caught up in the reverie that she barely heard the profanity. "Oh, yes!" she exclaimed. "Not a lot—most of us are stuck on matron duty for twenty years. But one day, I'm gonna be out there, like them."

A water bug the size of a sore thumb skittered down the hall. Marie winced and exhaled. *Someday*—but not tonight.

"You were so good in the lineup," the girl said. "'Careful, big fella!' Did you ever think about acting?"

"Oh, you know, just daydreaming. Once, in school—"

The girl cut her off. "Oooh, sorry, but I have to go. Gimme some toilet paper, wouldja?"

Marie opened a dented tin cabinet and took three sheets of newspapery tissue from a roll. The girl sounded hurt when she took them. "Thanks, but—three? I'm not feeling well. Could you just give me the roll?"

Marie hesitated. She felt bad for the girl, but the rules were the rules. "I'm only supposed to give you three at a time."

The girl groaned and swayed, stamping her feet as if struggling to hold it in. "Please! It's embarrassing to have to ask."

Marie was embarrassed, too, and she handed the roll through the bars. Was the three-sheet rule really a *rule*? She'd never seen it written down. She closed the door to the precinct lobby for privacy and moved her chair down to the next cell. She was grateful there was only one bulb in the hall. It wouldn't matter that she'd forgotten to bring something to read.

Marie hummed a tune to cover the splashing noise from the cell. *When they begin the beguine, it brings back the sound of music so tender*—Da-da, da-da-da-da-da. What in God's name was a beguine? The toilet flushed, but Marie barely heard it. She was trying to get back to the Hotel Astor. She'd been out of the police academy for six months, and she'd only done matron duty so far, aside from a few stray days on other assignments. Once, she helped detectives with an Italian burglary suspect, translating the interrogation. She'd been thrilled to do her bit, but the detective later told her that the perp was from Newark, not Salerno, and he'd only been playing dumb. There was the weekend at the beach at Coney Island, where she was supposed to be a reassuring figure if she came across any lost children. That was a change of scenery, at least, but she broiled in her heavy woolens, and several mothers seemed to take her for a free babysitter, dropping off junior—*Just for a minute, I swear!*—and strolling back hours later. Matron duty was better than DOA runs. It was considered inappropriate for a patrolman to search a female corpse. There had been a couple of stinkers. The toilet flushed again.

Marie was in awe of her boss, Inspector Melchionne, whose hand-picked gals were out and about doing all kinds of interesting things. There weren't a lot of them—thirty, maybe, out of two hundred and fifty policewomen—working pickpocket cases and con games, and detectives borrowed them for robbery stakeouts and drug buys. Just yesterday, there was a story in the paper about the one who locked up the Gypsy fortune-teller who swindled three spinster sisters from Flatbush out of their life savings; last week, another nabbed a would-be models' agent in Brooklyn who took plaster casts of girls' chests, claiming it was standard procedure: "All the major brassiere companies insist!" The headline was funny, if a little fresh: BUSTED! Marie had been in the papers when she was in the academy. She had the clip framed—a beautiful shot of her and her husband, Sid, beneath the caption "Two Cops in Every Family?"

The inspector was said to be fanatical in her attention to publicity. It was rumored that she approved every script for the new television program *Decoy*—the first cop show starring a woman, with opening credits that proclaimed, "Presented as a tribute to the Bureau of Policewomen, Police Department, City of New York." And policewomen were popping up on TV quiz shows like *Twenty-One* and *Dotto* and *Treasure Hunt*. Marie had wondered what consolation the public might take from learning that Policewoman Claire Falhauber knew so many state capitals, and then she realized that most people didn't know that policewomen existed. Marie hadn't herself, until recently.

Six months on matron duty. She didn't know how long it would be before she got a chance to do something else. It wasn't as if she'd get better at her job if it consisted of sitting down and doing nothing. She couldn't really say she was learning anything. And then she felt something at her feet. She heard the toilet flush again, and again. She looked down and saw the flood. *What was this?*

"What did you do?" Marie sputtered, clambering up on her unsteady chair.

The girl screeched and cackled, gripping the bars as if she might collapse from laughing. "That's for when you make the big leagues, honey! I'll never forget your face!"

WHEN MARIE DROVE home to the Bronx that morning, she didn't want to think about work. Her mind was as empty as the Sunday-morning streets when she arrived. It didn't really have a name, her neighborhood. The houses on her block were low-slung brick boxes, attached two by two— "mother-daughters," as they were called, accurately in her case. Most of the houses had some Jewish or Catholic testimonial, a mezuzah over the door, or a concrete saint in the yard. Mama had an elaborate shrine to St. Anthony of Padua in the back. Every year on his feast day, in June, there was a big party, prayers, a *processione*. When Marie was little, Mama got sick. Every doctor Papa took her to, they didn't know what it was. "Maybe some infection." "Maybe cancer." "Maybe you need to find a new wife, this one, she's not going to last." Mama had long black hair, down to her behind. She cut it off and wove it into braids, like lace, and she made a new frame for the picture of St. Anthony on the wall. She sent it to Italy, to the orphanage of St. Anthony of Padua. Did the orphans care that a lady in America cut her hair? Did God? She got better, though. All Marie knew was that Mama loved St. Anthony, and he loved her back.

It was a neither-nor place, stranded between highways. Hundreds of blocks had been bulldozed for the Cross Bronx Expressway, just to the north, and the Bronx River Parkway cut them off to the east. Whole neighborhoods were being paved over in the name of progress. The papers said that people were leaving the Bronx—Brooklyn and Manhattan, too—faster than they arrived, for the first time ever. Another highway had just begun construction to the west, on the far side of the foul wash of the Bronx River, just behind their house. Upstream was a coal-to-gas plant; downstream was a cement factory. Marie couldn't imagine any fish in the river, even the toughest fish, diving in on a dare. She wondered if she'd miss the place. She was willing to try.

There were four Panzarino sisters—Ann, Marie, and Dee, born two years apart, and then Vera, the baby, six years younger than Dee. Ann and her husband, Sal, had moved to Yonkers, following Dee and her Luigi, and Marie and Sid were looking at houses there, too. Vera would likely follow, whenever she got married. Cops were supposed to live within city limits, but that was one of those rules they didn't make much of a fuss about. At times, Papa grumbled about his daughters moving away, even if it was only a twenty-minute drive, but they'd been safely handed over to husbands. His say was no longer final once their names had been changed. He and Mama had traveled farther than any of his children would ever dream of going, and though they had met here in the New World, their marriage had been arranged from the old country. That was the way things were done then.

Marie usually took the subway in, but today she had Sid's car because he was having a Boys' Night in. Her father's venerable black Packard was parked in front, but she could usually find a spot no farther than three or four houses away. Cars filled the neighborhood the same way TVs had, creeping from novelty to normality without anyone really noticing. Everyone had TVs now, almost, outside of the roughest slums. Some said that kids would never leave the house, spending their lives staring pie-eyed at the box, and some said that TV was a godsend, a cure for delinquency, that would draw back the Jokers and Pharaohs and Tomahawks from their street gangs to huddle around Lucille Ball and Jackie Gleason. In the papers, you read that TV meant the end of radio, the end of movies, and the end of reading. You could read columns and letters saying so in the *Daily Mirror,* the *Journal-American,* the *Herald Tribune,* the *World-Telegram and Sun.* There had always been cars, of course, but now almost everyone had one. One of the casual miracles of the age, like the polio vaccine.

Marie mounted the concrete steps and stood beside the potted geranium as she dug into her purse for her house key. An iron rail separated her half of the stoop from Mama's. A twin house, joined side to side. She cast a furtive glance next door, as if Mama were waiting up to yell at her for being late for dinner. She opened her door and called softly, "Hello? It's me! Anybody awake?"

No one answered, but the smell hit her like—well, it hit her. The reek of sweat and ten-cent cigars and sloshed beer from the Boys' Night made her wonder if he'd hosted a prizefight along with a card game. She left the door open and went through the living room to the TV room—it didn't have a name before the TV arrived, as her parents just called it *lag-giù*, "over there"—and yanked open the windows. Even the Bronx River smelled better than the room, and she was glad for the breeze, taking it in for a moment before surveying the damage. Toppled beer cans and an overflowing ashtray covered the coffee table in front of the tatty old couch, and the rabbit-eared TV was tuned in to a test pattern. The living room seemed untouched, as always, with an immaculate white cloth over the table, a china cabinet full of dishes too good to be used. One of the pictures of Italy on the wall—the Leaning Tower of Pisa—hung askew, and Marie straightened it. The kitchen she didn't dare look at. And then—

"Mommy!"

Sandy came barreling out from the kitchen and vaulted into her arms. The crush of four-year-old love nearly made Marie faint. They kissed again and again, and Marie cherished the weight of her in her pink pajamas, the way she stared at her with dark, demanding eyes. Marie stared back, pretending to be angry, knowing that her daughter wouldn't be fooled. She didn't want to think about how late Sandy had stayed up, how much she'd overheard. "Sandy! This place is a mess! Did you have a party here last night?"

"No! Daddy did. They played cards."

"Did he win?"

"I dunno. What's for breakfast?"

Marie took in the horror of the kitchen then, with its littered beer cans and half-eaten sandwiches and still-smoking ashtrays, the coffeepot hissing on the stove. She marched forward and felt the broken glass crunch beneath her feet. *Reee*-verse march! She backed into the living room and set her barefoot daughter down.

"You stay out here, and I'll make you a bowl of cereal. See if cartoons are on."

Sandy was thrilled. "Can I eat in front of the TV?"

"Today's a special day."

"Is it because the place looks like a shithouse?"

Marie glared at her, more-than-half-pretending to be angry, and Sandy lowered her eyes, less-than-half-pretending to be contrite. "Sorry, Mommy."

That would have to do for now, Marie supposed. She went into the kitchen, picked up a towel, and flung the scalding coffeepot into the sink, where it sizzled in the dirty dishwater. She opened the refrigerator and saw the bottle of milk on its side, a white puddle below. Sandy called from behind, "The milkman doesn't come on Sunday, does he, Mommy?"

Marie turned around and forced a smile. "Did I tell you the prayer you say to St. Anthony? He's the patron saint of lost things."

Sandy ran a hand through her bangs with her right hand. Her black hair was in a bob. "I think. Can you tell me again?"

Marie stepped out of the kitchen, swept her up in her arms, and began to spin like a top. "Tony, Tony, turn around, something's lost that can't be found. Tony, Tony, turn around . . ."

After only three turns, she felt dizzy, so she set Sandy down. "But God helps those who help themselves. I'll make eggs."

Two hours later, Marie was dozing on the couch with Sandy in her arms. The house was clean. Some time had passed when Sandy nudged her. "Should I wake Daddy up?"

Marie looked at her watch: 10:10. "Let him sleep."

She must have slept again herself, because she woke when Sandy sat up. Marie heard Sid's heavy tread on the stairs and roused herself. He was in his underwear, his face unshaven and puffy, and he scratched himself as he ambled across the room. He was not having a good morning. Still, the boys called him "Hollywood Sid," and on his bad days he looked better than most on their best: six feet tall, broad-shouldered, built like a light heavyweight. He had thick black hair with a soft curl to it, a profile meant to be chiseled in marble, and a smile that could sell toothpaste. Not that he was smiling now. He surveyed the room and scowled. "Place looks fine. I don't know what you're complaining about."

Marie sat up, reflexively straightening the uniform blouse she still hadn't taken off, running a hand through the mushed side of her hair. *Complaining?* Had she been talking in her sleep? Sandy was still fixated on the TV. Sid stopped at the threshold of the kitchen. "Is it too much to ask for coffee?"

Marie turned off the TV, and Sandy followed her into the kitchen. Sid sat down at the table, and Sandy clambered into his lap as Marie put the kettle on. "You know, hon, the stupid coffeepot is no good. It's the cheap one we got from my cousin at the wedding. All we got is instant."

"If that's all we got, that's all we got." Sid exhaled heavily. He softened as Sandy nuzzled against him. "At least I got one girl who takes care of me."

"Daddy, who locks up more bad guys, you or Mommy?"

"Girls can't be real police, baby," Sid grunted. "It's a rough world out there, full of bad guys. They stay inside, so they can't get hurt."

Marie thought about bringing up the lady undercover at the Carlyle— not to argue with him, just so Sandy would know—but instead she said, "You want me to fry you some eggs or something?"

"Don't bother, I'll go out."

"Don't forget about Mama's later. It's—"

Sid looked at Sandy. "What's up?"

Sandy replied, "It's an extraspecial day for Aunt Vera. There's a boy she likes, and Nonna and Nonno have to see if he's good enough."

Sid laughed, and Marie laughed, and she went upstairs to shower and change. He was gone when she came back down, and she had to turn off the TV again so Sandy could dress for church.

MARIE AND SANDY had gone straight from Mass to Mama and Papa's. It was just like home, but in a mirror: the kitchen and stairs were to the left instead of the right, but the same spaghetti-joint prints of Venice and Rome adorned the walls, the dining room table had the same white cloth, the same china cabinet was filled with never-used dishes. In the living room, her brother-in-law Luigi sat with Papa, who was reading the paper. A public affairs program was on, with two men arguing about building a bus station.

"So, Pop, you mind if I maybe watch the baseball game?"

Papa didn't look out from behind his copy of *Il Progresso.* "Do what you want."

But when Luigi got up to change the channel, Papa growled, "But *la macchina* break, anybody touch."

Luigi hesitated, his hand inches from the dial. "Hey, Pop, me and Dee—I don't wanna spoil the surprise, but we're gonna buy you a new one for—"

"I like this one fine."

Sandy broke the stalemate, bellowing, "Nonno!" as she raced over to hug him. Papa was short and squat, and his feet didn't reach the floor when he sat on the couch. He had hard, small eyes, and a mouth that always looked as if he were about to spit. But he beamed at the sight of his granddaughter and climbed down from the couch. "*Cara mia,* you so pretty today!"

Papa had learned some Yiddish since his arrival, and better English, but he and Mama still spoke Italian at home. Their melodious speech was jarringly spiked with Americanisms, like "traffic jam, bad-bad" and "Buy one, get one free." The four girls picked up English from neighbors, the radio, and at school and mostly spoke it with their parents. Italian questions received English answers; Italian reproofs brought English apologies. The sisters traveled between languages, pulled between the little lost-in-time villages of the *Bel paese* and the big city in the New World.

Luigi was slight and trim, always dressed in the best from his midtown haberdashery, always ready to entertain, like the song-and-dance man he'd once been. Today, the costume was summer suit in pearl-and-gray herringbone tweed, and the show would be a melodrama, it seemed. As they embraced, he whispered, "Help me, please."

"Easy, kiddo. Is he being a pill?"

Luigi was a gem, but Marie knew that Papa was nervous. He might have to break Vera's heart in a couple of hours. Arranged marriages weren't done in this country, but he and Mama held the final and irrevocable right of refusal over their daughters' suitors. The day would end in banishment or matrimony. This wasn't a family dinner; it was a trial with catering.

"He could haunt a house," Luigi said.

Dee leaned out of the kitchen and barked, "Get the hell offa my husband! He signed the papers, it's too late for him to pick another sister. Get in here, Marie, we got jobs to do. Come on, Sandy, go play in the back, your cousin Anthony is there."

Marie followed into the kitchen, where she was astonished by the abundance of the feast and daunted by the labor required for it: peppers were scorching on the stovetop and mushrooms were being stuffed, focaccia baked, sardines dragged through a plate of flour. Sausages crackled in a pan, and Ann peeked at a pork loin roasting in the oven, poking it for doneness. Mama kneaded semolina dough for the *orecchiette*, rolling out the pasta into tubes, cutting the tubes into nickel-sized slices, pressing the slices into little cups with a stubby, masterly thumb. *Orecchiette* meant "little ears." Vera whacked away at a pile of greens. When Marie was young, weekday dinners were bird-food affairs of *pasta e ceci, o lenticche, o fagioli, o piselli*—pasta with chickpeas, lentils, beans, or peas—with maybe a cheap cut of neck meat for Sunday gravy. They'd been poor then, she thought, and then she thought again: *No! Papa had two houses, his own business delivering coal and kerosene, but money was for saving, not spending.* Funny what you believed as a kid, wasn't it?

Dee ducked as Vera waved the knife and wailed, "Do we hafta do all this? We went on three dates! All this, and I never even kissed—"

Mama barked—"*Basta!*" She didn't know much English, but she knew when the talk was about to turn dirty, at least as far as she was concerned. Mama looked like Papa, small and thick, with the same semipermanent *Don't-even-think-about-it!* expression on her face. She muttered, "*Che stupido.*"

"Come on, honey, it's all gonna work out in the end," said Ann, as she often did, reaching for Vera's wrist to take the knife. Marie shook her head and picked up an artichoke. Poor Ann had to believe that, didn't she? She was so lovely, so soft and sad, with a wonderful job at the UN, and a husband who was a bum. No kids, and the doctor said not to count on any. Marie looked over to Dee, who rolled her eyes before asking, "Where's Sal? Is he coming?"

"Some kinda big meeting he had. He's gonna try to come later."

Marie felt a wicked flicker of conspiracy with Dee, who'd just gotten out of the police academy. They were so alike in so many ways, though Dee had always been more confident and outspoken. Dee had two kids, Anthony and baby Genevieve, who was probably napping upstairs; Marie had only one, but Sandy was all she wanted. They'd taken the test together—it was Dee who pushed her to take it—but Marie had done better and had gone into the class ahead. And then Dee spoiled the alliance by asking, "How about Sid? He coming?"

Marie hated that Dee thought she was like Ann. Dee never liked Sid. Unlike Sal, Sid had a job, for one. He wasn't perfect, but there were plenty worse. She wouldn't let Dee get away with it. "You know he won't miss Mama's cooking. He's probably getting himself all pretty to make his grand entrance."

Mama smiled—she adored Sid—which prompted another eye roll from Dee. "Well, he's not gonna be the star of the show today. It's Vera's—"

Vera had two handfuls of greens and was about to drop them into a bowl when she knocked it onto the floor. It was a wooden bowl, and it landed on the floor with a harmless *Bonk!* But as far as Vera was concerned, it might have been a Ming vase that shattered, with all her dreams of love inside. She screamed, "I'm gonna kill myself, and alla you after!"

Mama bellowed, and Ann took Vera out to the back, to sit down and settle herself at the feet of St. Anthony. Marie dropped her last chunk of artichoke into the lemon water, and Dee took the sausages off the fire. They smelled done.

AT THREE O'CLOCK, everyone milled around the table, eyeballing the platters of *antipast'* on the table: hard *scamorza* cheese and soft *muzzarel,* salami, olives, fresh focaccia bread, crunchy fried artichokes and sardines, fried zucchini flowers stuffed with *rigot,* baked mushroom caps stuffed with sausage. It was only the beginning, and they couldn't begin. Two bottles of heavy, sweet homemade wine were on the table, courtesy of Mama's cousin Ugo. Papa reached for one. "*Sedetevi.* Sit."

Vera pleaded, "Can't we wait, Papa?"

"Three o'clock, you tell him?"

"Yeah, but maybe—"

"This Sunday, no? Not next week?"

"Yeah, but—"

"He got ten minutes." Papa said. "*Sedetevi.* Don't just stand around, like a buncha—I dunno."

Ann touched his hand. "Maybe we should say grace?"

"Why? We can't eat."

"Come on, Papa, you might as well say it now as later."

Papa made the Sign of the Cross, and heads bowed: "*Benedici, Signore, noi e questi tuoi doni, che stiamo per ricevere dalla tua generosità. Per Cristo nostro Signore.*" An awkward silence followed the Amen. Papa checked his watch and shook his head. When he extended his fork toward the mushrooms, Vera shot him a pleading look. The hand was withdrawn.

"So . . . we got two policewomen here," Ann began haltingly, like a comedian dying on stage. "Marie, Dee, anything interesting happen at work?"

"It's matron duty," Dee sniffed. "Babysitting for bad girls. Anything interesting isn't fit conversation for the dinner table."

"You got that right," Marie said, despite thinking, *How long has Dee worked now, two weeks?* Still, she wasn't about to tell about last night's toilet fiasco. "But matron duty isn't all we do. Inspector Melchionne, she's got her best girls doing all kind of crazy assignments. You got pickpockets—"

"And perverts," Dee interrupted. Again. "Some girls work on nothing but. They call it the Degenerate Squad."

Mama covered her ears. "Bah!"

Marie pushed on. "A while back, detectives brought a guy in. He said he didn't speak English, he was from Salerno, and I was the one who talked to him. They said they caught him trying to break into a store—"

Papa barked, "*Madonn'!* A million crooks in New York! Every color, they got crooks. Why the first guy you lock up, he gotta be *italiano?*"

Ann, Marie, and Dee shook their heads, exchanging looks: *You can't win.* Time dragged on until there was a knock at the door. Vera leapt up to answer it, and she couldn't conceal her disappointment when her beau wasn't on the other side. "Shit!"

Sid walked in, shaved and smiling, altogether transformed from the slovenly grump Marie had last seen. With his Ban-Lon shirt in robin's egg blue, he could have just walked off the golf course with Sinatra and the boys. *Ring a ding ding!* One arm was full of flowers, the other bottles of wine, and he didn't miss a beat at the greeting. "Hey! Nice to see you, too, Vera."

"I'm sorry, Sid, it's just—" Vera broke off, stifling a sob.

"What? Loverboy ain't here? Don't worry, maybe there was a subway strike. Hey, Mama!"

"Serafino!" Mama cried out. That was Sid's real name, but no one called him that but her. "*Così bello, come sempre—fiori? Come, la domenica?*"

Sid handed Mama a bouquet of tulips and baby's breath. "I got flowers on a Sunday, Mama, cause there's a florist on my beat, and I chased a guy who tried to stick him up. A Greek, but a decent guy. Lives upstairs, so it's no trouble for him to open up for me. I got some for you, Mama— of course!—and for Vera, and I couldn't forget my wife. Baby, you look gorgeous."

As Sid lowered a bouquet to Marie, she kissed him with fervor, wishing he were always like this. *Boy oh boy, did he know how to make an entrance!* Dee accepted a single lily with an indifferent hand. "It was a florist you went to, not a funeral parlor, right?"

"You're a pistol, you!" Sid laughed, before turning quickly to Papa. "I got you a little *vino.*"

Papa took the bottles from the paper bag and nodded approvingly. "Mmm, from a store. *Sid, apri la bottiglia. Ma ora mangiamo.*"

There would be no more waiting to eat. Everyone was too hungry to feel too sorry for Vera, but conversation was forced and spare. Mama pressed delicacies on Sid—"*Prova le alici, e i carciofi, e il formaggio*"—and Ann mixed compliments to the chef with inadvertent confessions of aching regret. "I try and I try, but I still can't cook like you, Mama. Sal would love this."

Luigi tried next. "A movie star came into the store the other day, Pop. Victor Mature. From *Samson and Delilah. The Robe*? Very religious pictures, very famous guy. He's Italian, his real name is Maturi—"

Vera wouldn't let him go on, captive as she was to other visions of martyrdom. "I just hope nothing terrible happened. But it had to be something terrible, right? He just wouldn't not show up. It'd be terrible if it wasn't terrible."

Marie was almost relieved to hear Sandy intervene. "Know what you should do, Aunt Vera?"

"What?"

That was Marie's question, too. Sandy stood up from her chair and began to spin. "Tony, Tony, turn around! Something's lost that can't be found!"

Papa, Sid, and Luigi laughed, and Marie covered her mouth, so she wouldn't. Vera began to bawl, knocking her chair over as she staggered to her feet. She started to run toward the front door when the telephone rang in the kitchen. She about-faced and ran back, still bawling, to answer it. The other sisters didn't have time to react when Mama stage-whispered, *"Ho fatto un sogno che è morto."*

Marie was horrified. "Mama! Stop!"

Sandy was frightened and looked pleadingly at Marie. "What did Nonna say?"

"Never you mind."

Mama leaned across the table and spoke in painfully clear English. "I have a dream. The boy Vera like, he die."

"Mama, please!"

Sandy began to cry, and then little Anthony followed, howling, and Dee and Luigi got up to hold him. *Why can't we have a regular goddamn dinner like regular goddamn people?* Sid was laughing too hard to help, and Marie was furious at him for a second—mostly at Mama—but before she could get around the table, she heard a scream from the kitchen: "NOOOOOO!"

The older sisters ran to the youngest, galloping in like cavalry. Dee grabbed the phone as Marie and Ann sat Vera down on a chair. She spoke as if in a trance. "A car accident, there was a car accident . . ."

Ann fanned Vera with a napkin while Marie got her a glass of water. On the phone, Dee was crisp and commanding. "This is Policewoman Dee, Vera's sister, with whom am I speaking? I see. Is there any—No, that's fine. Thank you for calling."

Marie admired Dee then almost completely. She'd done everything so splendidly—announcing her title in a Radio Free Europe voice, sticking to her first name so the probably-Irish nurse or probably-Jewish doctor wouldn't be put off by too many operatic vowels by another operatic Italian. The lines were perfectly delivered, and Marie should have been the one to deliver them. Instead, she just stood there.

Vera charged back into the living room. "I have to go to the hospital, I have to see him!"

Marie and Ann corralled her as Papa looked on dispassionately. *"È morto?"*

"No, he isn't dead!" Dee exclaimed. "The worst possible thing doesn't have to happen, every single time! He's in the hospital with a broken collarbone. He was driving here, got hit by a bus—"

"Dio salve il povero ragazzo!" Mama cried, not altogether convincingly. Marie wasn't sure if Mama wanted the poor boy to be saved, since he wanted to take her last daughter away from her.

"I have to go to the hospital!"

Papa wouldn't stand for any more hysterics. "What are you, a doctor? Sit down, eat your food. Big deal! He can come next week."

Vera froze, then obeyed with a sniffle. The women watched her with apprehension as she dabbed at her tears with a napkin; they exhaled with relief when she picked up a fork. Once the shock had worn off, the mood became suddenly festive—it wasn't such terrible news, after all. It was a stay of execution twice over: the boy wasn't hurt too badly in the accident, and Mama and Papa's judgment of him would be delayed for a week, and doubtless softened by what he'd endured in pursuit of their favor. Marie couldn't help thinking of it as a good sign, if not a good thing. When Mama brought out the *orecchiette* with sausage and greens, the talk was lively, and by the time the pork had been eaten, little more needed to be said. The women began to clear the plates, readying the table for coffee and dessert.

"Dov'è la grappa?" Papa asked.

"Hai avuto abbastanza," Mama replied, surveying the empty wine bottles.

"Go get it," Papa ordered. Mama shook her head, but she brought out a Coca-Cola bottle of clear liquor—also the handiwork of Cousin Ugo—and three little glasses for the men. Luigi waved a hand, demurring, but Papa glowered at him, filling his own cup, Luigi's, and Sid's. He raised his glass. "It's okay, Vera. If he love you, I love him. *Amore e famiglia.*"

"To love and family—" Vera wept and hugged him.

Sid raised his glass as well, emotion rising in his voice. "Hey, Pop, that's the sweetest thing I ever heard. You know, I was an orphan—my father left, my mother died, and my brothers were all adopted, except me. Before I met this family—"

Mama swooned, "Serafino . . ."

Marie surreptitiously surveyed the table: Papa, Vera, Ann, and Luigi were moved, visibly; Dee might have heard Sid reciting last week's minor league baseball scores for all the emotion she showed. Sandy was getting sleepy. She asked, "Nonno, was Sunday dinner like this when you were little?"

Papa grunted. "No. We didn't have food."

"What did you eat?"

"He means they didn't have a lot of food. Maybe just the pasta, maybe without the sausage," Marie explained. She turned to Ann, suddenly pensive. "I always wanted to go to Italy. Remember when I won that essay contest for the free trip, from the travel agency?"

But it was Dee who replied, "You said you wanted to go, since you never had a honeymoon."

Sid didn't react, and Marie tensed. Ann rushed to change the subject. "I remember! They gave you passage on the ship, a hotel in Rome for a week—for one person! Some honeymoon!"

"I'd'a been scared to go by myself," Marie said. She felt a little afraid, even saying it.

"That's my wife, the big tough cop," Sid snorted.

Everyone laughed, and Marie was relieved that he wasn't angry. Sandy began to doze, tilting in her chair, and Sid stood and picked her up. He looked at his watch. "Jeez, almost six already. I'll take this one home. I'm a little tired myself, and I got work tomorrow. You stay, relax, help Mama. I'll put her to bed."

"Thanks, honey. You're the best," Marie said.

Sid kissed her, then Mama, before making his exit. The benevolent mood resumed as the last of the almond cookies were eaten. Marie felt entirely stuffed, entirely satisfied, and she topped off her coffee so she wouldn't be tempted to put her head down on the table for a nap. Papa sipped his cordial, and a look of longing filled his eyes. "Why God no give me a son?"

That was the sign for the women to get up and begin to clear the table.

His melancholy after meals wasn't as regular as saying grace before them, but it was a frequent accompaniment to a second grappa.

"I could help in the kitchen," Luigi offered, sliding back in his chair.

"You sit."

MARIE WALKED DOWN the steps and back up, light-headed and light-hearted. She'd survived the night and the day, and now she could sleep and sleep. In the entry of her house, she heard something and stopped, half-whispering, "Hello? Anybody awake?" She looked upstairs and then across the living room, *laggiù*. Ronald Reagan was on TV: "General Electric, where progress is our most important product—" She turned it off and went upstairs. The bathroom door was slightly ajar, and she heard water running in the sink.

Marie cracked the door of the baby's room to peek inside. Not that Sandy was a baby anymore. Still, when she crept in and leaned over to kiss her forehead, she heard the soft music of baby breath, smelled the bakery smell that rose from baby skin. She was not without guilt for missing so many bedtimes. A family with one child could make do on a patrolman's salary, though a house in Yonkers would have to wait. She didn't know whether she dared admit it or dared deny it, but she wanted to work, she needed to, for her own sake. She would have died at home. Before this job, the story of her life hadn't been much of a story at all. Better for Sandy to miss her sometimes than to pity her always.

Marie went to the bathroom and waited at the threshold. "Hey, honey, that was something, wasn't it?"

And then she noticed that Sid was dressed to go out, in a blue sharkskin suit. She was confused. "You going someplace? Now? Where?"

Marie should have known better than to ask. There was no note of rebuke in her voice. He was free to come and go as he pleased, of course. But he wasn't dressed for his bowling league, was he?

In the reflection, she watched him tie a silver necktie into a Windsor knot over a baby blue crepe de chine shirt. Sid refused to turn, or even to catch her eye when he replied, coldly controlled. "You wanna know if I'm going out? You wanna know where? I swear to God, Marie . . ."

"Sorry, honey, it's just that—"

That was a mistake, too. This was not a conversation, or even an argument. He poured a splash of bay rum into a cupped palm, clapped his hands, and slapped his cheeks. "You're right next door! You're not in Italy! Not like you wanted—you never had a honeymoon! Like you're all alone. After all I done for you? I swear to God, Marie, I swear to God."

There was less coldness in his voice, less control, when he turned to her. What had she done? What had she asked that was so terrible? She had to try to find out *something*. She didn't throw out any backtalk. Nothing like, "You live in my family's house without paying rent!" God forbid. *I swear to God, Marie!* Always he said that, and she never, ever knew what he meant, whether he was keeping a promise or breaking one. She had so many questions, but the only one that came out was "Why is it you gotta impress everybody except me?"

She saw the white of his teeth and wished it meant that he was smiling. No, no more a smile than the raised hand would caress her cheek. He feigned a slap, just to make her flinch, then landed a real one when she ducked down. He grabbed her to make her face him before flinging her against the wall. She crashed into a framed picture of St. Anthony and heard the glass break when it hit the floor. She fell down beside it. She knew the prayer she was supposed to say, but she stayed still and kept quiet. Sid crouched down and put his mouth against her ear. "You're nothing without me."

She wanted to say, "Just go," or, "Do what you want," or even, "I'm sorry," but she knew there wasn't a syllable she could utter that he wouldn't construe as a provocation. She shuddered, hunkering down to seem smaller, and kept an arm up over her face. She was so stupid to have said anything.

From Sandy's room, there was a low wail, and then a call, "Mommy?"

Marie didn't move until she heard Sid stand. She hated herself for that.

"Unbelievable. Just unbelievable," he said. She hated herself for waiting to hear him stomp down the stairs, for the door to slam shut, before standing up and running to Sandy. She wiped her tears before she sat on the bed, and she didn't turn the light on. "It's all right, baby, Mommy's home."

"Were you and Daddy fighting?"

"No, baby. I slipped on the stairs."

"Why was he yelling?"

"He was scared I was hurt."

"Where is he?"

"He went to work."

"At night?"

"You know police have to work at night sometimes, baby. We're always here for people, to keep them safe."

In the dark, Marie couldn't see Sandy's face, couldn't tell if the child had fallen for the line. She wasn't sure if she wanted Sandy to believe her. How awful all of this was, all around. *Unbelievable, just unbelievable.* She didn't know what to believe. So many times, she'd tried to understand what he wanted from her, hiding her tears in a room with the lights off. Round after round, she played the game with all her heart, all her mind, but she hadn't a clue what the answer was, and she couldn't begin to guess. Nothing mattered, and nothing would ever change.

2 YOU KNOCK AT THE DOOR

"No one should come to New York to live unless he is willing to be lucky."

—E.B. White

JUNE 16, 1958
1400 HOURS

As Marie walked down the hallway in her pigeon-gray suit with the pencil skirt and matching trilby, white-gloved, faux-pearled, her police shield pinned to a lapel, she wondered what exactly it was she'd dressed up for. Many policewomen dreaded being summoned to Inspector Melchionne's office, with its churchy hush and scent of beeswax polish, and many had reason to fear, if their efforts were lacking, or if there was rumor of any act or attitude that might bring discredit to the bureau. "St. Theresa," she was called, among other things, not always with reverence. Her intimates referred to her as Mrs. M. There had been no hint of reproof when her secretary, Miss Emma Lehane, had called that morning, but Marie's confidence was not at a high point. She'd barely seen Sid since that awful little to-do on Sunday night, and they hadn't spoken. Whatever this interview was about couldn't have anything to do with that. *Could it?* No, and it was unlikely that the goof-up with the flooded cell merited a meeting with a figure as eminent as the inspector herself. The cops at the precinct had laughed when Marie ran out to ask for a mop. She hadn't done anything of significance, good or ill, so it was better to hope than to fret.

Still, Marie quailed when she saw the door with the frosted glass panel. POLICEWOMEN'S BUREAU. Below it, in smaller letters: INSPECTOR THERESA MELCHIONNE, COMMANDING OFFICER. She had never been inside before. *Goodness!* She straightened her posture and thought, *Come on, you're a big girl now! Let's see that brave smile!* She laughed when she recalled she'd said the same thing to Sandy before the kindergarten Christmas pageant. She was about to knock when a policewoman in uniform burst out, eyes brimming with angry tears. She looked at Marie and asked, "What did you do?"

Thankfully, the policewoman closed the door behind her. "What I do on my own time is my own business. I went on one date with the guy! How was I to know he's a bookie? I didn't place a bet!"

Marie could neither agree nor disagree, and the woman brushed past, shaking her head. "It's like she knows everything about you! As far as I'm concerned, St. Theresa can go to hell."

The encounter unsettled Marie, and she waited a moment to collect herself before knocking and going inside. The outer office was sizable, with three policewomen in uniform at a row of desks to the left, typing or talking on the telephone. On the right was a couch, a coffee table with copies of *Look* and *Life*, a vase of gardenias. Ahead was Miss Lehane, at her desk by the door to the inspector's office. She was older, taut and austere, her hair in a bun. She was on the telephone as well—"No, Inspector Melchionne is speaking at a luncheon for the Junior League that day, and at the Regina Coeli Society breakfast before"—but she waved for Marie to take a seat on the couch.

Marie smoothed her skirt and obeyed. She was afraid it would seem cavalier, even presumptuous, to pick up a magazine, and then she lost interest when she looked up at the framed newspaper articles on the wall: "LADY COP NABS PICKPOCKET," "UNDERCOVER MAMA TAKES DOWN SCHOOL DOPE RING," "GAL COP TELLS GYPSY'S FUTURE: JAIL!" Below the headlines were some of the great names of the Policewomen's Bureau: Peg Disco, the tennis champ and mother of five who'd spent years infiltrating the Communist Party for the Bureau of Special Services, rising so far as to head of some kind of Commie committee; "Dead Shot" Mary Shanley, who was no stranger to gunfights; Claire Faulhaber, who had been a college professor before becoming a cop. No wonder she knew her state capitals! She'd gone on the game show after taking down a ring of lady pickpockets who posed as mendicant nuns. Marie was afraid she was gaping, so she sat down and tried not to fidget. She was horrified to see a coffee stain on her left glove, and she covered it with her right hand. Just then, Miss Lehane beckoned her in to see the inspector, and Marie forgot about everything else.

"Hello, Marie. Please, sit down." Inspector Melchionne was seated at her desk, reading through a folder. She was a smallish, plainish woman with dark curls done up in a sensible bob. Was she fifty? No one who saw her pinching tomatoes at the grocery would have taken her for anything but a housewife. For Marie, however, there was no more regal creature east of Buckingham Palace. An Italian, too, when everyone else important was Irish, from the police commissioner to the district attorney to the mayor to the cardinal. She was the sole female in the department of rank, as only men were eligible to be sergeants and lieutenants, captains and beyond. Married but childless, the inspector had a nunnish air, and the propriety of her speech was such that you could picture it written in perfect cursive on a blackboard. The inspector hadn't looked at her yet. "Out of the academy for six months, top of your class, never sick, never late. Mother of a four-year-old daughter, married to Patrolman Scrafino Carrara of the 44th Precinct, sister of Benedetta Visconti, six months behind you in the Policewomen's Bureau."

The inspector paused, evidently expecting some comment. Marie's was minimal: "Dee—that's what we call Benedetta—she's the one who pushed me to take the test. We took it together."

The inspector put the folder down and smiled. "I hope she doesn't mind you got in the class ahead of her! Do you talk about work much around the dinner table?"

The casual manner set Marie at ease. "As a matter of fact, just last Sunday, we were just talking—about not talking about it."

"Well, matron duty isn't the most exciting work," the inspector allowed. "Still, moments do present themselves. I was delighted to hear about your translation efforts for the detectives. And I noticed you again, more recently."

Marie was thrilled. "Really? When? What for?"

"I picked you out of a lineup. Unfortunately, so did the victim," she said. "I wonder if I should have asked your sister, as well. I envy you having a police family, so to speak. They can be a great source of support. At the same time, families are never simple, are they?"

"No, Ma'am," she averred, warily.

"I took the liberty of calling your husband Serafino's commanding officer, to ask a few discreet questions. Would you like to know what I heard?"

The inspector reached down to find a paper in the pile, so she missed it when Marie twitched. "Uh—Sid. Everybody calls him Sid."

"Well, Sid does nothing but brag about you. Your score on the police test, that wonderful article in the paper when you were in the academy— 'Two Cops in Every Family?' He went to a print shop to make copies. I doubt there's a patrolman in the precinct he hasn't told about you."

"Huh."

"In any case, I bring all of this up for a reason. I wanted to get a sense if you would be comfortable with a measure of publicity. I take it you noticed the framed newspaper articles in the waiting room?"

"I thought they were wonderful—"

"I find most of them to be in spectacularly bad taste. They read like submissions to 'Ripley's Believe It or Not.' Still, the press is an absolute necessity for what I hope to accomplish, and backhanded compliments are better than none. Ours is a story that has to be told. Do you think you might want to try one of these assignments?"

Marie nodded with vigor. She'd have been shattered by the rebuke for her enthusiasm about the articles—*Really, if she didn't like them, why did she put them up on the wall?*—but she didn't have time. The inspector slid a sheet of paper across the desk. "Meet Mr. Todd."

Marie read aloud. "'President of the Todd Trust Company, President of Todd Shipyards, President of the Pan American Banking Company, President of the American Corporation of Lawyers Society . . .' Boy, that's a mouthful, that one. Member of nine private clubs. Very impressive."

"Indeed. You could understand how such a distinguished gentleman would need a secretary."

Yes! "I can type. Want me to apply?"

The inspector handed her another piece of paper. "This is from a previous applicant for the position."

Again, Marie read aloud, trying not to rush through it as her excitement mounted. "'Complainant states that at the time and place of occurrence, she responded to an advertisement in the *Herald Tribune* in the 'Help Wanted: Women' section. Asked by the above-listed suspect if she spoke Spanish, she responded that she did not. Complainant states that suspect then . . . free trip to Mexico . . . learn to speak Mexican . . . attempted to disrobe.' What's 'flamingo dancing'?"

"'Flamenco.' It's Spanish."

"I speak Spanish."

"My suspicion is that Mr. Todd has no interest in your abilities."

Marie nearly crowed, "So, I finally made it to the Degenerate Squad!"

"I prefer 'Special Assignments,'" the inspector replied, somewhat curtly. "I don't find the assault of women particularly amusing myself."

"Sorry, Inspector. I hate all the jokes. 'Do you have to be a degenerate to join?'"

The inspector nodded. "With twenty-five thousand policemen here, you'd expect a better joke now and then."

"Are you sure you want me? A lot of the girls talk about how they never get the chance—"

"I've sent three already. One said Mr. Todd had a toothache when she called on him, another said he wasn't home. The third told me that he apparently didn't care for redheads. If you don't succeed, I'll send someone else. Do you want to try?"

"Yes!"

"I don't want you to take any unnecessary risks. The woman in the complaint seems to have made her escape easily enough, but you never know. If Mr. Todd crosses the line, get out of there at once. We'll swear out a complaint with the district attorney and go back for him with patrolmen."

"Got it."

"Just be yourself, as much as you can. The best undercovers stick with one big lie instead of a lot of little ones. I can have you sit down with one of the more experienced policewomen if you—"

"I'm ready to go now."

The inspector didn't stop smiling when she noticed the coffee stain on Marie's glove; instead, she took a fresh pair from her purse and handed them over.

"Welcome to the Degenerate Squad. All the more reason to never appear as anything less than a perfect lady."

MARIE LEFT FOR uptown feeling lucky as a found penny. So what if she was just bait on a hook, a Gal Friday sent for a pickup on Perverts' Row? The confidence shown her was thrilling and steadying at once. The June afternoon was balmy and breezy. Soon enough, the city-summer heat would be upon them with its jailhouse ferocity, and the asphalt would sweat even though the hydrants were open, and the switchblades would glint like fireflies. Not yet: now, Central Park was as sweetly green as Eden. She was with a borrowed partner, in a borrowed car, but she was on her own in the big game, playing for keeps.

Adele was one of the three girls from the inspector's office, a still-cheery veteran of ten years, big-boned as a farm girl, with a wide, oval face. It had been arranged, somewhat laboriously, for them to take an Oldsmobile from the Detective Bureau motor pool for the afternoon. On the drive uptown, Marie learned that Adele was a widowed mother of three from Bensonhurst who would be forty-one years of age next September 12; that her favorite movie star was Lana Turner; and that she assumed Marie was an old hand at these undercover capers. She'd seen Marie's picture in the papers but had obviously forgotten that "Two Cops in Every Family?" was taken in the academy. Famous was famous, wasn't it? Marie resolved not to lie but decided it might jinx things to set her straight.

They were three blocks away from Mr. Todd's apartment when Marie asked Adele to pull over. The car was unmarked, and there wasn't anything coppish about either of them, though Adele was in uniform. Marie had heard stories of men arrested by policewomen who didn't believe they were real cops, even after the judge rapped his gavel and sent them to jail. *Yes, really! No, it's not a practical joke! You're not on "Candid Camera"!* But real undercovers were on constant guard against any odor of officialdom, and Marie decided that the habit of vigilance was worth cultivating, whether or not it proved necessary.

"This is good. I'll walk the rest of the way."

"You don't want me to come with you? Wait outside the door, in case he gets fresh?"

"No, Adele, it's a doorman building," she said. It wouldn't much matter if Adele was on the other side of the door, or across town. Marie would be on her own, and she didn't mind that, either. "The creep we're after could be paying the guy to keep an eye out. Besides, you're in uniform. What'd he think if he saw you?"

"He'd think I was in the Salvation Army."

Marie laughed, tugging at her gloves as if they were boxing mitts. "Gimme an hour with the schmuck. If I'm not out by then, knock the door down. I'll either be chloroformed or in love. Maybe both. If he tries something fresh, I'll slap him into next Sunday."

Adele let out an *Ouf!* as if she'd been walloped in the solar plexus. "Wow! I wouldn't want to get on your bad side!"

Marie was afraid she'd laid it on too thick, so the reaction satisfied her more than she could say, but her job wasn't to fool Adele, or even herself—mostly—but Mr. Todd. And he wasn't looking to hire a bodyguard or a bouncer. He was after someone young and soft, dumb and scared and eager. It was the part of an ingénue, which wasn't a stretch for her. "Just be yourself, as much as you can," the inspector had said. Marie had known better than to ask, *Which me?*

"Oh, honey!" Adele went on. "I wish I had your guts. Sometimes, when it's a slow day in the office, I think about it. Could I do it? I mean, I'm not a rookie—I don't hand over the whole roll of toilet paper, when a perp asks for it in the cells. But you? I guess it's why you're good at this stuff. Pretending you're not afraid. Or maybe not pretending! What if this miscreant says, 'Didn't I read about you in the papers a while back?' I'd turn tail and scram. You, I bet you just say something like, 'Jeez, was she pretty?' Or maybe, 'Nah, I just got one of those faces.' What I'd like is to see you do it, just once."

"Well, maybe next time, you'll come with me."

Marie felt small and guilty for allowing Adele to go on with her hop-head-high opinions of her gifts, but the pep talk steadied her. Besides, wasn't feeling guilty and small getting into character? Adele didn't seem to notice. "Are you kidding? Not today, not tomorrow, not ever, not even if they offered to promote me to Mrs. Police Commissioner Kennedy. I get such stage fright, I don't even sing in the shower.

"Anyways," Adele went on idly, "Everything happens for a reason. God took my Harold from me with the appendicitis, but my sons are healthy. My sister has a little girl, a cripple from polio, and a boy who's a Mongoloid."

"Sorry," said Marie, unsure if she was expected to agree. People did all kinds of funny arithmetic like that with their lives, working back from the sum to find the factors and terms. *Sorry?* Marie didn't know what to say, or how to say it. And it wasn't just that what Adele had said was strong stuff for small talk. For a moment, she wished the inspector had ordered an old pro like Peg Disco or Claire Faulhaber to drive her to Mr. Todd's, but that would have been a mistake: she'd have a million questions, and she'd have arrived with a head abuzz with half-remembered tips. The majority of policewomen worked as matrons, where they were solitary by design—one per precinct, per shift, as necessary—the only females on the premises not behind bars without a mop in their hands. Most of the rest worked with kids, in the Juvenile Aid Bureau. Marie and Adele were strangers to the task, to each other. It would have felt impolite, or unlucky, to ask real questions so late in the game. And then Adele asked one. "Do you hafta come up with a different alibi, each time?"

That was a cop word: *alibi*. The definition of the term escaped Marie at the moment, but she played cool. "How do you mean?"

"Not that I have to tell you, but nobody uses their own name. Not that anybody really believes we're cops, but you can't be too careful."

"Oh, you mean *alias*!"

Adele laughed, apologizing. But Marie hadn't thought of an alias, an alibi, or anything else, and when she touched her heart in relief, she felt her shield on her lapel. *Whoops!* She unpinned it and dropped it into her purse before she got out of the car. Adele honked the horn and held both hands up to show doubly crossed fingers, and Marie smiled, gave her the thumbs-up, like the fighter pilot to the bombardier in a war movie: *Bombs away!*

On the walk over to the apartment building, she almost lost her nerve. Three blocks! There was no need for her to park so far away. She was sweating as she fretted, and she almost walked into traffic—*Watch where you're going, lady!*—as she tried to guess the likelihood of Mr. Todd having a thing for sweaty, fretful girls. Why had she tried to show off so hard for Adele? The thumbs-up, like she was picking off Luftwaffen from her Spitfire or whatever. And then she started laughing. She wasn't the pilot, or even the bombardier. She was the bomb.

IN THE LOBBY, the doorman rose to attention, smoothing his lapels before offering a curt bow. He was a wheezing old doughball in threadbare crimson livery, and his accent had a Continental vagueness, more sad than sophisticated, like one of the two-line parts in *Casablanca*. "How may I be of service on this lovely afternoon?"

Marie was ready with her alias, at least: "My name is Miss Melchionne, I have an appointment with Mr. Todd in apartment 4A."

The mask of old-world courtesy vanished, and the doorman gave her a pitying look. Marie knew then that Mr. Todd was a keeper. The wily leer she'd anticipated from the doorman was dutifully supplied by the elevator boy when he took her to her floor. "I'm off at four," he said, winking and tipping his cap as he opened the brass cage.

At the apartment door, Marie pulled a compact mirror from her purse to check her face, telling herself that it wasn't conceit but craftsmanship that prompted the inspection. She mouthed the line that got her here: "Careful, big fella! It's not rush hour!" *Yes?* She saw a naive young woman, a striver from off-the-boat stock, desperate to impress. *Yes?* Nearly there, but her dark eyes might widen a bit: *Golly!* She practiced the pose and then put the mirror back in her purse with the cuffs, black-jack, and .32 revolver with the two-inch barrel. Her shield, too, which she'd never heard anyone call a "potsie," despite what the girl detective said on *Decoy.*

As Marie was about to knock, she saw that her engagement ring was poking up through the inspector's glove. She yanked it off and slipped the jewelry into her purse. It made her feel wanton. *What a wild woman I am!* She took a minute to let the giggles pass; this was serious business, wasn't it? *Knock, knock.*

When the door opened, she was greeted by a towheaded, bullish man of indeterminate middle age in a dark gray suit of worsted wool and a slightly daring violet tie. He sweated as if he'd just moved a piano and intoned his lines with wolfish welcome. "Well, well, well. Look at you."

"Mr. Todd?"

"And you must be—"

"Lana Melchionne."

"Where have I seen you before, Lana?" he asked, with a canny, cautious note that rattled her.

"I guess I just got one of those faces," she said, blushing. She'd have to thank Adele for that, later on.

"Melchionne. That's Italian, isn't it? You don't have any relatives who carry violin cases without violins, do you? You know what I mean, right?" In case she hadn't, he mimed shooting a machine gun—*Rat-a-tat-tat!* Marie shook her head. She had to win this one.

"Huh," he said. "And what brings you to my doorstep today? Are you selling Girl Scout cookies? I wouldn't mind a bite of something sweet."

"Well, no, Mister, I came here for the job. I called, but nobody answered. I guess that's why you need a secretary. I can type, and I can do shorthand, and I—"

"Ah, a *career* girl. How did you hear about me?"

Marie hesitated, and then a batty, breathy rush of bona fides came out of her mouth: "You remember my friend Adele, she was here a while back? She said you had this *unbelievable* high-class opportunity, going to Mexico, learning to talk Mexican, only her mother wouldn't let her go, on account of her having a dream somebody died, and her sister's boyfriend got hit by a bus the next day. He's okay, though, just broke his collarbone—"

"Enough! Come on in. We'll have a little chat and figure out what position might suit you."

Where had that come from? No matter—the blather had the intended sedative effect, and Mr. Todd asked for no further references. His head turned away before his body did, and his movements had a strained, stuck-in-gear quality, as if he were a machine operated by someone who hadn't read the instructions. Marie followed him down a long, dimly lit hall until he stopped and turned, this time his body leading his head.

"The Mexican position has been filled," he said. He regarded her legs for a moment before asking, "Do you have even the most elementary familiarity with horsemanship?"

"I was on a pony once."

"Lucky beast," he muttered. "Well, then, at least there will be no bad habits to unlearn. And I believe I have jodhpurs in your size."

The hallway opened up into a spacious room, largely bare, except for a plaid couch covered with a dingy white sheet, surrounded by an array of lights and screens on tripods. Todd took a seat at a handsome mahogany desk, just beside the entry, and directed her to the straight-backed wooden chair in front of it. His desk had stacks of papers, an open accounting ledger, and an adding machine, but the image of professional respectability was marred by a set of novelty-shop teeth, the kind that chattered when you wound them up. She'd taken him to be one of the numberless freelance gropers in the city, with his "Help Wanted" ad a bait-and-switch that should have been listed in the "Lonely Hearts" section. The photo gear made it likely that Todd Enterprises might actually provide job opportunities, though not the kind a legitimate newspaper would advertise. For now, Marie would maintain her *Golly!* face. She couldn't make an arrest on the basis of the décor, even when she noticed the leather cords that dangled from each corner of the back of her chair. "What sort of business are you in, Mr. Todd?"

"Well, young lady, we are an employment agency, and we are partners and advisers with a variety of different organizations in a variety of fields."

"That sounds wonderful. My father was in kerosene. He delivered it, but I helped. I can tell you, when they say you shorted 'em, you gotta check the lines, because it's usually a leak—"

"No, young lady," Todd interrupted, rubbing his hands as if the subject had dirtied them. "Educational programs, import-export, film production, chiefly in physical fitness and the modern arts. Can I be frank with you, Miss . . ."

Miss . . . Not-Marie. Her alias escaped her, and she had no alibi.

"Yes, Mr. Todd, please do."

She took out her notebook, as if she'd treasure his every word. She wrote, *Lana, Lana, Lana. Melchionne, Melchionne, Melchionne.*

Mr. Todd nodded in approval. "What I do—what we do here—is to understand the girl, and then we find the appropriate position for her. We want girls who are open to new ideas and experiences, girls with a certain savoir faire—"

Mr. Todd was interrupted by three ladies who burst out from a back room, brashly laughing. Each was wrapped tightly in a mock-mink coat, knee-length, and they carried themselves with a burlesque air, as if they were nude aside from their shminks and high heels.

"Chin-chin, Toddy!"

"Bon-swaa!"

"'Ta-ta! We'll stop by the kitchen for a quick pick-me-up. Is there— coffee?"

Marie was startled by their sudden arrival, and then she had to labor to contain her anger. They were certainly Todd girls, as per the announced requisites of athleticism, shamelessness, and foreign-lingo goodbyes, but they were also—all three of them—redheads: one ginger-blond, one chestnut, and the third flaming, nearly fire-engine red. The last undercover sent in by Mrs. M. had been wrong: redheads were very much a Todd type. Marie was now doubly determined to make the arrest, to show that it could be done.

"Yes—the coffee is fresh. Help yourselves."

Mr. Todd beamed at them and waved them on. His smile faded as the women left, and he returned his gaze to Marie. He shook his head. "No."

Before Marie could ask what he meant, two pinched little men with briefcases scurried from the same hall from which the redheads had come, their fedoras pulled low over their brows, like mourners at a Mafia funeral. Their departure occasioned no remark from Todd, nor did they acknowledge him. The three redheads followed soon after, laughing even more loudly as they went. They hadn't been away for more than a minute, Marie guessed: they must have gulped down their coffee. The men were a greater confusion to her. Was this a brothel, or a photographic studio for French postcards? Were the men accountants for Todd Enterprises, or something else? And speaking of accounting, the numerical mismatch between females and males baffled her. Three-of-a-kind, and a pair. Had someone been left out?

Marie didn't know anything about the sex trade. When her father saw a woman who went heavy on the eye shadow, he'd mutter that she was a *putan'*, but Marie had first seen a real-life prostitute only months before, on matron duty. She was shocked by the woman's plainness—she could have been cafeteria lunch lady—and then embarrassed by her naïveté. Marie didn't really know much about sex at all. She'd been a wife for five years, a policewoman for less than one, but her experience in both fields was narrow. She was a tourist in Gomorrah, without a guide or a map. All she knew was that she had to keep going, and she couldn't look back.

Mr. Todd continued to stare at her, pulling on his lower lip. He flared his nostrils, as if to take in her scent. Leaning forward, he planted his elbows on the desk, squinting, and then he eased back into his seat. He smiled, and then he stopped smiling. He repeated his earlier verdict: "No."

Was it over already? Marie stood to leave, but he held a hand up to stop her. And then he held up the other hand, drawing them together, palms out, thumbs extended, as if to see her face in a frame. When he moved the frame to the side, Marie reflexively followed. As he panned slowly to the right, she tilted in her seat. When he made a quick cut to the left, she leapt from her chair, knocking it over, to keep her face in the shot. She felt she had to follow, wherever it went. Todd shouted, "Yes!" As he moved his imaginary camera around the room, Marie chased it like a kitten after the beam of a flashlight. "Yes! Yes! Yes!"

He shook his hands loose, cracking his knuckles and examining his fingers, as if to check that the equipment remained in good condition. "Please sit, Miss . . .?"

"Melchionne," she replied brightly, picking up the chair.

"Yes, of course. Italian, is it? Oh, right. Sit. What I said 'No' to, earlier, was the idea of you in a behind-the-scenes position. Memoranda, correspondence, filing. I know as well as any executive that such mundane affairs must be tended to with efficiency. Still, I don't see you as a mere paper shuffler. Do you agree?"

"Yes, Mr. Todd, thank you, I do."

"Good. Why be a drone, when you can be the queen bee? And I do see you as a queen."

"I want to make the most of myself, to go as far as a girl can go," Marie said, flushing slightly. She knew how he'd twist her reply in his mind, but the flattery still flattered. She wasn't used to compliments.

"You'll find that I'm a very direct man, young lady. Very direct indeed. Does that present a problem for you?"

"No, not at all."

"Very well. Are you ready to proceed with the interview?"

"Yes, please."

"Naturally, all the heavy lifting, brain-wise, will be my department. Who would want to ruin that pretty face? Still, I can see you have more to offer than meets the eye. Very well, then. We'll start with the psychological tests. Are you 'inner directed' or 'other directed'?"

"What?"

"Very quickly, just answer. First thing that pops into your head. As I said, this is psychology. 'Inner' or 'Other'?"

"Uh, the second."

"That remains to be seen."

"Well, I—"

"Never mind. It's too late to change. If you could be an animal, what kind of animal would you be?"

The first animal that leapt to mind was Mr. Todd, with his sweaty paws. She wondered if she should flirt a bit, but then she decided against it. A defense lawyer would claim she was leading him on. She'd play it straight, as an ambitious young girl who was falling for his hustle about the high life. What kind of animal would that girl pick, to show her initiative and drive? "Oh, I know! A beaver."

The answer pleased Mr. Todd enormously. "I'll bet you would. You'd be a busy little beaver, wouldn't you? Do you know who sat in that very same chair, ten years ago, and gave the very same answer?"

"No, who?"

"Grace Kelly."

"No!"

"Yes. Princess Grace Kelly. Still, she'll always be just little Gracie to me. Ah well. I'd say you were a B-cup, yes?"

"Excuse me?"

"Vital statistics. Never mind your measurements, I'll take them later on. Your height and weight?"

"Uh, five-foot one, one hundred and ten pounds."

"I could just put you in my pocket right now. Date of birth?"

"September 5, 1938."

Marie had credited herself with an extra decade of youth. It was a bolder claim than it needed to be, but she knew that if Todd believed her, it would boost her self-assurance.

"Twenty. And a Leo! Very intriguing. Blood type?"

"O positive."

Mr. Todd sighed. "So common! It can't be helped. Am I correct in supposing that you think I might be interested in your qualifications?"

Marie knew the question was a trap, and that it was her duty to step into it. She was more cheered by passing for twenty than she was shamed by her common blood. And she hadn't known that Lana was a Leo, but she supposed that it made her brave as a lion. "Why yes, Mr. Todd, even though you've been talking about much more interesting opportunities, I do have typing and—"

Todd stood up and pounded his fists on the desk. "No!"

Marie shrank into her seat. When she clutched the back of the chair, she felt the leather cords, and then she let them go. The room shook from his pounding, and spittle lashed from his lips. Sweat streamed down his cheeks. "No-No-No-No-NO! Nothing you have done before matters! Nothing! You are nothing!"

Todd was putting on a show, but Marie was frightened by the real rage in his voice, the disdain in his eyes. Todd was Oz, the Great and Powerful, and Marie was Dorothy, come begging at his doorstep for his magic. Not Marie. Lana Melchionne.

"You are nothing," he went on, softening, as if in sorrow, before shifting again to a tone of consoling benevolence. "But with me, you can be anything. The possibilities are limitless! Come now, let's get you over to the couch. Let's see how you look in the light."

Marie tensed as she rose, clutching her purse. The attack was impending. She could smell it like spring in the air. It was what she'd come for, wasn't it? Better to have a trained officer here in Todd's lair, instead of some true naïf. But Marie hadn't done anything like this before. She saw Todd remove his jacket and place it over his chair. He loosened his tie. Yes, showtime was approaching. She tightened her gloves. *Let him try something fresh, I'll slap him into next Sunday!* She knew herself better than Adele did. Had an hour passed yet? No, not nearly. She hoped Adele's watch was fast. Marie and Todd were reading from different scripts. He thought he'd seduced her, and he wasn't wrong—her fear of failure outweighed her fear of assault. Just barely, for now.

Todd directed her to the near side of the couch, beside the arm. He'd try to pin her in the corner, she supposed. She sat down and unclasped her purse to take out her compact. Her hands were shaking, and she made only a cursory effort to powder her cheeks. She wanted the purse open, if any of its arsenal became necessary—*If! As if it would be "if," and not "when"*—and she placed it on the floor, by her feet. She would have preferred to have it beside her, but she didn't want to risk him moving it out of reach. She looked up to see the gray stains of his armpits as he fidgeted with a tripod. And then she couldn't see anything.

The blazing whiteness hit her like an avalanche. The light felt as if it had force and weight, knocking her back before she could shield her eyes. When the second light was trained on her, the blow was less, but she still hadn't recovered from the first. She placed her feet on either side of her purse. When Todd laughed, it sounded like he was moving around. She couldn't see him. She imagined an ant beneath the magnifying glass of a cruel child. She put her hands out like parasols in front of one eye, the other. She had to try to spot him, to know where he was, even with her shocked retinas. She was relieved when he spoke, though his voice was raucous: "Glorious! Just—glorious! How does it feel to be famous?"

Marie tried to smile but couldn't.

"Miss—I think we're past the formalities, aren't we? What is your name?"

"Lana. Lana Melchionne."

"Lana, your face was made for the camera, you pretty little liar."

Marie opened her eyes, despite how the light hurt. She couldn't let the remark pass unchallenged. "What did you say?"

When she didn't see him, she looked down again, raising a hand to her brow. And then she felt his hands on her shoulders. Her muscles clenched at his touch, but he kept on pressing down. She thought of the arcade game where a crane-claw nips a random prize from a pile. She tried to wriggle from his grasp. "Relax."

"If you think you can call me a liar—"

"Relax. Relax your body, and relax your mind. Don't be upset, don't take offense, but your name isn't Lana. No one's name is. Not even Lana Turner is really named Lana. Her real name is Mildred. Mildred! Spoils things, doesn't it? A pretty girl says her name is Mildred, it's like she smiles and she's missing teeth. 'Lana?' That's all Hollywood. And Hollywood starts here. Anybody can be anybody. That's the American dream. And I'll call you whatever you want, until I think of a better name. Do you really believe in yourself, Lana? Do you believe in this country?"

Marie lowered her hands and closed her eyes. She hadn't known that Lana Turner was an alias, or whatever they called it in show business—a stage name? She was highly doubtful that Grace Kelly had parked her royal rump in the chair across the room on her way to the throne of Monaco. But she was certain that if she didn't put Mr. Todd in handcuffs, very soon, she'd regret it, and not just at work.

"Yes, I do, Mr. Todd."

"I'm glad, Lana. Relax. I learned this technique in Shanghai. They have no inhibitions in the Far East, none of our ridiculous notions of shame. Let yourself go."

Todd seemed to be talking to himself. He began to sway behind her, and his touch lightened on her shoulders, becoming less pinchy, more of a soft kneading with his palms. It was less painful, but far from pleasant. The lights blazed in her face. Even with her eyes closed, she saw a haze of red through her lids, like blood in water. As Todd rocked back and forth, she felt the fabric of the couch pull with the movement of his hips. "Every girl who comes here, Lana, they want something."

Marie didn't think he expected an answer. Not the obvious one: a job. She wished she were somewhere else. Anywhere. Even Shanghai. She wondered if any girls had accepted his offers of foreign travel, and shuddered at the thought. If any found their way to Mexico, they weren't teaching men how to dance.

"Every girl who comes here, Lana, they want something from me. Every girl tries to show me something, to trade for what I can give."

Her nose itched. Would it be rude to scratch it? She didn't care. When she raised her hand to her face, his hands left her shoulders for a moment. She leaned forward and the hands returned, holding her more firmly.

"Some girls show me a little leg, some a little cleavage. Hmm, that's nice."

When his hands began to slip lower down her chest, she pushed them back. His body changed its rocking motion from side to side, to front to back. What was he doing? "One less button on a blouse, and you can see a whole new world. Yes . . ."

No, Marie knew what he was doing. She froze. She thought of what the inspector might say, if she didn't make this collar. No, that was stupid—she wouldn't say anything aside from, "Good try, Marie!" And then she imagined how St. Theresa would react to the sight of Mr. Todd humping the furniture behind her. No, she wouldn't think about that. She tried to think of what she could possibly charge him with. She could hear the cross-examination from the expensive defense lawyer: *What did you actually observe, Officer?* But Marie couldn't turn around. She couldn't look back. She couldn't speak, and she couldn't bear to listen.

"Not you, though. You're different, honey. Whatever your name is. You came in here with your imagination showing. *Yes, you did, yes . . .*"

Marie tried to push him away, and he seized her left hand, twisting it as he lifted her up from the couch. He had a grip like a blacksmith, and she knew her wrist would be black and blue tomorrow. An assault, that was. Unlawful imprisonment, too. Now she had misdemeanors! It took an enormous expense of willpower to see the upside of the situation. When she rose, she saw that his trousers were around his ankles, obliging him to waddle around to the front of the couch.

"Tell me, who you are, Lana! You can be anyone! Let your imagination run wild—you can be a geisha, a slave in the harem!"

At least he's giving me choices, Marie thought. The little joke gave her courage, and her head cleared. "I gotcha, Mr. Todd, but one thing I don't wanna be is pregnant. Let me just get to my purse, for my pessary—"

"Hurry up! Now, what are you? Be a princess, a cruel pirate queen!"

Todd still held her as she knelt, reaching into her purse with her free hand. She found her shield first, but she didn't think it would matter if she showed it. Hairbrush, compact, gun—no, no, and no. Finally, she found her blackjack, and she found her voice. "Get off me! Let go! I'm a policewoman! I'm the police!"

"That's what I want to hear! Yes! Yes! Yes!"

"You're under arrest!"

"Yes!"

Todd yanked her back up, and Marie lurched to comply, knowing that her wrist would break if she didn't. The soft heft of the leather-wrapped lead truncheon was repulsively similar to what she tried not to feel pressed against her. Todd seized a handful of her hair, pulling her face close. He loomed over her, staring down. When he pressed his mouth against hers, she was almost shocked that there was no liquor on his breath. His eyes were clear, if crazed, high only from his dog-in-heat desire. She pushed him away and brought down the blackjack on the front of his head, at the hairline. It felt like she'd kicked a curb. Mr. Todd frowned, and then he gazed at her with a quizzical expression. "That's maybe a little too much."

A single droplet of blood trickled down the center of his forehead, leaving a jagged trail behind. Its path zigzagged, as if it cutting through traffic. Mr. Todd's eyes crossed as he tried to see it. And then he laid his hand on her breast. She struck him again, on the side of the head. The blackjack landed with a damp slap, an almost gentle sound. He tilted forward like a building on a bad foundation before crumpling over on top of her, trapping her on the couch.

She squirmed out from beneath him, desperate to catch her breath. When Todd began to stir, she retrieved her handcuffs from the purse. He nearly woke up before they were fastened, and his once-wandering hands looked like little trapped crabs now that they were pinned behind his back, just above the pink expanse of his buttocks. She took the badge from the purse and fixed it to her lapel, and then she took out her gun, so he could see it when he awoke. It took some minutes of piggy blinking for him to realize his quandary. He managed to sit up. He glared at her and hissed, "You . . . *impostor!*"

Marie broke out in helpless giggles. He'd been lied to, of all things. Did this mean that she didn't get the job? The laughter incensed him, and he stood up to charge. Another wallop with the blackjack made his knees buckle, and he sank to the floor. She wished he'd get up again, so she could put another dent in his cranium. But he didn't move, even when she prodded his flank with her shoe. No, he was done for the day. Unlike Marie, who had hours of typing to tend to—all the clerical drudgery Mr. Todd promised she'd be spared, if she took refuge under his wing. She had a long night ahead of her, but she'd gotten what she came for: an arrest, her first. Whether she needed a hundred more, or a thousand, she was that much closer to her gold shield. And she could go back to being herself again, at least for a while.

WHEN MARIE CALLED headquarters to relate the results of her encounter, the reaction was not what she anticipated. The inspector seemed disturbed. "Are you all right? Do you need to go to the hospital?"

"No. Why? I'm fine. Really, it went down without a hitch. I never had any doubt. Anyway, Mr. Todd of Todd Enterprises is cuffed on the floor, with a couple of lumps on the head. Someone needs to put his pants back on, but—"

"Oh, dear. My poor dear Marie!"

There was pain in the inspector's voice, a note of nearly funereal condolence. Marie was still charged with adrenaline, but she'd won the fight. Hadn't she? Maybe she was still a little light-headed, but she wasn't the one who was facedown on the carpet, manacled, dozing, and drooling. The star pupil of Inspector Melchionne's Academy for Proper Young Lady Investigators had infiltrated Grabbyhands International and shut it down. She was bruised, and she was disgusted by the intimacy of the contact. But she wouldn't cry herself to sleep over it, or wake up screaming. A shower and a cup of coffee were what she needed, or maybe a little vin santo; not a sedative.

"I'm okay, Mrs. M., I really am. I wish we had a felony for all the aggravation he put me through. But we have the misdemeanor assault to charge him with, and Indecent Exposure, and Sexual Abuse in the Third Degree, right? Isn't that 'contact between,' um, male parts and the female body?"

"Let me think, my dear."

Male parts. The euphemism made Marie feel childish. And the inspector did not lack familiarity with the New York State Penal Code. Had Marie done anything wrong? She hadn't been ashamed, but she was starting to feel that she should be. "Inspector, I don't—"

"Indeed you didn't, Marie. I commend you, I truly do. I want my girls to have every opportunity that the men have. The case I make, within the department and without, that anyone even pretends to listen to is that women have certain talents—for conciliation, for communication—that many men lack. We are complementary. Husbands and wives within the police family, so to speak. Do you understand?"

"I do."

"But if we insist on every one of their rights, we have to accept their risks. And it's not as if we accept it, when policemen are attacked or killed. But we recognize it as a possibility, part of the honor of service. Do you agree?"

"Yes."

"But for a policewoman to be raped, or nearly raped, in the line of duty . . ."

The inspector didn't finish her sentence. Marie stopped thinking when she heard the word "rape." Had his male parts gone into her female parts, that's what it would have been. Why was she worrying about being impolite?

"What's even worse, my dear, is that—God forbid—had Mr. Todd succeeded, the District Attorney would not prosecute. They only proceed with a handful of cases a year. Had you seen him steal a dollar from your purse, your word would have been sufficient to charge him. But there are corroboration requirements for rape. Your injuries are . . . how shall I say it? They are inadequate to prove resistance. It would be argued that you didn't fight hard enough for your virtue."

Marie was aghast. "But what if he put a gun to my head? Or if I thought he had? I couldn't see him the whole time. I'm supposed to take a chance, he blows my brains out?"

"The District Attorney would inform me that he doesn't write the laws. It would not be a long conversation. And so you see why I need to think, Marie. What your husband would say, how he'd react, I'll leave for you to consider."

Marie flinched at the mention of Sid. The inspector went on, "You will be in the newspapers tomorrow, dear. And the article will go up on the office wall."

"Oh!"

"I could have managed the press if you killed him. Made something of it, even. But think of the editorials if this had gone badly. They'd argue that women mustn't be allowed to do anything more dangerous than operating a switchboard. Do you see my dilemma?"

"I do, but didn't you also say that what we do in the Policewomen's Bureau is a story that needs to be told?"

"Yes, but—not all of it," Mrs. M. replied, hesitating. "Not quite yet. In the early days, if a patrolman arrested a female, he'd summon his wife from home to search her. Or the duty fell to the station-house charwoman. It took the rape of a teenager by a policeman to prompt the state legislature to order the hiring of matrons. The department nonetheless refused to do so for several years. Moving forward is not the only option for us, I'm afraid."

There was much for Marie to take in. The future of policewomen, plus her marriage. She hadn't thought that her story could be reshaped, or that the script would require approval. Because Todd was in cuffs now,

she hadn't dwelled on how close she'd come to being raped. Without her
blackjack, she couldn't have fought him off. She'd gamely risked her safety,
but she could never gamble with her reputation. If that were lost, it would
be gone forever, like virginity. No, Marie wouldn't tell Sid what had happened today. Not even if she were under oath. Now that she thought about
it, there were other potential consequences.

"Mrs. M., he exposed himself, and he hurt my wrist. We have two
charges there. It isn't a lie to not mention what happened after. If this
goes to trial, though, I'm not going to lie to say that nothing else did. They
could lock me up for perjury. That's worse than anything this *cafone* is up
against."

"I would never ask you to lie, Marie."

"I've been lying since I walked through the door," Marie replied, without thinking. Had she really said that? And had she already started calling
her Mrs. M.? "I'm sorry, Inspector, but it doesn't make sense—"

"You're right, Marie, it doesn't make sense. But it might make a difference, if we tell the story the right way." The inspector paused for a moment.
"Welcome to the New York City Police Department."

"Am I?"

"No, not really. But I wouldn't let it stop you."

A low gurgle was followed by a pealing high note, like the call of an
exotic bird. Marie had never heard the inspector laugh before. That made
her feel a little better, and a little better would have to do for now. "Okay,
boss, I gotcha."

After hanging up the phone, Marie called the precinct for a patrol car.
She was tired, but she didn't want to sit down on the couch. She didn't
even want her shoes to touch the floor. But she needed a cup of coffee—vin
santo would have to wait—or she was afraid she'd pass out. Todd wasn't
going anywhere, so Marie went to see what refreshment could be found.
It was a galley kitchen, a narrow aisle of yellowing linoleum and elderly
appliances. There was no percolator, no pot on the stove, or even cups in
the sink. Had the redheads washed them? Marie put on the kettle and
found a jar of instant coffee in the cupboard. She poured a generous dose
of sugar from a container into the mug. On the counter was a little dish of
plastic stirrers—No, they were straws—and she took one to give the coffee
a few swirls. But she'd barely taken a sip before she spat it out. It was awful.

Had she just salted her coffee? Was this one of Mr. Todd's juvenile
pranks, like the wind-up teeth on his desk? There must have been eight

ounces of whatever-it-was in the glass container, the type they had in luncheonettes. She spilled a spoonful into her hand to examine. The white
powder was fine as talc, not the distinct grains of sugar or salt; when she
tasted it, it had an acrid flavor, astringent on her tongue. Didn't those
joke shops sell a chemical that turned teeth black? If she showed up at
the precinct looking like a hillbilly, she'd make Todd pay dearly for it. She
unscrewed the metal top and dumped the powder down the sink.

Nonetheless, she felt revived, and she set out to investigate the premises. Down the hall from where the redheads had emerged, she found a
bedroom with bare white walls and a queen-sized bed, the sheets and
blankets tossed and tangled. Nightclothes and other garments she couldn't
quite place—sheer things, lacy things, leather things—were tossed about,
and there were more tripods, more screens. Marie didn't know what to do.
She tried to think what Mrs. M. would advise, but instead Mama's voice
resounded in her mind: *Che schifo! Pulisci questo posto subito!* Six months'
training in the Police Academy was nothing next to thirty years with
Mama. Unable to resist, Marie straightened the clothes and made the bed.

When she looked at the next room, she could hear Mama scream, and
then fall silent. Marie couldn't describe what she saw. There were pictures, hundreds of them. Of women, sometimes in sheer or lacy or leather
things, sometimes without anything at all. Sometimes they were alone,
sometimes with men, and sometimes—*No.* Marie went to the kitchen for
the garbage can. She gathered up all the postcards and photographs, the
negatives, contact sheets, and film canisters, and dragged them into the
hall to dump down the incinerator chute. It took several trips before all of
it was gone.

She'd just finished her housekeeping when she heard a clamor-
ous banging. At last! It was Adele with two patrolmen, and she burst in
ahead of them when Marie opened the door. Profusions of sympathy and
umbrage poured forth: "My God, are you all right? Let me look at you!
Marie, you're a mess! Did he try to get fresh? *He did, didn't he!* Let me at
that crumb-bum, and—believe you me, I'll give him a piece of my mind!"

Adele locked arms with her and marched her down the hall. It was
a little much. The girlish abundance of emotion made her self-conscious.
Was she really a mess? She hadn't looked in a mirror yet. Was it her teeth?
No, Adele would have mentioned her teeth. Once they arrived in the parlor, Adele gasped again, taking in the vastness of the room—*Wow! It's like
a palace!*—and then the ass-in-the-air tenant, who remained on the floor

with his crumpled pants a wreath around his ankles: *Uggh!* Marie glanced back to see the two men regard each other with exaggerated restraint, as if they were put-upon television husbands dragged into another misadventure by madcap wives.

Adele leaned over Todd's prone form and slapped him. "Listen, buster, I don't know who raised you, but she didn't raise you right. That's not how you treat ladies, and it's not how you deal with police!"

Todd stirred. "Leave me alone!"

"Go head and cry, you big sissy!"

Woeful groans rose as Marie pulled Adele away. The laughter from the patrolmen was braying and broad. The notion of women doing police work must have seemed farfetched to them, but the spectacle of a lady trying her hand at police brutality was adorable—a carnival attraction, like a poodle standing up on two legs.

Marie had laughed, too, but this wasn't a joke to her, not least because she wasn't entirely in on it. When she turned to the men, her voice took on a casual gravity. "Thanks for coming, guys. We have our own car, so we'll meet you at the station house. This guy shouldn't give you any trouble. I blackjacked him a couple of times. He didn't have much brains to begin with, so no harm done. Let's get this show on the road."

Was that too much, she wondered? Among patrolmen, the girlier girls in the Policewomen's Bureau were considered useless, but the masculine ones were seen as unnatural. The men stared at her for a moment, fascinated, and then they turned to each other in bafflement. Marie realized that they hadn't been introduced. "Sorry, I'm Marie. And this is Adele."

She'd opted against saying "Policewoman Carrara" as too stiff and stuffy, but her informality made it sound like they were on a double date. One of the patrolmen extended his hand. He had a hungry look, and his grin had a belated aspect, as if he'd made it halfway out the door before he remembered to put on his hat. It reminded Marie that she still wasn't wearing her rings. He asked, "Don't I know you from somewhere?"

"No, I don't think so."

"You sure? I could swear. . . . Anyway, maybe we could maybe get a drink—"

"Well, I've got one of those faces," Marie replied, quoting Adele for the second time that afternoon. Adele took the hint and charged in: "Well, you just might have seen her before, in the papers. Or maybe you know Marie's husband, Sid, he's a patrolman in the Bronx. Know him? He's a giant of a man, a Golden Gloves heavyweight, but awfully sweet when you get to know him."

"Let's get this dope out of here," the cop said, no longer interested in palaver, now that his prospects for a date had dimmed. He tapped his partner on the shoulder, and they pulled Todd to his feet. He rose unsteadily, as if on roller skates. Marie looked at his blood-streaked pate and wondered how much damage she'd done to his brain.

"I n-n-n-never," Todd stammered.

"What gives, fella?" asked the second cop, warning in his voice.

"I knew, I knew deep down she wasn't on the level! I knew all along—"

The first cut him off. "But you didn't know, did you, jerkoff?" They helped him hoist his trousers and hustled him away.

At the precinct, all of the men's faces were strange to Marie, and few were friendly. The smallest towered over her, at the department minimum height of 5'8", and most had been in the military before joining the department. They saw her as a skirt who'd snuck into their locker room. Still, Marie preferred them to the ones who were all too happy to see her.

From floor to ceiling, she couldn't see a foot of space, a stick of furniture, that wasn't scuffed, dented, or dirty. Derelicts wailed from the cells. There was a miscellany of pop-eyed stares from random cops as they passed, followed by reliable guffaws, some politely stifled, when they noticed that Todd's fly was still undone. She supposed that should have been attended to, but she was—most certainly—not the man for the job. What Marie had accomplished that afternoon wasn't earthshaking. She knew that the press coverage of her escapade would be out of proportion to its significance. But she'd put herself in harm's way, and it wasn't a gag or a game.

The lieutenant behind the desk was a white-haired, white-shirted Irishman with eyes like chips of ice. He looked at Marie reprovingly when she told him that the charges were assault and indecent exposure. He inscribed their names in a leather-bound book with a fountain pen and asked, "Is it Mrs. or Miss Carrara?"

"It's 'Policewoman,'" Adele said. "They're not booking a room in a motel."

Marie felt a surge of gratitude until she realized she had to come back to the desk later on. Once she finished with her reports, she'd have to ask the lieutenant to assign patrolmen to transport Todd to court. She knew he'd treat her like a beggar with a tin cup when she returned.

Arrests by the Policewomen's Bureau were processed upstairs in the detective squads, where even veteran patrolmen knew to knock and wait at the half-gate until invited to enter. As a rookie chickadee from somewhere downtown, Marie didn't expect to be welcomed like Casey Jones on *Decoy*—the men on TV were always glad for her help—but the three detectives in the squad room made a show of their indifference. They were in their midthirties—two stout, one wiry, concentrating, respectively, on the telephone, a typewriter, and a newspaper.

"Lemme ask you again," said the detective on the phone. "Was she a hooker or not? I'll try to get your wallet back, either way. I never laid eyes on you myself, so do me a favor, take a look in the mirror, tell me if a young blonde would be swept off her feet by what she sees."

The thin man with the newspaper said to no one, "Ten bucks says the Dodgers are back in Brooklyn next year. It was all a big stunt. Trust me, I know."

Several of the department forms Marie needed were missing, and the typewriter she was assigned scarcely impressed the letters *e*, *d*, and *t*, without which the word "indecent" wasn't a word at all. When she had to fill in the caption for "Time of occurrence," she was stumped. She hadn't been looking at her watch when he jumped her. Besides, to pick a single instant didn't seem right. Had it begun when he placed the ad, or when she answered it? Maybe when she walked into the apartment. How could you specify—

"Three-ish. Say quarter-after."

Marie felt Adele's hand on her shoulder. She nodded and typed: 1515 HOURS. When it was time to fingerprint Todd, Adele escorted him from the holding cell and stood by his side. And now the third man, the typist—hefty, in shirtsleeves and a porkpie hat—began to stare at Marie with such avid interest that she missed the old, communal cold shoulder. She took out the three fingerprint cards and rolled ink from a pad onto the glass strip. Once she uncuffed Todd, he fidgeted and scanned the room. She knew that if he made a scene, she'd appear all the more trifling and unworthy in front of the men. She felt the third detective's eyes on her still. When she ordered Todd to give her his right hand, he extended it with a gentle flourish, as if she'd asked him to dance. "Anything for you, Lana."

Marie heard a chuckle from one of the detectives. It was the one with the newspaper, she suspected, though she refused to look to see. She took the thumb and rolled it in the ink on the glass.

"You have a lovely touch," Mr. Todd went on. "And I'd still like to make movies with you. Both of you. The dark ladies of the law, justice swift and sure, with a certain amount of spanking . . ."

There were more snorts of hilarity, and Marie ground her teeth. Though she'd hardly warmed to Mr. Todd since he'd been in custody, she had to admire his perseverance. And then his tone shifted again, from seduction to disdain. "Do you know how much money I make with those pictures? I bet I make more in a week than you do in a year."

Marie gripped his hand. She'd had enough. "Don't you worry, big shot. I found your dirty pictures, and I threw them out. Not to mention the funny sugar you had in the kitchen. What is that, something from a joke store? Does it make your teeth black or something? Whatever it is, it's gone, and the joke's on you."

"You what? You stupid little—"

Todd yanked his hand away. Marie stiffened, but then she saw Todd's head snap back. Had Adele done that? She heard a male voice behind her, and when she turned, she saw the porkpie hat. Todd was the larger man, by far, but the detective hoisted him by the collar and belt and flung him against the wall like a bag of trash. Adele joined the other two detectives in helpless laughter. In a tremulous whisper, Todd said, "I think I have to go to the hospital."

"Say that again, and you'll have to go to the dentist, too," the detective growled. "Go ahead, get in the cell. You'll feel better after you sit down a while."

The detective unlocked the cell door with a medieval-looking brass key. Todd went in, and the gate slammed shut with a mournful clang. Marie could see another prisoner inside, hunched in the shadowed corner. The detective smiled at Marie and Adele, extending an arm toward the exit. "All right, ladies, I'll print him for you later, after he settles. If you finished your paperwork, just leave it. I'll take care of the rest."

Marie wasn't especially troubled by the roughness, but she had to appear in court with Mr. Todd in the morning, and she already had enough things she had to keep from the judge. She tried to think about how she might convey that without sounding like a prissy schoolgirl. "Thank you, Detective. I appreciate your offer, but I can handle it. My name is Marie Carrara."

"I'm Marino. Call me Ralph."

Despite the brightness of his smile, there was a fixity to his eyes that made her uncomfortable. At first, she guessed he was going to propose they meet later for a nightcap, as the patrolman had done. Having two cops try to pick her up in one day wasn't typical, but it wasn't the record.

Still, Marino's expression seemed more particular, more reaching than a run-of-the-mill pass. Adele was on board with Marie's first take, and she attempted to run interference again, with the same breathless badinage: "You know, maybe you know her from the papers. Or her husband, Sid, he's a patrolman in the Bronx. A giant of a man—"

Marino blinked and shook his head. "All I'm saying is, I'll take him downtown later. No need to go ask the lieutenant for transport. I have a collar, too, and I have to spend the night in court anyway, so it's no trouble to take two perps."

Marie felt bad for being suspicious of him. Any cop might have made the same offer to a brother officer without expectation of payback beyond a backslap and a beer. Marino didn't seem lecherous any more, but plaintive, beseeching. He seemed to want something from her, but she couldn't fathom what it might be. "You know, Detective Marino, I gotta say—"

"There's no such thing as a free lunch," Marino cut her off, anticipating the objection. "Don't worry, Marie. I know you girls do Gypsy cases, like the one in the papers last week. I got another one for you. A con game somebody's running on a relative, the wife's side of the family. I done everything to try to figure out these Gypsies, even looked them up in the encyclopedia. What they got there, it's wrong. I really need your help. And please, call me Ralph."

Marie now felt twice as bad about the conversation. No cop had ever asked Marie to do a cop-favor before. It must have been embarrassing for him to ask her for help, and she didn't want to make it any worse. Both knew that to become a police officer was to enroll in a master class in petty indignity, beginning at academy graduation, when they charged you six cents for the shield. But what he was asking for wasn't in her power to grant.

"You gotta call the inspector, Ralph. I'm still new, and you know how it goes."

"I did, I called the Women's Bureau. They told me that a couple of you girls tried to get inside the place, but it didn't happen."

Marie's appreciation for the unpredictability of undercover work had grown considerably in the past hours, and she knew that even the best operators had bad days. She'd almost had a very bad day herself. But she'd be willing to bet that at least one of the ladies who had failed with Todd had been given the Marino job. Lazy people didn't last long in Mrs. M.'s special details, Marie knew, but informers against fellow cops were considered the lowest of the low. Better to begin again fresh than to dwell on who failed, or why.

"Call again next week," she said. "And say that you talked to me about it."

"Thank you, Marie! Trust me, I will never forget what you're doing for me. I owe you one, Marie. I owe you."

MARIE HADN'T DONE anything for him yet, but on the subway ride home, her spirits soared even as her thoughts scattered. Adele had kidded her about getting her autograph. Her first arrest! Famous Marie! And a real detective asked her for a favor—not a silly autograph, but a favor, the true currency of the job. Big shots did favors—bosses, like Inspector Melchionne, but also monsignors, union leaders, politicians and their brothers and nephews. Marie wasn't a big shot, but she was a different person now, she felt it. When had she changed? In the moment, it was so hard to tell the moments that mattered: *Three-ish. Say quarter after.*

When she got off the train, she felt fresh and ready, as if she were heading in to work instead of coming home from a long and daunting day. Now, she knew what she had dressed up for in her pigeon-gray suit with the pencil skirt and matching trilby, faux-pearled, with her second set of borrowed white gloves. She'd have to wash them, of course, though she secretly hoped the inspector would tell her to keep them as a souvenir. What should she wear tomorrow? She had to look her best for the newspapers. Her wrist hurt, and she'd be wise to ice it, but she needed the bruises to show. Would it be wrong to touch them up a bit with blush or lipstick, in case the judge asked to see?

As she mounted the front steps, it occurred to her that she'd never had to put on makeup to highlight her bruises before, only to cover them up. She stood in front of the door and stared at it. Suddenly, she was exhausted, as if the cares of the day had caught up with her, all at once. She was more nervous than she had been at the threshold of the inspector's office, or outside of Mr. Todd's apartment. She didn't know what she was fighting for here, or why.

And then the door flew open, and Sid looked at her, almost smiling, though his eyes were wet and mopey. He embraced her, kissing her cheek and mussing her hair like a child. She felt like a child when he held her, wonderfully small and safe, loved. Yes, things would be different now, she would be different, and things would be good.

"Baby, I'm sorry," he said. "You know how I get, you know how crazy you make me. Let's not argue again . . ."

3 YOU WILL MEET A STRANGER

The saints are like the stars. In his providence Christ conceals them in a hidden place that they may not shine before others when they might wish to do so.

—St. Anthony of Padua

AUGUST 22, 1958
1300 HOURS

Who could have predicted this? Last year, she was Mrs. Carrara, a first-class nobody, an outerborough housewife at loose ends; this year, she was Policewoman Carrara of the City of New York, a star in the making, Broadway bound. Who knew what anno Domini 1959 would hold? *The amazing Mrs. Abbie, that's who!* Marie felt bad that it had taken her so long to visit the fortune-teller in Silver Beach, but the past months had been so frenetic—a wonderful week up in the Catskills, an awful week with Sandy down with the croup, one crazy case after another, half of them making the papers. She'd started to save the clips in a scrapbook. Plus, all the fuss of trying to close on the house in Yonkers. And there were, *ahem*, those four evenings on *Treasure Hunt*. Telling Sandy about it cured her of the croup the next day, just so she could run outside to shout to her friends: "Mommy's gonna be on TV!"

And she was on TV, winning furniture and pots and pans and the car she was driving right now, a pool-blue Renault Dauphine. *Mon Dieu!* The pull-apart chunks of the burgundy velvet sectional crowded the house like ships in a harbor before a storm. Sid wasn't any less goofy about it than Sandy had been, and Marie suspected he'd only agreed to leave the Bronx because the couch deserved better accommodations. She was still basking in the afterglow of celebrity, at home and at work, and she'd never deny what it had meant—*Beep! Beep!*—but there was always a next thing, at home or at work, that she had to think about more.

The morning after her last TV appearance, Mrs. M. sent her to visit a dentist who was too free with laughing gas, and his hands. Marie had one question: *What's the address?* On the way out, she saw Adele, who gasped before she hugged her. "Oh, Marie! How can you go undercover, right after the whole country saw you on TV? Honestly, I don't know how you stand the pressure!"

On the set, Marie hadn't felt any pressure at all. The spotlights felt like sunshine on her skin. The producers went on and on about how the sponsors loved her. She had to beat out another contestant with a couple of easy-peasy questions, like "Who painted the *Mona Lisa?*" And then she got to take home free stuff. She didn't believe that she'd pick the Mystery Box that contained the bag of cabbages. The odds were in her favor—all but two or three held something she'd be happy to have. Astrakhan coat with sable collar? She'd take it. Vacation to Palm Beach? *Yup.* The audience wanted her to come out on top, and they screamed when she won the car.

Besides, how could other people recognize Marie when she didn't recognize herself? After she locked up the dentist, Mrs. M. put her on pickpockets for a few weeks, and then on lower-profile perverts. "We don't want you in the newspapers every day, like *Dick Tracy,*" she said. Marie wasn't any less busy, or any less content. She still played the ingénue for most cases, a damsel made for distress, but by convincing people she wasn't a cop, she started to believe she really was one. She followed Mrs. M.'s script for reporters: *Yes, police work can be a challenge, but I always make it home by six to make dinner for my family! They always come first!* That part wasn't exactly true, but the boss insisted that she say it.

SILVER BEACH WAS a onetime summer colony on a little bluff in the Bronx between the Bronx-Whitestone Bridge and the new one they were building farther east on the Long Island Sound. Mostly Irish, with some Germans and Italians. When the Depression hit, the summerhouses became year-rounders. There was a gate and a security guard, and uninvited guests—including two undercover policewomen, in the recent past—were turned away. Marie had never heard of a legally private neighborhood, though there were many parts of the city bound by tribal lines, beyond which it was unwise for outsiders to trespass.

Marie needed a diversion, a disguise. It was a Saturday, her day off. And since she hated to lose a minute of weekend time with her daughter, it occurred to her that she could kill two birds with one stone. Some experts said that juvenile delinquents were the last casualties of the war; they were the kids of Rosie the Riveter and G.I. Joe, left motherless and fatherless until Hitler and Hirohito were defeated. Others said the problem was caused by comic books. Either way, Marie wasn't taking any chances with Sandy. She loved their time together, and they'd rehearsed: "What does Mommy do for work?"

"Mommy doesn't work," said Sandy with some vehemence, before a warm and wishful note crept into her voice. "She's at home with me, all day."

"That's my girl."

Marie felt a shiver of guilt at the conviction with which Sandy spoke, at the loneliness it betokened. Despite the pains she had taken to keep her lives separate, wife-wise and work-wise, it seemed sensible to bring her daughter, using her as a prop in her latest scam-the-scammer play. This wasn't a caper with the Degenerate Squad, just an old-fashioned Gypsy swindle. Good clean fun. There wasn't any danger, and it was a gorgeous day, maybe the last beautiful Saturday of the summer, as Hurricane Daisy was gathering in the South. So why not make it an adventure?

Marie wanted Sandy to see another side of her, a better side, one that showed her as a woman of pluck and flair, like Casey Jones, not someone who cried alone in the dark. Not that Casey had a life outside of work, that anyone knew—not a husband, or a boyfriend, or even a cat. Anyway, it had been quite a while since the last "surprise slumber party," scooping up Sandy for an overnight respite with one of her sisters, but the baby wasn't a baby anymore. The kid wasn't deaf or dumb. Sid would never let Marie go for good. He's said so, more than once. Divorce was something for movie stars, not cops or Catholics. And Marie didn't want to leave him. She wanted her marriage to improve, and she had reason to believe that it could. Things weren't always so terrible, mostly—Sid was loving to Sandy, when he was around, and he and Marie hadn't had a serious disagreement in months.

Not since the night before she'd run into Detective Marino. In her purse was the torn-out page from the *Encyclopedia Britannica* he had sent her. Until she read it, Marie hadn't been sure that Gypsies existed outside of movies, but the article was circled, so that it was clear he wasn't talking about gypsum:

The mental age of an average adult gypsy is thought to be about that of a child of ten. Gypsies have never accomplished anything of significance in writing, painting, musical composition, science or social organization. . . . Society has always found the gypsies an ethnic puzzle and has tried ceaselessly to fit them, by force or fraud, piety or policy, coaxing or cruelty, into some framework of its own conception, but so far without success.

Marino's mother-in-law had outlived two husbands and had a sizable nest egg built up when she went looking for a third. Advice from a higher plane was sought, in the form of a certain Mrs. Abbie, who perceived dark forces surrounding them: "I see the letter 'R,' a man of power, something gold." Who could that be but Detective Ralph? Marie understood why he wanted to put a stop to it, but the situation didn't strike her as an emergency. Lots of ladies wasted time with palm-reader types with no harm done.

Still, it had been months since Ralph had first asked for help, and she called him right away when the article arrived in the department mail. She was too breezy in her tone. "So, Ralph, how much did the old gal take your mother-in-law for?"

"Eight grand that we know about."

Marie almost dropped the phone.

"It's not just the money, Marie," he went on. "She's like a loan shark, coming back for more. She's got my mother-in-law scared half to death, convinced everybody's against her. She hates her kids now. The witch put it in her head they might poison her food, and she doesn't eat. She was ninety pounds last week when we put her in the hospital. Her skin's hanging off her like old paint."

The next day, Marie and Sandy put on matching sky-blue sundresses with a white floral print and went to Silver Beach. They held hands. How could they possibly look more innocent? "Who wants ice cream?"

With scoops of chocolate in waffle cones, they were a sentimental juggernaut that no one could have withstood, even if a troop of Soviets manned the checkpoint. Marie realized that she'd never worked a real two-hander before, with a partner who was equally in the game. A smile lit her face as she neared the gate, and then Sandy cried out in delighted discovery—"Look, Mommy, a rabbit!"—and pulled Marie forward, like a dog on a leash. Marie had planned to tell the guard that they were there to see the Murphys, or maybe the Russos, depending on his complexion, but he made no remark on their passage. Once he was no longer an impediment, his features faded from view, vanishing except for his smile, like the Cheshire cat. They had breached the perimeter.

The streets of Silver Beach were pocked with potholes, the asphalt ending on either side in vague edges like a smear of butter on bread. There were no sidewalks. The notion of a private neighborhood had led Marie to expect manors and mansions, but the houses were cottages, often in need of a coat of paint. The house she and Sid had picked in Yonkers was bigger than the ones she saw here. Still, the place had its charms, and the hazy summer sunlight favored even the most ramshackle bungalow with a postcard glow: *Greetings from Silver Beach, August 1958. Wish you were here.*

Lanes of old elms provided ample shade, gulls wheeled overhead, and she could smell the tang of salt in the air. Men in shirtsleeves pushed lawnmowers, the whirling blades filling the air with a locomotive drone. Throngs of children milled and ran, and Sandy nearly lit out for a foursome of little girls in a game of hopscotch, like she had for the rabbit, but Marie held fast her hand. "Sorry, honey."

"But, Mommy, I want to play!"

Sandy was eager for a little brother or sister; that she would remain an only child was, for Marie, a matter of high probability and devout hope. Sandy's eyes grew avid at the sight of playmates, and Marie grieved to see it. "Maybe later, baby. There's somebody I want to visit."

"Who?"

"A lady."

"What lady?"

Marie knew she couldn't end the conversation with such a meager disclosure. She'd considered divulging that they were on a case, but it would overexcite Sandy; saying they were out to catch a wicked witch would terrify the child. Did Sandy know the Italian word for witch, *strega*? Marie spoke to her in English, her *nonna* in Italian, but God forbid if Sandy ever told Mama about it. "A lady who plays cards."

Sandy paused, quizzical. "What kind of cards?"

"I don't know."

"Go Fish?"

"Probably not."

"Can I play?"

"We'll see."

"How long will it take?"

"An hour."

"Huh."

The response seems to have struck an acceptable midpoint, neither interesting enough to tempt interference, nor tedious enough to provoke protest. Marie restrained herself from cleaning the chocolate smears from Sandy's face. At her destination, a modest blue-shingled colonial, an older gent was trimming the bushes. His back was to the street.

"I'm sorry," said Marie. "Is this the Abbie residence? Is Mrs. Abbie here?"

The old man's eyes tightened, but there was only so much suspicion he could maintain in front of a chocolate-covered child. "Do you have an appointment?"

"Do I need one? God, I'm so sorry—I should have known! I've heard so much about her, she must be so busy. Is she home?"

The effect Marie was striving for was one of harebrained adorability, and it worked like a tonic on Grandpa. He set his clippers down and went inside. "Let me see if she's in."

As Marie led Sandy across the lawn, she felt some resistance. She didn't have to drag her, but there was a counterpull, as if Sandy had suddenly gained ten extra pounds on her forty-pound frame. Marie saw the flaw in her plan—this was hardly the "better side" she hoped to show; it was another pathetic aspect, from a different angle. She was at a loss how to explain that this particular false face was an invention, a costume for a party. Marie might not have succeeded in concealing all her flaws, but Sandy knew that her mother wasn't a ditzy blabbermouth. Marie leaned down and said, in the secret-keeping voice, "It's a special kind of card game, honey. We have to pretend, but they can't know we're pretending."

Sandy squeezed her hand, relieved. A female figure appeared on the other side of the screen door, portly and diminutive, largely in shadow. Her accent was neither local nor obviously foreign. "May I help you?"

"Yes, I hope so—Miss Abbie? Mrs. Abbie?"

"Who are you?"

"My name is Marie—"

"Mommy is a housewife, she stays at home with me, all day."

Marie hadn't anticipated the contribution from her daughter. It wasn't a bad ad lib, but the encore might not be as helpful. She covered Sandy's mouth, as if to wipe away the chocolate. "Yes, Mrs. Abbie, it's true, and this is my daughter, Sandy, who needs her pretty face cleaned. I hoped I could talk to you, for advice. About *things.* I hear there's nobody like you. I couldn't—Well, I just had to come."

"Who sent you here? Who told you about me?"

"Do you know Sheila McGonnigle?"

"Never heard of her."

"No, of course not! What am I thinking? It's her sister-in-law, Mary."

"Mary who?"

"Mary, Mary, Mary—what is her name? I met her at the McGonnigle christening, months back. Brunette, very sweet, fifty or so, give or take?"

Mrs. Abbie shrugged, but Marie could see her shoulders slacken, as wariness left her body. Each had read the other, drawing the same conclusion: *What harm could this foolish woman do?* She went on, "Married to Phil? No, it's Sheila, married to Phil. My head, it isn't on straight today. Anyway, we're moving out of the Bronx soon, and I said to myself, I just have to talk to Mrs. Abbie, I just need some advice. It's been such a time—"

"It's twenty dollars for the consultation. Not a fee, a donation. You have it?"

"Yes," Marie replied. She'd be reimbursed, but she hadn't thought the advice would be quite so dear. Twenty dollars paid for eighty gallons of gas.

"Come in." Mrs. Abbie led them inside, down a hall lined with Persian carpet, to a curtain of multicolored glass beads. The old girl really had the Gypsy bit down, Marie thought. She kept a grip on Sandy, lest the dazzle prove too much for her. As Mrs. Abbie drew back the curtain for them, she seemed slyly prideful, delighted by their impending delight. Marie was awed by what she saw—it could have been a chapel in the Vatican. Candles flickered, making shadows dance on the wall; at the far end of the chamber, on a high table covered with gold cloth, there was a parade of porcelain saints, a foot tall or more, and a crucifix in the center. Marie noted the Madonna, the Infanta of Prague, and her old friend St. Anthony of Padua, with his lilies. The crucifix was brutal and baroque, with rivulets of blood streaming from nails and the crown of thorns. A green velvet couch faced the altar; beyond it were a black-lacquered coffee table and a throne-like velvet chair. Marie and Sandy were directed to the couch, the better to contemplate Mrs. Abbie against a tableau of the sacred and terrible.

Sandy believed they really were in a church, genuflecting before the altar and crossing herself. Marie wanted to yank her to her feet until she realized that the saints remained themselves, despite being suborned into conspiracy. She wondered if Mrs. Abbie had a Jewish room, too, full of menorahs and holy scrolls, or if this chapel could switch like a speakeasy when the constable knocked, the bar shelves reversing into bookshelves, the roulette wheels flipping into tea tables, cups and kettle glued in place. They took their assigned seats. Sandy seemed uncomfortable, and Marie held her hand firmly.

Mrs. Abbie must have been nearly seventy, with steel-gray hair in a tight bun and a face round as an apple. She wore a black housedress and a white satin shawl with intricately sewn beadwork. She had the somber mien of a woman devoted to seeking out hard truths for those in need. Marie had already supplied her with an abundance of information, and two mainstays of soothsaying were foreclosed upon from the outset: the rings she wore meant that Prince Charming had already arrived; Sandy was eloquent testimony to a functioning uterus. She'd even mentioned that they would be moving. It would be interesting to see how long it took her to repackage the real estate deal as a revelation. Time check: 1315 hours. Mrs. Abbie might have been working this hustle since the days of President McKinley. She withdrew a pack of cards from her shawl and set them on the table. They were larger than ordinary playing cards. "Cut the deck."

Marie complied, and Mrs. Abbie shuffled them. "Cut again."

The cards were fanned out in a line. Mrs. Abbie's touch was so deft she could have dealt blackjack in Monte Carlo. "Clear your mind, and breathe deep. Breathe."

Again, Marie obeyed, and she felt strangely lively and peaceful at once. There was no reason she shouldn't enjoy herself, even to allow herself to be slightly beguiled by the old shyster.

"All right now. Pick a card. Just touch the one you want. You will *feel* the right one. Don't hesitate, don't second-guess. When you know, show me."

Marie passed her hand from one side to the other, alert to any intuition. There were intervals of dullness and flashes of excitement, a kind of pull of warmth, in three places—no, two really—and she could almost hear Geiger-counter clicks from the one that emitted the greater radiation. She pointed to a card. Mrs. Abbie seemed pleased, though Marie had not done as she was told, hesitating and second-guessing both. When Mrs. Abbie turned the card over, Marie was confused. It wasn't any old playing card, but a picture of someone who looked like he was having a fit. Was it the joker?

Sandy leaned over, drawn in by the gravity and the ceremony. This was not like when her aunts played pinochle for pennies. "It's an upside-down man," she said, reaching to touch it before Marie caught her hand.

"Yes," said Mrs. Abbie. "The card is for the Hanged Man."

Marie felt light-headed. These must be tarot cards. She'd never seen one before. A few girls in high school had gone through a tarot fad for a couple of weeks. Marie kept her distance from them. Black magic had all the appeal of head lice. Hadn't the girls gone on to the Ouija board after that? And then what had happened? Alice Cantor got pregnant at sixteen; Frannie Angelini lost a leg in a car crash; and Jeannie Torrance must have gained fifty pounds overnight and grew little whiskers. Marie felt sick. She had brought her daughter here. What would Mama say now? *Strega! Strega! Strega!*

Sandy leaned in again. "What did he do? Was he bad?"

Mrs. Abbie smiled, cocking her head to the side. "It isn't what he did. He isn't anyone. He's a picture, a sign. And he isn't being punished. The Hanged Man means transformation, change. Don't be upset. It isn't bad at all. Let me finish. All of us, we need to know what the cards say."

Mrs. Abbie laid them out in a kind of hopscotch formation, one card at a time and then doubles, crossed over. Marie winced at the reminder of how she'd pulled Sandy away from the children playing, minutes before. The girl should have stayed outside, where it was safe. And yet Marie knew that she was being ridiculous. She would have had to stifle a yawn had the fortune-teller worked with an ordinary deck, where hearts meant love, diamonds money, and sevens and threes were lucky for this reason or that. Mrs. Abbie made a nasal noise, like cattle lowing. "Very, very interesting."

Marie didn't want to look at the cards. "What do they say?"

"Pentacles mean property, the nine here often means a house, as does the seven of cups. A house. You will move into a new home, very soon."

Sandy cried out, "We bought a new house!"

Mrs. Abbie stroked her chin. "Yes—but perhaps you haven't moved in yet. That is what the cards tell me."

Marie surreptitiously checked her watch: 1321 hours. Six minutes only? She had to give the *strega* her due. Marie had arrived as a disbeliever and would leave in the same condition, but, at the moment, she was tied up in knots. Knots, an old standby from the hag-bag of tricks: *Bring me a piece of string, so I can untangle your problems.* Eggs, too, to show the spirits in their true form. You'd bring an egg to the *strega*, and she'd cover it in special cloths. She'd say magic words, and then crack it open. The blood-red yolk meant that your money was cursed, and you had to empty your bank account so that she could cleanse and bless the cash. She'd wrap it up and do her abracadabras, with strict instructions not to open the package until the next day, when you'd find your money had turned to newspaper and the witch was in the wind. This was not Mrs. Abbie's way, Marie was sure. There was no need to run when the saps were begging to hand over their life savings.

"I see the letter 'M,' the number four," said Mrs. Abbie, her voice tentative, exploring. "The color blue. An older woman, who was a strong influence on you."

Sandy interjected, "I'm four!"

Mrs. Abbie nodded sagely. "Yes, that explains that. What else?"

Marie was unimpressed. Yes, she was one of four children, she wore a blue uniform and worked for Inspector Melchionne, but a woman eager to agree would have seen her mother, the sky, and the number of wheels on her car. *It's like you've known me my whole life!*

"When you were younger, you met a man at a large gathering. A wedding? There was dancing," Mrs. Abbie continued, her tone growing surer. "Maybe just a dance. The men there were in costumes. Uniforms? You were shy, you are still shy sometimes, even if people don't know? You are not always happy. And yet . . . tell me about the young man at the dance. Was he a soldier? Yes, I think he was."

"Let me think."

Marie didn't want to think. A soldier? A dance? Her estimation of Mrs. Abbie had improved considerably.

"This was not a good experience. And yet good did come of it."

"Let me think."

Marie, Ann, and Dee used to volunteer at the USO dances at the YMCA on 34th Street on Saturday nights. Mama would bellow at them as they left, *"Gard' i vestiti!"*—Watch your skirts!—and they always did. Still, it was patriotic to help, and it was fun to mix with the young men, mostly, though some got fresh, thinking city girls were easy. There were punchbowls of juice, cookies, a few donated trays of bagels that led to bitter remonstrations by country boys about how they didn't know how to make donuts here. A small band played their favorites: *Is you is, or is you ain't my baby.* Marie remembered when Dee punched a boy during that song, after he tried to touch her behind.

And then she felt Sandy pulling at her hand, as if she'd fallen asleep. Mrs. Abbie was speaking. Maybe she had been, for some time. "I was asking you about the dance, with the soldier."

"You know, there were several dances that were quite memorable."

Mrs. Abbie grunted and smiled. "This particular evening, it must have been of great consequence in your life. A difficult experience, but it made you stronger."

"Forgive me, I'm a little distracted. It's so long ago! But there must be some misunderstanding. I met my husband at a USO dance. It was the reason, really, for all the wonderful things that have happened to me since."

That wasn't entirely a lie, but it was a lawyerly way of saying that her two great blessings—her daughter and her career—ensued from that meeting. Mrs. Abbie seemed troubled by the rebuttal. Sandy perked up at the news. It hadn't occurred to her that her parents once were strangers.

"Hmm," said Mrs. Abbie. "That doesn't make sense to me."

"Me neither."

"The cards are rarely this clear. Your marriage—is it contented?"

"Very much so."

"Even when Mommy and Daddy fight, they still love me," said Sandy, with rote composure.

"That's true, baby," said Marie, laboring not to betray any anxiety. She hadn't just brought her daughter here, but every bad memory, in cheap suitcases that broke open as Mrs. Abbie jimmied the locks. Had she come alone, she'd have boo-hoo-hooed for an hour, swearing that her marriage was hell in a bottle. Which it was sometimes, but whose wasn't? She was adamant in her rejection of the tarot, and the cheat who worked the deck. She'd already won the game. In its stance on witchcraft, New York differed from old Salem only in the penalty phase. Fortune-telling was a Class B misdemeanor, punishable by up to ninety days in jail, and a fortune was being told for Marie.

Mrs. Abbie stared at the cards, and then at Marie, as if trying to decide which was lying. Marie wanted to reshuffle the deck and start again. Looking back at her life, it seemed to belong to someone else. She'd forgotten how much she'd forgotten.

Marie didn't know who first called him Hollywood Sid—for all she knew, he made it up himself—but no one could say that he didn't wear it well. The night they met, Ann and Dee hadn't come with her to the dance. When he asked to escort her home, she didn't refuse. Mama had been waiting up, and the three of them talked for an hour. It was after midnight when Marie went to bed, leaving Sid with Mama in the kitchen, drinking coffee; it was after four when she woke to go to the bathroom and found them talking still. Suffice it to say, Mama approved. Some months later, Marie and Sid were married.

In her mind, Marie hadn't said yes to Sid as much as she didn't say no. It didn't seem like a terrible idea. It didn't seem like an idea at all, but a circumstance that would arrive sooner or later, like winter or a rainy day. Her parents hadn't chosen someone for her, but they could refuse her choice, for any reason or none at all. Mama had been in love in the old country, but the family had decided otherwise for her. She lived through her daughters, saw in them a life she might have had.

Sid was made for Mama—motherless, with such a *faccia bella*, cheeks made for pinching. He was from Hell's Kitchen, on the west side of Manhattan. His father had walked out, and his mother had died young. And while his brothers were each adopted by different aunts, Sid was passed between relatives like a stray dog. He didn't have a job when they were married, but he was already living in the other half of the attached house, rent-free. Marie couldn't imagine how Papa agreed. The only time she remembered Mama crying in childhood was after she begged Papa for a nickel for soap—the girls' school clothes weren't just worn, they were dirty—and he muttered as he left, "Maybe tomorrow, maybe . . ."

For Marie to have refused the marriage would have taken more will-power than she possessed at the time, and the reasons only became obvious after it was too late. The reception was in her parents' basement, and everyone gave cash, as was the custom. There must have been five hundred dollars in the *borsa*, and Marie wasn't sure whether to spend it on a trip somewhere, or maybe on new furniture—there wasn't much more than an army cot in the place. Sid had his crowd up from Hell's Kitchen, and they were carousing like it was the stag night instead of the wedding. She was afraid something would happen to the money. She asked him, "Maybe I should hold on to the bag, honey?"

She never forgot the look he gave her, his eyes cold and wild, as if he were on the knife-edge of a decision to double over in laughter, or to punch her, or both. She touched his arm and said, "I guess if you want to hold it, that's fine, too."

Someone pulled her away to dance, and she wrote off Sid's reaction to wedding-day nerves. She was nervous herself, thinking about what lay ahead. Or trying not to think about it. She wondered whether it would hurt, whether he'd be gentle. Of the thousand ways she'd imagined her wedding night, ranging from Technicolor ecstasies to any number of ghastly embarrassments—What if she turned out to be *frigid*?—all of the scenarios included her husband being there.

Instead, when all the rowdies and relations cleared out, she found herself alone. She sat on the stoop in her white dress and tried not to cry, and her sisters felt too bad to talk to her. Mama withdrew, and Papa—well, it was no longer his place to say. Walking her down the aisle was a transfer of custody. Marie didn't see Sid for two days, and he lay in bed with a hangover for two days after that. The money was gone. Sweet Jesus, how this *strega* made her think about things!

Sandy tugged gently at her hand. "Mommy?"

"Yes, honey?"

"Am I in the cards?"

Marie laughed and leaned over to hug her. "Of course, baby!"

Mrs. Abbie drew more cards from the deck, placing them at angles from the arrangement on the table. "Yes, my dear Sandy. I see you here, where the swords cross the hearts. You were lucky, so lucky to be born."

"What does that mean, Mrs. Abbie?

"Only what I said, child. We are all lucky to be born."

Marie glared at Mrs. Abbie, who smiled in response. Did Marie catch a glint of spite? She braced herself for what the cards would tell next. While she knew the *strega* was a swindler and a thief, with the heart of a viper and the conscience of a gnat, she hadn't been wrong yet.

Marie was in no hurry to become a mother. Work was the best part of her life, before marriage and after. She was a secretary at the mason tenders' union, where she learned how to render the broken Neapolitan tirades of her boss—*Tell this cafone, he no gonna tell me nuttin'*—into "Dear Sir, regarding the matter discussed, I regret to inform you . . ." He'd tell her, "You got it *perfetto*, just like I say." He'd take her out for lunch at Luchow's with the boys, and he'd laugh at how she could tuck away the beefsteak. At work, no one dared disrespect her; work brought her into Manhattan, with its thousand daily diversions; work put money in her pocket and won her the freedom that money brought. But when she was laid low for a month with fever—St. Anthony was again enlisted for a cure—that was resolved with the removal of an ovary, Marie decided that it was now or never.

"Now."

The voice was not in her head. How long had Marie been gone this time? She checked her watch: 1340. Decades had moved through her mind in minutes, all her time in no time at all. Wasn't that supposed to happen when you were drowning?

"Now, now, now," said Mrs. Abbie. "I really don't see how I was wrong about the dance. Hmm! But maybe it would be better to move on to other areas."

Two months into her pregnancy, Marie felt like she was suffocating, in a caul of sadness. She ran away from home and took a room at the Barbizon Hotel, where only women could stay. She didn't know what she wanted, what she needed, what she intended, only that she couldn't be at home right then. After a few days, she called her sister Ann, who listened to her tearful screed with sympathy, as she'd always done. Ann pressed her to say where she was, swearing that she'd never tell.

An hour later, there was an army at the door. No, not an army, but a posse, of Ann, Mama, and the parish priest. Marie was brought home like an escaped convict. Ann wept when she left, saying she was sorry, but that it would all work out in the end. Marie found it hard to forgive Ann for a long time.

How long? Until Sandy arrived, and Marie was happy for a while. The baby was all she was supposed to be, a wonder, a refuge, love. But as the months passed, Marie felt herself decline. As the baby stretched out, Marie grew smaller; for every new expressive sound she heard, her own silences grew longer, her wants fewer. She didn't read books any more. On many days, she didn't dress. She cried as often as the baby did, and over much the same things. If the market was out of carrots, it was enough to make her sob. *Didn't anybody care?* One afternoon, she heard about how Radio Free Europe sent thousands of balloons behind the Iron Curtain, showering the captive nations with messages of hope. She spent the afternoon sobbing in bed. For a long time after, the sight of a balloon made her ill.

On July 4, 1955, at a picnic at her parents' house, Ann brought a copy of the physical fitness standards for the civil service exam for policewomen. None of the sisters had known that policewomen existed; none had been inside a police precinct. Sid, who had gone on the job just before Sandy was born, confirmed the truth of these unlikely creatures, though he assured everyone that they were kept far from the rough-and-tumble of the streets. "It ain't safe out there for ladies," he opined, to general assent.

The absurdity of the idea made everyone laugh, and even Marie joined in the improvised Olympics of sack races and horseshoe tosses to test their agility and strength. She-cops! The sisters might as well join the circus. Only Mama didn't think it was funny, muttering, *Che stupido, che stupido* as they kept up their antics through the afternoon. Other insults, as well, of which Marie only remembered one—*Masca-femina!*—meaning "man-woman," because she'd never heard it before. Marie didn't take it seriously. She'd enjoyed herself for a few hours, which was triumph enough, at the time.

Six months later, on a frigid Monday morning, Dee frog-marched Marie downtown to take the test. Dee had filed for her, knowing she lacked the drive to complete even the simplest tasks. Vera never seriously considered it, and Ann, who had several years with the United Nations, decided against giving up her seniority and pension rights. When a telegram arrived, announcing that Marie had placed third on the test, it was exhilarating and intimidating. As she was, she could barely do a sit-up. She spent a great deal of time in the gym before her academy class began, in June 1957, with five women and over five hundred men—Dee had placed ninth, and would follow her in the next class—and she hoped never again to be the person she had been back then.

"And yet I see there will be another child," said Mrs. Abbie.

Sandy cried out with joy. Marie did not.

Mrs. Abbie drew out more cards. "I see the number seven. Seven days, seven months, seven years, I can't say. But there will be another child. A boy. You will have a little brother, dear Sandy."

Sandy leapt up and ran to hug Mrs. Abbie. Marie refused to believe that the wretched woman had insight into anything beyond what feebleminded females disclosed to her unawares. Still, Marie would have handed over her last nickel, just to be sure. Mrs. Abbie could switch the money for shredded newspapers right in front of her. Marie didn't care, as long as she didn't have to go through another pregnancy. "It is quite clear to me," said Mrs. Abbie.

"There must be some mistake, but I can't really discuss it now," said Marie, inclining her head down to her daughter. "Come here, Sandy, honey."

Marie was thrilled to see that Sandy's hands were quite clean when she returned to the couch. Mrs. Abbie might have been able to see the future, but she failed to notice the brown smear that traversed her once-elegant shawl.

"I don't see any medical reason, at least from the cards," said Mrs. Abbie, with a self-assurance that would have made the head of the Mayo Clinic sound like a sophomore. "The future isn't fixed, like the past. With great efforts—many prayers, of course, but more than that—we may be able to change the course of events. It will not be easy, I warn you, if you take this journey with me."

"Oh, Mrs. Abbie, I would be so grateful for anything you could do," Marie gushed, rising to her feet. They were finished, each having obtained what they needed. Mrs. Abbie drew back the bead curtain, patting her chest on the spot where her heart should have been. Marie wished she had hand-cuffs. If Sandy hadn't been with her, Marie would have clapped them on the old monster right there. Hell, if she had Marino's copy of the encyclopedia, she'd have given her a great clout across the chops with it. This was a witch she'd be glad to burn. Others might claim that their card tricks were a harmless diversion, an entertainment, but Mrs. Abbie sold false hope on the black market, like the crooks who sold sugar pills as penicillin during the war. When the medicine is real, you don't need so many miracles.

Sandy asked to use the ladies' room, and Mrs. Abbie sent her down the hall with a dismissive wave. Mrs. Abbie turned to Marie and seized her wrist. "Call me in three days. No more, no less. Next time, leave the kid at home."

"I will, Mrs. Abbie."

"Now, be honest. Was I right about what happened at the dance? Are you happy in your marriage?"

Marie felt a tug toward a more candid reply, but it would have allowed Mrs. Abbie an equal satisfaction in her own gifts. She didn't think she was kidding herself when she believed that things could get better with her marriage. There was no choice but to hope, for one thing. For another, people did change, despite themselves. She didn't know why Sid hated her sometimes, but he was usually very sorry after; if he was an enemy to her, on occasion, he was a mystery almost always. Marie was a mystery to herself. She didn't know why the baby that had made her so miserable once delighted her now, or why she'd thrived in this often-awful job. Newborns didn't change as much as Marie had in the last two years. And Sid encouraged her to become a policewoman. He bragged about her when she was in the papers, and when she was on TV, though he laughed a little when he told people, to show that he didn't take it too seriously. Who knew what would happen to Sid, what might touch his heart? Greater wonders had been worked, though not through Gypsy spells.

And she didn't want to stop fooling herself altogether. Her job was a confidence game, and she was the primary mark—*I can do this!* Maybe she should reconsider how she saw the divisions in her life—the crackerjack cop and the weeping wife—and try to take herself on a case. She'd solved every one assigned her so far, hadn't she? At very least, none of the bad memories would go back into the cheap suitcases. She'd examine the evidence with cold eyes, no matter how it hurt to see, no matter where it led.

"No, my husband makes a wonderful living, he treats me like a queen. He bought these outfits for me and my daughter. Shopping runs in the family, you might say! But there has to be more to life than spending money."

Mrs. Abbie nodded piously at the mention of disposable income. Marie clasped her hands in gratitude. She would have preferred to have them around the woman's neck. Twenty bucks wasn't a bad price for all she'd been given to think about, but to rob an old woman of eight thousand, along with her family, her sanity, and her health? She'd show Mrs. Abbie no more mercy than she showed in turn, picking idiot pockets as she scared them into the graveyard.

"I noticed the dresses right away. They're quite fetching."

Gifts of clothing were Sid's customary apology after a dustup. He had excellent taste, and he never had any trouble getting advice from shop-girls. Hopefully, all of that was in the past. Sandy joined Marie at the door. "Thank you again, Mrs. Abbie. The next time, do you see—no, let's make it a surprise."

"Don't be fretful, my dear," Mrs. Abbie offered, as a parting gift. "Not all the news is worrisome. I also see much good fortune. New furniture, a car, perhaps."

Sandy crowed, "We just got that!"

"Yes, child?"

"Mommy won it on TV! Did you see her?"

Marie made an overbroad smile of false modesty. Could Mrs. Abbie be a viewer? Would she have to arrest a fan? "Yes, Mrs. Abbie, I was on a game show, *Treasure Hunt*, and I was quite fortunate. Did you see it, by any chance?"

"I don't waste my time with that nonsense," came the reply, with unexpected asperity. "They're all fixed. I could always tell. You read in the papers, everybody's investigating, even Congress! They say the pretty one always wins, so the audience is happy. I can see why you were successful, Marie."

Sanctimony was not something that Mrs. Abbie wore well. Yes, a grand jury had been hearing evidence that answers had been given out before-hand on *Twenty-One* and a few others, but Mrs. M. was still sending her girls to appear on the shows. Marie didn't quite understand all the fuss. Besides, *Treasure Hunt* was mostly a guessing game. Marie's first rival had been slightly older, a butcher's wife from Newark. A bit frumpy, she sup-posed. Now that she thought about it, there was a question about the Mona Lisa, and the travel magazine in her dressing room had an article about Leonardo. And the conversation she overheard in the elevator about the Hoover Dam also proved to be quite helpful. As for the boxes, well—any hustler in Times Square knew how to rig that one. But why was Mrs. Abbie so invested in her scorn? Perhaps to impress upon Marie that, no matter how much skill or luck she brought to the table, Mrs. Abbie ran the game.

Mrs. Abbie nodded sagely as they left. Had she a true knack for proph-ecy, she'd have seen herself in handcuffs a few days hence, shrieking as if the steel seared her skin. She'd have seen that Marie had arranged for three patrol cars to respond with lights and sirens, for the entire neighbor-hood to witness. She would have known that her address book would be "misplaced" in the precinct, so that she wouldn't have her clients' phone numbers any more. She would have foreseen her eviction from her little blue house in Silver Beach, so pretty in the August sunlight, under the shade of the elms, beside the sea.

When Marie and Sandy had walked two blocks, she clutched her daughter by the shoulder and said, "Do you know who that lady was?"

"No."

"Do you know what a *strega* is?"

Sandy gasped, but she saw her mother smiling and knew it was all in fun.

"We should tell everybody!"

"We should run!"

And so they shouted as they ran, hand in hand, madly laughing, "Strega!"

"Strega!"

"Strega! Strega! Strega!"

TWO
SISTERS IN ARMS

4 YOU'RE NOT HERE TO MAKE FRIENDS

The element of danger seems to make the policeman especially attentive to signs indicating a potential for violence and lawbreaking. As a result, the policeman is generally a "suspicious" person. Furthermore, the character of the policeman's work makes him less desirable as a friend, since norms of friendship implicate others in his work . . .

The element of authority reinforces the element of danger in isolating the policeman. Typically, the policeman is required to enforce laws representing a puritanical morality. . . . The kind of man who responds well to danger, however, does not normally subscribe to codes of puritanical morality.

—Jerome H. Skolnick
"A Sketch of The Policeman's 'Working Personality'"

OCTOBER 22, 1959
0700 HOURS

Going forward wasn't the only option, Marie knew, but she hadn't seen this coming. This wasn't just a step backward, but to the side. When she was told she'd have matron duty in the First Precinct, she was afraid that she was being punished for something. Confused, too, because she didn't see the point. The First, which covered the lower tip of Manhattan, was the financial center of the country, maybe the world. During daylight hours, it was swarming with stockbrokers, lawyers, clerks, secretaries, and every kind of worker bee; come sundown, most of the streets were so empty you could almost hear the crickets. Cops in the First were highly visible and rarely necessary. Marie was used to tasks that were difficult, delicate, even disgusting; it had been a while since she'd been told to do nothing. She'd been spoiled, in a way. So many city workers were like state inmates, looking at time as something to kill.

Marie had been on a shoplifting detail for the last month, and she'd made some nice grabs at the perfume counter at Gimbels. It wasn't the kind of caper that made for a gripping episode of *Decoy*, but it was a nice change from the degenerates, and she came home smelling better than when she left in the morning. In time, an opportunity to advance would present itself; of that much, she was certain. That there also existed a possibility of reversal—back to weary clockwatching with the hard cases and lost souls behind the bars, as one graveyard shift blurred into another— was sickening to contemplate. This was just a one-day deal, wasn't it? It had to be. Few policewomen visited the inspector as often as Marie did, dropping by to ask advice on a case, or to announce its victorious conclusion. But Mrs. M. was busy with meetings for an address to the League of Women Voters for a day before Marie managed to get in to see her.

The inspector greeted her in an off-the-cuff manner, without raising her eyes from the letter she was drafting. She didn't seem angry, but Marie relied on her for plain speech, even more than she did for praise. Mrs. M. had always been generous with explanation. Commands—arbitrary and absolute as lightning strikes—were the ordinary form of communication between ranks; for many bosses, to ask a question was an act of insubordination. Mrs. M. was wonderfully different in that way, as in so many others. But Marie hadn't heard any explanations, or accusations. Or thunder. She hadn't heard anything. "Does it present a problem for you, Marie?"

"No, not at all."

Mrs. M. folded her note and slipped it into an envelope. "I thought it might be convenient to be downtown in the morning."

"Oh?"

When Mrs. M. looked up, pride told in her gaze. Reaching into a stack of papers on the side of her desk, she extracted a teletype message. "It's Medal Day."

Marie blurted out, "Really? What am I getting?"

"Not you, my dear," said Mrs. M., as her face fell, barely and briefly. "For once! No, this citation is for Patrolman Serafino Carrara, of the 44th precinct. There are no other Carraras assigned there, and I checked to see he hadn't been promoted or transferred."

Marie was less abashed by her assumption that the accolade was for her than her obliviousness to Sid's achievement. Again, Mrs. M. knew what to say.

"There are so few marriages where husband and wife are both police officers that it doesn't bear generalization. Most policemen tell me they don't talk about work at home, aside from the occasional amusing anecdote. So much of what we do isn't fit for discussion around the family dinner table."

"When I do see my husband, work is the last thing we want to talk about."

That was no exaggeration. Marie's tours changed often and usually ran late. Patrolmen worked a cuckoo-clockwork of days, four-to-twelves, and midnight shifts, with weekends that might be Tuesday and Wednesday one week, Wednesday and Thursday the next. Marie wondered how they managed to keep track of time.

"I think that may be the wisest approach," said Mrs. M., pleased with how she'd rearranged the conversation. "And since you may presume that he escaped this ordeal unscathed, would you allow me to boast on his behalf?"

"Please do."

"He is being given the Medal of Valor."

Marie was bowled over. Department commendations began with the citation for Exceptional Police Duty, and then Meritorious Police Duty, and then a couple others before ascending to the Medal of Valor. Only the Combat Cross and the Medal of Honor were higher, and the latter was awarded posthumously, as often as not. Marie had won several EPDs, and other awards were pending. But she had once picked up Sid's handcuffs by mistake in the morning, and they were rusty, thick with lint. Their approaches to the job differed as much as their schedules did. Setting aside her second-class status, Marie had come to realize that she and Sid didn't have the same job at all. They shared an employer, but no common notion of what they did, or why they did it. Sid had a gig; Marie had a calling. He did as little as possible to collect his salary, while she gave more than she knew she had to give. Hadn't Mrs. M. once said that policewomen and patrolmen be complementary, as husband and wife? Still, their paychecks were the same. No other job in the country did that, as far as Marie knew; few employers saw any injustice, holding that men needed to earn more, as heads of the household. Neither Sid nor Marie regretted their respective approaches. In time, both met enough of the other species—the slugs and the strivers—to see that while each thought the other peculiar, neither was unique. Still, the Medal of Valor . . .

Mrs. M. read from the page: "'On August 9, 1958, at 0530 hours, in the vicinity of Depot Place and the Harlem River, Patrolmen Serafino Carrara and Michael O'Shaughnessy did effect the rescue of a person who attempted suicide by drowning, at grave personal risk to their safety.' Do pass on my sincerest congratulations."

"I will, Mrs. M. Thank you." Marie didn't know what else to say. Where to begin? *Good for Sid!* And what was good for Sid had to be good for her, for them. Though the incident had occurred a year before, she was sure he hadn't mentioned it. Sid never gabbed about the Job, not from the first, when Marie was still a secretary. She might never hear the story in any greater detail than what was summed up on the teletype. She was desperate to learn more, and not just—not mostly—because she found it so difficult to believe that her husband could be a hero. Hadn't that been what she'd been praying for?

"And I've given you matron duty at the First, so you'll be free to take a meal break at 1000 hours and come to headquarters for the ceremony. They have been notified. In the event that you are in charge of a prisoner, call me, and I'll arrange someone to fill in for the hour."

"Thank you, boss. But why—"

Mrs. M. waved away the question. "Because quiet days never happen when you need them to. Marie, if I sent you to the Central Park Zoo, you'd catch someone trying to steal one of the elephants. Besides, do you have any pictures of the two of you together, in uniform?"

"No, I don't think so. When I graduated from the Academy, he wore a suit."

"Very well, then. If there's nothing else . . ."

THE FIRST WAS a squat gray stone box on the East River. Old Manhattan was at the southern end of the island, a jumble of alleys and broken half-blocks jimmied into place, like mosaic tile; the symmetries of the city grid, clean and square, began farther uptown. Though Wall Street was only two blocks away, the smell of money was less distinct than the scents of river bilge and fish from the market on Fulton Street. Marie arrived in her pigeon gray suit, with her uniform on a hanger over her shoulder. The sergeant at the desk was plump, young, freckled. "May I help you, Ma'am?"

"Policewoman Carrara. Did Inspector Melchionne call?"

"Yeah, we heard. Congratulations to your husband. I guess you can get dressed in the ladies' room. I hope you brought something to read, to pass the time."

Marie thanked him and went on as directed to the door that was marked, in faded gilt letters, LA I S. Inside, the flaking plaster was painted an unwholesome shade of green, but the room was clean. She didn't cringe at the idea of setting her purse down on the linoleum floor. Some women put their uniforms on at home, to avoid the trouble of finding a decent place to change at the precinct. No patrolman ever did, and not just because they had locker rooms. The men didn't want to be recognizable as cops to their neighbors, let alone to strangers on the subway; the blue suit inspired too many questions, too many complaints. Not so with matrons: one told Marie that she were usually mistaken for a military nurse or stewardess. Once she dressed, she checked herself in the mirror. The suit looked as if it were put together by an amateur carpenter, bulky in some places, pinched in others; it accumulated around her like scaffolding. Every time Marie put it on, she wanted to lobby Mrs. M. to change it, to make it more practical and comfortable. The instant she took it off, the thought left her mind. She wanted to wear her own clothes at work, like a detective.

Once the day platoon spilled out into the street, Marie went to the empty muster room to flip through the newspapers that had been left on the table between the cigarette machine and the shoe buffer. She was tetchy and bored. She could offer to type or answer phones for the detectives, she supposed. It was almost nine when she went up to the squad, where she was told that they already had a man on light duty. The detective wasn't rude, but he blocked her from even seeing inside, as if she were selling encyclopedias, door to door. She told herself that she probably had little to learn here, anyway.

As she made her way down the hall, a stocky Irishman with red-blond hair and a flushed face whistled at her from the landing. He wore a black leather car coat over a fisherman's sweater. A toothpick twisted in his mouth as he bared his teeth. "You in town for a while, honey? Or is this just a layover?"

"Excuse me?"

"'Fly the Finest, Fly TWA.'"

A stewardess joke. Hilarious. "Oh, shut up."

The Irishman seemed as delighted by her annoyance as he would have had she been dazzled by his wit. Another man, also in a leather jacket, with a white turtleneck, arrived behind him and shoved him ahead, up the next flight of stairs. He was olive-skinned, with dark hair and eyes. A *paesan?*

"Leave her alone. She works for my friend, Inspector Melchionne."

Yes, a *paesan*. The second man shrugged an apology—*What am I gonna do?*—before continuing upstairs. Marie wondered who they were, what they did. The men's lockers were usually downstairs, and detectives wore suits. She waited until she heard the door shut before she tiptoed up to read the frosted glass door panel:

NARCOTICS BUREAU

DEPUTY CHIEF INSPECTOR EDWARD F. CAREY

COMMANDING OFFICER

Marie gulped for air and raced back down, forgetting to be secretive. She hadn't known that Narcotics was here. She'd somehow supposed they were in an underground hideaway, beneath the subway tunnels. They borrowed policewomen on occasion for undercover work, and she supposed she'd get a chance with them sooner or later. Now, she couldn't visit without looking like she just got the stewardess joke, and found it sidesplitting. *Layover! You're talking about sex!* To be seen as a little slutty, a little slow, was not the impression she cared to make. Still, the discovery gave her something to think about. When she bid adieu to the sergeant, the walk uptown lifted her spirits. The morning was cool and clear.

Most of the offices described as being in headquarters were across the street, in "the Annex," a drab former candy factory on the northeast corner of Center and Broome. Headquarters itself was quite grand, an ersatz *palazzo* with a great green dome and ornately carved stonework, wholly occupying a small, wedge-shaped block. The south end was wider, and the north had two small, paw-like extensions, so that if you pictured the dome as a head, it was sphinxish, in a way. Lard-assed, inscrutable, and curiously lovely, it seemed to Marie to be an appropriate home for the institution. She went inside to the auditorium, but she kept to the aisle and didn't take a seat.

The front rows were filled with cops in their dress uniforms, with long woolen coats and white gloves. Behind them were families in packs, with generations represented from infancy to near death. Many of the cops didn't have family there, aside from maybe a wife or a radio car partner, but the ones who did almost made it a second wedding. Marie had never been to this ceremony. Her awards had been of the lower order, and Mrs. M. had given them in her office, improvising remarks to create the sense of an event. Marie was so happy for Sid, and grateful—as ever—to Mrs. M. She heard the bagpipes lowing in a far corridor and looked out over the rows of blue hats to see if she could spot Sid. She couldn't.

When Marie felt a hand squeeze her arm, she turned to find her sister at her side. Dee wasn't in uniform, but in a perfectly tailored suit in a hound's-tooth check. She was always decked out in the latest styles from Luigi's friends in the garment district. Marie was delighted to see her. "Honey! You look—"

"Shh!"

Dee reacted as if they were about to be caught talking in church. Marie laughed—she felt the same way—but she pressed on with her effusions. "You shush! You look gorgeous! Are you working? Why—"

"Why do you think? I called Mrs. M. at the office earlier, and she left a message for me, saying to meet her here. And I am working, I have a new—"

The pipers entered the auditorium, their martial bray filling the room. The women straightened up at the sound, and then Dee leaned over to finish her sentence. "A new assignment, for the Brooklyn DA. They need someone to translate Italian wiretaps. I'm not allowed to say any more."

Marie rushed to hug her, in part so that Dee couldn't see her face, as she was unsure of the emotions that might show. Of the four sisters, Dee and Vera had loving marriages, while Ann and Marie had thriving careers. It wasn't as if they'd signed a treaty, but some notional fairness about their lots in life made it easier for them to get along. Marie was happy for Dee—she really was—but she was envious as well. If the DA had a job for an Italian-speaking woman, shouldn't the line for the job start . . . behind Marie? "That's just wonderful, Dee, I'm so proud of you. You must be thrilled."

"I am. I hope I never have to put on that uniform again. Why are you—"

"Mrs. M. arranged a day tour at the First, so I could come to the ceremony. Sid's getting a medal."

"What? Really? You, I could see, but—Sid? Really?"

"Shh!"

The ceremony was about to begin. After the invocations, patriotic and priestly, Commissioner Kennedy took the stage and began his prepared remarks. "Good morning, ladies and gentlemen. It is my great pleasure to welcome you here to recognize these officers, and the exceptional deeds they have performed. And yet I wonder if *exceptional* is really the proper word, given that they occur every day—every hour, perhaps—a fact often overlooked by the press."

Kennedy was a remote and austere figure, even by the Old Testament standards of the upper echelons. He was a man of absolutes, intolerant of misbehavior, within the department and without. Every Christmas, he'd order dozens of transfers of sergeants and lieutenants, utterly at random, to disrupt patterns of holiday gratuities. Modish and sociological explanations for juvenile delinquency were of no interest to him; criminals were not to be coddled, no matter their age. Cops who fell short could expect no quarter. There hadn't been a major scandal in the department since the business with the bookmakers ten years before that wound up driving Mayor O'Dwyer from office. The fact that O'Dwyer was once a policeman had not been an asset to his reputation. Kennedy had been public in his fight with Mayor Wagner to increase police salaries, which had won him some admiration among the troops, but it was undercut by his ban on moonlighting. That Kennedy was married to a Jewish woman, the former Miss Hortense Goldberg, also made him a peculiar figure to the rank and file.

"Please refrain from applause until all awards have been handed out."

As the names were read, the officers rose and took to the stage, saluting the commissioner and then shaking his hand, as the department photographer shot the portrait. Awards were given to one man or two; credit wasn't divisible among larger numbers, apparently. Kennedy recounted a succinct *précis* of each feat, usually in a single sentence. Most of the incidents involved gunfire—bank robberies that were intercepted, killers who went down with a fight. Otherwise, there were children pulled from burning buildings, lovelorn women and bankrupt men yanked from ledges. Sid and his partner had the only rescue from the water. Once the last cop left the stage, the crowd burst into fervent applause, and Marie took part with no less enthusiasm. Dee clapped listlessly.

And then Dee took hold of Marie's arm, leaning close, so no one else could hear. "I thought Sid couldn't swim."

Marie blenched. That was one of the reasons she wanted to hear more about the story, and one of the reasons she didn't. The citations were as terse as telegrams; you'd think the Job was paying by the word with its compliments. Maybe the partner—O'Shaughnessy?—had impulsively jumped in to save the man, and Sid kept his wits, wading in with a rope, so they weren't swept away. Not that they gave out the Medal of Valor for risking rope burn. Marie didn't know how to respond. Was she a cop here, a wife, or a sister? She couldn't be all three, not at the same time. Not even two out of three.

Here was Mrs. M., thank God. "Hello, girls! How was the ceremony?"

"Lovely!"

"Wonderful! Just lovely."

"They always are, aren't they? Dee, tell me, how was your interview?"

"I start tomorrow. Today. Really, I can't thank you—"

"You can thank me by representing our bureau with the ability and dedication you've always shown. So then, a red-letter day for both of you girls! I can't stay long, but let's go over to congratulate Serafino—Sid—on his—"

Inspector Melchionne led the sisters to the back of the auditorium, where the crowd had gravitated to the long tables laden with coffee urns and light refreshments. The cops with family entourages mulled around, most of the men holding children in their arms, their blue hats set on the little heads as flashbulbs popped. Relatives were shuffled and reshuffled for pictures. The level of photographic expertise was not high.

"Take off the lens cap—"

"And you have to put in a new bulb—"

"Take another one, just to be safe."

"Smile! Would it kill you to smile, just this once?"

Mrs. M. spotted Sid before Marie did, with the unaccompanied men who'd distanced themselves from the amateur shutterbugs. He was with one man in uniform, three others in suits. At first, Marie thought they were arguing, and then she saw they were laughing. She sprinted ahead to make sure that none of the remarks were off-color when Mrs. M. arrived.

"You should have seen Hollywood's face, when he dared him to jump—"

"Sobered 'em both up—"

"Flip a coin, he could have been fired—"

Marie prayed that her boss and her sister were still out of earshot when she bellowed, "Sid! Honey! It's me!"

The smile never left his face when he saw her, even as his hands gripped the shoulders of the men beside him tightly enough to make them wince. "Boys! Enough kidding around, guys, it's my wife! Hey, baby!"

"Hey, you! Look at you, how handsome!"

And Sid was, as always. He could have been on a recruiting poster. His dress uniform still fit as if he hadn't aged an hour since he graduated from the academy. When he embraced Marie, her head rested against the center of his chest. She whispered, "My boss is here. And my sister."

Sid looked down and tipped her chin up, for a kiss. His eyes met hers, and then his voice dropped to a low growl. "Did they hear any of that bullshit those assholes were saying?"

"I didn't hear anything, and they were behind me."

"Jesus, I hope so."

Sid sounded almost nervous, which was unlike him. Marie didn't want to guess what had really happened on Depot Place, though it sounded like the official version was distant kin to the truth. She doubted Sid had put in for the medal himself—he wasn't the type who raised his hand in class—and he didn't seem put off by his pals' jibes, but it was another matter altogether to lose face in front of females.

"Inspector Melchionne!" he bellowed, drawing out the first three syllables, so his pals would hear the rank. "What a nice surprise! And Dee, how ya doin'?"

"The inspector told me about the medal, Sid, me and Dee both," said Marie. "I wish you'd let me know."

Mrs. M. shook Sid's hand, holding on for an extra moment to reorient him toward the front of the auditorium. She had another surprise planned, it seemed. "You'll have to stand a few more minutes of attention, Sid. I've arranged for the photographer to get a shot of you and Marie together."

The photographer made an exaggerated show of looking at his watch when they arrived. He was old and brittle-looking, his suit shiny with wear, but he carried himself with the braggadocio of a tabloid lensman at a Broadway premiere. "This is them, Mrs. M.? The Spencer Tracy and Kate Hepburn of the New York City Police Department? Now I can see it, yeah. You kids are a couple of beauties. Get together, by the flag. Hop to it!"

The sudden invocations of authority and celebrity made Marie and Sid docile. Once they found the flag, they stood rigidly beside each other: *Present for duty, sir.*

"You look dead," said the photographer. "Why don't you close your eyes and cross your hands over your chests? Can we get the bagpipers back?"

Marie looked up at Sid, adoringly, leaning in close; Sid swept her into his arms, moving in for a kiss. Marie's hat fell off, and Sid caught it before it hit the floor. She began to laugh, too, and kissed him back. The flash went off: *Pop! Pop! Pop!*

"Great! You know what would be fun? A Tarzan-and-Jane thing. Honey, hop up into the big guy's arms, and we can—"

Marie was relieved when Mrs. M. interrupted. "That's enough, Mr. Lindstrom, you're not working for *Photoplay* any more. We should be mindful of the public resources involved."

Marie exhaled in relief. She and Sid took a very pretty picture. They always had. Now, it was time to leave. Mrs. M. wasn't entirely finished, however.

"Besides, Mr. Lindstrom, your next appointment is in Commissioner Kennedy's office, correct? You can escort Patrolman Carrara upstairs. He's on the list to be photographed with him," she said, turning to Sid to apprise him of her last gift. "It's a very stately setting, Sid. His desk was Theodore Roosevelt's."

Marie felt Sid stiffen. He stammered, "I, uh, don't know how to thank you."

Marie believed him. The three seconds that Sid spent with Kennedy on stage lasted at least two seconds longer than he'd have liked. Still, she guessed that the photograph in the commissioner's office would find its way into a silver frame in their living room. Sid might have sought to avoid official scrutiny, but he wasn't a wallflower. His nickname didn't just reflect his *faccia bella*, his pretty face.

"No need to say anything," Mrs. M. replied, checking her watch. "I have a meeting now. Congratulations, Sid. You, too, Dee. Marie, I'll see you soon enough."

Once the inspector left, Sid recovered his power of speech. "So, Dee, what's your good news?"

"I've been assigned to the DA's office."

"Good for you! Which DA?"

Marie thought that Sid's effort at civility seemed sincere.

"Brooklyn," Dee replied tartly. "They have a bridge there now. If you want to stop by, you won't have to swim. Bye-bye!"

Marie shut her eyes, so they wouldn't meet either her sister's or her husband's. What did Dee know? What did she mean? And how would Sid take it? Who was the patron saint of Not Getting the Joke? He must have heard Marie's prayer, because Sid joined in the eruption of laughter from his friends.

"Watch out for that one!"

It was time for Marie to go back to work, such as it was. "All right boys, it was nice to meet you all—"

She hadn't met any of them. "And I hope to see you again—"

She didn't. "But Sid has to go upstairs now to see the commissioner."

Marie kissed Sid and turned away. As she walked, she was careful not to hurry, and she listened for *one-two-three-four-five* paces, then ten, before she decided she didn't have to listen anymore. No dirty jokes, no Italian jokes, no digs against bosses had been uttered in front of Mrs. M.; no loudmouth would get a fat lip for blabbing any further exposé of the true events of August 9, 1958. Over and out. On the street, Marie found a pay phone and called the desk at the First to say she'd be back shortly. "Hello, sergeant. This is Policewoman Carrara, I wanted—"

"Oh, hey, is it eleven already? I'll put it into the book, you're going to headquarters. You told me already, didn't you?"

"Yes, I've already gone, I'm coming back."

"Sorry, you can't. Somebody from Inspections just came by to sign the log. I forgot to write that you left then, so I just did now. If they came back and you were here, it wouldn't look right. Right? You follow me?"

"No, not at all."

"You're probably right. Still, it's in the book that you're gone now, so if you could come back at twelve, it would be better."

"It's no—"

"See you in an hour."

The sergeant hung up. What a waste of a day it had been, what a waste of hope! Her husband wasn't a hero, not even for an accidental minute. His commendation was a fairy tale, while Marie was obliged to rearrange her reality to conform to official fictions. Her sister's transfer piqued her, more than she wanted to admit. And Mrs. M.? No, Marie couldn't be angry at her. Mrs. M. always had her reasons. Better to give a little hell to that sergeant, after she'd trudged around for an hour, in her stiff official shoes. Maybe she'd ask him to step outside and push him into the river. And then she'd rescue him, of course. They gave out medals for that kind of thing.

An hour later, Marie was readying a sharp remark as she opened the precinct door, but the sergeant bellowed at her from behind the desk. "There she is! I told you we had a matron today! Where have you—never mind, come here!"

Marie was early, and she wasn't in the mood to pretend. The two men from Narcotics were in front of the desk with a woman in a knee-length fox-fur coat. She was handcuffed, but she wasn't entirely in custody, lunging back and forth if either man tried to touch her. When she faced one direction, her coat and hair—also red, but darker—swung to the other, all awhirl, so that she seemed less a person than a phenomenon, a shape in the air, like a tornado.

"Get your hands off me, you rapist sons a bitches, or I'll—"

"Easy, princess! Nobody's gonna touch you!"

Marie raised her hands in harmless honesty, as cowboys did in Westerns when approaching wild horses. "Hello."

The woman turned to Marie, wild-eyed. She had striking looks, with high cheekbones, full lips pulled back to reveal gleamingly even teeth. She looked feral, but doll-like, too, with eyebrows plucked into perfect, last-of-the-moon circumferences, and the bridge of her nose could have been drawn with a ruler before the slight rise of its upturned tip. As her expression shifted from rage to desperation, there was an instant of indecision. Marie knew then that she was putting on a show, but it made her no less keen to watch.

"Thank God you're here! You better have a Midol and a maxipad, or—"

The woman shot fiery looks at the men, pivoting, as if readying a return to tornado mode. "I'm a bleeder like you never seen! You sons a bitches are gonna need galoshes if I don't get help. Right now!"

The sergeant cowered behind the desk, and the two men reflexively withdrew. Marie kept her hands raised and said, "I have what you need."

"You're a godsend!"

The woman stepped forward, as if to embrace Marie, but the Irishman held her sleeve. Marie saw from the ruddy smudge on his upper lip that his nose had been bloodied. He had scratches across his cheek as well, raking crimson diagonals, like a teacher's red pencil on a page of wrong answers. His earlier crudity had no bearing on the merits of this arrest, but Marie liked the lady for fighting him.

"Don't you go anywhere, unless I tell you," he snarled, toothpick clenched in his teeth. "If you were a man, Red, I'd have knocked you into next Tuesday."

"And if you were a man, Red, I'd have wanted you to try."

The other detective, the *paesan*, slipped between the two redheads to separate them. He looked at Marie pleadingly. "Would you mind searching her, before we take her upstairs?"

"No problem."

The Irishman said, "I gave her a toss, but you should pat her down before you go inside. This one's the type to have a switchblade. Keep an eye on her."

"Maybe an attack dog, too," said the woman, sucking her teeth. "And keep your eyes to yourself. You stare at me like I'm a French postcard."

"All right, honey," said Marie, playing the honest broker. "I just showed up at this party, so I don't know what's what. I'm going to pat you down out here, and then we go to the ladies' room, to check some more. It's actually very clean. Okay?"

The woman nodded. She threw her shoulders back, so the front of her coat fell open, revealing a black silk shift dress that fit snugly around her abundant bust. Marie reached inside and ran her hands around the lining of the coat. In one of the outer pockets was a purse, a black patent-leather clutch. Marie set it on the desk, to examine later. When she slipped her hand inside the other pocket, she jumped back. There was something alive in there. And it had bit her. "My God! What?"

As she looked at her hand, she was ashamed. She wasn't hurt. She'd just been startled. She didn't doubt either detective would have squealed like teenyboppers had it happened to them, but it hadn't. The woman tossed her head back, hooting and snorting. The Irishman gripped her shoulder with one hand, readying to fling her against the wall, and took Marie's hand with the other. "What is it, a hypo? Did you get stuck? Goddamn it, I knew it—"

Marie knew he'd hurt the woman unless she recovered her senses. Whatever inhabited her pocket—*Please God, let it not be a rat!*—was unlikely to survive a collision with the Irishman. "No, I'm fine, Detective, just wait—"

Marie refused to allow her temper to show. She could be in control of that, at least. She drew the woman away and kept her voice low. "What the hell do you have in there?"

When the woman indulged herself in a wry smile, Marie tried to glean whether there was a hint of malice in it. Yes? No? It didn't seem so. "I told you."

"No, you—"

And then Marie thought she understood. She reached a wary hand into the pocket and gasped as she withdrew it. The tiniest dog she'd ever seen nestled in her palm. Marie knew that, dignity-wise, it hadn't been a banner day for her. Still, she couldn't contain her reaction. "That is just the *most* adorable thing!"

And it really was, a Walt Disney sketch of a pooch come to life, with soft brown eyes, tiny white teeth, a little red bow around its neck. Black and tan, a terrier, maybe. It seemed impossibly miniature, the size of a frankfurter in a bun. The two detectives pressed in to see it closer. The *paesan* cooed, almost as sappily as Marie had. Even the Irishman seemed to soften. "Would you look at that!" He looked up at his prisoner, his eyes wide. "I bet he's a smart bugger. Does he do any tricks?"

"No, he's just a baby," she replied, melting as she gazed down. "He's smart as a whip, though, you can tell—"

The Irishman reached in to lift one of the paws with his pinkie. "Shake! Look, he can shake my hand. Isn't he something? Roll over, boy. Can you do that? No? Well, he's still just an itty-bitty bugger. Oh, I bet I know one he can do. All dogs can, it's in their nature."

The Irishman pulled the toothpick from his mouth, waved it in front of its nose, and then flicked it into the air. "Fetch!"

And the little dog let out a little yip and leapt—

"No—"

"You son of a bitch!"

The moment of terror was brief but acute. Even the sergeant yelled from behind the desk. Marie had cupped the animal in her hands, like a firefly, and it hadn't really left her palm when it bolted for the toothpick. She clutched it to her breast—*gently, gently*—and sprang back. As far as the redheads went, Marie far preferred the one wearing the handcuffs to the one who owned them. The woman began to buck and whirl again. "Sons a bitches, you hurt that dog, and you won't be able to have kids when I get through with you!"

The foursome paired off, man-to-man, woman-to-woman. The *paesan* bum-rushed his partner away from the desk, and Marie tried to soothe hers, holding up the pup to her face. "Listen, honey, why are you acting up like this? Any rough stuff, the dog's the first one to get hurt. You have to help me out here. My name's Marie."

"Charlie. Nice to meet you, Marie."

"You too, Charlie, even under the circumstances. Come over here and have a seat," she said, leading her over to a wooden bench on the side of the room. "I don't know what's going on. Stay put and relax, so I can try and find out."

Marie returned to confer with the detectives, positioning herself so that the woman and the Irishman wouldn't be in each other's sightlines. Marie gave him a cold look. "I thought you said you searched her. I guess you missed something."

The Irishman reddened further, and his mouth narrowed. His partner took Marie's hand, lifting it up to examine the fingers. "Yeah, sorry. Are you all right? Did it break the skin?"

The Irishman interjected, "I'd get a rabies shot. The little bitch could have caught it from the big one."

"No, I'm fine. It just gave me the heebie-jeebies, feeling something moving in there. I'm Marie, by the way."

Introductions were made by the *paesan*, whose real name was Paulie. The Irishman was, naturally, Paddy. Paulie stroked the pup's back, but when Paddy went to do the same, Marie moved it out of reach. When she gave him a hard look, he smiled, as he had when they first met. He was the type who didn't mind rubbing a girl the wrong way, she supposed, as long as he was rubbing her somehow.

"So, what do you need from me? What's the story?"

Marie kept an eye on Charlie as Paulie muttered a summary of their morning: Charlie was the *comare*—the mistress—of a heroin dealer named Ambrogino Bocciagalupe. Paddy rolled his eyes, as if the name was sufficient indictment. Little Gino—so he was called—also owned a bakery, in the Italian part of East Harlem. The detectives had watched him over the course of several weeks, and they'd discovered that he had a narrow and particular delivery service, involving very few customers.

Paddy took over from there: "And then, today, Gino has a beef with the little spitfire. We're tailing 'em downtown, to the Village, and they mix it up like nothing else. He gets in the car and takes off. A garbage truck cuts us off, and we lose him. We go back to your friend there, to try and talk, but—you mighta noticed—she's not the reasonable type."

Marie still didn't care for Paddy, but she was glad to have been included in the conversation. An ordinary matron didn't usually get many details on an arrest, although if narcotics were involved, brassieres would be lifted, pantie girdles unpeeled. Marie was unwilling to signal any alliance with him, just yet. "So, what did you get on her? Why is she locked up?"

"Listen, honey," said Paddy, flushing again, so that the scratches were even less visible. "If she wasn't a broad, she wouldn't be locked up, she'd be in the emergency room. I'm not going to tell you that this is the best collar I've made. But my rule is, nobody ever lays a hand on a cop and walks away free and clear."

Marie didn't disagree with what he said. But all of them knew that you didn't lock up a female for being hysterical, even if she scratched you. If a male did the same, he'd be half-dead by the time he was back in the station house. That was what a cop had to do, as a man, before submitting the matter to the abstract majesties of the law. Marie's indifference stung more than Charlie's fingernails. When she didn't respond, Paddy began to shout, "Nobody raises a hand to me, or any cop on this job!"

As he stormed out toward the stairs, he halted suddenly and turned to Charlie. Marie and Paulie both tensed, ready to effect another separation.

"So you're on the rag, are you? Is that your excuse? I think there oughta be a law, broads gotta wear a red hat outside, if they are. The city ain't safe, with you walking around!"

And then he turned to Marie, with no less spleen. "How about you? Where's your red hat today? Because, sure as shit, that blue one don't suit you!"

Marie and Paulie both rushed toward him, but Paulie beat her to him, and he hustled his partner up the stairs. "Come on, Paddy, let's not—"

"Neither of these broads—"

"Come on, Paddy—"

And they were gone. Marie was speechless. How could that *cafone* say those things? He should be suspended, at a minimum. Marie turned to take in the reaction of the sergeant. *Where was he?* After a few seconds, his head rose from behind the desk. Marie must have squeezed the dog, because it kicked and whined. *Sorry, baby.* When she picked up the purse from the desk, the sergeant didn't meet her eyes. As she led Charlie to the ladies' room, they exchanged amazed, indignant glances. Marie reminded herself that she shouldn't be too familiar, but she wanted to buy Charlie lunch for scratching Paddy in the face. She set the dog down on the floor. The pup chirped and gamboled, squatted and pissed. Marie felt her anger fade. "So adorable!"

Again, she steeled herself against letting her guard down. Charlie had shown she could take advantage of the moment. What Marie knew about her wasn't flattering. The outburst about her period—*Galoshes?* What woman would say that? She directed Charlie to the far side of the room, such as it was, as she went through the purse.

"Well, Charlie, let's take it easy on each other."

Compact, comb, tissues, lipstick. No hypodermic needles or razor blades. A ten-dollar bill, four singles, small change. House keys. A little bottle with a white stopper, L'Interdit. Wasn't that what Audrey Hepburn wore? It was time for Marie to leave the perfume counter behind. "I have to tell you, it wasn't such a nice trick, letting me put my hand in your pocket."

"You're right. I'm sorry."

The act of contrition wasn't false, Marie felt. She snapped the purse shut and opened her own, to take out the handcuff key. As she fished for it, she was reminded of Charlie's earlier request. "Is it really your monthly? I have Midol, and a Kotex."

"Please! Well, at least I'm not pregnant. That's the one upside, I guess."

This wasn't a conversation between friends, Marie reminded herself. "Huh. Let me give you a quick check, and you can take care of business. Have you ever been arrested before?"

Charlie seemed horrified at the suggestion. "God, no!"

"I have to check you for contraband. That's anything you shouldn't have. Is there anything you want to tell me about, to save me some trouble?"

"No! Please, I really gotta go."

There was mounting desperation in Charlie's voice, but Marie had been fooled before by claims of bathroom emergencies. "Sure, but once I uncuff you, I need to check your bra—"

"No problem! Just hurry—"

Once Marie unlocked the cuffs, Charlie dropped the coat and tapped the back of her dress, by the zipper. "Go—please—unzip me!"

Charlie shimmied out of the top, letting it slip below her shoulders. She yanked her bra up over her head and shook her bosom—*Nope, nothing hidden there*—while waving her hands like a burlesque dancer. "Please, can I go?"

Marie handed her the Kotex, and Charlie scampered into the stall. After the toilet flushed, Charlie emerged and went to the mirror to fix her hair. She wore a sad half-smile. Marie asked, "What did you get yourself mixed up with today?"

"Did you ever go out with your guy, expecting an engagement ring, and you get a punch in the kidneys instead?"

"I can't say that I have. I'm sorry."

Marie was sorry for her. Charlie retouched her lipstick before addressing her eye shadow. "I'll be a mess, tomorrow, when my eye swells up. Gino hit me with a cheap shot. Otherwise, I usually give better than I get. He has a cute little bump on his nose from when I hit him with a lamp."

When Charlie did her mascara, her hand seemed to tremble. She caught Marie's reaction in the reflection—a pitying tilt of the head. "No, I don't have the shakes, even though I could use a cocktail. You have to zigzag the wand when you do the lashes, that way you won't get clumps. Speaking of drinks, Gino was going to buy a cabaret for me to run. We had our eye on a place in the Village. Really just a bar, but it had a little stage, and a dance floor. That dream's down the toilet, too. Good riddance!"

Charlie examined her finished face and collected her cosmetics. "Are you married, Marie?"

"Yes."

Charlie stepped away from the mirror and slipped back into her fur coat. "So you're not in the market, and you don't need my advice. But if you were a single gal, I'd tell you not to fall for married dope-dealing gangsters. You know why?"

"Why?"

"Because they're not nice."

Charlie scooped up the pup, tucking her back into her pocket. "Then again, I'm not always nice, either. If that Irish bull wasn't such a prick, I'd give him Gino on a platter. I wouldn't spit on him now, not if his hair was on fire. But you, Marie? I'd be willing to tell you lots of things. You interested?"

Charlie placed her hands together behind her back to be cuffed again. Marie took Charlie's elbow and spun her, so they were face-to-face. She slipped her arm around Charlie's, as if they were chums, and began to escort her out of the room. This day on matron duty might not turn out to be such a waste of time.

"I'm a very good listener."

5 YOU WERE BORN READY

La donna è mobile, qual piuma al vento,
Muta d'accento, e di pensiero . . .
                    —Giuesppe Verdi & Francesco Maria Piave
                                                    Rigoletto

OCTOBER 22, 1959
1230 HOURS

As they marched up the stairs together, Marie hummed the tune from the opera: *Woman is fickle, like a feather in the wind, changes her mood, changes her mind* . . . The life Charlie had described—and had discarded as a pipe dream, at least with Gino—was exactly what Marie had. A career that engaged her; a home with a child who loved her; a husband who wouldn't leave her, no matter how he strayed. It wasn't altogether satisfactory, but no one wanted to hear you complain, any more than they wanted to hear you brag. Mama had told her daughters how to conduct themselves, at seven years of age or seventy: *Never let them hear a breath you take.*

Paulie greeted them on the third-floor landing. Seeing Charlie at liberty, such as she was, seemed to amuse him. He invited them into the office, which was no different from any other squad room, with a holding cell and a series of battered desks, all uninhabited. He pointed like a maître d' toward the interrogation room in the far corner, as if it were the best table in the house. Inside were three metal folding chairs around a wobbly wooden table. He asked how they took their coffee. It was a very civilized and equal-seeming trio, despite the fact that one of them was a prisoner, and two of them were women.

Marie didn't know the social conventions for this kind of occasion. A matron was delivering an inmate; a rookie cop with a potential informant

was being tested by a veteran detective; a young lady was being introduced to a suitor by her vigilant chaperone. Marie looked over at Charlie
again, wondering how old she was—twenty-two?

"I've had a heart-to-heart with Charlie, and she's agreed to talk about
certain matters of interest. And I'd like to help. I don't mean to be disrespectful, but I won't be disrespected, either. Charlie will not talk to your
partner. The same goes for me."

Charlie inclined her head in demure assent, and Paulie smiled. "I'd like
to apologize for Paddy. This won't be the first time, or the last. My partner
has a heart of gold, balls of steel—pardon my French—and a head of solid
rock. If you'd like to talk—and I hope you and Charlie will—I promise,
you'll deal with me alone. My mother told me—she still tells me—how to
treat a lady. I have sisters. I was raised right. Again, I'd like to apologize to
both of you. *Mi diaspace, dal mio cuore.*"

Marie glanced over to Charlie, and she seemed content. She didn't look
Irish, Marie thought. Was she even a real redhead? Whatever her background, Charlie took comfort in the courtesies. "Well, like Marie said, I've
come to a point where I don't see the point with somebody I know. Who I
guess you know, too. Gino. Whaddaya want to know?"

"Everything."

Marie felt herself recede from Paulie's sight. She didn't mind.

"What's everything?"

"Pretend I'm an idiot."

"Do I have to pretend?"

Paulie reached out and patted Charlie's hands as they rested on the
table. "I left myself open to that one, I know. I'm a big boy, and my feelings
weren't hurt. But your new friend Marie here, she just made such a nice
speech about respect. I took it to heart. Did you?"

Charlie didn't appear chagrined, but she took Paulie's hand and
clasped it. "All right, Detective. If we're going to talk as long as I think, I'd
like cigarettes, a cup of milk for my dog, scotch if you have it, rye if you
don't, and a Coca-Cola."

Paulie withdrew from the room. Charlie took the dog from her pocket
and set it on the table. She made a barrier of her purse, on the side that
adjoined the wall, and Marie did the same, making a kind of corral. Paulie
returned shortly with a pack of Chesterfields, a pint of Fleischmann's rye,
and the rest of the shopping list. The office apparently didn't lack for liquor
and sundries.

"All right, ladies. Are we ready?"

Charlie took a long sip of whiskey, and a short one of Coca-Cola. "Well, Detective, Gino tells me things, and sometimes he tells me more than he knows . . ."

Marie couldn't gauge Paulie's reaction. He didn't interrupt Charlie, and he lit her cigarettes as the need arose, which was often. Marie was fascinated by the presentation, by its breadth and clarity. As Charlie told it, the major heroin brokers in New York—mostly Italian, a few Jewish— bought it in bulk from syndicates in Montreal, Marseilles, and Beirut, fifty or a hundred pounds at a time, which they cut with milk sugar and laxative powder. Heroin that was 70 or 80 percent pure would be half that—at twice the cost—the next time it changed hands, to gangsters across the country, or midlevel dealers in New York. By the time it moved through the middlemen, the heroin might be one part in twenty, and the price might be thirty times what it was when it arrived. A pound of heroin cost more than gold, wholesale; when it hit the slums, it approached the value of diamonds. Charlie rubbed her ring finger at the mention.

"Now, like I said, the closer the junk gets to the streets, the money gets crazy, but the scene gets crazy, too. That's where you get the stickup guys, the fiends, the ones who'd sell their mother for a fix. It's where you draw the cops' attention."

Charlie smiled and held up another cigarette. Paulie lit it, and she continued. "Nobody hates junkies like the mobsters. Not even cops. Funny, isn't it? The big boys, the ones who pony up a hundred grand for their friends in Montreal and Marseilles? If they found out that one of their kids—or their friends' kids, or even a cousin on the wife's side—if one of them ever touched the stuff, that would be it. They would be dead to them. Maybe dead to everybody.

"Tell me, Paulie," Charlie went on, suddenly coquettish, maybe warmed by the whiskey. "When are you gonna have a drink with me? I guess you know, I have a soft spot for Italians."

Charlie held up another cigarette, but Paulie slid the lighter across the table. His tone remained even, and his eyes remained kind as he replied. "Maybe when we have something I can drink to. What you told me, it could be part of a news program, like *See It Now*, with Edward R. Murrow."

"That's not on anymore."

"Well, I'll miss it. You learned a lot of things about the world from Mr. Murrow. And what you told me, it matches up with what I know. But what it's like I'm looking for a stolen car, and you're telling me that the Ford Motor Company makes 'em, and the steel comes from Pittsburgh, and the rubber on the tires comes from trees. That and a dime would get me on the subway."

"It's fifteen cents now."

"Like I said, you're good with the big picture. And I know we're just getting started here, but you haven't said much about Gino."

"I don't have anything good to say."

"I'm not here for good things. What does he do? Deliver packages? How many, how big, to who? When and where?"

"He delivers packages maybe twice a week. I'm in the car, so we look like a nice loving couple. At least a pound of dope, usually to Brooklyn or the Bronx. For his cousin or something—you know how these Italians say everybody's a cousin—"

"What's his cousin's name?"

"Nunzi."

"Big Nunzi or Little Nunzi? Nunzi from Delancey Street, or Nunzi from Mulberry, or Nunzi from Arthur Avenue, or Nunzi from Canarsie? Nunzi Farts, or Cross-Eyed Nunzi, or Crazy Nunzi?"

"Nunzi from Astoria. But Nunzi from Astoria, his cousin is on Pleasant Avenue. He's Frankie."

"Big Frankie or Little Frankie? Frankie Whiskers, or Frankie Blue Eyes—"

"Pleasant Avenue Frankie."

"Now we're getting somewhere."

Marie recalled Paddy's expression at the mention of Ambrogino Bocciagalupe, and she was relieved it was Paulie who led them through the cavalcade of Nunzis and Frankies. Did Nunzi Farts's friends call him that? Did his mother? She realized her mind had wandered as Paulie began the next round of questions: "Did you ever meet Pleasant Avenue Frankie?"

"No."

"Did you ever meet Nunzi from Astoria?"

"No."

"The packages, does he deliver them the same days?"

"Sometimes, there's two on the same day, but we never had more than one package in the car at a time, in case we got ripped off or stopped by cops."

"Did that ever happen, that you got ripped off, or stopped?"

"No. Gino drives careful."

"What car does he drive?"

"There's a couple different ones."

"Who does he deliver them to?"

"I never met the gentlemen. I stay in the car. And wherever he goes, he parks around the corner."

"Is there anything concrete you can give me?"

"Isn't what I just—"

"No. And my guess is, today wasn't the first time you and Gino had cross words. You're hot as a stove now, but how do I know he won't send you flowers tomorrow, and you'll take him back? Are you willing to do whatever it takes here? Are you in for the long run?"

"You don't know anything about me, if you think—"

"Does he stash anything at your place? You're on 88th Street, just off Third, right? Second floor of a brownstone?"

"How did you—"

"I'm a detective," Paulie replied, as if he were straining to remain jovial despite his deepening disappointment. "It's my job to find things out. But the only news you gave me today is that the subway fare went up. The city doesn't pay me much, but, in all honesty, I can't say that I've earned my day's pay. You sit tight, have a drink and a smoke. Take the dog for a walk around the ashtray. I'm gonna step outside with Marie for a minute."

Paulie rose and led Marie from the interrogation room. Charlie seemed shaken before she laughed and began to talk baby talk to the dog. Marie felt foolish. She'd been so taken with Charlie, impressed and intrigued. Had they wasted Paulie's time? You had to take chances, and not every chance panned out. He had to know that. Didn't he? He continued to watch the door, as if he expected Charlie to make a break for it. A minute passed, and then another. Paulie walked to a nearby desk and picked up the phone. His voice was low, as if to keep Marie from overhearing. "Yeah, it's me. No, not much—Damned if I know. I'll be right there."

Paulie hung up and walked out into the hall. Marie endured a few more minutes of awkward solitude before returning to the interrogation room.

"What happened, Marie? What did he say?"

"I swear to God, Charlie, he didn't say a thing. Not to me. He talked on the phone, and then he left. I felt like a dope standing there, so I came back in with you."

Charlie reached for her whiskey but put it down without drinking. "Are you being honest with me, Marie?"

"I am. I said, 'I swear to God,' and that's not just an expression. If I couldn't tell you something, I wouldn't. I like you—that's the truth—but I won't pretend we're old friends."

"What if I wanted to tell you a secret?" Charlie asked, with an unexpected earnestness. "Just between us. No cops can know. Would you keep it?"

"No."

Marie might have hesitated, had Charlie not put it that way: *As a matter of fact, Charlie, I happen to be a cop.* It was just as well. Charlie held her breath, and then she let it go. She held her cigarette up, as if she expected Marie to light it. When Marie failed to oblige her, Charlie lit it herself. "Is this guy Paulie serious? Why's he playing hard to get? I'm not supposed to be the one who asks him to dance. I'm leaving Gino, and I want to hurt him. But I'm not gonna hurt myself, if you guys are just running a game. Gino and his friends, they play for keeps."

Marie was in unknown terrain, managing an informant, and in too-familiar country as a wife who'd taken her punches. She had always kept two sets of books in her head, as a human being and as a cop, and the steady gains from the second helped offset the losses of the first. Charlie had no business being with Gino, for love or money. Could it be that there was no conflict, that what Marie wanted to say was exactly what she should—as a policewoman who wanted to become a detective, and as a Catholic who hoped to avoid hell? She promised herself that she'd stop if it felt like she was lying. Acting was a talent, but lying was a sin.

"To me, what you said was incredible. Paulie mentioned *See It Now*, like it was an insult, but I thought it was great. I never knew anything about heroin. At the same time, I understand why Paulie says it doesn't really help him. The DA needs evidence to make a case. The way the law works, you have to see something yourself, before you can say it in court."

The mention of judges and courtrooms seemed to unsettle Charlie. "Am I in much trouble, Marie?"

Marie nodded slowly. "Yeah. You're in big trouble, but it isn't with the cops. I'll make a big stink to let you go home from here, no matter what, and I think they'll listen. But you've made bigger mistakes than smacking Paddy. You're with the wrong guy, doing the wrong thing, and the road you're on—you and I know—it doesn't end with you owning a nightclub. You're such a smart girl, such a pretty girl, with so much going for you.

It makes me sick to see you throw your life away over a bum like Gino. I don't want to push you to do anything you don't want. I can try to help. But only if you're telling me the truth. There's nothing in your apartment?"

"No, I told you. It's in his place, I guess, or the bakery. The family owns the building. All of them have apartments upstairs, the mother and father, brothers. Gino, his wife, his kids. Two little babies, both boys."

"And what Paulie said about you going back to him, if he makes nice? What if he says he's sorry? Not for the first time, right?"

A wistful look crossed Charlie's face. She watched the thread of smoke writhe like a snake before a snake charmer before grinding out the butt. When she didn't reply, Marie pressed on. "Sooner or later, Gino's going to prison. You want to be one of these girls who think a special day—Valentine's, whatever—is an eight-hour bus ride to the middle of nowhere? Sitting across tables with a hundred other inmates, the guards yelling if your hands touch? That's if you don't go to prison, too."

Charlie sat still and looked down. There was a reckless emptiness in her eyes.

"My husband is a policeman, too, Charlie. But I have my own pay-check. If anything happened, and he wasn't around—God forbid—the world wouldn't end. Not money-wise. I wouldn't be out on the streets. You talked about a nightclub. Could that still happen?"

"I still work a couple of nights a week, and I know the business. I have my savings. A nice little bundle, but not enough for a club. Gino pays for the apartment. Another good reason to move. To go downtown, to the Village. I like it better there."

"That reminds me, Charlie. You said that you took the packages to Brooklyn, the Bronx. But these guys grabbed you in the Village."

"Yeah, that. That's nickel and dime. Gino skims from the packages, he does his own little side thing. Half an ounce on two pounds, maybe, and not every time, not with the same customer. He cuts it again and packs it up into capsules for a couple of small-timers. A luncheonette on Barrow. There's a newsstand, on Ninth and 20th, a night clerk at the YMCA on 23rd, and a couple of bellboys at—"

"Charlie! This kind of stuff is exactly what Paulie was asking!"

"Are you kidding me? I gave him Nunzi from Astoria, Frankie from Pleasant Avenue! They make millions! Half the heroin in the country comes from them!"

"All you said was their names."

"Saying their names could get me killed."

"I appreciate that. But pointing a finger doesn't make a case. What they need is facts, times and places. Things that you saw, with your own eyes."

"Well, I saw fifty capsules of heroin go into a sugar bowl at the Flegenheimer Luncheonette. It's in the back. White china bowl, blue flowers, third shelf on the left. We just delivered it to the owner. He cooks, too. Name's Artie. He's Greek, short and fat, tattoo of a bluebird on his left arm. Is that the kind of thing you want?"

"Yes, Charlie, it is. Let me find Paulie, see if we can let you be on your way. Tell me, though, why you'd never go back to Gino. Why is this time different?"

Charlie didn't answer, but as Marie made to leave, Charlie held her arm. "How does what I told you hurt Gino?"

"It doesn't, really."

"Then we got to figure this out together, Marie. The only way I can really do this is to put him away. I don't want to go to prison. Nobody does, I guess. But what I really hate is long bus rides. Can we talk again?"

"I'd like that."

Marie went out to look for Paulie. As it happened, he returned to the office just then and beckoned her to follow him into the hall. His expression of discontent had vanished; now, he grinned like a kid. In the hall, Paddy awaited them in a similar state of elation. "Nice job, honey! I knew if I put you two broads together, you'd get what we needed! I knew you'd break her—I mean, she wanted to talk, so it wasn't so hard, but you had her wanting to come back for more."

Marie couldn't speak. She'd been set up. And she'd been spied on. Several notions occurred to her at once, but a Christian woman couldn't put them into words. She looked at Paulie, who didn't appear to be ashamed of his complicity, or his partner's. Hadn't she told him that she wouldn't work with Paddy? As several blasphemies began to take shape in her mouth, Paulie and Paddy both interjected.

"Listen, Marie, you did great," Paulie began.

Paddy cut him off. "I know it was a dirty trick, what I did downstairs, but I got the both of you to hate me, didn't I? Didn't I? You and her were on the same side, after that. I wouldn't have been so rough, unless I knew you could take it."

"I didn't like it either, Marie, I don't talk to ladies like that, even if they're perps. But you gotta admit, it worked."

"That's the thing, the only thing," Paddy continued. "It worked."

"And I called Mrs. M.," Paulie went on. "I called her when I left the room. I asked if you could be assigned here, to handle Charlie as a confidential informant. A couple of weeks, at least. Who knows where it could lead?"

Marie managed to persuade herself that cowardice was the lesser part in backsliding from her hard line on a Paddy-free partnership. It had been typical of her experience in the department that opportunity and indignity arrived hand in hand. It still steamed her to recall the crack about the red hat, but she'd heard worse. *Sticks and stones.* Still, it felt like she had to swallow a thumbtack to agree.

And then Paulie said, "Congratulations, by the way, on your husband's medal. But I know you have it in you, too. You'll get there."

Another thumbtack—a rusty one—even before Paddy piped in, "Listen, honey. I know I owe you an apology. Let me make it up to you. Let me take you out, buy you a cup of coffee."

Marie had been assuaged by the mention of Mrs. M. and the transfer, but Paddy needed his head examined if he thought they were friends now, or that they ever would be. She'd rather eat red-hot, three-inch nails than have coffee—

"I wouldn't go out with you if—"

"I was thinking of the Flegenheimer Luncheonette."

MARIE TOOK DOWN Charlie's contact information and escorted her out of the precinct. They parted, each convinced that they had done well by each other, and that they would do better still. Marie hurriedly changed back into her civilian clothes and joined the detectives in an elderly green DeSoto, shabby even by cop standards. She assumed the car to be Paddy's from the lumberyard of toothpicks she had to brush off the back seat. She liked how fast things were moving, but the speed of events had also outpaced her ability to forgive the men. She had so many questions, but she didn't feel like talking to them, just yet. It was a relief she didn't have to relate the particulars of Charlie's information: Artie, Greek, short and fat. Bluebird tattoo. Blue-and-white china bowl, third shelf on the left, in the back.

They didn't speak until they arrived in the Village. Paulie turned to Marie, and he made his proposal in a tentative, gentle voice. "Marie, what

I want us to do, is—if you don't mind—is we'll just put a couple of eyeballs on the set for a bit."

Marie took in the phrase *the set*. She liked how it made them seem like they were in a play, and she planned to use it herself at the earliest opportunity. She nodded as Paulie went on, "Give Paddy fifty, a hundred feet when you tail him. Once he's inside the diner, wait a minute, so you're not together. We don't know the layout—is it one long counter? Crowded or empty? Paddy's gonna try and pick a spot where he can see inside the kitchen if Artie goes to the sugar bowl. If Paddy has his back to the door, you sit where you can watch behind him. I'll be outside. If somebody makes a buy, follow him out, and I'll follow you. I'll grab the buyer, Paddy grabs Artie. Okay, Marie?"

"Fine."

"I asked Inspector Melchionne if you were ready," Paulie said. "You were born ready, she said."

Marie might have smiled, but she could see Paddy smirking in the rear-view mirror. No, she wouldn't let him see her soften, not yet. She checked her watch: almost four o'clock. "Is there anything else?" Marie said evenly. "If not, let's go."

"Play for time," Paulie counseled. "Stall for as long as you can, and maybe we'll get lucky, and somebody interesting drops by."

As Paddy opened the car door, Paulie reached over to take hold of his sleeve. "Paddy, you didn't tell any of your newspaper friends about this, did you?"

"Who, me? This is a penny-ante dope spot."

Marie could tell that playing coy wasn't Paddy's strong suit, but Paulie didn't seem too bothered, whether he took it as admission or denial. After Paddy departed east on Barrow Street, Marie followed at a leisurely pace. She kept his obnoxious red head in sight, half a block ahead of her. He walked like a cop, with an unrushed, ambling gait. Why hadn't Paulie gone in to sit at the counter? Maybe Paddy would have stood out too much, loitering outside. After a block and a half, she lost him behind a newsstand, and then she picked him up again, crossing to the north side of the street. There it was, the luncheonette. Once she saw him go inside, Marie stopped at the newsstand. She'd read all the morning newspapers twice already. *Life* had a photograph of Nikita Khrushchev on the cover, angrily shaking an ear of corn. If the counter was crowded, it would take up too much space. *Reader's Digest* was too small, and it wouldn't stay open, even if she cracked the spine. She felt like Goldilocks, trying the bowls of porridge. And then she saw *Time*, with the president of Chevrolet on the cover: *Two Cars in Every Garage? Detroit's Compacts Arrive.* This one was just right.

A bell rang when she opened the door, but no one looked up. No one was there, aside from Paddy. The counter was L-shaped, with a dozen red vinyl stools planted on the linoleum floor, slightly askew, like dandelions. Four narrow booths crowded the wall. None of the seats allowed for a clear view of the door, but the bell sounded a warning for any new arrivals. Marie chose a counter seat at the narrow end. She was closer to Paddy than she would have preferred. He had a cup of coffee and a menu in front of him. She opened the magazine.

Could she see a menu, please? She was getting hungry, and she wanted something else to read. She wouldn't look at Paddy. A man shuffled out from the kitchen. He was short and fat, with a bluebird tattoo on his forearm. He plucked a menu from the far side of the counter and placed it in front of Marie.

"Sorry," he said, with a harried, affable smile, "The waitress had a problem with her kid. She had to go home. We close in half an hour, but I'll take care of you, whatever you want."

"Thank you."

Artie turned to Paddy and said, "Hash and eggs, over easy, right?"

"That's right."

As Artie disappeared into the kitchen, Paddy winked at Marie. *Really?* She couldn't decide whether it was more ridiculous as a cop-signal, or a come-on. *Yes, they made it inside the diner!* She liked Artie better than Paddy now, too—that list was lengthening by the hour—even as the flicker of sympathy she felt for him flustered her. Drug dealer or not, he seemed a decent boss to his waitress. That he had a good side was sad, in its way. Recalling Paulie's admonition about playing for time, Marie decided against a sandwich, or a dish that was ready to serve, like stew. When Artie reappeared, he asked, "What's it gonna be, honey?"

"Do you have any soup?"

"Chicken noodle and split pea."

Marie bit her lip, as if torn by the choice. "Pea soup. No! My mother makes that, and nobody could make it better than Mom. No, I'll take a cup of chicken noodle, for now. All of it looks so good . . ."

"Coming right up," said Artie, warmed by the compliment. As he dashed back into the kitchen, he called out, "Take your time, dear!"

What an amateur that Paddy was, ordering hash and eggs—three minutes, from griddle to plate! Not that there was much on the menu that would take time. They weren't at the 21 Club. Not meatloaf, not goulash. Not a steak; not here. There, she had it—liver and onions. That had to take longer than a hamburger. As she flipped through her magazine, Paddy reached for a *Wall Street Journal* on the counter and half-heartedly pretended perusal. "My own investments are fairly conservative," he intoned. "General Motors, General Electric, U.S. Steel."

As small talk went, this was microscopic, and even Paddy seemed to realize it. He slid the paper away. "Whatcha reading? Anything good?"

Marie shook her head. He didn't seem to require her participation in the conversation. "Not much of a reader myself."

Marie raised her eyebrows and turned the page.

"I'm more into music. I like to take a girl out dancing, Friday nights. How about you, honey, you like to dance?"

Marie kept her eyes on the magazine and held up her left hand. When she tapped the wedding ring, he hissed: "Take it off! Take the ring off! Don't be stupid!"

Marie refused to look at him, but she had to concede that Artie was more likely to take a shine to a single gal than a married one. She lowered her hand beneath the counter and slipped the rings off. Still, she was sure Paddy was working a double hustle, trying to pick her up even as he put her down. She only had to join him in one of the games he was playing. Once the rings were safely in her pocket, she allowed herself to concentrate on the magazine.

President Eisenhower had just entertained the Soviet premier at Camp David. She didn't care to read about it, even if it explained why Khrushchev was shaking an ear of corn. Turning the pages, she found something more in her line—

CRIME: Knights v. Crowns

Outside a slum-neighborhood high school in The Bronx, a cluster of Puerto Rican teenagers, members of the Royal Knights street gang, waited for their victim. When school let out, the hoodlums swarmed around John Guzman, member of the enemy Valiant Crowns gang, and started shoving and punching him. Guzman fled back toward the door of the school building. Royal Knight Edward Peres, 16, drew out a shortened .22-cal. rifle and shot him in the chest.

When Artie reappeared with Paddy's hash and her soup, she gave her order. She was more demonstrative with her hands than she had been earlier, so that he might notice her newly naked finger. "Is it good? I was thinking about the stuffed cabbage, or the chipped beef. But I think I want the liver and onions. Do you recommend it?"

"Absolutely. Best you've ever had, or it's on the house."

"Great. Let me have it with French fries, instead of the boiled potato."

French fries should take longer. Plus, she could douse the plate with ketchup if the liver was too livery. She was doing well, so far, if she had to say so herself. She looked down again at the magazine and didn't respond to Paddy's pestering.

"I bet you like to dance. I can take you anywhere—the Palladium, the Peppermint Lounge. How 'bout the Copa? I don't got much use for Puerto Ricans, but I like Latin music. Latin girls, too."

Marie tasted her soup, and she was pleased.

"What's your favorite song? Who's your favorite recording artist? I bet I can guess."

Marie continued with her reading. She was glad that she'd moved to Yonkers. Fear of crime hadn't figured as a motive, only opportunity—the city meant crowds and concrete, while the suburbs promised an unattached house, fresher air. But in the past years, acres of tenements had been bulldozed in Manhattan in the name of slum clearance, sending tens of thousands of poor people to the South Bronx, where the slums grew larger by the day. That's where the Royal Knights did their jousting.

And those ridiculous names! The old fogeys who blamed comic books for delinquency might have been on to something. With a little make-believe, random kids from rough streets become Buccaneers and Egyptian Kings, Dragons and Savage Skulls. And once you called yourself something—Policewoman Carrara, for example—you had to act the part.

Marie stiffened, alert to the sudden noise in the room. The bell at the door hadn't rung, but the sound was far more alarming. She hadn't noticed the jukebox on the wall. Paddy hadn't guessed her favorite singer, but it was a very pretty song.

> Every night I hope and pray
> A dream lover will come my way
> A girl to hold in my arms
> And know the magic of her charms

Bobby Darin? Yes. She didn't want to hear it. Not here, not now, and not from Paddy.

'Cause I want—A girl—
To call—My own—
I want a dream lover
So I don't have to dream alone

When Artie returned, the dish he set before her had a sharp aroma—it was made with vinegar, the Italian way—and she looked forward to keeping her mouth full, not least to avoid conversation with Paddy. Both men seemed pleased with themselves. Artie asked, "So?"

"The best," she said, in complete candor. "You didn't exaggerate. I wish I didn't have to pay for this, but I do."

As Artie loomed over her, she smiled and chewed, biding her time. A new song played on the jukebox. She didn't have to guess who it was—Sinatra—and she didn't want to contemplate its message.

Just what makes that little old ant
Think he'll move that rubber tree plant?
Anyone knows an ant—Can't—
Move a rubber tree plant.

"Sinatra, everybody loves Sinatra," Paddy opined. "You like Sinatra?"

Yes, everybody loves Sinatra, you jackass. *Jackass!* Marie dipped her head down and filled her face with liver. She tried to keep her mind on the game. *On the set*, as they said. On the part she'd signed up for, and not Paddy's private sideshow. Why wouldn't he let it go? Still, he'd boxed her in beautifully, and she had to admire his cunning, if nothing else. She had to pretend not to hate him. If she made her feelings clear—*Shut up, jackass!*—Artie might throw Paddy out, and their chance of a collar would go from slim to none. And who would be blamed? Paddy would say she couldn't think on her feet. He and Paulie were partners, and this was her first day. They didn't need any reason to kick her off the team.

As it was, she saw Artie look over at Paddy, and the clean plate in front of him. He cleared it and wiped the counter with a rag. His tone was less welcoming, Marie thought, when he asked if there would be anything else. Paddy considered the matter, planting a fist beneath his chin, his pose all the more absurd as the slaphappy anthem plonked away.

> *But he's got—*
> *High hopes, he's got—*
> *High hopes—*
> *He's got high, apple pie, in the sky hopes—*

"Well, I'll have some apple pie, I guess," he said, breaking into a grin at the inspiration. When Artie turned to lift a slice from under the glass bell, Paddy treated Marie to another wink. She didn't believe she had much to learn from him as an undercover. Would he have ordered an ant or a rubber tree plant if he were asked during the verse instead of the chorus? They were playing for time. What would pie buy them, another two minutes? Her plate was nearly empty. She made a point of eating her last fries, one by one.

> *Once there was a silly old ram*
> *Thought he'd punch a hole in a dam*
> *No one could make that ram—Scram—*
> *He kept buttin' that dam!*

Artie set the pie down in front of Paddy before turning again to Marie. "So, sweetie, anything else for you?"

"You know, that pie looked good. But you know what I read in one of the magazines? That I should try it with a slice of cheese melted on top."

"Seriously?"

Artie seemed perturbed, but Marie pressed on. "Yeah, it sounded crazy to me, too, but I like to try new things. 'You only live once.' That's my motto."

"Are you sure? It doesn't seem normal."

Artie was rather parochial in his tastes for a man who sold heroin. But pie with melted cheese would take more time than pie without, and she'd have the upper hand on Paddy. "It was in *Good Housekeeping*. Maybe *McCall's*."

Paddy butted in, "Say, Artie, I'd like to try a little cheese on my pie, too."

> *So any time you're feelin' bad,*
> *'Stead of feelin' sad,*

Just remember that ram—
Oops! There goes a billion kilowatt dam.

"You know," she mused, eyeing Paddy. "That's a pretty funny song you picked, mister. Why should we be rooting to knock down a dam? A billion kilowatts. Don't we need the electricity? Where's the American taxpayer in all this, I'd like to know?"

Artie harrumphed in assent, glaring at Paddy as he picked up his half-eaten plate. When the kitchen door closed, Paddy stage-whispered, "Don't make things so complicated! Cut out this shit about taxpayers!"

Marie shot back, "What's with calling him 'Artie'? He never told you his name. Stop trying to pick me up. I'm married, and I hate you."

"*Hate* is a very strong word, honey."

"Don't call me 'honey.' And stop talking, the song is over."

"I'll put another one on."

"No, I will—"

But Paddy was closer to the jukebox, and he was there before Marie could leave her seat. At least she'd have a minute of peace while he made his next ever-so-clever selection. Besides, how many songs were there about girls who weren't interested? Better to let Paddy waste his nickel. When Artie returned with the desserts, Paddy flashed Marie another grin. Artie watched them both anxiously as they took their first bites, as if he risked poisoning them. Marie didn't care for it.

"Not bad," she said. "Interesting."

It wasn't, really. What was interesting was the song that began to play. There were martial drumbeats, and a volley of trumpets, and then a massive choir. She recognized the song, but the valentine was difficult to discern.

Mine eyes have seen the glory of the coming of the Lord;
He is trampling out the vintage where the grapes of wrath are stored;
He hath loosed the fateful lightning of His terrible swift sword;
His truth is marching on.

Marie looked over at Paddy and saw, for the first time, shame in his face. The expression passed quickly, but knowing that he had the capacity for it was a comfort. Artie coughed. "Let me know if there's anything else."

Marie wasn't unhappy to wrap things up, even if it meant her first day at Narcotics hadn't finished with the hoped-for flourish. She wondered how many heroin capsules Artie sold every day. Would there be forty-nine left tomorrow, or three? Paddy ate his pie. The two of them wouldn't come back here again, at least not together.

"Oh, shit, I forgot," Paddy said, his mouth full. He held his hand up and chewed for five seconds, ten. Marie was interested in his gambit. He'd piggybacked on her cheese-on-the-pie line; maybe she'd jump on whatever bit he had now. What was good for the goose . . .

"Let me get a cheeseburger and fries, to go," he said, before his voice softened and slowed. "It's for Ma. She's at home. Can't get around, not lately, poor old gal."

"Your mother! I'm sorry, I'll get that packed up for you," Artie said, rushing back to the kitchen as he called out, "What's the matter with her?"

The door closed before Paddy answered, fixing Marie with a look of malevolent satisfaction. "Crabs. Real bad crabs. A filthy old whore, me old Ma is."

Marie shook with disgust. It sickened her that anyone could even think of such a thing. Worse, he hadn't left her room to improvise any further delay. She'd considered ordering a cup of coffee, but now, she only wanted the check. The pot was right in front of her, and it smelled fresh. She tried to shut everything out of her mind except the music.

> *I have read a fiery gospel writ in burnished rows of steel:*
> *"As ye deal with my contemners, so with you my grace shall deal;*
> *Let the Hero, born of woman, crush the serpent with his heel,*
> *Since God is marching on."*

Marie was so desperate to leave that she didn't hear the bell ring when the door opened, as Artie emerged from the kitchen with a brown paper bag.

"Here you go—"

All of it happened so fast, and her wits were so scrambled by Paddy's crudity, that her first apprehension of trouble didn't come from the two teenagers who charged into the luncheonette, but by Artie's face, which was—what? Shocked, was her first thought—actually electrocuted. Had he touched a live wire? Marie must have looked shocked, too, when she saw the first teenager holding a gun. He kicked Marie, sending her spinning around on her stool. As she neared completion of her circuit—*nine o'clock, ten*—she saw the second teen behind Paddy, holding a knife to his throat. The motion didn't make her dizzy; she found it oddly head-clearing. The first teen had vaulted over the counter during her gyration. "Give us the sugar, baby," he said, gun pointed at Artie. "Everything else, too."

When Marie came to rest, she was furious—at Paddy, mostly, for his nasty distractions; at Artie, for his heroin; and at the thieves, of course. She found herself angriest at the first teenager. He was in charge here, making the demands, holding the gun. That he'd pointed it at Artie made sense. That he'd sent his sidekick to contain Paddy with a knife wasn't a bad plan, either. But didn't Marie deserve more than a kiddie-ride spin on a stool? Didn't she deserve to be threatened as well? She leaned over the counter and picked up the coffeepot, splashing it into the first teen's face, and then she flung the pot at his head. He screamed like a girl—*Yeah, like a girl!*—and collapsed. The pot hit Artie, bouncing off his temple, but he didn't react, aside from dropping the takeaway bag with the hamburger to the floor. Paddy's dirty mother would go hungry tonight.

> *Glory, glory, hallelujah*
> *Glory, glory, hallelujah*

Marie heard a gunshot. When she saw Artie hadn't moved, she guessed the scalded gunman hadn't pulled the trigger. No, it had to be Paddy. She saw the man with the knife fall before she heard him scream. Paddy raised the first of many fists to pound the lights out of him. "Hold a knife to me, will ya?"

"Please, mister, stop—"

And then there were flashes of light outside of the windows of the luncheonette. Were they shooting outside, too? No, no sounds accompanied the lights, aside from muffled shouting:

"Hey! Get out—"

"No, you get out of the way!"

Marie knew she wouldn't understand what had happened until later on. And she knew that if she stopped to figure things out, it might end very differently. She hopped over the counter to get the burned man's gun. When she pushed Artie back, he tipped over. She picked up the gun from the floor—a snub-nosed .38, just like hers—as the teenager bawled, clutching his face. As she put her foot between his shoulder blades, the bell at the door rang again.

Paulie was inside, barricading the door with his foot, his body, as if the greater threat remained outside. He looked at Paddy, and then at Marie. "You okay?"

Marie nodded. "I need cuffs."

Paulie pulled a pair from his belt and tossed them over to her. She caught them and knelt down, yanking the boy's hands behind him. The shouting from outside the luncheonette was growing louder than the music.

He is coming like the glory of the morning on the wave,
He is Wisdom to the mighty, He is Succour to the brave—

"Who's out there, Paulie?"

"The press. Paddy does that. You should get out before they come in."

"What? Why?"

"If you're gonna work this case, with Gino, you can't—"

Marie understood at once. She left the gun on the counter.

"There should be a back way. Before you go? Do me a favor, and—"

"Yeah."

Marie stepped over Artie into the kitchen. Inside, she looked to the left, to the third shelf, and saw the blue-and-white sugar bowl, filled with capsules. *Yes?* Yes. She gave the thumbs-up to Paulie and found her way out through the alley.

6 YOU WHILE AWAY THE HOURS

Once the wife knows there is another woman in the case, she frequently makes every conceivable mistake. . . . Ideally, she should behave as if the situation did not exist. . . . Finally the wife's mistake is to assume that the catastrophe which has befallen the marriage is entirely the fault of the husband . . .

One of the best ways a wife can help her husband grow emotionally is to eliminate her own childishness. Significant evidence of maturity is the ability to compromise and adjust to a difficult or even a hopeless situation.

—Paul Popenoe and Dorothy Cameron Disney
Can This Marriage Be Saved?
From material featured in the *Ladies' Home Journal*

DECEMBER 16, 1959
1500 HOURS

Marie knew how to pretend to be in love, but the meeting with Gino in the coffee shop had been hard on her. It had taken some time to arrange—Charlie had gone away to Atlantic City for a week, to calm her nerves, and then she wanted to play hard to get for a while. She was sure Gino would beg her to take him back, and she was right. Marie trusted Charlie to play the part as she saw fit. She wouldn't be a stage mother, barking at her little starlet to smile, smile, smile, or an acting coach, urging her to remember when her dog died to bring a tear to her eye. You couldn't force these things. Charlie was a volunteer, which was unusual. Unique, even—Paulie had explained that every other informant he'd known was either facing prison time, or hustling for petty cash. Nonetheless, he impressed on her his view of how the relationship was to be overseen. For him, it was less like managing an actor than handling a rattlesnake.

111

"Remember, Marie, these people are the lowest of the low. They've turned against their own. I've have had snitches give up their best friends, their own brothers. My view is, it's better to be nice than not-nice, but never too nice. With a rat, the most important thing is control. Never turn your back on them. Never let your guard down. And never make a move without asking me first."

That didn't seem right to Marie, in many ways. Both cops and crooks seemed to hate informants, calling them the same names—*snitch, rat, fink, stoolie, squealer*—as if sticking to your side was what mattered most. Couldn't bad people try to do good things? Besides, if Paulie knew how to handle Charlie, Marie wouldn't be involved. She was heavily invested in the case—if Charlie didn't deliver, Marie wouldn't remain in Narcotics— and she should be coolheaded, she knew. But she suspected that a lot of the men who held that informants violated the natural order of things thought of lady detectives in the same way. Not that she was entirely on the same page with Charlie, either.

"Believe me, Marie, I've seen his wife. I stopped at the bakery once, to check out the competition. I'm surprised they got any pastry left to sell. Fat as a house, and she could pass for forty. If Gino had something better to go home to, he wouldn't be all over me, like he is."

Marie didn't want to debate the theory and practice of adultery. She didn't want to dwell on their rival roles as wife and mistress. But man trouble was what had brought them together, and she believed that they could be genuinely friendly, even if they weren't genuine friends. She could work with Charlie without living through her. The only personal case Marie was taking on was her own. It wasn't as if she were practicing with Charlie, as such—she still believed her marriage was a fixer-upper, not a teardown, as they said in real estate—but if she learned something she could take home, so much the better.

The chance meeting in the coffee shop had begun as scripted: "Charlie! How are you! You look terrific! And this is your fella—"

"Gino, you're not gonna believe it! This is Marie, I know her from the beauty parlor. We've been talking for months about getting together for lunch or coffee, but we never did, and now . . . here we are!"

The coffee shop had been chosen because it wasn't busy; the beauty parlor scenario allowed them a frothy measure of affection without any real knowledge of their backgrounds. Charlie wouldn't have to memorize many details, and Marie didn't have to commit to a story that might prove inconvenient. It wouldn't do for her to be married, but she didn't want to be completely up for grabs, so to speak.

"Gino, take a look at her. Isn't she adorable? You gotta fix her up with somebody! Somebody decent. Let me think . . ."

"Wouldja look at you," Gino said, approvingly.

Marie blushed as she took the seat across from them in their booth. "Now, Charlie, you know I'm engaged."

Charlie slapped Marie's hand before taking hold of Gino's. "Marie's supposedly getting hitched to a guy named Sid. Only problem is, she barely knows him, and she's not gonna see him again until next year."

"Is he doing time?" Gino asked, solemnity in his voice.

"No, he's in the Navy."

Gino sucked his teeth and frowned. Sid the Inmate might have been deserving of respect; Sid the Sailor was a chump. Charlie went on, "Me, I think you should live a little. God knows when you'll see him again. You know what they say about sailors, having a girl in every port."

"That's not all they say about sailors," added Gino, eyes gleaming as they bore down on Marie. "Some of them, they don't like girls."

Charlie let out a cackle, and she gave Gino a shove before turning her attention to the menu. "Honey, don't be such a tease! I'm starving. Let's eat."

As Gino smiled, Marie imagined what Sid would have done, had he been here for the wisecrack. She laughed, and Gino looked at her with new approval. She could read his mind like a billboard. Three simple sentences, all fatheaded fantasies: *This is a broad with a sense of humor. I could see spending time with her. Who knows where it could go?*

Marie didn't know where it would go, either. She knew where it wasn't going—to bed, with Gino or any of his friends. Gino was handsome, but she wrestled with her revulsion toward him. He reminded her of Sid, with his doggy need for female approval, his confidence that he'd win it. Sid had six inches and seventy pounds on Gino, and the self-assurance that came with the size, but dogs they were, the both of them, always sniffing the air, showing their teeth.

Though Marie told Charlie to just be herself with Gino, what she witnessed set her on edge. Charlie was doe-eyed and doting, and her hands seldom left him, fluttering adoringly from his hair to his hands, his cheek to his shoulders, like songbirds in a cartoon. The about-face from avenging angel to chirping cherub was stomach-churning for Marie, who also had to pretend affection, laughing at his jokes, nodding at his opinions about politics and baseball and whatever else. Gino had an infuriating habit of tossing out a line of conversation for Charlie to run with, then yanking it back after she took her first steps. "I can pick a horse, Marie, I got a sixth sense. Come to the track with me sometime, you'll go home rich. Tell her, Charlie, tell her about Belmont, last week."

"Oh, that's a sweet one. Last Friday, we went out, and on the racing form, I saw a horse called, of all things—"

"She saw a horse called 'Charlie's Day,' but it was fifty-to-one. There was another one, 'Pleasant Dreams,' and I live on Pleasant Avenue. Besides, I got a friend at the track, and I already know it's the horse to pick. The funny thing was, what I heard him say was 'peasant-something,' 'cause there was all this noise in the background. So when it turns out to be 'pleasant,' I figured it had to be. A sixth sense, and a friend at the track, that's how I do it."

Marie nodded, a rapt expression on her face. Gino had to remain a little hopeful, a little hungry for her; without the enticement of sex, there was no reason for him to see her again. The smell of smoke always, but only smoke; never fire.

When they left the restaurant, Gino stripped a bill from a wad of fifties to pay the check. Marie shook Gino's hand and kissed Charlie good-bye. After she turned to leave, she heard him remark, "Not a bad caboose, either."

Charlie must have pinched or punched him, because he offered a jovial protest: "Hey! Take it easy, baby! You know you're one of a kind!"

Charlie was indeed a rare bird. No other gal pal was a partner or even a party to the drug schemes of Gino's crew. If the couple met another gangster at a nightclub, the men would excuse themselves from the table if business needed to be discussed. She had been with Gino for two years, but it was only in the last few months that she'd joined him with the deliveries. Marie didn't have that kind of time, and she'd never earn that kind of trust. She really had no idea what she expected to accomplish. She'd show up, shut up, listen, and smile. The project had begun with such ambition, bandying talk about shipments from Marseilles and Beirut, but what they'd gotten their hands on so far hadn't filled a sugar bowl.

Ah, the sugar bowl! An interesting afternoon that had been, at Flegenheimer's. It still smarted that Marie's part hadn't just been overlooked; it had been erased. She understood the reasons for her invisibility.

She couldn't work a case against Gino if she was in an article about his customer's arrest. And she couldn't help but smile when she remembered how one of the papers ran with the story the next day.

COPS FOIL DOPE-DINER ROBBERY
Mystery Beauty Sought

Paddy was quoted extensively: "There was a very pretty girl there. New in town. She asked me about the sights. Statue of Liberty, Grant's Tomb, I told her. She didn't know I was a cop. I guess I just got one of those faces. Trustworthy."

Marie threw the newspaper across the room, and it took some time to put the pages back together. Her hands shook so that she had to leave the paper on the kitchen counter to continue reading: "When these thugs busted in, they came from behind. One with a gun, one with a knife. I hate to admit it, but they got the jump on me. Not on this gal, though. She was fast as a jackrabbit, and she saved my life."

The sudden injection of fact into the fable startled Marie. She really had saved him, she supposed. It had happened so quickly, and she'd left so soon afterward. It still felt like he was trying to flatter her, sending her messages in the newspaper as he'd done with the jukebox. As she read on, she realized that she wouldn't have to recalibrate her assessment of a newly honest Paddy: "What she did, it'll be with me 'til my dying day. The one guy yells out, 'Gimme the sugar!' and this little lady picks up the pot. I'll never forget what she said—'How'd you like some coffee with that?!'"

He never did know when to stop, did he?

"She sure knew how to handle herself. I wish she stuck around, so I could thank her. Somehow I don't think I'll see her again."

And why was that, pray tell?

"She was a stewardess, here on a layover."

Marie threw the paper across the room again. She had the house to herself, now that Sandy had left for school. Friday was not her usual day off. She had briefed Mrs. M. after she'd left Flegenheimer's, rushing back to headquarters from the Village. Marie would be home until Tuesday, at least; Mrs. M. had conferred with Inspector Carey at Narcotics, and they had decided that she should make herself scarce for a while, so she wouldn't be associated with the arrest. Carey had sent someone to deliver her uniform to the Policewomen's Bureau, in case a cagey reporter decided to stake out the office for the "mystery beauty."

"Whatever you say, Mrs. M., but I don't like to burn up my vacation. I don't have plans to go to Paris. It's just in case Sandy gets sick or something."

Marie had enough time banked to stay home the rest of the year, but she was as thrifty with her minutes as her father was with his nickels, especially since she wasn't paid for half the overtime she worked.

"I understand. Inspector Carey will have you signed in, on 'special assignment' for those days. Call on Tuesday morning, to see if he wants you then."

"Really?"

"Really. They work in mysterious ways in that office."

Marie had become accustomed to increasing degrees of freedom at work. The kindergarten regimentation of matron duty was behind her—so it seemed, and so she prayed—and she was able to make her own hours as she saw fit. Some pickpockets worked the morning rush, and some degenerates didn't get out of bed before the afternoon matinees. She worked all over the city, calling in to report on duty or off from where she had to be, rather than making extra trips downtown to sign the attendance ledger. That was the adult way to handle things, of course, but it wasn't how the department managed its men, its patrolmen especially. From what Marie had picked up in her precinct travels, there was a fair amount of hide-and-seek by beat cops and their sergeants—at least with the lazier cops, and the stiffer bosses, who tended to bring out the worst in one another. Still, to be told to stay at home while being paid to work seemed thrillingly criminal. "If you say so, Mrs. M."

"Also, I'd like you to take down my home telephone number. Call me at any time. Good news or bad, I'd rather hear it from you first."

That confidence was heady as well. Before, Marie had always reached the inspector through the switchboard at headquarters when there was some urgent matter to be discussed. She was touched by the trust, and suddenly alarmed as well; was this a kind of farewell? Marie had always hoped—was determined—that the day would come when she'd leave the Policewomen's Bureau. But the notion that the day had already arrived, that it was already over, felt unwelcome, even unfair. Was she saying goodbye, here and now? And then Marie realized that she might be getting ahead of herself.

"Thank you, Mrs. M. I can't thank you enough. All of this is so sudden. What do you think? Do you think I might wind up staying at Narcotics?"

Mrs. M. looked down and then away, toward the window. It almost seemed as if she were grieving.

"Do you want me to stay? I'll stay if you need me here."

That brought a smile to Mrs. M.'s face. "Of course I want you to stay, dear! And, of course, you won't. Not forever. What happens in Narcotics is out of my hands, and likely out of yours. I don't doubt your work will be exemplary. They've routinely borrowed my girls, just like the other commands that need undercovers. You've done a number of gambling cases, haven't you? But you've always come back after a week or two. Frankly, I'd refuse the requests if I could. I'm tired of them calling me like they'd call the Automobile Club if their car battery died. These commands need women. And women deserve to be assigned to them.

"My dream for the Policewomen's Bureau is for it to go away. Matrons could be assigned to precincts, and many women will gravitate naturally to more motherly areas, such as working with juveniles. But there are no women in any of the precinct detective squads. None in Robbery, none in Homicide. One of my predecessors, Mary Sullivan, spent three weeks in jail befriending a female murder suspect. That was in the 1920s. No other woman has been assigned to Homicide since! That will change, and I hope you'll be part of that change. As things are, however, I have to look out for my girls, and to speak up for them. I'm not as irrelevant as I aspire to be.

"I'm not sure if I told you, but I have decided to return to school, for a master's degree at City College. My subject will be, perhaps unsurprisingly, our profession. Much as I wish this might be our last day together, my dear, I'm afraid we may be seeing more of each other."

When Marie arrived back in Yonkers that night, her evening threatened to be eventful as well. It was past six when she pulled into the driveway, prettily littered with leaves from the oaks and elms that canopied the streets. She'd rake them over the weekend and play campfire with Sandy when they burned the piles. The driveway was behind the house, which was on an odd piece of property, sharply sloping in the front, with steep slate steps cutting down through a tangle of pachysandra; the backyard didn't back up against another yard, as others did in the neighborhood, but a street. Marie loved the place, though the house had been sold to her as "Tudor moderne," and she'd since found out that it was a Craftsman.

Sid's car was there. The sight dismayed her, as if it were an ambulance in the driveway. Why wasn't he out celebrating? Two or three nights a week, he was home late, if he was home at all. She reproached herself for being alarmed. She'd become more adept at managing him lately—*Show up, shut up, listen, smile*—and there shouldn't be any reason to fear; his day had been one of accolades and applause. No act of valor had occurred on Depot Place, but he didn't know that she knew. Still, the loss of the esteem in which she briefly held him left her with less than when she began, as if she'd bounced a check. She remained on guard.

When Marie opened the back door, Sid was in the kitchen, sitting at the table with a can of beer. She noted the ashtray with six or seven crushed butts piling up inside. He'd been there for some time. His fedora was on the table. He was in his midnight-blue silk suit, the jacket on the back of the seat beside him, so it wouldn't wrinkle. He looked dashing, and he looked dangerous. Marie smiled. "Hey, honey!"

Beyond that, she wouldn't venture any comment or question, no matter how innocuous. Not, "What a wonderful ceremony!" Not, "What was the commissioner's office like?" Not even, "Go out and have fun, you deserve it!"

Sid looked at her steadily, his gaze varying between the appraising and accusatory. He was using the silence to his advantage: *You know what you did. If you didn't, you're even stupider than I thought.* There was no audience here, no one for whom they needed to maintain any appearance of civility, although the sound of the TV in the living room suggested that Sandy wasn't far away. That sometimes helped.

Marie laid her uniform over the back of a kitchen chair and sat down across from her husband. The table was circular, white Formica with gold flecks. She noted the salt and pepper shakers in the center of the table, white ceramic with a pale blue windmill design. It had become a habit to evaluate her surroundings for potential weaponry. She wasn't sure if the tactic was something she'd picked up at work and brought home, or the reverse, but it had become second nature. A coffeepot had served nicely, hours before. She put it out of her mind that both she and her husband carried guns.

Marie smiled again and took a breath. If Sid had something to tell her, she'd wait for him to say it. In the meantime, she put her mind to work: Sid had come home to change, obviously, and he might have had a nap as well. Had he sent the babysitter home? Yes, most likely. She smiled again and looked at Sid. He was getting ready to speak.

"You got a call."

"Really? From who?"

"A guy."

Sid seemed more sullen than angry. Though Marie was curious about what he'd say next, she stuck to the program and kept her mouth shut.

"Were you expecting any calls?"

"No. Who was it?"

Sid went on, "Guy named Paulie."

Marie nodded. *And?* At least it hadn't been Paddy who had telephoned. Sid might not have appreciated his sense of humor. But where was this going? She hadn't known Sid to be jealous before. Controlling and demeaning, yes, but both knew that Marie was as likely to be unfaithful as she was to be a Soviet spy. And yet the nature of these arguments had never been matters of logic.

"He said he has your shoes."

Marie was at a loss. What was Sid trying to make of this? She thought of Cinderella and her missing glass slipper. Except Marie had lost two flat-soled clodhoppers of petrified horsehide. Such was her version of the fairy tale. Marie replied in a soft, even tone. "I must have left them at the First, after matron duty."

"Is that what happened? Unbelievable. It's just unbelievable! You really think you're something special, don't you?"

Marie still didn't know what she'd done. But even if she offered abject and absolute contrition, if she pled guilty to this offense and whatever might offend him in the future, her apology would resound in his ears as shouted obscenities. He translated what she said into a language she didn't recognize.

"I didn't ask for you to be there today. I didn't want you there."

Marie didn't have to tell him that Inspector Melchionne had orchestrated her attendance; he already knew that. And for her to say that she'd have been just as happy to skip the ceremony would not have been well received.

"What made you bring your goddamned sister, with her wise remarks? The mouth on her! 'It's in Brooklyn, there's a bridge, so you don't have to swim.' If her husband was a man, he'd have cracked her in the mouth, a long time ago. A woman won't open her trap to show how smart she is if she's missing teeth."

Marie tried not to cringe at the recollection. Dee should have known better, even if the jibe had come across as casual cattiness, rather than a threat of exposure. Sid had laughed at the time, as did his friends. None knew that Marie knew that the Medal of Valor should have been a Pulitzer

Prize for fiction. And she still couldn't guess what it had to do with Paulie and the missing shoes.

"Your sister, I don't expect much of her. She's not my problem. Thank God."

Marie could imagine Dee's response to that. "Thank God" would not have sufficed as a prayer of gratitude; novenas would have been offered, night and day. Marie needed to get Dee's voice out of her head. It would only make things worse. She supposed she should be grateful that he seemed to be arriving at his point of contention. Her curiosity, at least, would soon be satisfied.

"But you? My own wife? One day I get as a cop, when they want to make a big deal about something I did. Did I ask for it? No. Me, I go about my business. I do what I can. Day by day. Not looking for attention, not looking for a pat on the back or my name in the papers. Just a paycheck. That's good enough for me."

Marie tentatively dipped her head. A nod, barely—agreeing with him, but only if he wanted to see it that way.

"So, I decide to do the right thing. Even when your boss swoops in to take charge of everything. She's a nice lady, nice to you—I don't argue with that, she means well—but she sticks her nose where it don't belong. Why is she getting involved with me? Did she ask me? Do I want to get marched upstairs to stand next to that prick Kennedy, who hates cops? Who wakes up every morning and asks, 'Who do I eat for breakfast today?' Standing next to him, for the picture, I smiled like I had a gun to my head. Why did you let her do that to me?"

Nothing, nothing, nothing. There was nothing Marie could say.

"And I thought that was the worst part. That the rest of the day, it would be good, it would be fun. Nope. Not with my wife! Can she let it alone? Can she let this one goddamned day just finish, so it's mine—one day for me in the police department? When I get the goddamned Medal of Valor? No, she can't let it go. She can't. It isn't in her, to let it go. To just let it be a nice, simple, happy day for me."

Here it was, it was coming. It was new for Sid to talk about her as if she weren't there, to call her "she" as if he were telling the story later, to someone else. That couldn't be a good sign.

"No! That's not enough for her! Nothing's ever good enough for my wife. She has to go out and call attention to herself. Today, of all days, she has to volunteer for Narcotics. Today, of all days, she finds guys there who—all of a sudden!—want to work with a broad. Today, she sets up a stickup, and a dope bust. Guns going off and hot coffee for everybody! And how your new boyfriend goes on about you—'She handled herself like she's in gunfights every day, takes care of business and disappears out the back door.' That's what he says. 'There's gonna be a big deal in the press, but she don't mind being left out of the story.' That's what he says to me! 'Getting the job done, that's all a real cop cares about.' Like I was looking for attention with my goddamned Medal of Valor!"

Now Sid was shouting, and Marie was trembling. What pained her was that she was able to follow the thread of reason in his tirade. It made so much more sense than most of them. She really wished Paulie hadn't called, to let her know that her shoes were safe.

"I don't know how you can stand yourself. You ought to be ashamed. Don't think I don't see right through you."

And then Sandy came running in from the living room, calling out, "Mommy? Mommy, are you home? Daddy, is Mommy home?"

"Yeah, she came home to pose for a statue," Sid sneered, picking up his hat. "I'm outta here. Unbelievable!"

Sandy rushed to embrace her mother, and Marie scooped her up into her lap. Neither said anything until they heard the car start. "What's for dinner, Mommy?"

"You know what? It's a special night."

"I know! Daddy won a medal."

"That's right! Daddy won a very important medal, for being a hero."

"What did he do?"

"He saved a man from drowning."

Sandy furrowed her brow. Not out of suspicion, as Dee had done, but out of the practical challenge of making sense of things. "Daddy never goes swimming."

"That's what makes it so special. Whaddaya say—Wanna go out for pizza?"

And so the prospect of spending several days at home, on "special assignment," had less appeal than when it was first proposed. On Saturday, Marie took Sandy into the city to see two movies, and then to FAO Schwartz to shop for toys; on Sunday, after church, they spent the day at the Bronx Zoo. On Monday, she cleaned the house from top to bottom, and then she went to the beauty parlor to have her hair set. On Tuesday morning, she called Inspector Carey, who couldn't be reached. Nor could

Mrs. M. Unsure what to do, she drove down to the First, to present herself for duty. When she ran into Paulie outside of the precinct, she was glad to see him, until he started shouting. "Are you kidding me, Marie?"

"What are you talking about?"

"Why were you there? Didn't they say to lay low? Who told you to come in?"

"They pay me to work, Paulie," she replied, managing to maintain her temper. "They don't pay me when I don't."

"There's a whole big book of rules for this police department, Marie, and on top of that, there's seniority, meaning you should listen to people who have been doing this for more than a day. Weren't you told to stay away?"

"Yeah, for a day or two, and then nobody said anything."

"You should have asked me!"

"I don't know how to find you, Paulie. There might be a big book of rules, but your phone number isn't in it."

"All right, that one's on me," he said, calming down slightly. "We have our own switchboard, I call in five times a day. But listen, this is a chance for something big. Shipments like Charlie talked about, the president himself would tell you, they're a matter of national security. I don't know if your girl's ever gonna deliver half as big as she talks, but we'll give her a run for her money. And we're gonna do it right. That means that nobody knows about you or her. Stay in touch with her. Stay on top of her. And stay away from the office. We're making a play against people who have a lot of power, a lot of money, a lot of friends where they shouldn't have friends. Do you know how many guys in the office I trust?"

"None of them?"

"No! Why would you ever say a thing like that?" he cried, exasperated again. "Jeez, Marie, you can be cynical. I trust all of 'em! They're great guys! Some I know better than others, and some I like better than others, but I'd trust any of 'em with my life, and they'd do the same for me."

"Oh," said Marie, entirely at a loss.

Paulie went on, "But I only got to be wrong once. And, between me and you, if this case goes bad, if somebody on our side spills something to somebody on theirs, it looks twice as bad for you and me. A couple of Italians blow a case against Italians, some people are gonna draw their own conclusions. You follow me?"

"But that's not fair, nobody could—"

"They could and they would. And who told you life was fair?"

And so, Marie found herself at home for much of the next month. She found it difficult to reconcile the urgent sense of mission Paulie inspired—they'd march into battle together, upholding not just the Stars and Stripes, but the Italian tricolor—with the fact that he hadn't bothered to let her know anything. It was important enough to call her at home, to tell her that he'd found her crummy old shoes. With the fate of nations at stake, not a peep?

Every morning, Marie called in to the switchboard, reporting on duty, special assignment, as per Inspector Carey; every afternoon, she called off duty, special assignment, as per Inspector Carey. There were no messages for her. She repainted Sandy's room, and, after much discussion with her daughter, she agreed to do the ceiling in a deep blue shade. They cut out stars from gold foil, pasted them to paper backing, and borrowed a stepladder from a neighbor to tape them up to make a night sky. The next morning, she borrowed a different ladder, from another neighbor, and she cleaned the gutters. She hated to think of her dilemma as a contest between her patience and her patriotism, but at least she was home to put her daughter to bed every night.

Once Marie was back in touch with Charlie again, they'd spend an hour or two in the afternoon together, talking about things, getting comfortable with each other. There wasn't much more that Marie could do. When Gino resumed his deliveries, they were episodic; if there had been a routine, Charlie hadn't noticed. Every couple of days, Gino would call to say that he'd be there in twenty minutes; Charlie would call Narcotics to leave messages for Marie and Paulie, but even if they had been waiting by the phone, they wouldn't have made it there in time. Marie offered to wait outside of Charlie's apartment in her car, but Paulie decided against it. For the time being, it was resolved that Charlie would keep a diary of times, dates, license plates, and destinations, to see if a pattern could be discerned. The detectives wanted to nab Gino with one of the heavy packages, not the two-bit side trade he had with newsies and bellhops. That made sense, Marie supposed, but her workweek dwindled from fifty-odd hours to a couple of lunch dates.

Charlie went on about Gino, with roundabout sentimental reminiscences—*Once we took a drive in the country*—that tended to end in hard landings: *Turned out to be a stolen car.* Marie couldn't trade complaints in quite the same way, much as she was tempted. *I'm just an old married lady, there's nothing much to tell.* Talking about marriage would have strained her ability to dissemble, and telling too many cop stories made the relationship seem purely practical. She did regale Charlie with an incident from the past summer, in which she'd found herself in a high-speed chase after a drunk smashed into her car as she drove home. Several gunshots were required to make him pull over.

"My God, I wish I could have been there with you, blasting away!"

The intimacies Marie was willing to share were about growing up in the Bronx with her sisters. "Weeknights, we wouldn't eat until Papa got home, at eight or nine, and he plopped himself down in his chair for one of us to untie his old-timey shoes, laced tight as a football. We were half-starved, half-asleep . . ."

Charlie never tired of these childhood tales. She rarely mentioned her family, beyond sour and glancing references to coal towns in Pennsylvania. "I wish I had your sisters, Marie. I had one, and she was a bitch. My father always went on about how he always wanted a son."

"My father always said the same thing."

"Did he? Oh, honey, I knew I liked you. Did you ever want to go back home, show them what you became, what you were?"

"I never went too far away. What was fun was when I was on TV, on a quiz show. *Treasure Hunt.* It's silly, and I don't even know if it's on anymore, but I won prizes—furniture, a new car. I don't—"

"I know that show! It had the 'mystery boxes,' right? I'm so jealous! I'd love to be famous. Just for a minute. It would be so exciting."

"And your life isn't, Charlie? Are you kidding me? You're a secret agent working behind enemy lines, getting messages to the underground. Like 'Voice of America,' or 'Radio Liberty' behind the Iron Curtain. You're the star. More! You're the whole station. It's 'Radio Free Charlie.'"

Charlie laughed and squeezed her hand, a little hard. Had Marie overdone it? She hadn't lied. Charlie looked at her intently, and her grip was unforgiving.

"When they make the movie, Marlene Dietrich is much too old to play me," Charlie said, and then she smiled as she let go. "I do like to be noticed, but I don't let people get close. You're pretty much the only one now. You and Gino. Me and Gino, our first date, we went to the Copa. A bunch of the Yankees—Mickey Mantle, Whitey Ford—got in a fight with guys who were heckling Sammy Davis. Made all the newspapers, and me and Gino both threw a few punches, but we got out before the cops came. That's

Gino, always in in the middle, in the mix. If we went to the fights, we were ringside. After, it was Toots Shor's, or Jilly Rizzo's, where we'd meet *Mister* Sinatra, or *Mister* Gleason. First class, all the way. Romantic as the movies. Crazy fun, at first, and then regular crazy, after."

"Sounds like it."

"Even so, Marie, you have to admit—isn't getting killed by someone you love so much better than if it was some stranger off the streets?"

"Are you—What? Are you out of your mind?"

Marie was aghast, and then Charlie laughed. Marie shook her finger as Mama would have, with much less provocation. "Don't scare me like that, Charlie."

"Well, I don't think you scare too easy. 'Whatever it takes,' right?"

"Whatever it takes."

Marie became less bored over the weeks. It wasn't part-time work, no matter when she punched in and out. For every hour spent with Charlie, Marie spent eight going over what had happened, and what it might mean. Charlie went on wild emotional flights as she talked about Gino, but she'd always boomerang back, and talk of romance always circled round to talk of revenge. Marie was confident Charlie could be depended on to remain faithful to their conspiracy.

As November turned to December, Marie had one other distraction that took her out of the house. The Detectives' Endowment Association had an annual Christmas gala at one of the hotels, and policewomen were a traditional part of the pageant, dancing on the stage. In the past, Marie hadn't had time for the twice-weekly rehearsals. She'd felt overlooked lately, and she was eager to see the inspector for a holiday helping of praise. And she wanted to be among detectives. The dinner was also a legendarily good time, with politicians aplenty in the crowd, and celebrities popping up on stage. It wasn't a surprise when Sid asked her if he could come with her, though his courtesy was of a degree she'd rarely seen since they married. "Honey, you know what? I think I can get off for the thing next month."

"What thing?"

"The Christmas party. With the detectives. You're involved, right?"

"Yeah."

They were in the kitchen, just before dinner. Marie was at the sink, washing lettuce for the salad. He stepped behind her and slipped an arm tenderly around her waist. She turned and saw Sandy at the door, staring at them, beaming.

"Well, unless you got another date," Sid went on, "I'd be happy to escort you."

Sid kissed her cheek, and Sandy stood, staring. This was a moment that the child would cherish, and Marie wouldn't spoil it for her. She turned around and kissed him. It shamed her to be so grateful for such small mercies, but it guaranteed his decency through the night of the party. He couldn't even think about hitting her until after. "I wouldn't have it any other way."

The day before the dance, Marie and Charlie had an appointment at the beauty parlor. They really did get their hair done together, and Paulie had insisted that the receipts be submitted for reimbursement. Whatever it takes, as they said. Outside of the salon, Charlie was pacing on the sidewalk, and she rushed over as soon as she spotted Marie, breathlessly unburdening herself of the news: Gino had set up a double date. A blind date, for Marie. In two days.

"Are you kidding me?"

"No, believe me, I—"

"Who does he think—"

"I know, I know!"

"Where are we—"

"He'll pick us up at my place. We'll go from there."

Charlie had nothing more to tell her. She'd done everything she could to pry it out of him, she swore, but Gino was adamant that her beau would be a surprise. "For what it's worth, Marie, Gino's acting like the cat who got the canary. He's very, very happy with himself. He thinks you're gonna fall head over heels for this guy. Not that he said it, but I can tell. He's got friends who blow their noses in their neckties. This isn't one of them. Gino, he's showing you off, and he's showing off to the guy he's bringing. Believe me, I know him."

Charlie opened her purse for a cigarette and then closed it. Her voice lowered and slowed. "He's a romantic, in his way." And then she crowed, "He thinks you're a catch, honey. That's what I love about this gimmick! Because he's the one who's gonna get caught."

To say that Marie was rattled was an understatement. What did Gino think her type was? How dare he presume? And what should she wear? Marie collected herself: *This was not a real date.* She was an officer on an unconventional assignment, just like Mary Sullivan spending three weeks in jail to catch a killer. But the department would have the same questions as Mama: *Who is this guy? Where were they going? What did she think would happen? What would she do, if things went wrong?* Paulie couldn't know until the last minute. If she decided not to go, it would be her choice. Charlie couldn't see her losing her nerve. She marched inside the beauty parlor and took slow control of herself as her hair was washed, combed, clipped, and curled, but she almost lost it again when she overheard a conversation between the women next to her.

"It's just like that episode of *Decoy* when she had to go undercover at the Coney Island boardwalk, as a shimmy dancer. And the guy who falls for her, his name was Willie, she thought he gave her a stolen necklace, but it turned out to be from his mother, and—"

"Don't spoil it!"

"I might as well tell you, because—"

"Don't!"

"Why not? The show's over."

"Why?"

"I dunno. It was canceled. People didn't watch."

Marie was grateful when the hair dryer blocked out the sound. Her blood pressure was almost normal by the time it was done. As the blue gray steel bonnet was adjusted back on its armature, freeing her curlers from the jets of hot air, Charlie was in a pensive mood. "So. Whaddaya think?"

Charlie's bonnet had been lifted a moment before, and she waved her hands to cool her curlers before the manicurist took them from her. There was no need for Marie to ask, "About what?"

"About me and him. What I'm doing."

Marie didn't want to have this conversation in public, no matter how obliquely they spoke. Another manicurist had seized control of Charlie's hands.

"Well, you know, you made a decision," Marie opined. "It's the right decision, if you ask me, and now you have to follow through. You've got your life to live."

Marie's woman harrumphed in assent. Charlie's was much younger, squat and pale, sweet-faced but with a determined set to her jaw, like Dorothy when she upbraided the Cowardly Lion for frightening her dog. It seemed that they had disagreed over the subject of men before.

"Don't get me wrong," said Charlie. "I'm not saying I'm getting cold feet. I'm still in, like I told you. In for a penny, in for a pound."

"I wouldn't be here if I thought different, honey."

"It's just that I wonder when I should have known, what I always knew. You know? If I had half a brain, so much could have been different."

"Yeah."

"It wasn't like it wasn't always there, right in front of me. Plain as the ring on his finger. After a while, you can't blame him for trying. You gotta blame yourself, for not trying. Know what I mean?"

Marie understood better than she could admit. It took effort to find the right cliché to deaden the depth of her feeling: "'Fool me once, shame on you. Fool me twice, shame on me.'"

"Still, if you didn't pretend a little, pretend things were a little better than they were, or that they'd get better, how could you get up in the morning?"

"Oh, please!"

Despite the vehemence of her interjection, the older woman didn't miss a stroke as she applied the chosen color—orangey-pinkish, "Georgia Peach"—to Marie's nails. Charlie waited a moment before pressing on, yanking her hands back in irritation from her own girl, whose hands shook so that Charlie's cuticles were dabbed with vivid crimson. Charlie cast a wary glance at the older woman, and then a catty one at the younger, who began to sputter in protest, "Just because nobody loves you, you—you don't have to hate whoever is in love, even if . . . even if . . . "

Marie saw the corner of Charlie's mouth rise, unkindly; tired of her old role as plaintiff, she assigned herself to be the judge in this new proceeding. "'Even if?' And what do we have here? Callow youth against hard-won wisdom? Do tell!"

"My fiancé, he—"

"He's in the Navy," interrupted the older one, whose hands remained steady on Marie's. "Always has been, always will be. This one, she'll never learn. Hasn't heard from him in months."

"You don't know anything, you never—"

Charlie cut off the young woman's outburst. "How wonderful! And what a coincidence! Marie has a fiancé in the Navy, too. Maybe they know each other."

The woman looked pleadingly at Marie. She saw the blue eyes well with tears, and she tried to take in her figure, to see if she was starting to show around the belly. Marie couldn't tell. She didn't want to know. "Um, well, it's a very big Navy, isn't it? Ah . . . what ship is he on?"

"The USS *Abraham Lincoln*."

In the second she took to think before she replied, Marie reckoned that whether the girl had a good life or not was out of her hands, but she had it in her power to grant her a day, a few days—weeks, maybe—without pain. "Really! My fiancé, he's on the same ship. I'll have to write him, to see if he knows him. Not that I got any letters lately. They're on some kind of top-secret mission, and they can't write stateside, because it might give away their position. 'Loose lips,' you know. Maybe your fiancé has a stack of letters ready to go, just waiting for the 'All Clear.'"

"Maybe! Yeah, that must be!"

The younger woman snarled at the older, "See? There was a reason. You don't know as much as you think you do."

The older woman didn't believe a word that had been said, but she knew better than to argue with a customer. The rest of the beauty treatment was completed in silence. Marie remembered to take the receipts from the cashier, and she tipped both beauticians with guilty extravagance. One for believing her lies, the other for not believing them. She would never come back here. That ship had sailed, like the USS *Abraham Lincoln*. When Charlie parted from Marie outside, she hesitated, and then she hugged her, kissing her quickly on the cheek.

"Marie, I honestly don't know whether what you told that girl was the sweetest thing I've ever heard, or the rottenest."

Marie laughed, a little. She didn't know, either.

"Listen, Marie, Gino might be a crook, a drug dealer, a liar, and a thief, but one thing he isn't is cheap. Don't dress like we're meeting for rhubarb pie at the Automat. Put on your gladdest glad rags, we'll be somewhere in café society. Another thing he isn't is late. He'll pick us up at my place, six-thirty sharp. See you Friday."

7 YOU BELONG TO ME

3. There must be no love interest. The business in hand is to bring a criminal to the bar of justice, not to bring a lovelorn couple to the hymeneal altar.

—S.S. Van Dyne
"Twenty Rules for Writing Detective Stories"

DECEMBER 18, 1959
1645 HOURS

Marie kept reminding herself that the only remotely romantic aspect to the evening was that maybe, someday, this gentleman might persuade another gentleman to give her a gold shield. That was the jewelry she dreamed of at night, when her dreams were sweet. She didn't have the jitters of a single gal, wondering if he'd like her, or she'd like him, but the mail-order bride's dread of the postage due upon delivery. Marie had no idea what that felt like, but she couldn't ask Mama at this point. Or any other. She'd been terrified from the moment Charlie had told her about the date. Not that it was a date.

"Mommy, are you going out with Daddy?"

Sandy had just arrived home from her after-school gymnastics program. Seeing her mother getting all dolled up—she'd opted for her turquoise chiffon—wasn't such a rare event. There were weddings, cop affairs like last night's, in which she and Sid took it upon themselves to attend in costume as a loving couple. But two nights in a row was unusual, and she was going out alone. The night before had gone so beautifully that she didn't want to think about it, didn't want to jinx what lay ahead. How could tonight's show match it?

Last night, she was one of twenty girls playing showgirl on stage at the

Hotel Astor for the Detectives' Endowment Association Christmas Dinner Dance, feeling sexy as sin and holy as the holiday. Before the show, she'd peeked past the curtain to take in the mass of dark suits and pale faces in the ballroom, smelling the Brylcreem in slicked-back hair, the Old Spice and bay rum slapped on flushed cheeks. All the blather and gab, all the dirty jokes and war stories somehow harmonized into a sweetly muddled roar. A thousand detectives smoked a thousand cigarettes. Rival chiefs kibitzed with their wives at white-draped tables with bottles of rye in the center, all grudges buried for the occasion. When the curtain rose, the girls kicked and turned and pivoted in perfect unison, *tight-tight-tight*, and the applause filled the room in a soft percussive rush, as if it were part of the music. Afterward, Sid had a star turn, too, as the devoted husband. He swooped in just as Mrs. M. introduced her to Inspector Carey, her boss in Narcotics, who raved about how well she'd done so far. She couldn't have asked for a better night. But she had to, didn't she? Didn't tonight matter more?

"As a matter of fact," Marie replied, pausing to finish her lipstick. She had no idea how to complete the sentence. She wiped off the rosy hue and then tried on the ruby, wiping it away as well. *Any ideas yet?* No.

"Which color do you like better, Sandy?"

"The red one."

Marie turned from the mirror to see if she could detect any irony in the response, but she couldn't tell. Was six too young to be that kind of wiseass? Sandy had an intent look, half-smiling. She wore a blue jumper, a white blouse. Marie smiled and grabbed her. "How come you haven't given me a kiss yet?"

Sandy kissed her, stepping back quickly to resume her half-smiling scrutiny.

"Mama?"

Now, Marie was on guard. She'd always been "Mommy" until a few, very recent occasions, all of which involved special pleading for favors: a doll, a dress, a dog. All had been denied, though the dress had been acquired, last week, and the doll would come for Christmas. They weren't getting a dog. Marie might have folded a bit quickly, though she didn't see the harm in the occasional indulgence. Sandy had picked up *Mama* from Marie and her sisters—the intonation sounded *barese*—but what she intended to gain was obscure. Mama always said no, even if you asked her for the time: *Who do you think you are? It's time for you to mind your business, that's what time it is.* Where was Sandy going with this? "Yes, honey?"

"Where are you going with Daddy?"

Marie turned back to the mirror to work on her eyelashes. "I'm not going out with him, baby. I'm going to work."

"Don't, Mama."

The anguish in her voice made Marie freeze, the mascara brush an inch from her eyes. She was going to try the zigzag Charlie told her about, to avoid the clumps. She placed it back in the bottle and turned again to her daughter. "Why not, baby?"

"Just don't."

Sandy bit her lip, and her eyes darkened with tears.

"Why?"

"Please, Mama?"

"Come on, honey. You can tell me anything."

"Because when Daddy dresses up fancy to go to work, you get mad, and then he doesn't come home for days and days."

Sandy fell into her arms, sobbing. Marie didn't know what to say. She couldn't tell Sandy that she was wrong, exactly, without telling her that she was stupid. Marie didn't think that Sid's disappearances troubled her as they once had, but they didn't please her. Sandy wasn't imagining a change in the indoor weather when her father put on his nightclub attire. Marie might have to lie to Sandy, but there was no point in lying to herself. She still didn't know what to say. Not that "going to work" was just a figure of speech when Daddy said it, but not when Mommy did.

When "Mama" said it. Was that what Sandy was after—the good old days, when Marie grew up with *Nonna* and *Nonno*? It was true that her parents hadn't spent a night apart since they married, but . . . No, that was another conversation they wouldn't have now. Mommy had to go to work. Yes, she was painted and perfumed, in her party frock, heading out for a dalliance with a lovelorn stranger at some chic boîte, but fun had nothing to do with it. One day, Marie would sit her down and explain it all. Maybe when Sandy was fifty. Or fifty-five.

"I promise, honey. You'll see me bright and early in the morning, just like always. And tomorrow, if you're good for the babysitter, we'll have a special day."

Sandy wasn't entirely mollified. "Who? Bernadette? Aunt Ann?"

"No, it's Mae."

"Oh."

"Don't you like her?"

"She's all right, I guess. We watched *The Battle of Bataan* on TV last night. It was sad. That's why Mae hates Japs."

"Well, maybe we'll give Mae a rest for a while, after today. You be good, and I'll see you in the morning."

Marie had plenty of time before the six-thirty pickup, but she had an errand to run beforehand. She drove to the precinct on the Upper East Side where she'd arrested Mr. Todd. He'd been in the news lately, too, when the FBI arrested him for producing pornography. And cocaine possession—ounces of the stuff, in the sugar dispenser. Marie felt foolish when she heard, remembering her fear it might turn her teeth black. What a rookie she'd been then, what a kid! She called the squad from a pay phone and asked for Detective Marino. "Tell him, Marie's on the corner . . . Marie who? Just give him the message. He'll know."

Ralph Marino appeared presently, doffing his porkpie hat. He beamed at her, rushing forward but halting abruptly, like a nervous teenager unsure if he'd earned the right to more than a handshake. "Holy cow, Marie! Look at you! If I wasn't married, I don't know what—"

Marie shook her head, smiling but wondering—*Was this another one, who thought he was on a date?* No, Ralph hadn't asked for a date when they first met, and he wasn't asking now. Couldn't she take a compliment? He'd looked up to her when she barely had a year on the Job; now, she was a seasoned veteran, with well over two. She hugged him like a brother. "C'mere, Ralph. I appreciate this, I really do."

"Forget it. Are you kidding? After what you did for me? Did'ja know, we got three thousand bucks back from the old Gypsy? This is nothing. I'll meet your snitch. She'll know my pretty face, and she'll have my number if she gets in a jam."

"Thanks, Ralph."

Marie wanted Charlie to have another police contact, if she or Paulie couldn't be reached. Ralph knew that Marie was with Narcotics, and that her assignment was of some sensitivity. He stuck to small talk as he drove to Charlie's apartment. His admiration was steadying; Ralph, for one, seemed to believe Marie knew what she was doing. It wasn't true, but it was nice to hear. It had been a week since Marie had spoken to Paulie, but he'd called a dozen times today.

"How do you know it's not a regular guy? His cousin, his neighbor? You want us to spend the night on somebody who could be an insurance adjuster for Metropolitan Life, or the assistant principal at Evander Childs High School?"

The prospect of a pleasant evening with a respectable man hadn't figured in her nightmares. "I don't know who the guy is, Paulie. I'm telling you what Charlie told me. She said Gino didn't have any legit friends. Not that she's met."

"That's all you got, Marie? Don't tell me—"

"That's all I got, Paulie. And I'm not asking for anything, or telling you what to do. But if I don't take a chance with this, I really don't see the point. Either Charlie can do something for me, or she can't. I jump in, or I quit. Two choices. Which one would you pick?"

"Come on, Marie! There's ways of doing these things. We have rules. Me and Paddy, we've handled some complicated cases—"

The mention of Paddy and rules in the same breath struck a nerve. "You can cover my back, or you can get off it."

Marie was proud of herself when she hung up the phone. She felt a little bad, too. Paulie's concerns—aside from the fear of wasting time on a solid citizen—were ones she shared. There was no reason to expect anything to go right. She was relieved that he didn't seem to be offended when he called back.

"Remember, Marie, with an informant, you always gotta be in charge. What you say goes. If it's a hundred degrees outside, and you say, 'Looks like it's gonna snow,' your CI, he better start putting on mittens."

"Got it. Always in control. What's a 'CI'?"

"Jeez, Marie! It's an abbreviation. Short for 'Confidential Informant.' Didn't anybody teach you anything? Anybody asks, pretend you already knew that."

"I will."

Ten minutes later, he called again. "Have you ever been inside there before, with the Charlie Ida?"

"No, I haven't. And it's just 'Charlie,' not 'Charlie Ida.'"

"Are you kidding me?"

"I'm not kidding you."

"'Charlie Ida' is shorthand. Radio code, like in the Army. 'Charlie' for 'C,' 'Ida' for 'I.' Charlie Ida means CI, as in Confidential Informant."

"I wasn't in the Army, Paulie."

"Well, it's too late for that now. But when you're inside, look at everything. If there's letters on a desk, see who sent them. Any bills, how much and who from. Open the refrigerator. And even if you don't have to go to the can, go to the can. Look in the medicine cabinet. Every pill, every drop and dram, you should write down."

That last advice was useful. Marie admired Paulie, and she knew she had much to learn from him, but the pattern of their relationship—extended periods of neglect, interrupted by moments of intense attention—reminded her too much of her marriage. Just before she left her house, there was a final call: "And don't drive yourself crazy over all this stuff. Relax! You sound nervous. Don't be nervous! Just act natural. Be your regular self. That's the worst thing you could do is be nervous!"

Marie was grateful that Ralph kept it light as they drove. "I don't know how it is where you are, Marie, but my lieutenant, he lives and breathes how his kids do with the baseball, and the football, and every kind of running around. Five boys he has. You'd think he was managing the Yankees. The kids have a bad weekend, the squad guys have a bad Monday, and Tuesday, too. We follow how Bishop Loughlin High School does against Xaverian as if we got a grand riding on the point spread.

"And here we are. You want me to stay in the car? Tell me how you want me to be. Tell you the truth, I never handled anything like this before. I got snitches, here and there. Rummies, mostly. Maybe they have a tip about who broke into one of the saloons on Second Avenue. Nothing like you got going, whatever it is . . . Anyway, what do I call your Charlie Ida?"

"Just 'Charlie.'"

They parked around the corner from Charlie's place. The neighborhood was middle-class, mostly German and Hungarian. Not the kind of place where people were wary of cops, but it was best not to be lackadaisical. When Marie called, Charlie sounded frazzled. "Marie, it isn't even five yet! What are you doing here? Why don't you just come up, I gave you the address."

"It's five-thirty. And I told you, there's a guy I want you to meet. Somebody local, who you can trust, in case you can't get hold of me."

"Oh yeah, I remember. Couldn't we do it another day?"

"Charlie, he's here. I can't send him away. I'll bring him up."

"Don't! The place is a mess!"

"Come down then."

"I can't! I haven't put my face on yet, and my hair, it's—"

"Put on a kerchief, and come down. He doesn't have to fall in love with you."

"Easy for you to say! Me, I'm gonna be in the market, soon enough. And why not try somebody from the right side of the tracks, for once?"

"He's married, Charlie."

"So?"

"Stop. Try a single guy next, for a change. Come on downstairs, it'll just take a second. Come over to Third, we're in the blue sedan, east side of the street."

"Fine."

Paulie would have approved of how she handled that, Marie supposed, but the bickering rattled her. *Women!* Had she said that aloud? No. But she didn't know what Charlie had to be skittish about. Marie was the one on a blind date. She returned to the car and stood beside it. Charlie appeared presently, in a white silk scarf that covered her hair like a nun's wimple; fresh crimson lipstick made her seem less devout, as did her Riviera-style sunglasses. When Marie tapped the window, Marino got out of the car to meet her. "Detective Marino, this is Charlie."

"Marie, you didn't tell me he was Italian," Charlie purred, extending a gloved hand, as if she expected Ralph to bow and kiss it. The gesture reminded Marie of a dog offering its paw, but Ralph seemed smitten.

"Nice to meet you, Charlie. You look out for my friend here, and I'll look out for you." He turned to Marie and said, "Nope. Not a bit like any of mine."

When the women went inside, Charlie disappeared into the bedroom to resume her beautification. The little dog came out to bark greetings before returning to its mistress. Marie had forgotten about the dog. Charlie hadn't brought it out on any of their excursions, though it hadn't outgrown her pocket. The sitting room was cheery, even in the winter dusk. There were Persian carpets, a couple of leather club chairs, and a French Empire settee. Though the pieces were handsome, the glamour of the tenant made them appear dated and dowdy. Marie supposed the apartment had come furnished. Charlie hadn't lied about it being a mess—there were stockings and lingerie strewn about, a half-finished cup of coffee, a mostly finished plate of cake on an end table, and a toppled stack of magazines on the floor—but would take all of five minutes to tidy the place. Marie called out, "Honey, I'm going to clean up a little out here. Not because I think you're a slob, but because I have to do something to take my mind off things."

"I have a French maid outfit, if you want to put it on."

"No thanks."

Marie started with the magazines. *Vogue, Photoplay,* and *Quick,* which she expected; *Paris Match,* which impressed her; *Modern Bride,* which saddened her. She checked the cover and saw that it was this month's issue. A girl could dream, couldn't she? Marie reflexively touched the ring finger of her left hand, double-checking—really, it must have been the tenth time—that she'd left her matrimonial knickknacks at home. She felt nosy, even when she reminded herself that she was under orders to snoop around.

Marie collected the ashtray, the cup and plates, and brought them to the kitchen. There was a single plate in the sink, mottled with dried specks of gravy. Dinner for one. Marie pictured Charlie during her nights at home, opening a can of Dinty Moore beef stew as she browsed *Modern Bride.* Once the dishes were washed and set on the rack to dry, Marie checked the icebox. Bottles of milk and buttermilk; a carton of eggs—ten of them—half a loaf of Wonder bread, butter; elderly jars of capers, mustard, marmalade. A decaying head of lettuce in the vegetable drawer, which Marie threw out. In the freezer, there were ten ice trays, two frozen steaks. The only thing of interest was an open bottle of champagne, with a teaspoon dropped into the neck. It had an occult aspect, like a charm meant to ward off the evil eye. Marie brought it out into the living room, where she collected the scattered garments before approaching the bedroom. She knocked at the open door.

"Come on in."

"Tell me, Charlie, do you have a regular girl who cleans for you, or do you just invite fidgety policewomen over now and then?"

Marie laid the stockings and nightclothes over the back of a chair and set the champagne down on the vanity. It was twice the size of Marie's, with a three-part mirror in the center, banked with pitiless fluorescent bulbs. The trove of atomizers and stoppered cut-glass bottles inspired in Marie the same childish fascination she saw in Sandy when she readied herself to go out: *This is what a grown-up lady can do.* And Marie could hardly argue with the result. Even in the harsh light of the vanity, she was amazed at the skill of Charlie's hand, the palette of pale shades that played up her high cheekbones, the vibrant colors that set off her lips and eyes. She wore a boldly low-cut dress of emerald silk. "Charlie, you're a vision."

"Thanks, hon'. You're a knockout yourself! I meant to tell you before, but your call shook me. Even having you come here early, it's a break from my routine. I like two hours solid to put myself together. Meeting a strange man when I'm not even halfway ready, I felt like I was getting pushed out of a plane without a parachute. And thanks for the champagne. You read my mind. I have a glass here. Get another for yourself, would you?"

"I know how you feel, with the 'pushed-out-of-a-plane' bit. What's with the spoon in the bottle?"

"It's supposed to keep it fresh, after it's open. Gino explained, it's science. He isn't stupid, you know. Something about metal and electricity keeps it bubbly."

Marie was dubious, but she said nothing. She had to get into the habit of not finding Gino so awful. She felt her stomach tighten. "Does it work?"

"Tell you the truth, the bottle never lasts long enough to find out."

In the twenty minutes that remained before Gino was to arrive, Charlie drank three glasses of champagne to Marie's one. The spoon-experiment would remain unproven. They kept the conversation light, avoiding cop talk, and confining the girl talk to styles and prices and how to combine two different kinds of eye shadow, rather than the fix in which they'd shortly find themselves. One of them would soon be without a man, and the other would have one more than she wanted.

When three long blasts sounded on a horn downstairs, Charlie rose, and Marie followed. As they left, Charlie glanced around the room and said, "I wasn't crazy about this place when Gino first moved me in here. But I think I'll miss it, when I go. Life can take you to some crazy places, you know?"

"No argument there, Charlie."

When Gino met them on the sidewalk, he approved heartily of both women's appearance. Marie thought he looked dashing as well, even if his cream linen suit and Panama hat were wrong for the season, or the latitude. He opened the passenger door for Charlie and pushed the seat forward for Marie to get into the back of a sporty little coupe. Was it one of the new compacts she'd read about in *Time*? She'd forgotten to note the plate number. She could get it later, she supposed. Were Paulie and Paddy tailing them? She wanted to turn back to check, but she stopped herself.

As they drove downtown, she tried to remember the night before. There were a few jitters then, too, weren't there? No, it was worse than that, much worse. What was the kamikaze impulse that drew people to amateur theatricals? The awful costumes, with the itchy gloves and spangled silver tops that shed scales like old fish. The backstage panic that spread like a flu with the touch of every damp hand, every humid, hurried whisper, as they waited for a choreographer who never showed up. It was more than ordinary stage fright—they were there to show the boys that real ladies could be real cops. *Che cosa?* What would it prove if these women in mannish jobs looked good in leotards? If they kept time like Swiss watches as they kicked up their heels, would the detective squads fling open their doors to them? And would nondancing lady investigators be welcome as well? There was not a scrap of sense to it. All the while, she knew Sid was out working the room, trading knuckle-cracking handshakes with hard-ass Irishmen, *paesan* cheek-kisses with *paesani*. He wasn't a detective, and he wasn't dancing for his dinner, but no one would question his right to be there. It was a kind of campaign-stop for him, to pose for the cameras with her, as if he were running for husband. What had she been thinking?

"Here we are, ladies!"

Gino roused Marie from her reveries at 51th Street, east of Broadway. He held the door for Charlie and extended a gallant hand to help Marie clamber out. They were by the Winter Garden Theatre. Were they going to a play? The marquee was dark, but *The Miracle Worker* had just opened, and Marie would have loved . . . No, a story about a woman who couldn't see anything, hear anything, or say anything wouldn't be uplifting at the moment. Was *Guys and Dolls* still playing? Even a lout like Gino would have enjoyed that one. As they walked down Broadway, Marie hummed, *Luck be a lady, tonight.*

At 50th Street, Gino stopped and flung a hand out. Marie looked up to see a blue neon sign on the corner, the letters descending as if they'd spilled from a waterfall: Hawaii Kai. Charlie let out a thrilled coo, and Marie couldn't suppress her pleasure. There had been Tiki bar fads over the years, but Hawaii had just become a state, and the Polynesian theme had come back with a vengeance. There were lines around the corner to get in. Gino cut through, palming cash for the doorman as they shook hands. Perhaps some reappraisal was due him, Marie mused, before opting to wait and see what else he'd arranged. At the threshold, Gino stepped between the women, slipping an arm through each of theirs, and escorted them in.

"Aloha!"

There were girls in grass skirts bearing trays of drinks, some the same azure hue as the neon sign; the booths were framed in bamboo, with thatched roofs, as if they were huts on the beach; there were palm fronds and twists of crepe paper and gaily colored plastic lanterns everywhere. The orchestra played music of a lovely, driftingly lazy quality, as if to wake you from an afternoon nap, or to lull you into one. It reminded Marie of the make-believe of Sandy's bedroom, with the night-blue ceiling and the twinkling foil stars. Only a *cafone* would complain that it wasn't real.

"Aloha!"

Gino broke away from the women when he noticed a man in a white dinner jacket at the bar. Marie blinked when she saw him, unsure how her sight might have been affected by the colored lights, the strain of the day. It looked like Tony Bennett, it really did. It couldn't be, could it? *I know I'd go from rags to riches, if you would only say you care . . .* No, she knew it wasn't him. The man was as handsome as Tony, though, tall and dark-haired, with strong features and soft, kind eyes. Could it be him? The nicest people sometimes had not-nice friends. Wasn't Marie proof of that?

"C'mere! Marie, meet Nunzi!"

Marie extended a hand, and Nunzi turned it to the side, kissing it, as Charlie had expected Marino to do with her. Marie tried not to think of the dog's paw. It was gracious when Nunzi did it, she had to admit. His left hand lifted her right, which prevented her from a glimpse of a wedding ring, if there was one.

"Pleased to meet you, Marie."

"Likewise."

"Gino told me a lot about you."

"I can't say the same. I was kept in the dark, like a mail-order bride."

Nunzi laughed, almost shyly. "He said you had a sense of humor."

When he snapped his fingers, half of the hula-skirted waitresses turned around. "Should we sit down?"

"Sure."

At the booth that had been reserved for them, Marie was placed against the wall, with Nunzi blocking her in; Gino and Charlie took the opposite positions, across the table. Boy-girl, girl-boy, as was appropriate, although the arrangement blocked Marie's escape, and from exchanging whispered confidences with Charlie. The dictates of etiquette didn't often coincide with optimal police tactics. Nunzi hadn't been anything but a gentleman, so far, but the night was young. Charlie lit a cigarette, and then Gino did. Nunzi asked Marie if she wanted one, and then if she minded if he smoked, before he lit his own.

"Not at all."

"Would you mind if I ordered for the table? It's a little unusual here, but the manager's a friend. He'll steer us right."

Gino spoke before Marie could: "We'll put ourselves in your hands, Nunzi. How do you like this guy, huh?"

"I like him fine, Gino," replied Charlie, with a chill in her voice that cut through the tropic balm. "Maybe you can introduce us, sometime before dessert."

"Gino! What's the matter with you?" Nunzi cried out, affronted by the lapse. "You got me so distracted with this beautiful girl, you forget to say what's-what with your own. *Madonn'!* One's prettier than the next!"

The objection was made with humility, an old-country sense of propriety, and both Charlie and Gino seemed distressed by the distress they had caused him.

"Nunzi! Where's my manners, you're right!"

"Nunzi! My Gino, he forgets—"

"Nunzi, this is Charlie, the light of my life!"

It wasn't as if Marie hadn't heard the name before, but now she'd never forget it. Nunzi, Nunzi, Nunzi. And it brought her back to the Paulie grilling Charlie: *Big Nunzi or Little Nunzi? Nunzi from Delancey Street, or Nunzi from Mulberry, or Nunzi from Arthur Avenue, or Nunzi from Canarsie? Nunzi Farts, or Cross-Eyed Nunzi, or Crazy Nunzi?* This Nunzi didn't seem crazy, and he certainly wasn't cross-eyed. He was medium-sized. Marie supposed she could ask him where he was from, when the opportunity arose. Until then, the farter couldn't be excluded. Marie shifted ever so slightly away from him on her seat.

Drinks were ordered for the table, Pink Ladies for the ladies, Blue Dolphins for the gents. The cocktails were sugary and delicious, and Marie was careful to sip hers, and to spill what she could, as successive rounds of Mai Tais and Kon-Tikis and Scorpion Bowls followed. The scene was fascinating, and Marie couldn't find fault with the company, Gino included. His eagerness to please Nunzi may have been a little obvious, but the genteel tone set by his—Friend? Boss? Supplier?—limited his tendencies toward vulgarity and self-regard. A reference he made to Charlie's "knockers" inspired a stern glare, and a shake of the head. A waiter arrived with a tray of shrimp and spare ribs and announced crisply, "This called 'pu pu platter.'"

Gino asked him to repeat it, and the waiter obliged.

"Pu pu platter."

Gino looked around the table, but Nunzi was studying the menu, and Marie and Charlie were engaged in a discussion about the blueness of the drinks. Marie peeked at Gino and saw the gravity of his predicament. A foreigner—an Oriental!—had just walked up to them and said "poo-poo." *Twice!* And he was supposed to just . . . let it go? Were they still in America?

"I can't think of any blue fruits, aside from blueberries."

"There's a blue liqueur called Curacao."

"Do you think it's just food coloring?"

Charlie asked Nunzi, "Do you mind if I try a taste of your cocktail?"

"Please do."

Nunzi didn't look up when he answered. Marie thought it odd Charlie hadn't asked Gino, but he hadn't been paying much attention to her, and she wasn't pleased. As for Gino, his unspoken joke stuck like a bone in his throat: *Is there no justice in this world?* Marie was certain that Nunzi was neither an insurance adjustor nor an assistant principal. By biting his tongue, Gino had testified eloquently to his importance. This matchmaking business was more than just business for Gino—his heart was in it, and he didn't care if everyone saw how soft and large his heart could be. And he had a right to be proud. Marie and Nunzi were plainly taken with each other. She was impressed by the effort he made with her, asking her opinion more often than he offered his own. Sid had never deferred to her like this, even during their courtship. By acting as if she were interested in Nunzi, she found herself interested in him; even if she was only pretending, the pleasure she took made the pretense all the more persuasive. At worst, she'd have a lovely dinner out in the city. How long had it been since she'd had one?

"Try the roast pork, Marie, it's the best thing here."

"Please! I have my older sister's wedding next month. The way you feed me, I'll never fit into my dress. Twenty-three years old, she is, and she acts like she's twelve. I guess every girl gets a little silly then, but still."

"Silly? Marie, she's more than silly, if she thinks you have to watch what you eat. Besides, I like a woman who looks like a woman."

"Here's to that," Charlie broke in with some volume, raising her glass. "Let's everyone toast to that!"

Gino tensed for a moment, but when Marie held up her mostly empty Kon-Tiki—the straw had allowed her to spit most of it into the bamboo—Nunzi followed suit, and they toasted to womanly women.

"I'm thirty years old, and to be honest, I'd like to settle down," Nunzi said. "But I'm willing to wait for the right girl. I've been engaged twice. One girl, I found out later, she wasn't . . . suitable. The other, her parents sent her back to Palermo."

"Really? Why?"

"I guess they thought I wasn't suitable," he said, his eyes narrowing briefly before he laughed. "I'm an American. I'm an old-fashioned man, but this is the New World. Lots of opportunity here."

"How nice for you. Where do you live?"

"Queens. College Point. A nice big place. My parents live with me. We're originally from Mulberry Street."

"How wonderful!"

Marie was too effusive in her response, but she was relieved to have finally learned which Nunzi sat beside her.

"Do you know Mulberry Street? You're not from there, are you?"

"No, but I get pastries from Ferrara's, on Grand, now and then."

"They're the best! The *sfogliadel*?"

"The *sfogliadel*!"

"Marie, would you mind if I asked you to dance?"

"Not at all! But give me a minute to freshen up. Charlie, are you coming?"

Nunzi rose to allow Marie out of the booth, and he bowed when she left, arm in arm with Charlie. They walked from the dining area, past the dance floor, and down the hall toward the powder room before they spoke. Charlie punched a wall.

"Holy shit, Marie! I don't know how long I can take this. I think Gino wants to screw Nunzi even more than Nunzi wants to screw you! And that son of a bitch is head-over-heels in love with you. Sons a bitches, the both of 'em! I want you to put 'em both in prison, Marie, and let 'em bang each other black and blue. I'll send Gino one of my negligees in Attica. What a bitch he turned out to be! I can't stand this—"

Marie was startled by the outburst, not least by the raw language; she could hardly imagine how Nunzi would have reacted. Gino had ignored Charlie during the meal, but the jealousy caught her by surprise. Gino needed Nunzi, and Nunzi wanted Marie; the unfinished business was between the three of them—Charlie's job had been done. But this wasn't just a job for Charlie, after all—she was in this for . . . love? It must have been painful for her to witness the kindling of romance, as her own affair was ending. Marie regretted having been sharp with her when she flirted with Marino. What business was that of hers? There was nothing in Paulie's snitch-maintenance manual that would be of value in this situation.

Marie hugged her and let Charlie weep on her shoulder. Three

convulsive sobs led to two deep breaths—that's all it took, thank God—
and then Charlie stepped back. She shook her head and lit a cigarette.
"Sorry, Marie."

"Don't be, Charlie. It's a crazy situation we're in. Who knew that Nunzi
would be such a nice guy?"

"I know! He's *wonderful*. And he loves you. You want to switch? Gino
hasn't looked at me all night. I'd really love to be there when you finally get
him, just to see his face, so he knows it's me who did it."

"Honey, I'll lock 'em both up. That's the point, remember? And it's just
my luck to fall for the nicest heroin dealer in the world. Who looks like
Tony Bennett."

"Doesn't he? I was wondering all night who it was! First, I thought
Victor Mature, or even Tyrone Power, but it's Tony Bennett."

Charlie took a drag on her cigarette and then stomped it out on the
floor. She had regained her composure, but she clearly had more on her
mind. Marie braced herself as Charlie took her hand. "But Nunzi isn't Tony
Bennett. And I'm not in love with Gino, and you're not afraid of fitting into
any bridesmaid's dress. For your older sister, who's twenty-three! Him you
could fool, but not me. I'm a big girl, and I told you I'd play this game to the
end. But I need to know about you."

"What do you mean, Charlie?"

"You know what I mean. Tell me why you're here, why you're doing
this."

"You know, I'm happy to talk, but I really have to *go*, and—"

Marie began to step away, but Charlie held on. It reminded Marie of
when they first met, in the ladies' room at the precinct, except their positions were reversed. *Just a quick strip search, honey, and you're on your way—*

"Me, too, Marie. But neither of us is going anywhere until you tell me
what your deal is. You don't seem like a mental patient, or suicidal. But
here, tonight? With Nunzi and Gino? It's flat-out batshit. A happy woman
would never do this. God bless you for it, and I thank God I met you. I
believe in you, I do, but I need to know who the hell you are, what the hell
you're doing here."

Charlie's grip was firmer than expected. Marie didn't want to fight
her. The hallway wasn't the place for this discussion, and Charlie wasn't
the person to have it with. On most days, Marie refused to admit how bad
her life could be, even to herself. She'd so dreaded the idea that someone
might see through her, that she'd be exposed as the wretched creature Sid

had so often told her she was. Could she keep on fooling everyone? Now, suddenly, she didn't want to. She was sickened at the thought that no one would ever know what her life was really like. She'd lived this lie so long, so well, wore it as if it were cut to fit, like second skin. How could she ever escape it, if she couldn't tell her tragedy from her talent?

Marie shook her head and placed a hand on Charlie's, where it held her wrist. "My husband? He makes Gino look good. I wish I had half your guts, Charlie, getting out, getting back at him. Can we go now, please?"

And so they ran into the ladies' room together. Thankfully, there were no other women inside. Marie felt an immense sense of calm, an ease so deep she could have dozed off in the stall. She didn't know if she'd made a terrible mistake in telling her secret, but she didn't care. And she didn't care that the criminal who had fallen for her might have been a better match than the one she'd made with a cop. She didn't think she was suicidal, but maybe Charlie was wrong about her not being cracked. It was crazy for her to be here. For tonight, at least, Marie might as well let it all go and enjoy herself. After washing their hands, they touched up their faces.

"Charlie, what I said, it's just between us, right?"

"Of course, darling."

"For what it's worth, at least you know where you're going with Gino, you know what you want. With the guy I have . . ."

"Your husband?"

"Him, too. But he's tomorrow's problem. Nunzi is who I'm here for, tonight. He's tight as a clam. I could be married to him for twenty years, he'd never tell me about his business."

Marie watched Charlie pucker her flawless lips and bat her flawless eyes in the mirror. As they walked down the hall, Charlie took her arm again. "I think you might find Nunzi a little more chatty from here on in. A lot of men loosen up after a couple of cocktails."

"Even if these drinks are stronger than they seem, I don't see—"

"Just you wait, just you watch. You didn't notice? The secret ingredient to blue drinks is red pills. At least for him. Nunzi ain't gonna sleep until next week."

Marie was stunned. "You can't—"

"I can't drug a drug dealer? Really, Marie, you have to fight fire with fire, and you weren't getting anywhere with him. My days as a chaperone are numbered. 'Whatever it takes,' remember?"

They were back at the table before Marie could think of anything else to say. Nunzi rose to meet her, and he extended a hand toward the dance floor. Marie curtsied and smiled, gazing deeply into his eyes to see if his pupils had begun to dilate. He mistook the look for infatuation. His cheeks were damp with sweat. As he led her onto the dance floor for a rhumba, his rhythm was a little ahead of the band.

"I hope you don't feel I'm being forward, Marie, but I care for you. When I saw you, I had a strong feeling, and now? Now, I think I could pick you up in my arms and run from here to Yankee Stadium."

Marie felt his perspiration pour down, but she was afraid to push him away. She should be demure, she supposed. "Well, we're not even at first base yet, are we?"

Nunzi stopped short, his voice dropping an octave. "That's not sex talk, is it?"

"Excuse me?"

Marie was alarmed by the change, but the injured innocence of her reaction assuaged him. She wondered how many pills Charlie had dumped in his drink. He held her close again, and they resumed their dance. *Bésame, bésame mucho—*

"I'm sorry, Marie. Please forgive me. I shouldn't have said that. My first fiancée, she wasn't pure. It was almost too late, before I found out."

"I'm sorry, Nunzi. That must have been terrible for you."

"I'm glad you're understanding. You seem like the understanding type. I'm not. With me, I take sides, I make decisions. You're everything to me, or you're nothing. But opposites attract, don't they?"

"They do, I really think they do."

"What would you want in a husband, Marie? I mean, what qualities should he have? Personal qualities, his character."

"Well, let me see . . ." Marie knew he wanted to some version of the self-portrait he'd painted for her, as a man of power and tradition. She'd give him that. More, too, though she wasn't sure if it was for his sake or hers. "I can't say I've never thought about it, but I don't know if I've ever put it into words. Strength, of course. A husband, a father has to be strong. I'd like him to be old-fashioned, I guess, because I think of honesty and good manners as old-fashioned. And he'd have to be kind."

"Kind? Why? How do you mean?"

"I think kindness in a man is a beautiful thing. In a strong man, especially, because he doesn't need to be kind to get his way. Someone who helps you when he doesn't have to. Someone who doesn't hurt you just because he can."

Marie hadn't wanted Sid to be so much on her mind as she spoke. She was afraid she sounded pitiful, damaged. How had Nunzi taken it? Some time passed, and then he lifted her chin to gaze into her eyes. "Is it too soon to meet your father?"

So, the speech had gone over well. Marie hesitated before she replied. She tried not to cower as she danced with him. She could feel his body heat through his dinner jacket, the strength with which he held her in her arms. His breath steamed on her neck. No one had held her with such hunger, such heartbreaking need, since—when? It didn't matter. Marie wasn't a kid anymore; she was a cop on a job. This would be her last dance with Nunzi. She wasn't leaving with him, and she wasn't giving him her phone number. She did want his, for a wiretap. She nuzzled her forehead on his shoulder.

"I'm honored you think of me this way, Nunzi. And Papa, he'd be proud to have a son-in-law like you. I know it! But he's very old-fashioned. He lives in America, but his mind is still in Bari. *Sai com'è.*"

"*Lo so, e io lo rispetto.*"

"I'm the baby of the family. I'm Papa's baby girl. He'll want to know how you'll support me, if you're good enough. 'You'll have my name, until you meet a man with a better one.' Sometimes, he acts like I'm Grace Kelly. Only a prince is good enough for me."

Marie felt Nunzi's chin jab against her neck like a jackhammer. "I want to meet him. Can we go there now?"

"No, it's too late. He gets up at four in the morning. But I want you to talk to him, soon. You want me to tell you what he'll ask?"

"Please!"

"What do you do for a living?"

"I own five apartment buildings, six laundries, a restaurant."

"My father would tell you he respects your accomplishment. He's a businessman himself. Coal and oil, but he owns some property, too. He'd tell you, these businesses can take as much cash as they give out. They can make you poor just as quick as they make you rich."

Nunzi looked at Marie with even greater appetite. "Marie! I always knew our kids would be beautiful, but now I see, they'll be brilliant, too. Three days from now, I'll have more money than I know what to do with."

Marie nestled her head against his chest. She felt a quiver in the muscles of his back. He would tell her more, she knew. *Three days.*

"I speculate on the stock market. I have a very good tip."

"My father says the stock market is like gambling. He lost some money on some tips before. It's always some friend of a friend, who knows some inside deal in Canada. He learned his lesson. From now on, it's General Electric, General Motors, U.S. Steel. Slow and steady. But you, I'm sure you know what you're doing."

Where had Marie picked up that line? What did she know about stocks? And then she remembered it was Paddy's, at Flegenheimer's luncheonette. She'd never thank him for it.

"You're so right! You're right, and he's right. I really want to meet your father, Marie. I have to laugh, I have cousins in Montreal, that gave me the tip. But I won't talk about Canada or the stock market with him, I promise!"

"Please don't! I don't know what to say, Nunzi. Three days is Monday? You want to come over on Monday night?"

"No, I meet my cousins at seven."

"No, of course, nobody has company on Monday. You can't come on Sunday?"

"Lemme think. After is better. I really want to make the right impression. I feel a little light-headed. Best to wait. We can't go now, to see your parents?"

"No, it's too late to visit with Mama and Papa. Would you mind if we sat down? I'm a little flushed."

"I could sit."

Marie could feel the sweat pouring off him as they rejoined Charlie and Gino, where a round of rum and cokes awaited them. When Charlie took pains to hand a particular glass to Nunzi, Marie glared at her, but Nunzi drained it to the bottom. He dozed off soon after, waking suddenly to vomit into the bamboo. Marie was relieved that Charlie's concoctions wouldn't remain in his stomach. As Gino fanned Nunzi with the menu, he looked pleadingly at Marie. "I wish—I thought this was going so good. Nunzi, he really likes you, Marie. I've never seen him get like this. I gotta get him home. Would you mind taking Charlie back uptown? I swear to God, I'll make it up to you."

8 YOU'RE A BIG GIRL NOW

31. Q. What is a mystery?
   A. A mystery is a truth which we cannot fully understand.

—Baltimore Catechism

JANUARY 7, 1960
1210 HOURS

The scraps of information Marie had gleaned had been put to use. She thought them slim pickings when she reported them to Paulie, but he was delighted.

"Are you kidding me? Yeah, it'd be nice to have the passport numbers of the guys coming down, but telling me that Nunzi from Mulberry Street is doing a deal with Canadians at seven o'clock, Monday night? Guys around here work for years, without getting close to a guy like that. You land him practically overnight!"

Nunzi was arrested that Monday evening, with two men from Montreal and ten kilos of heroin. They really were his cousins, it turned out.

What a whirlwind romance it had been! More whirlwind than romance, she supposed, although now that it was over, Marie could admit, at least to herself, that it had been a date. She didn't have to admit anything to anyone else. They'd always have Hawaii, she and Nunzi.

When Inspector Carey called her in to his office, he was long on compliments, short on questions; Inspector Melchionne had asked only if Marie was happy with her assignment, and if she thought it might suit her to remain at Narcotics, once the business with this informant was concluded. Marie nodded with vigor. "Definitely. It doesn't seem like I've even gotten started. I want to do the regular work everybody else does, making buys, making cases. Right now, I don't feel like I'm a police officer. They're handling me like I'm an informant they don't trust. No matter what happens from here on in, I think I've earned my place there."

"Let me know when this investigation concludes. I'll see what I can do." The inspector looked at her carefully. "Remember, call me at home if you need to, any time, night or day."

That Marie wasn't altogether satisfied with how things had gone at the Hawaii Kai didn't bear mentioning. She had no desire to return to Gino's social rotation. She doubted she'd meet another heroin dealer as important as Nunzi, or as gentlemanly. She hadn't told Paulie that it wasn't only her charms that had inspired Nunzi to be so forthcoming about his affairs, but a generous dose of amphetamines. Had she told him, she didn't know whether he'd scream, "You could go to jail for that!" Or if he'd shrug and say, "Oh, we do that all the time." And she wasn't sure which reaction would trouble her more.

No one had troubled Marie with anything for the past weeks. She was the Employee of the Month—so she was told, over and over—but it felt like she'd been fired. She called in, and she called out. Charlie was in a sulk after the dinner, keeping Gino at arm's length, punishing him for his inattention: *He loves to dance, but he wanted us to wait at the table until you and Nunzi got back.* She was distinctly unreceptive to lectures about the impropriety of playing Lucrezia Borgia with little red pills. And Marie was less than pleased that it was Charlie who informed her of Nunzi's arrest.

When Paulie finally called, two days later, he began with more migraine-inducing advice: "From here on in, I want you to keep on getting closer to Charlie. Real close! But not too close. Always keep pushing her. You gotta wring her dry, because they always have more. But never tell her anything about yourself, not anything personal, because these people, they're animals. I'm glad you've been patient. It's been hell with that partner of mine, holding him back through this. He wanted to lock up all the small-timers your snitch gave up, at the newsstands and whatever. You've been a big help, though, and I got some great news—"

"If it's about Nunzi, I already heard," Marie interrupted. She'd been defrosting the freezer when the phone rang, and she'd just banged her elbow trying to chop out a pack of frozen peas with a screwdriver. "Not from you guys, though. Tell you what, Paulie, give me your address, so I can mail you a check for ten cents. That way, in case anything big happens, you won't be out a dime for the phone call."

Marie was afraid that she sounded as snitty as Charlie had, complaining about Gino not asking her to dance, but it rankled that when Paulie referred to his partner, he wasn't talking about her. What was she again? "A big help." What had she done for him, packed his lunchbox?

"You know, Marie," he began, exasperated, before catching himself. "What can I say? You're a pain in the ass sometimes, but you're right. It was a crazy couple of days after that collar, but I should have called. Without going into detail, we have other sources, and we picked up stuff about what happened that night. The first story was that Nunzi got food poisoning from the bad chop suey. Gino bragged about how he saved Nunzi's life. How he brought Nunzi home, and him and Nunzi's mother stayed up all night holding his head over the toilet, giving him ginger ale. 'Anything for Nunzi!' That's Gino's national anthem. After Nunzi gets locked up, Gino changes his tune. Fingers are pointed, the guys are starting to sniff around. They smell a rat."

"Really, Paulie? They didn't say anything about Charlie, did they?"

"Nah, nah, nah. Are you serious? These guys, the way they think? Nobody would ever pay attention to a broad. Don't worry."

"Thank God!"

"That's when Gino starts spreading the word about how drunk Nunzi was. 'And you know how drunks talk.' And then he goes on about how funny it is, how he picks out this fruity chink place, for dinner. 'What's wrong with a goddam steak?' And how he doesn't lay a hand on you, but he gives Gino the *mal'occhio* when he talks about tits. 'What's the matter with that guy? Thirty years old, and he still lives with his mother—'"

"That's just *wrong*, Paulie. Nunzi might be a criminal, but—"

"Yeah, I know. And Gino knows, too, he could get killed for saying it, if it ever got back to Nunzi. He should be more careful, running his mouth. I'd like for him to stay alive, long enough for me to lock him up. Maybe him and Nunzi, they'll be cellmates, and they can figure out who the real man is."

Marie laughed. "You know, Paulie, Charlie said the same thing that night."

Paulie didn't laugh. It wasn't the kind of joke a woman should make. "She should know better, Marie. Call a man a *fanook*, he can't let that go. She should be more careful, too."

"Yeah, Paulie, I know. I know, and you know, and Charlie knows. Everybody knows, but some people, they go ahead, anyway. The careful ones, they don't get involved with all this, do they?"

THREE WEEKS LATER, Marie was at Charlie's apartment again, picking up lingerie. Charlie was primping for their lunch date, and though her daylight beauty regimen required no more than half an hour, she tended not to get out of bed before eleven. Marie had visited several times since, and the room was always slovenly. The issue of *Modern Bride* was new, but the same dinner-for-one dishes were in the sink, the same lonely sundries in the icebox. This time, the champagne hadn't been opened, and there were a dozen decrepit roses to throw away, sent by way of apology by Nunzi the Monday after their dinner. They'd held up longer than expected, since Marie had told Charlie to put a little bleach in the water. Marie couldn't give him her address, for obvious reasons, and she didn't have to worry about where to divert subsequent gifts of flowers or candy or singing telegrams.

As Marie bundled up the roses for the trash bin, she decided to have a serious talk with Charlie about what they should do, where they should go from here. She caught herself: *They?* Both had decisions to make, but they wouldn't be together much longer, either as Charlie and Marie, or Policewoman Carrara and Charlie Ida Charlie. Marie had imagined two ledgers when this started, separate books for cop ambition and human obligation. The accounts had become commingled. They weren't really friends, she'd think, and then she'd wonder. They could spend hours together in small talk; they'd entrusted each other with their most awful secrets. Marie didn't regret her confession outside the powder room, and she ached with admiration for how Charlie was standing up to Gino, how she was fighting back, even in its backdoor form. Marie didn't care if Gino was caught, as long as Charlie escaped. That wasn't how a cop was supposed to think, but Marie didn't care about that, either.

The careful ones, they didn't get involved in these things, did they? Marie had begun to doubt Charlie was as in control of her emotions as she claimed. She tried to persuade her to take Gino's calls in the days after the double date. Charlie had been almost persuasive in her explanation why she wouldn't: "Sorry, honey. He was a jerk, and he has to pay. Like you told me, I have to act the same as always. Natural and normal, just another day, *la-di-da*. So I gotta crush him like a bug, make him come crawling. Not because I want to, but because he'd get suspicious if I didn't. It's the only way I can get him back."

"You mean, 'Get back at him,' don't you, Charlie?"

"That's what I said, isn't it?"

Marie was relieved that all of it would be over, soon enough, when Paulie and Paddy moved on Gino. Even if they hit the jackpot, with pounds and pounds of dope in the package, Gino probably wouldn't flip—no man like him ever had. And if he decided to make history by cooperating, neither woman would remain with the case. Gino couldn't know who'd betrayed him, for his sanity and Charlie's safety. Besides, Marie wanted to begin again in Narcotics, with partners who thought of her as a partner. She was going to suggest a fresh start for Charlie as well. There were nightclubs in every city, from Hawaii to Havana, and men with money to back her in all of them. Maybe even some without wives. Wasn't that kind of planning what made a bride modern?

The telephone in the kitchen rang, but the door of Charlie's bedroom was half-closed. Marie called out to her, "Should I get it, Charlie?"

"No, just unplug it. I don't want to talk to him."

Marie went into the kitchen and pulled the cord from the box. She'd thought Gino was already out of the doghouse. Had there been another spat since? She washed and dried the dishes and returned to the bedroom to hurry Charlie along. She was tempted to make the bed, but she resisted the urge. "Not taking any calls?"

"Not from you-know-who."

"What's the problem? I thought you patched things up."

"We did. And then yesterday, he called me by his wife's name."

Marie wasn't sure if she was being sisterly or coppish as she chose her words. "Well, I'm sorry. But you know, whenever you're not talking to him, you're stopping the clock. It's going to be that much later, that much longer, until you don't have to talk to him at all."

"And when do you suppose that great day will finally arrive?"

"Soon. I'll sit down with Paulie, push for him to make a move. A week, maybe two. We've got weeks of your diaries. Did you notice anything about when the deliveries happen?"

"To be honest, I don't pay attention. I just write down where and when, like you said."

"Well, Thursday seems to be the day for the big stuff. And when it doesn't happen Thursday, it's on Friday."

"Was yesterday Thursday?"

"It was."

Charlie nodded. Her mouth tightened as she glared in the mirror. "We were in Brooklyn when he called me . . . *Giaconda*. That fat cow!"

Marie tried to block out Paulie's voice in her head, telling her that Charlie was just another stool pigeon, to be controlled and exploited. This was getting trickier, but Marie thought she could say something useful that was nonetheless true. "Giaconda is his wife?"

Charlie nodded.

"Was he mad at you at the time?"

"What does that matter?"

"Look, if he said her name when you were being intimate, it's an insult. But if you were arguing about something—if you were driving him nuts, if he hated you, just for a second—and that was what came out of his mouth? That's not so bad. You know what I mean?"

Charlie laughed, and then her expression shifted to something like pity. "Thank you, sweetie. I wish you didn't have so much practice, looking on the bright side of shitty situations. I go back and forth about missing Gino, when this is over. But I will miss you. Can we stay in touch? We really are friends, aren't we?"

Marie was sorry for both of them, but she managed to force a smile. "I think of us as friends, Charlie. And let's talk about your plans, over lunch."

"You're paying?"

"The city is."

"Then let's go somewhere nice. And I'm having champagne."

"I don't see why you shouldn't."

This was city business, and champagne for Charlie was a better investment than most of the two-bit buys the boys made, but Marie would never submit the receipt. She'd pay out of her own pocket, and maybe she'd have a few glasses herself. As they collected their purses and put on their coats, someone began to pound on the front door. Neither doubted who was outside. A rapid traffic of meaningful glances ensued. *Him?* "Yeah." *Really*—"I know!"

When the banging stopped, they heard Gino call, "Come on, Charlie! Let me in! I know you're in there! Let me in!"

Charlie rolled her eyes, and Marie shrugged, but their indifference was affected. Something of consequence was about to happen, they knew. Neither moved their feet, so the floorboards wouldn't betray them. They barely whispered as they spoke. "Do you want me to answer, Marie?"

"Is he gonna smack you around? If he is, let's go out the fire escape."

"No, he's sorry, I can tell. He's gonna throw himself at my feet, swear how he loves me. He'll cry like a baby and beg me to take him back. Doesn't Sid do that?"

Marie thought of the weeks of avoidance from Sid after the bad nights, the shopping sprees of compensatory clothes. The only tears shed were hers. She and Charlie were not as alike as she'd assumed. "Yeah."

"I'll let him in. I'll talk to him for five minutes, and then I'll send him on his way. But don't leave, okay? Promise me you won't leave. I want to have lunch with you. You promise?"

"I promise. But promise me, Charlie, not to fight. Settle him down. You'll get him back, but good. Make it count. Next week, or the week after. Are you with me?"

Charlie nodded and yelled at the door, "Relax already! You're gonna get the cops here on us!"

Marie wasn't sure whether to disappear or to join Charlie at the door, in case Gino became violent. She had her gun in her purse, but she'd taken out bigger men than him without it. She decided to remain in the parlor, withdrawing ten or fifteen feet, so she'd be seen without appearing confrontational. When Charlie undid the lock, Gino pushed inside and began to yell, "You're driving me crazy, you crazy bitch! I told you, I'm sorry! I love you, Charlie! How many times I gotta tell you? Are you crazy, you—"

Gino never noticed Marie. He grabbed Charlie, kissing her face all over. And then he fell to his knees, clasping his arms around her waist. "You're killing me, Charlie. You kill me, when you do this."

Charlie raised a hand to strike him. The fist clenched, unclenched, clenched again. She held it up for a time, as if struggling to bear the weight. As if she knew that she had the power to shatter him, but the blow would break them both. And then she lowered it, unsteadily, to muss his hair, stroke his cheek. Marie could barely stand. She wasn't sure if what she'd seen was love, but it was more like it than anything she'd ever known. Charlie twisted Gino's ear. "You hurt me, Gino."

"I know. I'm sorry."

"Get up. Marie's here."

Gino lifted his head from Charlie's hips, peeking across the room, even as he held her. Though he remained in genuflection, his height made him seem less childish than his smile, which was that of a boy lost and found. "Hey, Marie!"

"Hey, Gino."

"I gotta talk to Charlie for a couple of minutes. Do you mind?"

As Gino stood, he began to playfully push Charlie toward the bedroom, pinching and patting her, still humble in his approach, but needy, and greedy, and grateful. Marie didn't know who she wanted to shoot most. Should she start with herself? Charlie turned to her as she led Gino by the hand. "This is gonna be a very short talk, honey. Remember what you promised. Me and you, we're going out for lunch. And the champagne's on you."

They disappeared into the bedroom and the door slammed shut. Marie sat down on the couch. The door opened again for the dog to be let out. It barked in protest, and then it charged Marie's feet until she picked it up and put it in her lap. A pretty little thing. Why hadn't she ever asked its name? She needed to read something, to pass the time. Marie knocked over the magazines she had just stacked on the table back to the floor. It wasn't her job to clean up here. She heard grunts and groans from inside the bedroom. Wasn't there a radio she could turn on? Marie slid the dog off her lap and went in the kitchen to wash the dishes again. She really had just given them a casual rinse before. Now, she'd give them a scrubbing. Marie opened the tap to full flow and began to sing to herself as she worked. *La donna è mobile, qual piuma al vento, muta d'accento e di pensiero.*

After the dishes were done again, and the pots and pans were pulled from the cabinets to be properly scoured, and the last rotten half-head of lettuce was dumped from the bottom drawer of the icebox, and the drawer was cleaned as well, Marie returned to the sitting room. She didn't hear any boudoir festivity, which was a relief. When she heard the shower go on, she hoped that it was Gino, cleaning up. If it was Charlie, she didn't have the patience to wait for another half-hour of makeup. And then she heard someone else banging on the door.

That was confusing. Had Gino been locked out somehow? No, she knew that it wasn't Gino at the door. Marie knew she was falling into old, bad habits of believing something wasn't true because she wished it wasn't so. The oak door wasn't thick enough to stifle the war cry of a wronged wife, baying for blood. "Open the door, you prick! I know you're in there! I'll kill you both!"

It occurred to Marie that, while Mrs. Gino—*Giaconda, wasn't it?*—was aware of a rival, she might not know her face, and that was one more reason, aside from the obvious ones, why Marie shouldn't be the party to receive the uninvited guest. Marie went to the bedroom door and pounded it with her fist. When there wasn't an immediate response, she turned around and began to kick it with her heel. Gino opened the door, just a crack. "What is it?"

"Company."

"What?"

"It isn't the goddam milkman!"

Gino smiled, and he opened the door. He was naked, which shouldn't have been as surprising to Marie as it was at the time. "I seem to be a popular guy today."

Marie didn't care about what a smart cop might do, how Paulie would have called this play. This was not a circumstance that she was prepared to address. Did Giaconda understand that Marie wasn't Charlie? That Marie was also a wife, at least as dutiful in her vows, perhaps even more wronged than Giaconda? No, that might not be apparent, at first glance. Marie ran to hide behind one of the club chairs. Gino didn't put on shorts or a bathrobe. Marie was ashamed to see his nakedness, but she had to keep watching. It wasn't his physique that held her eye, but the confidence in his body. He walked to the door and threw it open, shouting, "What the hell are you doing here? What the hell is wrong with you?"

Giaconda said nothing, at first. Marie was embarrassed by her own first reaction: *She really is as fat as Charlie said.* And then Giaconda found her voice: "You bastard! You stupid *cafone*! How could you embarrass me like this, in front of everybody! Where is she, your bitch! Let me see her, with my own eyes, and let me tell her—"

Giaconda tried to charge past Gino, but he blocked her. He slapped her, and she slapped him back. He laughed as she screamed. There was a flurry of uselessly flapping hands before he shoved her away. "Get the hell out of here!"

Giaconda lunged forward again, but she'd lost heart. "Just let me see her, just let me in. Let me see the *putan'* who's taking my family from me, who makes my children grow up without a father—"

Gino struck her again—quickly, twice, in the face—and then shouted, "Who's watching my kids? Did you leave those kids alone? What kind of woman are you, who would leave little babies alone? You call yourself a mother? If anything happens to those kids, I swear I'll kill you! Who's watching them?"

He kept on slapping her, and the she started to cry. "I'm sorry, Gino, I shouldna left 'em, I'm sorry—"

Giaconda tried to embrace her husband, but he shoved her away. She fell to her knees, as Gino had done, but he refused to forgive her as he'd just been forgiven. He pulled her up by her hair and threw her against the wall. "You disgust me. Go home and take care of my children. If anything happens to them, it's on you. You better say a prayer, not a hair on their heads is out of place. I'll kill you if something happens to them. You should die of shame, as it is."

"I'm sorry, Gino, I'm so sorry—"

"Get the hell out of here. I'll deal with you later. Go home."

"I'm sorry—"

Gino slammed the door. When he turned and walked toward Marie, who was still crouching behind the chair, she looked down at the floor. She could hear his footsteps, and then she could smell his sweat as he knelt down to set a beckoning hand on her shoulder. He stroked her gently, back and forth. "Come on up, honey. I'm sorry you had to see that. Are you okay?"

His hand moved through her hair.

"I'm okay. I have to go."

"You want to come lie down with me and Charlie? Just for a little while?"

Marie reached for her purse, touching the outline of her gun. She wanted to shoot him. She couldn't, could she? She wanted to run after Giaconda, and to keep on running. The two of them, they could run away together. And then she heard Charlie screech from the bedroom doorway, "It's about goddam time, Gino! Tell that fat bitch off!"

Ten dead seconds passed before Charlie laughed again. "Not you, Marie! I didn't mean you. If I had your body . . ."

Marie hadn't thought that Charlie was talking about her. Even if she had, her feelings wouldn't have been hurt. The only aspect of her appearance that concerned her was her hair, which had the hand of a naked man in it. Nothing Charlie could have ever said hurt as much as the fact that she said nothing, for nearly forever, before she shouted, pretending to be shocked, "Gino, leave her alone! What kind of animal are you? Get the hell over here, come back to bed! Marie, let's have lunch tomorrow, honey. Gino!"

Gino pinched Marie's ear, as Charlie had pinched his, and he walked away. The bedroom door closed, and Marie threw up. There wasn't much in her stomach, but it made an ugly, sticky stain on the carpet. She didn't want to come back here, ever again, but she supposed that she'd have to, at some point. She'd clean it up then.

AS IT HAPPENED, Marie visited one more time. Charlie had put off meeting for days, complaining of the flu, headache, cramps. When Marie dropped by with homemade soup, Charlie said she hadn't seen Gino since the last time the three of them were together. Marie didn't think Charlie looked ill, but she was inclined to give her the benefit of the doubt until she noticed that the house was spotless. Marie apologized for the intrusion and said she'd be on her way after she put the soup in the refrigerator. When she did, she saw soda and beer, cold cuts, cheeses, a tray of lasagna. As Marie left, Charlie withdrew to the bedroom, thanking her for the soup, waving her away without a handshake or an embrace.

"Don't come close. Believe me, you don't want to catch what I have."

Marie stared at Charlie, hoping that there would be some recognition of what had happened between them, what was happening now. Nothing needed to be said, as long as there was some small sign that they knew it was over, that they respected each other enough not to lie. With that one little gesture, it would be so much easier for Marie to look back on all of this as . . . what? Maybe just as a story that wasn't so sad. But Charlie looked down and away. Marie left. She didn't think that what Charlie had was catching, but she wasn't taking any chances.

The show was over: *Radio Free Charlie will be concluding its final broadcast this evening* . . . Charlie had abandoned the case, the cause, but to call her a traitor wasn't quite true, or fair. She reminded Marie of the POWs paraded before cameras in North Korea, stammering scripted denunciations of Uncle Sam. Regardless, she was lost forever behind enemy lines. Marie left a message with the switchboard for Paulie, telling him that she needed to see him, right away, and he was waiting for her in front of the First Precinct when she arrived. They walked around to the back of the building as a sour, icy wind washed over them from the river. She said that Gino had moved in with Charlie, and that they could no longer rely on her. Paulie said that he'd heard.

All in all, he said, it had worked out much better than anyone could have expected. "With women like that? You look at who they're with, it tells you who they are. They think they can change, but they never do. The habit they have, being with the wrong guy? The way they fool themselves, they'd be better off on heroin."

The remark pierced Marie, and she shivered, grateful that the river wind made it seem as if she'd reacted to the cruelty of the elements instead of the opinion.

Paulie spat in the street. "These snitches, they gotta know, if they cross us, they're finished."

That brought Marie back to the matter at hand. "How do you mean, finished? She's finished with me, with us, right? That's all you mean, isn't it?"

"I don't understand, Marie. That's what you came here to tell me, isn't it? You caught her in a lie, and you want to cut her loose. Me, I'd do the same thing. But just because you're done with her, doesn't mean we are. We didn't really have anything on her when she started cooperating. Now, we got some real leverage. She don't decide when the music stops."

Marie wasn't cold any more. When Paulie said "we," she knew she wasn't included. She wasn't even a helper anymore, big or little. Though she realized her news about Gino wasn't news to Paulie, she couldn't berate him for holding back on her—again—until she understood what he meant by leverage, and how it might be applied. It sounded more like blackmail. "What are you telling me, Paulie? What do you have in mind?"

"Well, we sit down with her, remind her who her friends are. Tell her that she can't just back out whenever she feels like it. Tell her that if Gino found out—"

"Paulie! You wouldn't! That would be a death sentence, and you know it!"

Paulie shrugged. "She'll know it, too. You gotta show 'em who's in control. Sets a bad example if you don't."

"Who's she gonna tell? Why would she ever say anything to anybody? Ex-snitches aren't like ex-drunks, they don't have meetings in church basements."

"I can't say what's gonna happen, Marie, but I do know we won't protect her. She moves packages with Gino, and we're gonna lock him up, sooner or later. If she gets collared with him, she gets collared. No special treatment."

"That's fine. Just don't make it worse, because she didn't help us as much as we wanted." Marie didn't want to be outside anymore. "And as long as we're talking about special treatment, what's next for me? Where do I go from here?"

"If I was you, Marie, I'd go see Theresa Melchionne. You did good work here, everybody knows that. Whether you stay a little longer, or go back with the other women, I don't know. Theresa has to talk to the big bosses, to Carey or maybe even Kennedy."

"A 'little longer,' Paulie? You're the one who told me I did more in weeks here than most guys did in years. And who's 'everybody'? Nobody

knows what I did. Your rotten partner told the papers that I was a stewardess. Did he put in for a medal for that one? Was my name included in the
paperwork?"

"If it was up to me . . ."

Marie raced to headquarters and parked herself in Mrs. M.'s office.
Calls were already being made, she guessed, and she wanted Mrs. M. to
hear the story from her first. Once Emma granted her entry, Marie strained
to remain calm as she recounted what had happened with Charlie—most
of it, or much of it. She probably wasn't as calm as she hoped. Mrs. M.
waited a while before making any comment.

"Your reputation is held in high regard among the powers that be, and
I have a bit of capital I can try to invest here. You may not get everything
you deserve, sadly. But tell me your primary concerns. I should be able to
do something for you."

What did she want most? Marie couldn't recall being asked an easier
question, but she held her tongue. The gold shield would have to wait.
"Well, the first thing is, I don't want this girl killed. I liked her, even if she
let me down. What she did was out of weakness. I'd like to get Narcotics
off the warpath with her."

When Mrs. M. nodded, Marie pressed on. She hadn't been asked for a
wish list, but three was the customary number when they were offered. It
couldn't hurt to ask, could it? "One of the things that really bothered me
was that the guys got all the credit for my work. I know why nobody could
know about me, but still. I'd like to have something to show, for my family's sake. I don't know if I'll ever tell my daughter half the things I've done
here, but . . . The raise I'd get for being a detective is one thing—and I'd like
it, for my family—but this was an investigation that I made happen. From
nothing. And I should have been in charge. I have what it takes. Next time?
Next case? I want to run it myself."

"Very well, Marie, I think I understand you. Go out and get some
lunch. Come back in an hour, and I'll see what I can arrange."

Marie passed the time in anxious perambulation, briefly escaping the
cold in drug stores for half-cups of coffee that tested the limits of what her
stomach could bear. When she returned, Mrs. M. was on the phone, but she
signaled for her to come in. It appeared that the inspector wanted her to
witness the drama from backstage: "Yes, Ed, I see . . . No, I wouldn't quite
put it that way . . . Certainly not. I do not count any members of the press as
friends. I do not dine with them, or drink with them. There has never been

a newspaper story about the Policewomen's Bureau that the commissioner hasn't approved. No leaks in this ship. Few can make the same claim."

Mrs. M. looked at Marie as a smile briefly passed her lips. Was that Inspector Carey? Had the jibe about press leaks referred to Paddy? Marie hoped so. She remained anxious, though Mrs. M. seemed pleased as she hung up the phone. "First things first. Your informant will not be troubled any further. Not by the police department, in any case, with any undue prejudice."

"Thank you!"

"You will not continue your assignment with Narcotics, however. It was suggested that you became somewhat attached to this informant, sentimental about her. That she's an immoral woman can't be denied."

Marie was too indignant at being called a softy to dwell on the morals charge. "My job was to befriend her, Mrs. M. And I don't think it's sentimental to want to keep her from getting killed."

"I don't doubt you, Marie, and I don't believe any explanation they might concoct to find you unready, or unsuitable. As for the matter of your advancement, I have arranged a new investigative portfolio for the Policewomen's Bureau. I don't mean to diminish your past efforts, but we will not be pursuing lonely deviants or petty thieves. No one will be taking credit for our accomplishments. We will consult with the Homicide Division, as necessary, but the primary responsibility will be ours. Yours, if you choose. Are you interested?"

Marie was very interested. She wasn't sure if two wishes had been granted, or one and a half, but it was better than nothing. As she left, Mrs. M. had one last benediction to offer. "The next time you have to wear your uniform will be for your promotion. And you can tell Sid the same. He's being transferred to plainclothes duty, in the Public Morals Division. It's a step toward his detective shield. It was a bit of an effort—apparently, his record as a patrolman isn't quite up to par—but his medal was of value. To be honest, it might not have been enough, without your recent endeavors. 'Reflected glory' is the expression, I think. He will rise to the occasion, I hope. It wasn't all that I wanted for you, to be sure, but I did try to bear in mind how you took such pains to say that it was all for your family's sake."

THREE

THE CASE OF A LIFETIME

9 YOU'RE ONLY AS YOUNG AS YOU FEEL

When a bird loves a bird he can twitter,
When a puppy falls in love he can yap.
Every pigeon likes to coo when he says I love you,
But a bear likes to say it with a slap.

—"Say It With A Slap"
Words and music by Buddy Kaye and Eliot Daniels

MARCH 14, 1963
0815 HOURS

The ingénue act was over for Marie. Not by any order, or for any formal reason, and certainly not because she couldn't still carry it off, she insisted to herself. Circumstances just didn't call for it, in her present assignment. Today was the debut of a new look. Marie had never spent as much time on her makeup as she'd done this morning. She ventured a few expressions in the mirror: Woe is Me, Check; Happy Old Bat, Check; Absolute Bewilderment, with a Side of Tremors, Check. She felt like she was in a silent movie, but she wasn't a character today; she was scenery. All of this toil had been undertaken to make sure she wouldn't be noticed. Vanity of vanities, to think she could make herself into nothing at all. Still, she'd done well. She looked nearly as bad as she felt, with aches and shakes unfeigned.

At the door of the bedroom, Sandy squawked, "Mommy! You look horrible!"

That was the vote of confidence she needed. Marie cackled, "Mirror, mirror, on the wall, who's the fairest one of all?"

"Not you, by a long shot."

No argument there. Marie wore a wig of long gray hair in a loose bun, with stray bobby pins dropping like pine needles from a Christmas tree in January. Her eyebrows were silvered. Putty, powder, and liner gave her bumps and furrows, and purple eye shadow around the lips made her look like a cardiac case. Seventy-five cents at the Salvation Army bought her shabby black wool suit, five sizes too big. Ace bandages were wrapped around her knees. Her clunky black uniform shoes completed the outfit. "Want Mommy to walk you to school?"

"No!"

"Want to kiss Mommy goodbye?"

Sandy shook her head. Marie didn't want to press the joke too far. She was proud of her technique, but there was no need to inflict any more distress. Sandy was nine years old now. Who knew what she knew? Theirs was a house that operated under wartime censorship, with subjects avoided, opinions suppressed. Blackout curtains were drawn daily at dusk, so no signs of habitation were visible to hostile outsiders. As if outsiders were ever the threat.

"Not when you look like that."

Marie would have made Sandy come close, made her see through the costume, but her ribs ached, and she'd wince if they hugged. The bruise on her cheek was real. She'd iced it to limit the swelling and slept with a beefsteak on her face. What she couldn't hide she might as well deploy. Cheap shoes and a shiner, that was the contribution from the real Marie, lending authenticity to the performance. "All right, honey. But you know, this is just make-believe, pretending for work. And it means you'll have to give me extra hugs and kisses later."

"Okay. When will you be home? For dinner?"

"Maybe. I hope so, but I'm not sure."

"What about Daddy?"

"He may be working late, too. You and Katie will have to figure out what to have for dinner. Can you get her, can you have her come up?"

Sandy bellowed, "Katie! Mom wants ya!"

"Sandy, I could have yelled myself. Go downstairs and ask. Or I'll kiss you and walk you to school and make your friends think your mama is the oldest and craziest *strega* there is."

Marie rose and held out her hands, and Sandy ran, fake-shrieking, to get Katie. Marie had turned again to the mirror when the young woman arrived at the door, announcing herself with a horrified intake of breath. "My dear Lord, ma'am! You should have . . . I nearly spanked Sandy for telling me how awful you looked this morning!"

Katie was a twenty-year-old Londoner who had been with them for a year. She was an unmixed blessing, one of the few good choices Marie had made in her domestic affairs. She was determined to spare herself the agita of the incessant last-minute babysitting rearrangements, and she wanted stability for Sandy. That Sid had been passed like a hot potato among grudging aunts may have also figured in the calculations. *Just look how he turned out.* Few were the days when Marie didn't spend either breakfast or dinner with Sandy, but Katie was adored as the sister she very sensibly never expected to have.

"Thanks for sticking up for me, Katie, but the kid's telling the truth. The question isn't if I'm pretty. It's 'Am I real?' What do you think?"

Katie swiveled her head owlishly from side to side. She was barely five feet and thin as a mop handle, with brown hair in bangs and a ponytail. She had an ordinary kind of prettiness that was made beautiful by her invincible cheer. Katie stared judiciously as she stepped close and then reversed her paces until she was back at the threshold of the room. "It's good, ma'am."

"I'm glad, I thought—"

"Only . . ."

"Yes?"

"Only the hands. They're your own. I don't know if anyone will be studying you so close, but for me, they do stand out."

"Ah, Katie," said Marie, picking up a pair of tatty black cotton gloves from the dresser. "I am in agreement with you once again. I wondered if I should cut off the fingertips."

"You'd have to ruin your nails."

"True. Since my daughter won't be seen with me, would you take her to school?"

"I'd planned to. Right away, I think. There's a woman at the front door."

Marie held her breath. Only strangers used the front door, but she'd bet that the visitor wasn't unfamiliar altogether. "Did Sandy see? What did she look like?"

"No, Sandy was upstairs. The lady was young and dressed up. Too nervous to be selling anything. I told her to wait and closed the door."

"Thanks a million, Katie. You'd better go."

"Yes, ma'am."

Marie turned back to the mirror and closed her eyes, so she could think without seeing anything. Who should she be? At first, Marie thought about stripping off the mask. She'd descend the staircase in an evening gown, hair up like it was Jiffy-Popped, spackled with diamonds. As if she were the host of a variety show, and a celebrity guest surprised her on stage to sing a duet.

"Oh, Carmen, you shouldn't have! I didn't expect to see you here! Ladies and gentlemen, this is Carmen, a lady I've known about for a while, but I've never met. What a special surprise to have her here! Carmen is a Puerto Rican whore from the Bronx. What are we going to sing tonight, Carmen? 'Please Release Me,' that's just too perfect. Maestro?"

No, that song wouldn't do, Marie thought, opening her eyes to see the sad old woman in the mirror. They already sang that one last night on the phone. Marie and Sid were in bed. Both were asleep, until the phone rang at midnight.

"Is this Marie?"

"Yes."

"Marie, who's married to Sid?"

"Yes. Who is this?"

"My name is Carmen, and me and Sid are in love. I know this must be hard for you, as a woman, but I'm begging you to let him have a divorce."

Marie first thought she was dreaming. Late-night calls filled her with dread; good news could always wait until the morning. Long ago, when she was a newlywed, she feared that such a call would bring news of Sid's death in the line of duty. They wouldn't call, she knew now; the message was delivered in person.

"Okay," said Marie.

"What did you say?"

"Honey, he's yours for the taking. I'm not kidding. Have fun and good luck. Pick him up in the next hour, and I'll give you a free toaster."

"You shouldn't joke. I know you love him, too, in your way."

"I don't."

"You shouldn't joke."

"You shouldn't call. Ever, let alone this late."

Marie shoved Sid's shoulder from across the bed. He slept on his back, arms splayed. She dropped the phone on him and sat up. "It's for you. Why don't you take it downstairs? Downstairs, outside, just go."

Sid took the phone and said, "Unbelievable, you are just unbelievable . . . "

For once, she agreed with him. But he broke the phone after. There had been occasions when he'd taken pains to avoid hitting her in the face. Not last night. He left an hour later.

Marie had been thinking about doing the old lady getup for a while. This morning, the war paint did double duty as camouflage. Staring into the mirror, she tried on the Happy-Old-Bat expression again. "How convenient! I didn't want to be pretty today!"

When she heard the back door slam, she was grateful. Carmen spoke as if there were procedures for off-loading a secondhand husband, like the rigmarole of buying a house. Did they have to set up an escrow account, until Sid was inspected for termites? *Sign here, initial here.* Hadn't Marie agreed to be rid of him last night? Nothing made sense. There was no point in avoiding Carmen now, and there was reason to make clear that she was never to come here again. Marie removed the wig, but she'd taken far too much trouble with her makeup to do it over again. She lumbered downstairs, her legs stiff, her tread leaden. "Coming! Coming down! Shut up, you!"

Carmen couldn't hear her, but Marie was already easing into character. When she realized she'd forgotten her gloves, she didn't go back upstairs; she'd already started down, and the show was live. Marie opened the door but left the chain on, leaving three inches of space for Carmen to see inside. "What do you want?"

"Marie?"

Carmen was in silhouette, the early light behind her, in a dark suit and broad-brimmed hat. She had spent time putting herself together, maybe as much as Marie. Was she pretty? Marie didn't care. She didn't see her as a rival, or even a woman, but mud on Sid's shoes that he'd dragged to her doorstep. "What do you want?"

"I want to talk to you."

"There is nothing to talk about."

"There is, though, I need for you to hear me, I need—"

"You need to go home."

"I need for you to let Sid go, we are so happy, we—"

"You need to shut up and get the hell out of here. I told you last night, the bastard is yours, take him."

"We want to have children!"

Marie unchained the door, so she was thrown into bright relief. "I don't care if you have kittens. Take him! Good riddance, and go to hell, the both of you. Listen to me, you idiot, I do not love him. He's all yours. But if you ever show up here again, if you ever disturb me or my family, I will kill you."

Carmen took two stunned steps back, and then a third. Marie couldn't guess what Carmen had been told, aside from that Sid was the poor prisoner of a sham marriage, when he had so much love to give. Having said her piece, Marie noticed the woman for the first time. Her suit was conservative and well-cut, dark gray, the kind worn for a job interview or a funeral. Her figure was voluptuous, her bust and behind full and round. Young, no more than twenty-five. Pretty, too, though it looked like she'd been crying. She'd also taken pains to cover being smacked around last night. Not much in common between them, aside from Sid and bruises. And yet this one wanted so much more of him. Didn't she know that the bruises were part of the package? "I'm laying it out straight. I don't want him. Is there anything else?"

"Oh, my God, you're prettier than he said!"

Carmen began to cry. She turned and stumbled down the narrow steps, nearly falling before she reached the street. Marie slammed the door.

Did that tramp really say that Marie looked *better* than Sid had said? That son of a bitch! Marie hadn't lied when she said that she was finished with him. This time, she'd call a lawyer. This time, the resolve wouldn't melt with the passage of time, the bonds and burdens of tradition and reputation, church and family. She'd been ready to make the move for a while, but Sid had failed to supply a persuasive reason since . . . when? Had it been two years since the last beating? They saw each other infrequently, given their schedules, and their lack of effort to do otherwise. Having Katie helped, to be sure. Still, they'd been cordial, even warm lately, and coexistence had begun to seem oddly agreeable. Did Marie dare to dream it, that marriage could feel no worse than a pebble in her shoe? That Sid might have grown more devious, rather than more decent, hadn't occurred to her. She'd thought he'd settled down. Apparently, he had.

Part of it had to do with an improvement in finances, since Sid went from patrol to a gambling squad. Clearly, there were men in headquarters with an eye for talent! Half of Sid's childhood friends from Hell's Kitchen were hoodlums. He could have made a dozen major bookie cases from guests at the wedding. Marie didn't approve, but she was in no position to object. She was content to open the newspaper and not read Sid's name in it. Years had passed since the last major corruption scandal. Were they overdue? A scrapbook of clips about Sid could become thicker than hers in no time, and it wouldn't be good for either of them. Not that Marie asked, or Sid would ever say. He could have been a grocer or a test pilot for all the shoptalk that passed the dinner table. Work was one of the richer strains of the unspoken in the many silences of their marriage.

The exception Marie had made was in telling Sid about his transfer. Had that been three years ago already? For once, she'd been tough-minded. She didn't just fling herself like a virgin into a volcano, desperate to appease. There was danger in suggesting she was better-informed—better-anythinged—than he was, but the gambit had paid off as extravagantly as one of Gino's bets at the track. She'd framed the news as a reward for his medal, with the early tip-off a favor from Mrs. M. Marie claimed no credit, but Sid knew she'd been responsible. He didn't have to love her as a husband, or to respect her as cop, but this time—*Finally!*—he'd understood that she could be of value to him. That he should be a little less loose with his temper, less fast with his hands, was a breakthrough. Marie would have looked back on the months that followed as a second honeymoon, had there been a first.

Did that tramp really say what Marie thought she said? *Enough.* She had to get ready for work. Halfway up the stairs, she realized she was still doing the old lady walk. Was it nine years of marriage or five years of policing that made her feel ancient? Or maybe there were so many heavy thoughts in her head that she was getting bowlegged from carrying them. *Enough.* So many people had said to Marie, "How amazing! You and your husband, both police! The stories you must have, the adventures, it must never be dull!" Did they ever work together, did they ever compete? Did they ever practice with the handcuffs at home, ha-ha-ha! Over time, random cop comments that passed her way painted Sid as a likable loafer and a petty grifter, never passing up an opportunity for a laugh, a buck, a dame. Few cops respected him, but most liked him. A charmer and a joker. One thing that a few said at social events over the years—often with whiskey on their breath, hastily added after indiscreet hints about his being lazy or a ladies' man—was that he was never mean. Marie supposed she was glad to hear that. No one else got hurt.

Marie had never been mean, but no one would accuse her of being soft anymore, not even in Narcotics. Cowering less at home had been good for her posture; the grueling and often gruesome nature of the "new investigative portfolio" had thickened her skin. She had too many cases to form sentimental attachments, even if she were so inclined. She hadn't cried in a long time. She didn't cry last night, or this morning. A black eye wouldn't kill her. That Sid cheated was old news. She'd told him off last night, and she'd chased away his mistress this morning like a neighbor's dog on the lawn. The old Marie couldn't have done that.

She grabbed a blouse and business suit from the closet. One outfit for the morning stakeout, the other for the afternoon meeting in Queens, at the DA's. Maybe she'd get a referral for a divorce lawyer there. She had picked out a charcoal suit, but put it back when she realized that was what Carmen had been wearing. *Blue today, yes.* Other lady-friends of her husband had called the house, but none had ever visited. This one wanted kids with him. *Good luck with that plan, sister!* The prospect of more children was about as appealing to Sid as an iron lung.

Marie had no regrets that her diaper-changing days were behind her. She tried to picture the conversation between Carmen and Sid: *Of course, baby, I'd love to have kids with you, but my bitch of a wife won't let me go, and I won't have bastards.* That had to be his pitch, the reason Carmen showed up in her Sunday best, with a face looking like it had been in the Friday-night fights. Marie did like the hat. She had one like it. The hell with it, she'd bring it along. It went with the suit. And with the bruise, covering it with a little shadow.

And so off to Queens, to Union Turnpike in North Jamaica Estates, where she would spend the morning observing the office and residence of one Dr. Harvey Lothringer, obstetrician and gynecologist. One small comfort in the absence of professional conversations with her husband was that he wouldn't get Lothringer's name if he did knock up Carmen. Still, Sid had to know that Marie had been working the abortionist racket. Several cases had been in the papers—though none lately, with the newspaper strike—and other cops would have brought them up. Wouldn't he look foolish, not knowing? Oh, Sid always had a line. Maybe, "You know, these cases, they're just so sickening, Marie doesn't like to talk about them. We just have the one kid, and we'd like more, so it's hard for her."

That wasn't hard at all. Was it possible she learned to lie from Sid? He was a master, after all, and she amazed herself with the brazenness and fluency of her deceit as an undercover. Did she have reason to be grateful to him for that, too? That would make three things she owed him for, aside from Sandy and her job. Maybe she'd give him Harvey Lothringer's number, in a pinch, if the good doctor wasn't locked up by then. No, Sid wouldn't spring for the five hundred dollars Harvey charged. More likely to go for the twenty-buck job from the uptown country granny with a branch from a slippery elm tree, who'd learned the old remedies and knew about female innards from her days on the farm. For all Marie knew, she'd wind up tailing Sid as he drove Carmen to some veterinarian's assistant at Belmont racetrack who owed him a favor. She shuddered at the thought. She couldn't wish anything like that on anyone, even Carmen.

When Marie first started working abortion cases—ABs, they called them—she had been so exhausted by the episode with Charlie that she told her sister Dee that the work was "a breath of fresh air."

"Marie," Dee had said, hesitating.

"Yeah?"

"I translate wiretaps for the Brooklyn DA. Nine-to-five, no bodily fluids. I get bored sometimes. But you? You *really* need a change of pace."

Since then, Marie had visited too many teenagers in emergency rooms to let her heart break for any of them. Not just teenagers. She had learned to decipher the scrawled handwriting on the charts, which told of puncture wounds, blood poisoning, infection. Girls who didn't want to have babies now, and never would again. Girls who made mistakes, and then made bigger ones, trying to fix them. Marie refused to see herself in them. She'd done that with Charlie, and it wasn't something she'd ever do again. As she saw it now, the separation between her lives made both halves possible. She'd rebuilt the wall between them to be unbreachable as the one in Berlin.

Marie didn't have to be a detective to understand her life anymore, but she had to be a cop to keep the peace on its rougher corners. She was a real cop now, and whoever didn't believe her could go to hell. She worked to fix things in the city, day after day, and if they weren't set right by the time she went to bed—whenever that was—she still slept like a baby, because she needed her sleep if she was going to try again the next morning.

Besides, the women were never in trouble with the law. None were arrested, at least. They were treated as if they'd attempted suicide, more or less; they didn't have the right to do what they'd done, but they were to be pitied, not punished. In New York, it was a misdemeanor to obtain an abortion, and a felony to perform one, but the city only went after the abortionists. The women were enlisted as witnesses against those who gave them what they'd begged for, what they'd paid for. None of the girls refused to cooperate, and few required much persuasion, feeling guilty relief at having escaped both arrest and pregnancy. Only the dying ones kept their secrets. Marie remembered the last words of a fourteen-year-old as she hemorrhaged in Kings County Hospital: "She made me promise not to tell."

No such effort against empathy was required with the abortionists, whether they were washerwomen or Park Avenue surgeons. None that Marie met had shown an interest in anything but money, in making the most that the heartless market would bear. And the market talk she heard often worked its way into her nightmares: "It's thirty-five bucks."

"I only got twenty-five."

"Tell you what, find another girl with the same problem, I'll do you both for fifty."

"But what if I can't—"

"The longer you wait, the worse it is."

That much was true. The woman who offered the two-for-one special knew that much about biology.

Marie had met both girls the same night in a Bronx hospital, where they were treated for sepsis and chemical burns in the uterus. One was terrified that her mother would find out; the other had no family at all. Marie indulged herself in a moment of pity then: *Poor kids* . . . Most of the hospital cases were poor kids. They were the ones who could only afford the home remedies. Girls who could come up with a hundred bucks usually could find a doctor, and they were spared all manner of butchery. Still, the amateurs were somehow less cold-blooded than some of the professional men, whose conversations Marie heard on wiretaps.

There had been Doctor D., in Brooklyn, who refused to work on women after the first trimester, because of the risk of complications. He didn't turn them away, however; for a fee, he referred them to a nurse who was willing to gamble with the old catheter method. On a Monday afternoon, Marie stepped into the basement of the candy store where she had a wiretap plant and listened to the weekend's talk. Sunday morning began with a call to the nurse about a fifteen-year-old he was sending her. She was at least four months pregnant. The girl would be with her grandmother, and the nurse was to decide whether the AB was worth the danger.

Marie covered her ears as Dr. D. complained to his mother about why he didn't want come to dinner at his brother's. "I don't know what's worse, the pot roast, or hearing his stupid wife go on and on about how much money he makes!"

And then the nurse called, screaming, "They brought it back to me, and it's breathing! It's—"

Alive. Marie wanted to stop the tape and replay it, hoping she hadn't heard right, but she couldn't move. "Calm down!" he barked. "Tell me what happened."

"Doc, when I examined her, I figured she was at least five months. But the grandmother insisted, and offered an extra two hundred. I did the job, sent 'em home, told 'em it would pass. Twenty-two years, I've had sick ones, ones who died, never ones . . . It came out breathing. They called. What do I tell them?"

"You tell them to shut up and calm down! That's first. Then, you tell them to cut the cord. Put a pillow on its face for a couple of minutes, and the problem's over. Make sure you get the girl penicillin tabs tomorrow, and we're all riding easy."

Marie stopped the tape and went to the bathroom. She needed to splash water on her face before she listened to the rest.

"Holy shit, Doc, they brought it to me: it's in a pillow case, and it's still breathing. They just left, they left it with me. It's a boy. A goddam boy. I feel sick. I don't know what to do. Can I bring it to you?"

There was a pause before Dr. D. responded. Marie guessed that he'd panic, that he'd hang up and run, but the crisis made him decisive. She was almost impressed. "Listen, you idiot, you bring that thing here, and you'll wind up in the dump with it. You understand me? You're not thinking. Sit down and listen to me. Put the thing down. Don't touch it, don't do anything until I tell you what to do."

Dr D. took a long breath, and then he told the nurse to tie it up in news paper. She was to take the bundle for a long walk and leave it in a trashcan, somewhere far away. And the plan worked. Marie spent the next several days with the Homicide Squad, the Brooklyn DA, and the Department of Sanitation, excavating garbage dumps. They never found the body.

Since she'd been on the abortion wiretaps, Marie hadn't gone back to her own doctor. Though her constitution was strong, her diet healthy, and her habit of exercise maintained since the academy, she routinely worked herself to exhaustion. When she caught a cold, she toughed it out with orange juice and salt-water gargles. She'd begun to think of doctors as worse than ordinary people, and she strained against the assumption. These were not typical doctors, she told herself. No one on a wiretap was a typical person, though she supposed that the men Dee listened in on were typical gangsters. She'd filled in for a while when Dee was out on maternity—her third, Michael—and found the conversations grindingly mundane, mostly gripes about traffic and indigestion and kids. She'd expected to hear about nonstop murder plots, and the banality was a shock. Hearing physicians brag about cheating on taxes and wives, laughing in contempt for patients, was sickening. She'd had to renegotiate her earlier, unquestioned views of several institutions—marriage, the police department—although she remained faithful to both. Yes, there were bad husbands, bad cops, but it didn't mean that love and justice were lies.

Marie had interviewed hundreds of women over the years about how they found their abortionist. A few said that their own doctors would have done it but wouldn't risk their licenses. Other doctors demanded such extravagant fees that the women resorted to the next tier of medical competence—a nurse, maybe, or a pharmacist. Even a mortician, once. Among the doctors, there was a never a hint of any principle in effect; profit was all that mattered. Marie was delighted to work the MD cases. They were educated men, privileged men, with choices available to them; they were respected men, sworn to do no harm.

Marie parked her car four blocks away from Dr. Lothringer's house, so no one would see the bag lady get out of a car. She had her cane and a bag of breadcrumbs to feed pigeons, in case she found a park bench. Also, a few dog biscuits, which an old cop had taught her to carry. If she found a good observation post where a neighbor's mutt raised a rumpus, she might make a peace offering. This was a pro forma surveillance, requested by Mrs. M., should the Queens DA have any questions.

Marie had gotten AB wiretaps in the Bronx, Manhattan, and Brooklyn, but never in Queens, where the DA, Frank O'Connor, was a celebrity of sorts. He'd been a defense lawyer, and one of his cases had been made into a movie by Alfred Hitchcock. *The Wrong Man,* with Henry Fonda. Marie had seen parts of it, working the theaters for the Degenerate Squad. It was the story of an innocent Italian musician mistaken for a holdup man. A sad story—the real robber was arrested in the end, during the second trial, but the musician's wife went crazy and wound up in an institution. O'Connor was supposed to be tough on cops, routinely tossing out cases he didn't think passed legal muster. Marie wasn't worried. This one was ready to go, as far as she was concerned. She had more than enough evidence for a wiretap.

Ordinarily, Marie posed as a patient to visit a doctor and ask for the

AB. If they agreed, she applied for a wiretap. The doctor's name might come from a hospitalized patient, or a talkative perp eager to make a deal. Anonymous letters came in, and occasionally even a signed one, from an ex-wife or girlfriend. When Marie went in to see one of the doctors, her favored imposture was that of a bookmaker's girlfriend, a good-time gal who didn't mind who knew it. Short skirts and go-go boots, hair up in a beehive if she had the time. She mostly called herself Lana, for old time's sake, except for when she wore her red wig. Then, she was Charlie, and she'd come on even stronger. It was a more fun than playing an ingénue. The conversation ordinarily followed the same script.

"Undress and get up on the table, so I can examine you."

"Fat chance. I'm a big girl, all grown up, and I'm less than two months along. I got a lab report. I've been to two of you bums after my own coward doctor, and the way they stare and grab around in there, I should be charging them. Look, I got the cash. Look! Don't touch. That's today's rule. But I don't want to do it today, because my fella—he's in the sporting world, if you know what I mean—he got us ringside seats for the fights Friday at the Garden, and we'll be going to Toots Shor's after, for a party with *Mister* Jackie Gleason. All I need from you is a yes or a no for Monday, and we can both be on our merry way."

Marie guessed that Charlie would have been pleased to be of assistance, but she didn't care much, one way or the other. Some doctors paid no mind to her half-a-whore folderol, as long as the money was green. Others raised a knowing eyebrow when she talked about men whose pelvic exams had a note of tourism to them. More than one suggested they ought to have some fun now, since she couldn't get more pregnant. Often, they gave her attitude right back at her. "Spare me the baloney about how you can't stand to spread your legs for a guy. You wouldn't be here in the first place, if that was true. Be here Tuesday, 10 a.m."

There was no need for that with Dr. Lothringer. Marie had two witnesses, a young unmarried couple from the Bronx named Helen and Benny. Helen's name had come up on a wire in the Bronx, on a doctor who usually steered his girls to an AB shop in Manhattan. Lothringer had dealt with them as if they were Soviet agents delivering microfilm. They were given a number to call, and then directed to an apartment lobby near Grand Central, just after midnight; they would show five hundred dollars to a strange man with an accent, who sent them home again. Within the hour, they would receive another call, from a woman, giving them final instructions regarding the time and place. After scribbling down the information, Helen asked, "What's the doctor's name?"

"You don't need to know," said the woman, hanging up the phone.

The next afternoon, Helen and Benny went to the address on Union Turnpike, where Marie trudged now. An ordinary ranch house on a corner plot, with an attached garage, adjacent to a supermarket parking lot that was separated by an eight-foot-tall wood-slat fence. Dr. Lothringer—male white, approximately forty, five-ten, two hundred pounds, eyes brown, hair brown, no distinguishing characteristics—had barked at them for being fifteen minutes early. The maid was still there. Waiting in the house or even outside in their car was forbidden. They were to drive around until the precise time of the appointment.

When Benny and Helen returned, the cash was handed over. Benny was directed to a waiting area, Helen to the examining room. The doctor told her to go to the bathroom to undress and empty her bladder. He gave her an injection for pain, and she took her position on the table with her feet in stirrups. "I'm a dental hygienist, you know," Helen said. "I understand how the procedure works. I appreciate how clean everything looks here."

"All the instruments are autoclaved," said Lothringer, briskly indifferent to her endorsement. "You're about six weeks pregnant. Do you feel anything?"

"There's no pain."

Once he was finished, he gave her some tablets of antibiotics, as well as sleeping pills, should she need them. Calling Benny in, he told him to get in his car and park underneath a railroad crossing, six blocks away.

"What? Doc, I—"

"Do as I say."

"Why?"

"Do as I say. Go."

After Benny left, the doctor led Helen to a door that connected to the garage. His dog, a Dalmatian, joined them beside a station wagon, taking the passenger seat as Helen was ordered into the tailgate: *Lie down.* She crawled into the car and lay flat, still groggy. They drove a while and then pulled over. "Get out. Walk two blocks east. Your boyfriend is waiting for you."

"Can't I—"

"Get out now. There's a door handle on the inside, you don't need me. Go."

The dog barked. At her? Maybe not. Helen scrambled out of the tailgate and watched the car depart. She felt a woozy dismay. The sunlight bore down on her face. She just stood there. East? Where the hell was that? She walked half a block, and then came back. East? She sat down. Some time later, Benny found her.

As Marie traipsed through the neighborhood, she wondered whether she should look for the railroad crossing, but she decided not to bother. What she needed was an observation point, a spot to sit and watch from. There were no benches nearby; a synagogue had broad stone steps, but it was a couple of blocks away. She went around the corner to check out the fenced-off area next to the garage—a parking lot. She meandered among the cars when the fence opened up by the Lothringer house. No, it didn't—the garage had a back door that opened into the lot, a secret exit.

A station wagon crept out slowly. Marie saw the Dalmatian with its spotted white head out the passenger window, pink tongue lolling. The door closed behind them, and the car disappeared onto the side street. Marie blew him a kiss when he left. *What a sweet setup!* Watching the front, you'd never see the patients leave. She wondered how he'd come by the odd garage, if he'd had it custom-built. This caper would be a challenge. Once the wiretap was up, she'd have to put together a surveillance team. The Lothringer house would be a technically difficult set, with two entrances; in a neighborhood without a lot of people walking around, watchers would stand out. Still, Marie knew she could manage. She was determined to win.

The law said that abortion was like murder. Like it, but not exactly. Abortion was covered under Article 125 of the Penal Code, which spelled out the varieties of homicide. The DA usually wanted evidence of ten or twenty abortions—documented with sworn complaints, bank statements, prescription records, and other evidence—before they moved to take the case down. Marie wasn't a detective yet, but as far as she was aware, the boys at Homicide didn't wait for a killer's body count to hit double digits before making an arrest. When cops raided an AB location, they always brought a police surgeon, in case they caught him in the act. Once the abortionist was in handcuffs, it would be the surgeon's job to complete the operation. Not to stop it, or to repair whatever might be repaired, but to finish the job. The woman stayed on the table. That's what happened when they broke into Dr. D.'s office. They were lucky to catch him then, since they didn't have the baby's body from the dump. His last abortion was a crime when he started it, but not when the police surgeon finished. It didn't make sense, but Marie had grown accustomed to a measure of unreality in the law, as she had in life. The make-believe sometimes felt like dreaming, and it sometimes felt like lying. Always, it felt like a game.

And the rules of the game were just as strange when it came to wiretaps. The taps were invaluable. They were also inadmissible. Federal law said no one could "intercept and divulge" telephone conversations; in New York, it was decided that intercepting was fine, as long as there wasn't any divulging, at least to civilians. Cops asked DAs for wiretaps every day, and DAs gave them to judges to sign, and untold legions of mopes and mutts were locked up because of them. Cops overheard plots to commit kidnappings, bank robberies, murder, but they could never say why they happened to be in the right place, at the right time, to stop them. Juries were ignorant of the most meaningful facts in the cases they had to decide. Still, Marie was glad they were able to take some advantage—the Feds couldn't listen at all.

An investigation might take weeks, or months. There may have been a dozen active AB wiretaps across the city, half of which were Marie's. Once the judge signed off, the techs at the Criminal Investigation Bureau set to it with their bag of tricks, picking out the paired screws in the feedbox, running a wire from the line up the telephone pole to the plant, wherever they set it up to listen. The plant could be anywhere with a little privacy—a vacant apartment, the basement of a grocery store, storage space at a hospital—but the closer it was to the target site, the better, in case there was need to get there in a hurry.

Marie waited in the parking lot for the station wagon to return. She looked at the specials in the supermarket windows: Land O'Lakes Butter, eighty-nine cents; Kraft Deluxe Dinners, thirty-nine cents each; veal cutlet, sixty-eight cents a pound. The veal was a good price, but she didn't want to leave meat in the car all day. After forty-five minutes, the station wagon emerged again from the garage, the Dalmatian's head hanging out the window, moving at the same creeping pace. Lothringer could have returned by way of the front entrance, but to see the departure repeated so soon gave it an aspect of déjà vu. Two pregnancies had ended within the hour. Two human possibilities would never be, and two women had been spared all manner of pain, shame, and fear. Harvey Lothringer had made a thousand dollars. There were days when the world seemed to be spinning faster.

Marie was startled by a light touch on her elbow. She turned to see a boy from the market, thickset, dark-haired, seventeen or eighteen years of age. He had a white shirt, a black bow tie, goggly black-framed glasses with a patch inside the right lens. "Are you okay, Ma?"

He had the faintest moustache, like eyelashes that had drifted down to his upper lip. Marie wanted to brush them away. The world spun faster still. "What?"

"Are you feeling okay?

He had a deep voice, slightly adenoidal but assuredly mature. It did not fit his baby face. "You look a little lost. Can I get you a drink of water?"

"Thank you, no. I was just resting. I have to go now."

"Well, take this, anyway."

He pressed a small object into her hands. A spool of thread?

"It's an ointment with camphor, my Ma used it, it helped with the circulation. Her hands were cold all the time, like yours."

Marie didn't feign trembling as she clasped his outstretched hands with her threadbare gloves. That he'd fallen for her disguise touched her vanity, even if his eyesight was obviously not top-notch. But his compassion nearly moved her to tears. She slipped the tin of ointment into her pocket and touched his cheek. "You're very kind. Your mother is a lucky woman."

Marie swept strands of gray hair from her eyes and began her arthritic shuffle out to the street. She didn't look back until she'd gone several blocks. She had to stay in character until she was out of sight, taking a roundabout route to her car to make sure he hadn't followed, out of concern for her welfare. She dreaded the prospect of his discovering she'd deceived him, seeing the kindness leave his face. Later on, he might learn to be cynical about ragged strangers, to be quicker to judge, slower to help, but she hated the thought that she might be his teacher. She was pressed for time, but she didn't lengthen her stride or unhunch her posture until she was back at her car. Once she was in the clear, she pulled off her wig and sped away.

Marie clutched the tin of ointment as if it were an amulet, as if it held the same precious compassion with which it had been offered. There wasn't much of it, so she knew she might have to make it last a while.

10 YOU DIDN'T SEE THIS COMING

Only the work of women spies is comparable in the need for long-sustained acting. . . . A woman detective who falls down on her character work might be thrown downstairs, or find herself looking into the business end of a pistol. We're good at make believe. We have to be.

—Mary Sullivan
My Double Life: The Story of a New York Policewoman

MARCH 14, 1963
1400 HOURS

Marie found Helen and Benny waiting for her in the lobby of the DA's office. She was early, and they looked as if they'd been sitting for a while. Both of them were birdlike, slim and fine-featured, each with their own fluttery tic—her eyes darting, his fingers drumming like pistons on the wooden bench. They dressed alike in dark suits, and Helen wore white gloves. Benny jumped up when Marie arrived. His black hair was carefully combed, except for a section on the right temple, which was cowlicked from scratching. "We're not late, right?" he asked. "She said we were late, but we're not, I told her. And here you are, getting here after us. So we're not, right?"

Marie assured him they were all there at the appointed time. She thanked them for coming, as if she'd invited them to lunch. As she took Helen by the arm, she could feel the rat-a-tat of her pulse, fast as beating wings. She was glad Helen had worn gloves. They made her look younger, more old-fashioned. Helen was twenty-three, three years older than Benny. It shouldn't have mattered that Helen looked respectable, but it always helped. She wasn't a victim of Lothringer—she'd jumped through hoops to find him, had borrowed money to pay him. As had Benny. And she wasn't a victim of Benny, either, but their mutual reliance on dodgy condoms from his cousin in the Army. They had dated for two years, and both were students at City College. He was in the accounting program, and she was taking night classes after her day job at the dental office. They had planned to get married next year, after he graduated. They still planned to marry, and to have children. Marie didn't doubt that they would. She could picture them dancing at their wedding, he in a white dinner jacket, she in her white gown, the image of innocent promise, these past weeks banished from their memories.

They reached their floor and made for their destination at the far end of the hall. The young couple gasped when they looked at the sign on the door:

ASSISTANT DISTRICT ATTORNEY ALFRED PATTEN

DEPUTY CHIEF, HOMICIDE BUREAU

"Oh, my God," cried Benny. "We're not going to be arrested, are we? Just tell me if we are. I'd rather know—"

"Not knowing is worse," said Helen, clutching Benny as she touched a gold brooch on her lapel. "This was my grandmother's. I wouldn't have worn it if I was going to prison."

"Nobody's going to prison," said Marie firmly. "At least nobody here. You're very nice people who made a mistake. Like I told you before, you're not in trouble. But the doctor, he's a bad man. All you're going to do is tell this district attorney—Mr. Patten—what happened. Just like you told me."

Maybe the judge, too, but Marie decided against mentioning that. Their fear was so extreme, so unfounded, that it was almost funny, but she didn't much feel like laughing. Helen sank her head into Benny's shoulder.

"Do you know this Mr. Patten?" Benny asked. "Is he a good man, a nice man?"

Marie was about to assure them that he was when Benny added a third query: "What does he look like?"

"I've never met him, but—"

"Oh, God—"

Marie took a schoolmarm tone, forceful but not mean, as she separated the couple. "Benny, get a grip on yourself. Stand up straight now, and let me see you both. Good. Benny, I've spoken with Mr. Patten on the phone, and he seems like a very nice man. Helen, that is a beautiful brooch. I don't want to hear another word from either of you, you'll drive each other crazy. Let's go in."

The receptionist looked like a sterner version of Marie's character from this morning, gray within and without, but steely where Marie had been ashen. A tissue was tucked in the cuff of her right sleeve. Nice touch, Marie thought. She'd do that, next time. When Marie stated their business, the receptionist didn't look up from her typing. "Please have a seat."

They took their places on a brown leather couch. Benny resumed his finger drumming. The receptionist hadn't announced their arrival. Waiting wasn't the hardest part of a case, but too often it was needlessly dispiriting. So many hours wasted, watching doors that stayed shut so the man on the other side could feel more important. Helen began to play piano with one hand on the arm of the couch. Marie decided to join their imaginary orchestra, tapping against the wall. She didn't notice when Benny stopped his drumming. "Jeez, I'm sorry, Miss, I didn't even notice," he said. "I mean, Officer. How'd you get the shiner? Who'd fight a lady cop? I hope whoever did it to you, he got the beating of his life. Do you see, Helen? With all this, with us, I didn't even see—"

Marie was startled but recovered quickly. She always kept a couple of excuses handy, like the dog biscuits in her purse. "It's nice of you to say, Benny. But this isn't a war wound. I was playing catch with my daughter, who's only ten but has a heck of a fastball. That's my last inning for a while!"

Benny chuckled as the receptionist picked up the phone. "Mr. Patten, your two o'clock. Yes, all here. You may go in."

ADA Patten's desk was a vast table, littered with mountainous stacks of papers that gave it the look of a city skyline, midearthquake. He was an imposing man, gray at the temples, with handsome, slightly outsize features—brow, nose, cheekbones, chin—that made his face seem as if it had been put together for the benefit of jurors in the second row. His voice was deep and smooth—"Do come in, so glad . . ."—and his blue serge suit was tailored. He stepped from behind his desk to greet them. "Sorry about the mess. Very busy here, but I'm sure we all are. Thank you for coming."

Patten directed Helen and Benny to a couch, and Marie to a chair beside it. "I'm sure this fine officer has explained why you're here. What I'll ask you to do is to tell me, in your own words, what happened regarding this incident. Beginning to end. Mainly with you, Helen, though I may have questions for Benny. And, of course, this fine officer is free to speak. Once we're finished, I will have a stenographer come in for the official statement. Do you have any questions?"

Marie had dealt with many prosecutors over the years, but never with a deputy bureau chief. She admired his lack of sanctimony or sentiment. Some of the men were contemptuous of the fallen women before them. Many were well-meaning, but so ill at ease in discussing sexual matters that they sounded like stroke victims: "And . . . young lady . . . did this individual . . . this instrument . . . Where am I? No, of course, with regards to the lower, the nether regions, of you, of your person . . ."

"Now that you ask, mister," Benny began, his head rotating between Helen, Marie, and Patten, "is there any chance, we might get our money back?"

Marie watched Patten's eyebrows rise, his mouth narrow.

"No," he replied. "Illegal contracts are unenforceable, as a rule. Please, go on."

Helen lowered her head, her voice shaking, "If my parents found out, they'd die, they'd just die of shame—"

Patten broke in, "Can I get you a glass of water?"

"Yes, please."

Patten looked at Marie, inclining his head toward the water cooler in the corner, and she obliged him. After Helen regained a measure of her composure, she recounted how, when she realized she was late, she couldn't go to the family doctor. In desperation, she confided in a girlfriend, one of the other hygienists, who recommended another doctor in the Bronx to confirm the pregnancy. Even if he wouldn't help, he might know someone who could. As Helen detailed the skullduggery that followed, Patten was attentive but gave no sign if he found one part offensive, or another part odd. He didn't take notes or ask questions, save for a periodic "And then?"

Helen became emotional when she talked about being ordered out of the tailgate: "I didn't know where I was, the sun was so bright, the medication . . ."

"And then?"

"And then he said Benny was a few blocks to the east, and he drove away."

"East!" Benny protested. "East! What are we, Apaches?"

"I found him very strange, very disturbing," Helen submitted, still nervous. "I wasn't happy with . . . so much. With everything."

"And then, from there," Patten continued. "You found Benny in the car."

"I found her," Benny said, stung.

"All right," said Patten. "And then?"

"And then I drove her home. She went to bed, because she had to work the next day. A couple of days after that, the police lady came to the door."

Patten asked if she had any contact with Lothringer since, or if she required any medical treatment as a consequence of the procedure, and then he summoned a stenographer. He stood, and his tone was crisp and businesslike, warning Benny that he was here now only for moral support. He tilted his head at Marie, indicating that she should keep silent as well.

"Ready? Now, for the record. Present in the Queens District Attorney's office, One-Twenty-Five dash Oh-One Queens Boulevard, Room Four-Two-Four, on this date, March 14, 1963, at fourteen twenty-one hours. Twenty-one minutes after two. I am Assistant District Attorney Bernard Patten, Deputy Chief of the Homicide Bureau for the District Attorney of Queens County, in the State of New York. Present is a court reporter, and a Miss Helen M—, from whom I will take a sworn statement regarding events which occurred on the sixth and seventh of March of this year, within but not exclusively within the county of Queens. Good afternoon, Miss M—"

The story would never be boring to Marie, no matter how many times she heard it. She was alert to every shift in nuance, wary of any potential contradiction, any signs of strain. Helen's earlier rehearsal had calmed her; Patten's even tone helped, as did the genial speed of the dialogue. An up-tempo pace worked best with certain witnesses—slow down, and they start to wobble. Just like riding a bike. Marie felt like an agent who'd brought a young talent in for an audition—*With this one, I think you'll be impressed*—and Helen was hitting all her marks. Showing the money to a stranger near Grand Central. Autoclaved instruments. The Dalmatian. Marie blinked in sympathy when Helen was kicked out into the merciless sunlight. She felt warmly toward Benny when he found Helen in his car.

"Thank you, Miss M—. Is there anything you'd like to add?"

"No, sir. Thank you."

With her white gloves, the hat with the little black veil that fell over her forehead, Helen looked chaste and penitent. She was perfect. Marie was certain that she'd cinched it, that they'd move ahead to the next round.

"No, I thank you, Miss. And this ends the statement. The time now is fifteen-thirty hours. I thank you all. Officer, you may escort them out."

Marie didn't know why he didn't have them wait, in case the judge had questions, but she supposed that she could answer them herself. Clearly, they did things differently in Queens. Maybe she'd discreetly ask him for a referral for a divorce lawyer, "for a friend." She guided Helen and Benny down the hall and into another elevator. Four detectives were arguing inside.

"The hell with O'Connor, if he don't go with it."

"If that isn't murder, I don't know what is."

"The hell with him."

"Knowing it ain't the same as proving it, being able to prove it."

"The hell with him. He's got a baby dead from an overdose. I don't care whose drugs they were. Lock up the stupid whore of a mother."

"Lock 'em all up."

"Does O'Connor think they're gonna make another movie about him? *The Wrong Man.* He's the wrong man for this job."

"Where do you want to eat?"

"I dunno. The Greek?"

"God no, the German maybe. I need a beer."

"And if he don't charge this broad with murder, I got friends at the papers—"

"There's a newspaper strike. What are they gonna do, write it in their diaries?"

"Well, when they get back to work, they're gonna ask him why. O'Connor doesn't understand, cases aren't always neat and clean, like in the movies."

When the elevator reached the ground floor, Helen and Benny were near collapse. Marie watched as one pair of terrified eyes locked on the other before searching for the exit. They were working to make their way in the world, to build something for themselves before having kids. Two years, maybe three. They never imagined that they would be in a place like this. Marie walked them through the lobby and shook their trembling hands. "What now?"

"What next?"

"I'll let you know. This was the hardest part, though. You did good."

Benny's mouth formed an awkward kind of grin, with the right side of his lip rising up, his jaw going sideways. "Thanks for being so nice to us, miss. And watch out for those knuckleballs."

"What?"

Benny traced a finger below his eye. Marie wished she'd seen him smile before, to know if this was what it usually looked like. Was he insinuating that he saw through her story, or was he making a joke? "You can bet on it," she said, winking and walking away. The elevator was empty when she returned. She was glad for the privacy, the moment to think. There was no risk of exposure, even if Benny had read her mind. He'd never say a word to anyone about anything that had happened today. She exhaled in relief.

Marie found Patten behind the paper-stacked desk, writing on a legal pad. He gave her a quick wave, a half-nod, and part of a smile. "Officer, that was wonderful work. Thank you."

"I'm glad. Where do we go from here?"

"Well, we have it on the record. Thanks to you."

"You're welcome. And?"

"And we will be in contact if anything else is required. Thank you again."

He didn't look up from his pad. Was he writing about this case? A lawyer could take fifty pages to say yes, a hundred to say no. Patten hadn't asked her for any of her paperwork, now that she thought of it. Marie's stomach was heavy. Three thank-yous: that wasn't good. "When do we go to the judge?"

"As soon as possible. As soon as feasible and necessary. Thank you."

And now a fourth. Did he not like her witness, her ill-concealed black eye, or her hat? When the detective in the elevator threatened to go to the press, it sounded peevish—*I'm telling Daddy!*—but now she wondered if their case or hers would have been decided differently if public opinion were in play. The newspaper strike had shut down the seven daily papers since Christmas. No one knew what movies to see, or if there was a sale at Macy's, or a protest in Harlem. When the presses stopped, any number of ordinary activities seemed to have been suspended as well; florists were going out of business because there were no obituaries.

Marie returned the half-smile, pulled up a chair, and sat down. He finished a page, and he flipped to another. He looked at Marie without the smile and cleared his throat. Marie slowly rose, as if cowed, and walked over to the water cooler. She filled a paper cup and set it on Patten's desk. "Sounds like you got a cough."

Deputy Bureau Chief Patten didn't appear to be amused. "Officer, we have no further business here today."

"Counselor, I got that when you said, 'possible, feasible, and necessary.'

If you meant it, you would have said, 'soon.' People go on like that when they're bluffing. I don't mean to be rude. I just want to save time. I have wiretaps all over the city, more than I can keep up with. But when Inspector Melchionne asks me what the problem is, I ought to be able to tell her. Before I leave, I want to know two things. The first, you can guess, so I'll save that one."

Patten evinced annoyance and curiosity in equal measure. Marie was satisfied he wouldn't call security before they finished. "When I took the witnesses down in the elevator, four detectives were up in arms over a case. A dead baby. Drugs were involved. I know they just came from a meeting, though obviously not with you. Still, why wouldn't you charge the case like they wanted, with murder?"

"Detective," he began, "I'm not sure you're entitled to an answer on either issue. But I appreciate you pointing out that particular verbal mannerism. I play poker, not as well as I'd like, and now I have an idea why. And so, I'll tell you."

Marie didn't know if he intended to flatter her by calling her "Detective," or if her insubordination had made him forget how insignificant she really was.

"In this case, the mother was a sixteen-year-old prostitute with an IQ of seventy. She had a two-year-old son of unknown paternity. From what we know, she lived with someone she described as an 'uncle,' in a garage near a junkyard. He sold heroin, and he sold this young woman. The child ingested heroin at some point and died. The police were notified when the woman went to a neighboring garage, asking for a shovel to bury him."

"I see."

"I'm glad you do. And while I am extremely sympathetic to these detectives' frustration, there are two kinds of murder, as you know: to intentionally cause the death of a person, or to cause a death by conduct evincing a 'depraved indifference to human life.' Like firing a gun into a crowd, or poisoning a well. We have depravity in abundance here, to be sure. Given her age and intellect, Mr. O'Connor is inclined to charge Manslaughter in the Second Degree, under the theory of gross negligence. That is a failure to exercise a reasonable level of care, by someone with a specific duty to the deceased. Everyone knows what a mother should be, what a mother should do, keeping her baby safe. Might I ask you, Detective, do you have children?"

Marie knew that Patten was practicing with her, rehearsing a speech for a jury. And she had been persuaded. Patten had made a skillful argument, a thoughtful argument, but the bid for cheap sentiment was insulting. *Do you have children yourself?* That was what the car salesman said when he tried to steer you to the bigger models on the lot. She'd listen to him, but she wasn't going to ask him for a divorce lawyer. "Yes, I do. I have a daughter. Do you have children?"

"Yes, two boys and a—"

Patten glared at her, inspecting her face for any signs of mockery. "That is neither here nor there. But I hope I've given you some perspective on the situation, how the police might see this case one way—a very human, natural, normal way—but the law is the law. Nothing can interfere with our duty to it. Still, I understand why the police might not be happy with Mr. O'Connor. Did they make jokes about the movie, about *The Wrong Man*?"

"I'm with you, Counselor, on the manslaughter charge," she deflected. "A hard call, but it seems like you made the right one."

Patten set an elbow on his desk and planted his great, jutting chin in his hand. "I'm glad you agree, Detective. Your opinion matters. It does. I'm not a superstitious man, but I wonder about the coincidence, when you ask about what you overheard in the elevator, and this matter with Dr. Lothringer. Think of this sixteen-year-old girl, who was the definition of an unfit mother," he intoned, his rhythm quickening. "An imbecile, a prostitute. Hopeless and nearly helpless, unable to care for herself, let alone a bastard child, of whose father nothing can be said except that he must truly be of the dregs of humanity. Who else would couple with a creature like that?"

Patten paused for Marie to assent, which she did with a forceful nod. His gestures became stagey, but his disgust was unaffected. "Think of this child. What hope did it have? Was there any chance it could have grown to be anything but a criminal, a lifelong burden on society? Think of the bloodlines! With its mother an idiot, its father an animal, the wretched thing truly never should have been born."

Marie nodded again, with less vigor. Talk of lower orders and lesser breeds made her ill at ease, having been accounted among them on occasion. At least Patten was working toward his conclusion: "Let me put it this way, Detective. Had this sixteen-year-old girl met Dr. Lothringer, early in her pregnancy, would it have been such a terrible thing?"

Marie didn't have an answer.

"I put it to you, it would have been better if she had."

Marie knew she was unlikely to prevail in debate against a man of

Patten's talent and training. Arguments in her house weren't won by ora-
torical skill. Still, she wasn't about to roll over for him. "No, I'll give you
that the two-year-old probably wasn't going to cure cancer, or help us beat
the Russians to the moon. But Helen and Benny, their kid would have
grown up to be a taxpayer, don't you think?"

"That's a fair point. Let me ask you then, do you think Helen should be
arrested? You can still go arrest her, if you want."

Marie didn't care for the new course of conversation. "Why? It's not as
if you're going to prosecute."

"Come now, Detective. Do you think Helen should be arrested?"

"That's not the way we do it. I don't make the policy."

"Suppose you did? Suppose our places were reversed, and you were
on my side of the desk, and I was the cop. Obtaining an abortion is a misdemeanor, and you are empowered under state law to prosecute. You have
a duty to prosecute. You're sworn to prosecute. Go ahead, send me out to
lock her up!"

Marie didn't know why the city had decided to only partially enforce
the law. It seemed wise to her, and kind. Who decided what rules were
to be followed, and which were to be ignored—the five district attorneys,
the police commissioner? Was it Mrs. M.? Patten saw her discomfort, and
he pressed his advantage. "Tell me, do you think what Helen did was
wrong?"

"How I feel doesn't matter, Counselor."

"Come on, Detective! Yes, it's a big, rough city, full of raw deals and
rotten compromises. But we try to do good, and we feel better when we do
it, don't we? We both know that stealing is wrong, but if someone cheats
on the electric meter, our outrage is not the same as when someone takes
the poor box at church. You're happier to make that arrest, we're happier to
prosecute, and that thief, I can assure you, will get more time than anyone
fiddling with the meter. I saw you with Helen. You are professional, I'm
sure, even with witnesses you don't care for. But you didn't look down on
her, you didn't have to swallow any disapproval. Am I right?"

"No, I didn't."

The policewomen who worked these cases talked about "AB witnesses," as if they were bystanders at a car crash. Marie felt no scorn for
Helen. She liked her well enough. Under other circumstances, they might
have been friends, both of them Bronx girls from modest backgrounds,
aspiring to better lives. There was pity for the obviously pitiful—the girls

of promise and potential, whose bodies had been scarred. And pity for those without promise, like Patten's sixteen-year-old, whose lives stood out like surveyors' flags, mapping the outer boundaries of earthly misery. But there was little contempt for the others, either. The ones who got away with it, so to speak, ending their unwanted pregnancies without incident. Women like Helen.

"Well? What does that tell you? What are you telling yourself? Look, we're in the 1960s. The world is changing, faster than we know. You mentioned the race to the moon. The stuff of comic books, not so long ago. Even the Catholic Church is joining the modern world. Thousands of its finest minds are in Rome for the Vatican Council. A generation ago, it would have been unimaginable for a lady police officer to sit where you sit, aggravating a bureau chief because they don't like the way a case is going. Many of your colleagues, maybe even the four you met in the elevator, see you as proof that the police department has gone straight to hell. Am I wrong?"

Again, Marie had no reply.

"I'll be up-front with you, perhaps more than I should. Mr. O'Connor has decided that this office will not pursue abortion cases against doctors. Where there are persons without medical competence performing medical procedures, we will prosecute. With professional men, no. Without them, these unfortunate women will go to the black market, where they can be preyed upon by hacks and quacks."

Marie thought he'd made an interesting speech, an inspiring speech, and she liked how he'd gone from Rome to the moon before circling back to Jamaica Boulevard. But she'd listened to too many wiretaps to hold the professionals in higher regard than the hacks and quacks. She could tell him about Dr. D. and the baby in the dump. "Thank you for giving it to me straight. I don't know if I agree with everything you've said, but it's not my job to agree or disagree. I'll tell Inspector Melchionne, and if she has any questions, I'm sure she'll call you or Mr. O'Connor herself. For what it's worth, I never met Dr. Lothringer, but I can promise you, he's no humanitarian."

"The man has no criminal record. Not even a traffic ticket."

"You tend to stick to the speed limit when you have an anesthetized girl stuffed in the back of your station wagon."

Patten pursed his lips. The conversation was over. He hadn't persuaded Marie, but he'd unsettled her. It would take some time to sort through her thoughts.

"Thank you for all your fine work, young lady."

Officer, detective, and now "young lady." It was time to go. Once she took her leave, so many thoughts crisscrossed her mind that it went blank. She doddered through the lobby as if guided by a kind stranger who led her by the hand. Outside, the heedless crowds shuffled past on the sidewalk. She took her hat off to fan herself, and the brim struck her bruise. The day had been a disaster at home, a travesty at work. Her eye started to tear. She put her hat back on and started to walk to her car.

They weren't going to get a better witness than Helen. Anywhere else in the city, prosecutors would have been thrilled to put her on the stand. Helen wasn't a slow girl with a new stepfather, a deaf mute grabbed by a pack of ghetto kids when she tried the shortcut home down an alley. Not on her tenth pregnancy by an alcoholic husband. And then Marie stopped short on the sidewalk, even as people bumped into her as they passed. Helen was in the least desperate circumstances of anyone Marie had encountered in this work. She wanted to marry Benny, and he wanted to marry her; they wanted children, but not yet. Had they married in 1963, out of obligation, rather than in 1964, by choice, their marriage may have been harder, their prospects fewer, at least at first. Maybe Benny would have had to quit school to work, and he'd never advance as he'd hoped. Or maybe the couple would have moved in with one of their parents for a year, so Benny could finish college, and Helen would have help with the baby. And they'd have the life they wanted, except a little sooner. Not quite as planned. Which was how life happened, as far as Marie understood, even for people who planned better than she had. Did Helen and Benny really think that life was *intentional*? Ah, to be young and naive!

And yet Marie didn't think the worse of Helen. Marie had run away to the Barbizon when she was pregnant, with a baby she wanted, at a time of her choosing. She hadn't gone back to Sid by her own free will. She knew the terror of feeling trapped, betrayed by her own enemy body; the seasickness inside that made her want to drown; the hard hope that the next hell couldn't hurt worse than this one. Those might have been the most trying days in a life that didn't lack for trial. Marie wouldn't allow that Helen was right to do what she'd done. She didn't really know what she thought, or even if she wanted to know. "They don't pay me enough to think," as the old cynics said. That wasn't Marie's attitude, to be sure. But her job had trained her to see Helen as a prospect more than a person, part of a solution to a problem. The collapse of the investigation had rendered

Helen uselessly human. Marie wished her well, but she wasn't unhappy that they wouldn't meet again.

Not even Paulie could have found fault with how Marie had handled her, being nice instead of not-nice, while maintaining control. *Two o'clock? Yes, please, thank you! Can we be early?* Marie wasn't looking to make new friends, and she didn't have a shortage of problems to solve, of cases to work. She didn't understand why she was so angry with Patten for lightening her workload.

And yet she was angry. She was convinced that Lothringer had to be called to account. She resented having her time wasted. She even resented the waste of Helen and Benny's time. Patten had been more adept, more respectful than most DAs, but the process itself was disrespectful, making Helen repeat her ordeal, confessing over and over, as if she were a criminal. Which she was, Marie supposed. But if Mr. O'Connor didn't think anyone committed a crime, why did his deputy bureau chief take half the day to talk to them? Didn't all of them have better things to do? Marie hated the hypocrisy, the way different big shots made up their own rules. "The law is the law," Patten had said. Except when it wasn't. It was as if the chiefs had made peace, but they hadn't bothered to tell the warriors to stop fighting.

Marie went to a phone booth and fished in her purse for dimes. She didn't want to see her chief. Mrs. M. wouldn't be disappointed in her, but Marie wasn't used to losing. The inspector would make her own calls, but the worst she'd learn was that Marie had been pushy with Patten. And it wouldn't bother Mrs. M. to hear that Marie had given them a bit of what for, as long as it had been done in a ladylike way. When Marie was put through, she spoke at vehement length. Mrs. M. was impassive when told of Patten's decision, of O'Connor's policy.

"Well then, we won't waste any more time in Queens. We are in great demand in the other boroughs, and we're already stretched thin. You are, certainly, Marie. I can hear how tired you are. Go home and have a nice dinner with Sandy, and tell her I was asking about her. Take tomorrow off, too, as a commander's day. You've earned it. I'll tell roll call. Start your weekend now, and enjoy it."

"Thanks, Mrs. M. I will."

Marie nearly wept with gratitude. With exhaustion, too, which swept over her. She wouldn't cry over what happened today, not with Carmen and Sid, or Helen and Benny and ADA Patten. She was glad that she didn't have to fix her makeup. Mrs. M. would have noticed the bruise, and she wouldn't have fallen for the line about playing catch. Marie wished she could have told the boss about Sid, but she was afraid of so many things, of everything. What was Marie supposed to be—a cop, ready to take on whatever rolled her way? Or a cop, who knew that you never gave up another cop, right or wrong? An Italian woman, taught that family shame should be kept within the family? Or an Italian cop in an Irish department, protective of the reputation of her kind? She was at an intersection, with nothing but bad roads to go down. Dead ends, every one of them.

Marie looked across the street and saw a deli. She dropped a few more dimes in the phone and called Katie to discuss dinner arrangements. "We can have hot roast beef sandwiches, Katie, I know you like them. Do we need anything else?"

"No, ma'am, we have the rest. The milkman came today. We have half a loaf of Wonder Bread, and the Chips Ahoy cookies, for dessert."

"Lovely. Tell Sandy I'll be young again when I get home. Not as old, anyway."

"Yes, ma'am, I'll tell her."

In the deli, she took her number and waited to order. She asked for the end cut, which Katie liked. The counterman made a face when she insisted on coffee from a fresh pot but backed down when she glowered at him. She could handle certain men, most men. There was really only one she couldn't manage.

When Marie arrived home, she was relieved that Sid's car wasn't in the driveway. She didn't expect to see it. After a blowout like last night's, he'd wait a few days for the air to clear and return loaded with shopping bags from Gimbels or Bonwit Teller. Marie hoped he'd stay away the whole weekend, so she could have a real rest. On Monday, she'd be the picture of health when she went back to work.

Marie collected her empty coffee cups and the deli bag and began to gather up her costume from the back seat. Her arms overflowed with gray hair and tattered clothes, and she dropped her uniform shoe. Leaning over to get it, she dropped the other and then flung everything to the ground. The pile of sorry rags could stay where they were. The light had begun to soften into evening, and she took a stroll around her little garden. The forsythia would soon be bursting with yellow flowers, and then the azalea would follow, pink and purple. And then the peonies . . . She touched the trunk of the fig tree, still swaddled in burlap. It was a gift from Papa, who had told her that a house wasn't a real home without one. He'd wrapped his trees every October, to keep them warm for the winter. This weekend, she'd plant her peas and spinach and mulch the beds. Sandy loved to help her in the garden. Katie could have some time to herself, if she wanted. A wonderful weekend, it would be just wonderful. She flung open the screen door and called out, "Mama's home!"

Footsteps scurried on the floor above. Marie put the meat on the kitchen counter. She took out a can of brown gravy and a box of potato flakes from the pantry, a pack of peas from the freezer. Dinner could be on the table in less than fifteen minutes. The convenience still made her marvel. She'd bought the meat fresh, but it would have been fine defrosted. She could go shopping twice a month if she had a big enough freezer. When she thought of the hours her mother spent cooking every day, the hours at the market, Marie wasn't nostalgic for the old days. The instant food tasted better than her childhood's endless round of lentils, chickpeas, and beans. And her mother was a fine cook, after all. Once the dread of poverty had finally lifted, dinners in the Bronx had become feasts. But they took a day or more to prepare. Tonight, Marie could be a good mother again in minutes.

Katie walked into the kitchen with a mild grimace on her face, an expression that signaled some lesser trespass on Sandy's part. "She was up in your room."

"And?"

"She'd forgotten your disguise from this morning. But when I told her you were coming home, as yourself—like you asked—it reminded her. The thing was, she seemed so pleased I didn't have the heart to be sharp with her. She wants to make a grand entrance. I know she shouldn't be in your things, but—"

"How does she look?"

"I don't have the words for it."

"Well. Have her come down. We might as well see."

Katie went back upstairs. Marie looked inside the refrigerator and saw that there was half a bottle of wine. Sid had opened it the night before. She filled a glass and had a sip. She heard Katie and Sandy exchange whispers outside of the door.

"What do you want me to say?"

"I want you to introduce me, how I said! Shh! She can practically hear us!"

Katie entered the room with her arms folded behind her back for her announcement. Sandy strolled in before it was complete. "And now we have the winner of the Miss America pageant, Miss Sandy Carrara, from Yonkers, New York!"

Marie took another sip before setting her glass down. It was her daughter standing before her, but it was also another creature altogether, adorable and awful in equal parts: Marie's turquoise dress swaddled Sandy like a general's greatcoat; her little hands—in white gloves—hiked up the hem, so that black high-heeled pumps were visible below. Marie tried to hold back laughter at the costume, at its darling failure to appear all grown up. But the makeup was another story, a garish clown-face of red lips, white powder, and blue eye shadow, plastered on in profusion. To complete the ensemble, she wore one of Marie's fedoras, white with the black tiger stripe. Her daughter was a vision. An apparition, really. Katie hadn't prepared her for the sight. Sandy was clearly thrilled with her handiwork.

"What do you think, Mommy? Don't I look just like you?"

Marie couldn't ignore the sincerity of the tribute. She wondered if she'd always been clear with Sandy, as she left her house in her sundry masquerades, that she intended to look appalling at least as often as she meant to appeal. Maybe she should make the distinction clearer, leaving by the front door when she was a society dame, through the back when she was a tramp. Or she could have Katie take Polaroids of every outfit, pasting them into separate scrapbooks, labeled "Do" and "Don't." Right now, her task was to find a compliment. She didn't always have one at hand, as she did her excuses. "You come here, Miss America."

Sandy rushed forward, stumbling into Marie's arms. Marie picked her up and spun her around. She didn't have to say anything, as long as she kept giddily turning. One shoe, and then another fell away from Sandy, and then the hat. Marie wanted to keep on spinning and spinning, so all the paint spun away from her face, and her clothes, and the years. She could imagine Sandy as a little girl again, fresh from the bath, laughing in her arms. Both needed to catch their breath when they stopped.

"This is the way you dress, Mama, when you dress pretty. You should be like this, every day. I didn't like how you looked this morning."

All was well again in the world. Katie started on dinner while Marie walked Sandy back upstairs to change and wash. They gabbed as they ate, and then all three did the washing-up. They watched *Ozzie and Harriet* at seven-thirty, and then Marie brought Sandy up to bed to tuck her in and say prayers. Katie stayed downstairs to watch *Perry Mason*. Marie was about to retire when she remembered she had left the heap of tatters and gray hair in the backyard. What would the neighbors think of that if they saw it in the morning? That a witch had been killed? *Strega, strega, strega!* Marie collected the pile and returned to her room. She put the wig on the post of a chair and hung up the old suit in the closet. It would have made sense to leave it on the floor, to make it look slept in, but enough was enough. When she checked the pockets of the coat, she found the tin of liniment from the boy at the supermarket. She rubbed it like a lucky penny and set it on the nightstand.

Marie washed her face and went to sleep. She didn't remember turning the light out, but she must have. The click of the switch made her stir, pulling her back toward consciousness, and the brightness felt sudden, severe. She didn't open her eyes. She felt a heavy tread on the floorboards. The shoes dropping to the floor with a clunk. The shuffle as the socks came off. Marie kept her eyes closed. If only it were a stranger in her house, a burglar. She would know what to do with a man like that. No, this would not be a good day. Not at the beginning, and not at the end. She felt old and broken again, even more than she had in the morning. No costume was necessary anymore; no costume was possible. Her heart nearly broke when she heard Sid laugh. "Holy shit! I knew it didn't make sense. You dressed like an old bat, an old bag when Carmen came here? Holy shit, I wish I'd seen that. Unbelievable!"

Marie blinked her eyes open for a second. It was a mistake. She didn't know why she had to peek. It was a mistake, even though Sid wasn't facing her. He was laughing at the wig on the chair, pulling off his tie, throwing off his suit jacket. He had three shopping bags from Macy's. The curled ribbon that erupted from their tops made her sick. They had arrived too soon. The timetable she'd assumed, with the whole weekend free—No. She closed her eyes again and rolled over, feigning unconsciousness. This wouldn't work. She didn't know why she tried. She heard his suit come off, the slip of his belt. He came into bed with her. "Hey, baby."

Marie tried not to move, but she flinched at his touch. She couldn't pretend to be asleep anymore. There was a kiss on her cheek. "Sorry we fought."

He reeked of scotch. Marie didn't like where this was going. He pressed against her back. His skin was hot, a little wet, as if he'd just chased someone. Marie wanted to run now, too. What was about to happen hadn't happened in a long time. She had to get out of bed. 'I'm sorry, too, honey," she said. "Are you hungry? You must be starving. Let me get up, fix you a plate of something."

She tried to slip out from under his arm, but he wouldn't let her. She had to think of something to say. Outside—on the street, anywhere else—she could always think of something. Diversions, distractions, delays. She labored to turn and face him. She kissed him and smiled. He laughed. "That wig," he said. "The old lady act. I'd'a given a million bucks to see that. Didn't know what the hell she was talking about. You are something, honey. What, I don't know. But something."

Sid shifted in the bed, but he still kept an arm around her neck. His breathing slowed, and Marie thought he might sleep. And then he laughed again. He slid on top of her, his body heavy, radiating heat. He smelled differently. Maybe it was just that it had been so long since they'd been close like this, skin against skin, that she mistook him for a stranger. She did better with strangers, she could talk to them.

"So you like the old lady getup, do you? I gotta tell you, there was a kid from a supermarket, he came up to me today. What a nice kid! His mother raised him right. When you were a kid, didn't your mother always tell you how—"

"Shut the fuck up."

Sid didn't hit her. He covered her mouth with one hand, pulled her hair back with the other. It hurt. When she closed her eyes, he moved his hand away from her mouth and opened one, scratching her with his thumbnail.

"Look at me. If you ever try to leave, I'm the last thing you'll ever see."

There was no way to not see him. There was nothing she could say to move his heart, to move him away. She had to find a way out, to try. What did she have, that could help? She stretched out a hand toward the nightstand, to take hold of her token of mercy. She couldn't reach it.

11 YOU KNOW HOW THIS ENDS

"Crawling at your feet," said the Gnat (Alice drew her feet back in some alarm), "you may observe a Bread-and-Butterfly. Its wings are thin slices of Bread-and-butter, its body is a crust, and its head is a lump of sugar."

"And what does *it* live on?"

"Weak tea with cream in it.'"

A new difficulty came into Alice's head. "Supposing it couldn't find any?" she suggested.

"Then it would die, of course."

"But that must happen very often," Alice remarked thoughtfully.

"It always happens," said the Gnat.

—Lewis Carroll
Through the Looking-Glass

APRIL 16, 1963
1700 HOURS

The newspaper strike had ended, but Marie didn't care. She didn't want to know what was happening now, what would happen next. She knew she had to see the doctor the day she vomited. She knew that she was pregnant. It wasn't flu season, and she hadn't eaten anything risky the day before—minestrone for lunch, an overcooked pork chop for dinner. That was . . . yesterday? *Yesterday, yesterday . . .*

The life she'd made was over. She'd feared it from the first, from that night when Sid came home. He left the next morning, early. Marie had the weekend to herself, as she'd hoped, planting peas and spinach in the garden. She didn't open any of Sid's gifts but delivered them to the same Salvation Army store where she'd picked up her bag-lady duds.

Yesterday, Marie had driven back from her two wiretap plants in Brooklyn to the office and decided to grab lunch in Chinatown. When she got out of the car on Pell Street, the fishmonger stink overwhelmed her. Marie didn't have a delicate stomach. Not since she first carried Sandy. It had been just over a month since the night with Sid. She felt ill again when she realized, but her stomach held. Yesterday, yesterday, yesterday. She might have been able to get away with the ingénue act yesterday, one last time.

For the first time in her life, Marie hated her husband. She wanted to call the police. With past beatings, she could have had Sid arrested—possibly, if she was hurt badly enough, and the right cop responded—even though it would have done more harm than good. After a night in jail, Sid would be bounced back to patrol, maybe put on a desk for a while. There would be chaplain visits for both of them. This time, it wouldn't have mattered. There were no charges to press. What Sid did wasn't a crime. A husband couldn't rape a wife, even if all the burdensome corroboration requirements had been met. And it was Sid's stupidity as much as his malice that infuriated her. Why didn't he just stick to his fists, the way he had before? Didn't he understand what could happen? This injury wouldn't heal in a few days, and it couldn't be covered up with cosmetics. He'd planted a bomb inside her that could destroy them both. *Ticktock, ticktock.*

And now, Marie couldn't leave him. The realization made her more nauseated than any smell. With another child, she'd have to take sick leave, starting in August, September at the latest. Unpaid, of course. Four or five months before the birth—she wasn't up-to-date on the regulations, since she hadn't thought she'd need to know—and then six months after. A year without a paycheck, without a purpose beyond the four walls of her house. A year of living only on his dirty money, of having to ask him for it, just to keep a roof over their heads. She remembered how miserable she was after her last pregnancy. And that was with a baby that she wanted. No, she had to try and find someone who could defuse the bomb.

Marie didn't go to her own doctor. She'd flipped through the yellow pages and picked a random name. Not entirely random: Not Irish, or Italian, or Polish, or Spanish. Not Catholic. She didn't recognize Dr. Levine's address, or his telephone exchange, "AS9." Was it in Astoria? She hadn't made up her mind about what to do. And she didn't really know if there was any urgency to decide.

That was a lie, she knew. Her lying mind refused to believe her body, which was speaking louder and louder. She was an unreliable informant, who could neither be trusted nor controlled. What she knew was that they didn't do wiretaps on doctors in Queens.

"MRS. MELCHIONNE, DR. Levine will see you shortly."

It turned out to be in Astoria, after all. An Italian and Greek neighborhood, mostly. Marie was Lana again, for luck. Marie had driven through the neighborhood to find the address she'd claim as her home. She didn't see any big apartment houses, where the vast anonymity of New York life might seem natural. People on the street stopped to chat, slapping backs and shaking hands. Did everyone here know everyone else? Where were the solitaries, the strangers? Marie found a desolate block off the far end of Steinway Street, noting the nearest deli, pizza place, beauty parlor, in case she was asked. Had she made a mistake being a Melchionne here? Of course, she was using it as a married name. Marie could have been born Lana Levin . . . ski. Yes, Levinski might work, almost a cousin of the doctor. A *meydele* who married into the wrong tribe, and wanted to return. Maybe he'd look kindly on her. *Nu?*

Dr. Levine was in his sixties, with an air of genial distraction. He wore bifocals that slid down a long, slender nose. Marie didn't know which angle to work. Should she do the kicked puppy, mewling and woebegone? Or lay it on the line as a tough cookie looking for a quick fix? *Let me know now, Doc, I got the cab outside, and the meter's running.* But that worked when the only issue on the table was the price. Could she just be herself, for a change?

"How can I help you, Mrs. Melchionne?"

"I'm pregnant."

"I will not offer congratulations, until we are sure."

The doctor took her blood pressure, checked her pulse, and made notes on his chart. He asked her height and weight, rather than taking measurements himself. Maybe that showed a willingness to cut corners? He didn't wear a wedding ring. Was a playboy better than a mama's boy? She was grasping at straws, she knew.

"We'll need a urine sample."

"I know," Marie said. "I just don't want to have to wait five days to find out if the rabbit died."

Dr. Levine laughed and set the chart down. "Young lady, the rabbit always died, whether the results were positive or negative. Is this your first pregnancy?"

"No, I have a daughter, she's nine."

"That explains it," he said, pushing his glasses back up his nose. "They don't use rabbits anymore. There's a new test. The 1960s have been good to rabbits."

"I'm delighted for them."

"Rabbits replaced rats, frogs, and toads," the doctor went on, as he scanned the bookshelves behind him for the relevant volume. "It was the same principle, injecting the creature with urine, watching for ovulation. Miraculous, really, the advance it represented. I was already out of medical school then. Anyone who said they knew how to detect pregnancy before was practicing witchcraft. But it must have seemed like witchcraft after— rats and toads! At least they didn't use black cats. Science, young lady, it moves very quickly. Who knows what 1970 will bring, 1980? Maybe cancer will be like the common cold by then. We should live so long!"

The talk of witchcraft reminded her of Mrs. Abbie. She'd foreseen a son, by another man, after Sid had gone insane. Three predictions for twenty dollars. Only time would tell if it was a boy, but the witch was dead wrong about the daddy. As for Sid's sanity, Marie wasn't sure if she had the perspective to judge, given that she was an inmate in his asylum.

The doctor handed her a paper cup. Marie withdrew to the lavatory and produced her specimen. The cup felt as hot as if she'd filled it from a kettle. It didn't feel normal, although she knew it was—body temperature, 98.6 degrees. Still, the intensity of warmth was unsettling. She set the container down carefully in the center of the sink, as if it were unstable, incendiary, a grenade with a loose pin. Marie stood up and then sat down again, closing her eyes. She could picture a glow inside her. When the city was a hundred degrees, there were fights in the streets, and old people died panting in their beds. A hundred degrees didn't seem natural at all. Who could live inside themselves, in such fevered heat?

When she returned, she set the cup down on the counter. Could she leave now? She hadn't even hinted at what she wanted. He seemed to be a decent man, but decency didn't work to her advantage. "How long 'til the test comes back, Doctor?"

"Tomorrow, because it's late," he said, his eyes bright with cheer. "Had you come this morning, you'd know by now. Are you very anxious about the good news? It's very natural. I can give you something to help you sleep."

Marie wanted to tell him that he was right about her anxiety, but wrong about the cause, not to mention the cure. Instead, she had an overwhelming feeling she had disappointed him. Spasmodic sobs left her mouth, and tears her eyes, and she covered each with a futile hand, as if the doctor could not see behind one, or hear behind the other. She felt like a child. She did not want to be a mother again.

"Please sit down, Miss," he said, guiding her to a chair. "Would you like a glass of water? A cigarette?"

He took out a pack of Lucky Strikes from the pocket of his lab coat. Marie shook her head. She sat down and leaned over, breathing deeply until the emotion passed. She decided to dispense with her stratagems and confess what had happened to her, why she felt as she did. "I'm sorry. This pregnancy is not what I wanted. My husband and I . . . our circumstances are not ideal. He is violent with me. He was violent with me, when this child was conceived."

"I am sorry to hear that," he said softly, lighting a cigarette. "You poor girl. You don't deserve that. No one does."

Marie didn't know if she expected more. What could he do, order a strict regimen of not being beaten for the next eight months, along with vitamins and bed rest? She felt better for having spoken, and she was glad for the simple compassion of what he said in return. A little shot of sympathy—straight up, no chaser. Did he have anything else for her? When she looked at him, his eyes remained kindly, but nothing came out of his mouth but smoke. "Thank you, Doctor. Do you have kids?"

Marie had to draw him out. Dr. Levine turned away, as if to look for an ashtray, and stepped back, five or six paces, taking her in from a broader perspective, noting her shoes and clothing, to see if they were cheap or not, clean or not. He walked back to her and sat down, his gaze trained on her cheeks, her neck, and then he picked up her hands to examine them. "Yes," he said. "Three daughters, one of whom, like yourself, was married to a man who . . . did not appreciate her. How long have you been married?"

"Eight years. Ten, I think." Marie smiled weakly, abashed that the flubbed number wasn't done for effect.

The doctor nodded. "And the violence, it has been going on for some time?"

"Since the beginning."

"What I mean to ask is if any particular misfortune—like losing a job, say, or a death in the family—that could be a factor. Did anything like that happen?"

"He has a steady job. His family, he isn't really in touch with them."

"Does he abuse alcohol?"

"He drinks, but I wouldn't say to excess."

"Does he hit you when he's sober?"

"He has."

"Then I'm sorry to tell you, Lana, that there isn't much hope. Getting drunk or being broke, they aren't good reasons for a man to beat his wife, but they're reasons. If he wasn't himself because he lost his job, he could get another one. If he was a brute when he drank, he could stay away from liquor. But it sounds like your husband is being himself, and he's just plain mean. Deep down, mean to the bone. You could live to be a hundred and fifty, and they still won't find a cure for that."

Marie felt weak, and her sight went hazy. She felt oddly relieved to hear that her pregnancy wasn't her worst problem.

"Do you work, Mrs. Melchionne?"

"Yes."

"What do you do?"

"I'm a secretary, a legal secretary."

"What does your husband do?"

"He's . . . in sales." Marie hadn't expected the second question, and her lack of preparation showed. Marie could see him making the calculation: Italian surname plus evasion about her husband's livelihood equals *you-know-what*.

"Well," he continued cautiously, "I'm glad you have a career, the ability to make a living on your own. I don't know if you're religious or not, but I'm friendly with Father Miglione over at St. Francis Assisi, and you'll find him very easy to talk to. And even though . . . how shall I put it? Let's say that, even though many people from your background are reluctant to go to the authorities, especially with intimate issues, family issues, the police can help. They really can. As it happens, my brother-in-law is a lieutenant at the precinct."

The doctor watched closely for her reaction, but Marie remained stone-faced. She felt like laughing, just a little. *Che bella fortuna!* What wondrous chance had brought her here to this wise and humane physician, who could provide her safe conduct to the authorities, secular and sacred? "My brother-in-law was very helpful with my daughter, and I'd be happy to call him. Go see him, you can sit down and talk. Nobody has to get arrested. Sometimes, just a word of warning, it can help."

Again, he sought to gauge her response, but she betrayed nothing. He advanced gently from sentence to sentence, pausing between them as if wading with her, step by step, into deeper water. "I could call him now, if you want. He's at work, I believe. Not that you have to talk to him, right away, but you'd feel better if you do. It's no trouble, and—"

"Thank you, Doctor, but I don't think—"

"Let me be frank, Mrs. Melchionne," he said, his voice suddenly firm, knowing that she would follow him no further. "You're going to have to face some facts about your life, your marriage, and you're going to have to make some hard decisions. He has to change his ways, or you have to leave him. It doesn't sound as if he's likely to change. I think you know that."

The doctor placed a tender hand on her shoulder. "Otherwise . . ." He drew on his cigarette and dropped it, exhaling, and then breathed again, as if the weight of his words needed the full force of his lungs to be uttered aloud. "Otherwise, you could lose the baby."

Marie's eyes widened before she lowered them. Her mouth tightened, but she wasn't smiling. She didn't think that she was smiling. She hid her mouth with her hand, just to be safe. Her hand felt as if she'd fallen asleep on it, and her face did, too. She was numb, head to toe. A tingling nothing-ness, inside and out. She kept her head down. Over the years, her head had become a filing cabinet of reasons why she couldn't go to the police with her problems. Now, this stranger wanted to make an appointment for her? Under her alias, which also happened to be the name of the Director of the Policewoman's Bureau? And the miscarriage of which he warned—this direst of consequences, this worst-case scenario—would have been a wish come true for her. And if Sid beat the baby out of her—well, she'd been beaten so often for nothing that she might as well get some benefit, for once.

"All right, then, Mrs. Melchionne. Go home, have a nice dinner, get some rest. We won't know for certain about the pregnancy until tomorrow morning. No need to make an appointment, just come in. Positive or nega-tive, those are the two possibilities. But the other condition that afflicts you? Without treatment, so to speak, you may have a long, unhappy life, or a short one. A bad bargain, either way."

"I see, Doctor."

"I sincerely hope you do."

As Marie drove back to Yonkers, she allowed herself to weep for the entire ride home. She had an idea that grief would pass, that it would leave her body like morning sickness, and she'd feel better after some fresh air. But even as she drove with the windows down, and the salt breeze bathed her face as she crossed the bridge, tears poured from her eyes. She imagined so many of them falling from her that the rivers rose below. She could cry forever, but she could only bleed so much. Dr. Levine's prescription was simple: Stay, and you'll die. Leave, and you'll live. Marie wished she could have stayed as his patient. There was a beautiful confusion to him. He could be so perceptive, even profound, while being so mistaken about what she wanted, who she was. Of course, she hadn't told him the whole truth. And he wasn't half wrong in thinking that she was married to a criminal. She was nearly home before she stopped crying.

Tonight, of all nights, she had to go over to Dee's, to see the new car. Over the past few years, vehicle purchases had come to occasion a family gathering, as fixed in ritual and mandatory in attendance as Easter dinner. The tradition had begun when Marie had won her Renault on the game show, back in 1958. None of them had owned a new car before, but once Marie had hers, secondhand would never do again for Papa. And then the rest had to assemble to view the latest Ford or Chrysler when it arrived at one of the sisters' houses.

"Look at the chrome!"

"What color's the leather? 'Cream,' you said? It's just beautiful."

"I can see why they call it the 'Executive Model.'"

"*Che bella.*"

All of them would be there tonight. Vera had three children now, and a genial goliath of a husband who doted on her. Italian, of course—Vera was now Mrs. Gaetano Calabrese. Guy managed a construction crew and would doubtless rise further still. The old homemaker-breadwinner split suited them fine. When Guy and Vera looked at each other, the love in their eyes always made Marie's heart break a little, despite herself.

As she parked in the driveway, she inspected her face in the mirror and wiped her tears. At least she was better off than Ann, she thought, in a moment of guilty cheer. Marie hated to admit it, but Sal made Sid look like a bargain. Sal's employment history was checkered—Marie didn't know if he had a job now—and whenever the subject of their lack of offspring arose, he'd bellow, "Alls I know is, ain't nothing wrong with my *brazziole*—ask anybody!"

What a *brazziole* Sal was, Marie thought, unwilling to even think the word in English. The sense of fraternity among the brothers-in-law was haphazard. Luigi and Guy didn't go to ball games or bars together, but they were well-disposed toward each other, as the "good husbands." For Sal and Sid, bars and ballgames were just the beginnings of their nights out. Marie didn't want to know about the middles or the ends. She'd done well enough at not-knowing until Carmen called.

Marie left the car and gently stroked the branches of the fig tree before she went inside, glad to see new buds. She felt better, but the emotional toll of the day still showed in her face, and she readied a ruse as she walked in. "Anybody home?"

Marie heard a tattoo of footsteps coming downstairs and waited until Sandy was almost in sight before she declaimed, "Achoo!"

"Hang on, honey," Marie said, ducking down, covering her face with her hand. "I have—ah, ah, ah—" She held out a hand to stop Sandy's charge. "Achoo!"

"Do you have a cold, Mommy? Are we still going to Aunt Dee's?"

"No, just a little hay fever," said Marie, standing again, flicking imaginary tears away from where so many real ones had just run. She waved at Katie as she emerged from the living room. "And yes, we are going. Get me a tissue, and—Sandy, you look like a coal miner. What have you been doing?"

Sandy was in purple corduroys, a yellow sweater, both mud streaked, as were her cheeks. "Dodgeball at the Walshes'. Can I wear my new pink dress?"

"No, it's a casual affair. Katie, would you go with her to wash and dress? I'd like to freshen up myself, and we should get going. And take the car, go see a movie. Of course, you're welcome to come to my sister's, if you want."

The women proceeded upstairs for their ablutions. Marie was sitting in front of her vanity when Sandy joined her, having been made presentable again with surprising dispatch. Katie hovered at the edge of the door. Sandy began to pick and poke through the cosmetics.

Marie hoped she wasn't too indulgent with Sandy, but she tended toward leniency, recalling the austerities of her own childhood. Mama always handed down the maximum sentence, no matter how slight or inscrutable the offense. Sandy wouldn't be pelted with shoes for roller-skating, or sent off to school every day with the baffling admonition to "guard her skirt." Matters on which Marie was inflexible were also inspired by her early life, such as the rule that Sandy have dinner at six every evening, with Katie or whoever was there. Marie knew that her childhood hadn't been miserable, by any means. It just could have been much happier. Her household had escaped the worst deprivations of the Depression, the sacrifices of war. All of them loved one another fiercely, in their own ways. Was it possible that Sandy's childhood was less happy than her own? There was enough food here. A bigger house, in a prettier place. Katie, an indispensable angel, night and day. If Katie left, Marie didn't know what she'd do, especially if there was another baby. If? *God forbid, God forgive me.*

"Mommy, do you have to sneeze again?"

"I think I—Achoo!"

"Bless you, Mama."

"My goodness! That's what you get, with an early spring. Anyway, now I'll do my lipstick. Watch, Sandy, how it's very light, and then you blot with tissue."

Sandy leaned in close. "Can I try?"

"I'll put it on, and then Katie will show you how to blot."

Katie took a tissue from the box and tore it in half, as not to waste it.

"Wait, don't move!"

As Sandy kept her mouth open in a perfect, just-saw-a-ghost O, Marie traced its contours with the slightest smear of pink. Katie folded the tissue paper and held each edge at the corners of her mouth.

"Close now, slowly," Katie said, her tone grave and momentous. The two women were so synchronized, so simpatico, that Marie thought of Katie as something like a sister and something like a comother. She had to remind herself, in humility, of their differences. Katie had been an orphan. Sandy doubtless heard nights of her parents' shouting from behind closed doors, but Katie had heard real bombs drop. Perspective wasn't the least of Katie's contributions to the household, but it was the only one for which Marie couldn't forthrightly thank her.

"I'll take that lipstick now, Sandy dear. Katie, hit the road, go out and enjoy."

Dee lived three blocks away, and it was a pleasure to walk there on a spring evening, beneath the towering old oaks that lined the sidewalks. The neighborhood the Panzarino sisters had colonized was called Crestwood. Most of the houses were Tudors and Dutch colonials, built in the twenties and thirties, sturdily handsome, with a well-settled air. Marie's house was almost as close to the Bronx River as her parents' had been, a few miles downstream, but there it was a sewer; here, you could feed the ducks from the grassy banks. It was a favorite Sunday walk for Marie and Sandy. If she left Sid, would she leave all this, too?

As they made their way beneath the trees, Marie wondered how long Sandy would be content to hold hands as they walked. Nothing could be better than this child; nothing could be worse than having another, right now. She had been so sick, so ruined, so sad after Sandy was born. She had made so much of herself since. To begin again? She didn't know if it was possible. She'd heard of other mothers having the "baby blues" for a few months, despondent except for when they were crazy-angry. Was that what Marie had? She didn't remember being angry, and it went on for two years. She was a dishrag until Ann brought that test to the cookout, and Dee twisted her arm to take it, and even her son-of-a-bitch husband drove like a madman to get her back home from Florida for the physical.

"Are you going to sneeze again?"

"No, baby. Tell me about your day. How was school? What did you do?"

"A boy got sick in gym."

"I'm sorry about that, but what did you learn today?"

"State capitals."

"Really? What's the capital of Maryland?"

Sandy squeezed Marie's hand. "C'mon, Mommy. Can't we just have a nice night out?"

Marie started to laugh before she felt a chill in her heart. Sandy had picked up one of Sid's lines, one of his milder dismissals of a subject not to his liking. There was something awful in the imitation, worse than when Sandy had put on the frightful face paint, which could be washed away. It troubled Marie to think about how Sandy might take after him. Sid's better qualities were few enough—he was tall, handsome, charming to everyone else, not stupid—but aside from hoping Sandy inherited some of his height, Marie prayed his influences would be minimal.

"Annapolis," Marie said. "We'll only do three."

"But Ma . . ."

"Enough. New York."

"Albany."

"Good. California."

"Sacramento."

"Good. New Jersey."

"Who cares?"

"Oh, Sandy!"

At Dee's, a car-shaped object in the driveway was covered with a tarpaulin. When had they changed from humble savers to proud spenders? *Welcome to America!* And here they were in the backyard: Mama and Papa on aluminum folding chairs that unsteadily held their weight, at the far poles of two picnic tables set end to end. Vera brought out a second tray of *antipast*, salamis and cheeses, olives and roast peppers, focaccia. Luigi was at the barbecue, tending to steaks, while Sal stood beside him, a highball in his hand, offering advice. Children stampeded around, and Mama held Vera's infant. Sandy was about to join the donnybrook, but Marie led her over to pay respects to her grandparents first.

"Ciao, Nonno!" Sandy cried out, running to embrace her grandfather.

"Cara mia, Zandy! You so big now!"

Sandy went to the far side of the table to hug her grandmother, kissing the infant in her arms. "Ciao, Nonna! And hello, little Joey! Can I go play now?"

Mama asked, *"Perché lasci questa ragazza vestirsi in pantaloni, come un uomo?"*

Why did Marie let the girl dress in pants, like a man? None of the next generation took in half of what their grandparents said. Papa's effusive affection didn't need subtitles. With Mama, Marie's translations were faithful neither to the letter nor the spirit of what was said. "Nonna says your outfit is very pretty, Sandy."

"Thank you, Nonna!"

Mama looked down at Sandy's new Keds, bright red with white laces, and shook her head. *"Quelle scarpe, una puttana non le porterebbe al circo."*

Even if Mama believed that a whore wouldn't wear those shoes to a circus, Marie felt no obligation to say so: "Nonna bets you run faster than all the boys, with your new sneakers."

"I do! I can!"

And off Sandy skipped, cheerfully oblivious. Mama didn't object to Marie's renditions of her remarks, confident that the point had been made. She asked after Sid, as she always did. *"Dov'è Serafino?"*

Mama's end of the picnic table was close to the barbecue, and Sal leaned over to respond before Marie could. He wasn't a bad-looking man, tall and reasonably fit, with black hair slicked up in a pompadour. He dressed as if he'd come from a resort, in a white short-sleeve shirt, sky-blue slacks, white loafers with gold buckles.

"Mama, Sid's working. Didn't I tell you?" Sal said, winking at Marie as if she were a glad player in the game. "Very big case, it may go all night. In Harlem, with the colored people. He was so sorry he couldn't see you tonight. He told me your knee was not so good. He wanted to know, how is it feeling?"

Mama fanned herself and cast a glance toward one end of the yard, then the other, as if adversaries might be listening. *"Che Dio mi sia testimone, è gentile da parte sua chiedere. Il mio ginochhio? Sono contenta di essere viva, credo . . ."*

Whatever. Marie kissed Sal quickly, making the barest contact of lips on each cheek. *Cafone,* she cursed silently. *Stronzo! Faiscifo,* you prick of misery. It rankled that Sid felt his mother-in-law was owed the courtesy of an RSVP, that his brother-in-law was updated on his nightly whereabouts, when his wife would have been punched for asking. It pained her that he and Sid got on so well. Ann held herself responsible for her husband's wandering eye and heavy hands, because she couldn't have children.

"Is it a case in Harlem?" Marie asked sweetly. "I thought he was handling something Puerto Rican, in the Bronx."

She walked past him to Luigi, who crossed his eyes and laughed before he dropped his two long forks on the grill to embrace her. He was the smallest of the husbands, slightly stocky now but still light on his feet. He had soft, rounded features and an alert, mostly droll air. Luigi picked up the forks and checked the steaks before setting them down again, so he'd have both hands free to tell his story. "You know who came in the shop today?"

Sal angled in closer, and even Mama was eager to hear.

"Richard Burton's understudy in *Camelot.*"

"That's something, it is. Really, that is something else," Sal offered, a statement that Marie couldn't find fault with, aside from its utter emptiness.

Mama asked, *"Chi è, lui?"*

"Richard Burton, Mama," said Sal, "A movie star, he was in *The Robe.* About the Bible, in ancient Rome. Very classy."

"Ah, *sì,*" said Mama, content to withdraw from the conversation. Marie didn't know if Sal was lying, or if the meaning of the term "understudy" had eluded him.

"Does he need insurance?" Sal ventured, with a hungry look. "Do any of them need insurance? When they come back, can you ask?"

Luigi suppressed a wince and offered a bland demurral—*Uh, I didn't maybe*—before reaching down to the cooler to pull a beer from the ice. He punched two holes in the top of a can of Schaefer and drained half of it at a gulp.

"Marie, where's my manners?" he burst out, when he finished. "Let me get you something to drink, a little wine? Let me go—"

But Marie was ruthless in cutting off his escape. "Thanks, but I ought to help out the gals in the kitchen."

She strode briskly toward the house. Guy sat on the back steps with his two-year-old, tossing him into the air. The child looked like a toy in his massive hands. There was concrete dust on his boots, but he had on a clean T-shirt. Marie could picture Vera badgering him to change, and Guy throwing his dirty shirt at her as he chased her around the house. She leaned down to kiss him as she passed. "Hey, Guy."

"Hey, Marie."

She tousled his hair and headed into the kitchen. Dee was at the stove, Vera at the table, chopping onions for the salad. Ann stood to the side with a cigarette, in a blue-and-white tennis dress that Marie thought fetching until she recalled that it matched Sal's outfit. The humidity of the room broke on her like a wave, and the odors of sausage, garlic, and cigarettes choked her. It was hot as a body here, 98.6 degrees. Marie felt her stomach curdle, and she thought she might be sick; the nausea dissipated, but then she felt light-headed. Ann clasped her arm and ushered her to a seat next to Vera, who cooed, "What is it, honey?"

Ann hovered, touching Marie's brow with the back of her hand. "You don't feel feverish," she said. "Maybe a little. Can I get you a drink?"

Vera found a vacant space on the forehead to take her own reading. "No, she's fine. Is it your stomach, do you want something to settle it?"

Dee fixed her with an appraising stare. "Are you pregnant?"

The other sisters took the question as a joyous announcement. Vera would have had a child every year, and Ann would have given anything, just to have one.

"How wonderful! My God!"

"Look at you! Just look!"

Marie looked up at Dee, impassive at the stove. Her expression was neither accusing nor celebratory; instead, it had a clinical clarity that made the emotion of the other sisters seem shallow and primitive. "Don't get ahead of yourselves," Marie said, taking a glass of water from Ann. "Don't start knitting little booties just yet. I had a long day, and I skipped lunch."

"Well, then, either way, you could use a cocktail," Ann volunteered, touching her to check for fever, one last time. "An Old Fashioned? Anybody else?"

Dee accepted, while Vera shook her head, and Ann disappeared to the bar in the living room. Vera left to make Marie a little plate of *antipast*. Marie was apprehensive about being left alone with Dee. A timer went off with a *Ping!* on the stove, and Dee hoisted the heavy pot to drain. When she nearly dropped it, Marie jumped up to help her—*Stop! You want to kill yourself?*—taking hold of one of the handles to empty it into the colander. Their faces were flushed with steam, but the heat didn't bother Marie as it had, a moment before. Dee dumped the pasta, greens, and sausage into a bowl. She gave it a stir and then turned to Marie, her gaze still direct, though there was a kindness in her eyes. "See? You don't even know your own strength. You can get through anything. Sit down now, have a little something."

As Ann arrived with the drinks, and Vera with a plate, all three began talking again, as if nothing had happened. Which it hadn't, Marie supposed. She felt better once she started to eat, and she was no longer the center of attention. She didn't want to be pregnant. And she couldn't even think the other word anymore, training herself to stick to the shorthand, "AB." If she slipped and said the letters aloud, maybe they'd mistake them as code for something innocuous, like an atomic bomb. Her sisters would forgive her divorce. Dee would throw her a party. What would Mama and Papa say? It would kill Mama, at least. Her options became jumbled in her mind: *Stay and go and live and die—*

"All right, let's get this show on the road," Dee said, satisfied that the pasta was as close as it would ever come to passing maternal muster. Mama would have spent half the day making it. Dee's had come from a box. "How many are we? I'm only putting out real plates for grown-ups. What's the count? Mama, Papa, Ann and Sal, Marie, Dee and Luigi, Vera and Guy. Nine. And I ought to put out a tablecloth, even if it's plastic."

"You know you'll hear about it, if you don't," said Ann, as they all set to their tasks. Proper plates and paper ones, glasses and plastic cups, metal cutlery and plasticware were deployed for majors and minors. Outside, the trays of *antipast* were lifted to lay the tablecloths. Dee set out the big bowl of *orecchiette*, a little one of grated cheese. Luigi took the meat off the grill and set up the record player on a card table, plugging it into an extension cord. He put on *The Great Caruso*. He always started dinner with Mario Lanza, who had once been a customer.

Most of the children rushed to the table before they were called. Marie gravitated toward Papa's end of the table, calling Sandy to sit beside her. She was surprised to hear her order countermanded by Mama: "Zandra! Sit by Nonna."

Sandy looked at Marie, less than delighted, but she did as she was told. It wasn't as if she didn't love her Nonna, but she was jealous of her time with Marie.

"Zandra!"

Mama had never approved of Sandy's name, knowing of no saint who shared it, but Marie had been determined in her choice. Refusing to call the baby "Stella" had been one of her few early acts of resistance. There was nothing wrong with the name; Marie thought it beautiful, the Italian word for star. She loved Sinatra's "Stella by Starlight"—*My heart and I agree, she's everything on earth to me.* But Stella was Sid's mother's name, and Marie would have no sooner agreed to it than she would have suffered a brand on her child's flesh. She thought of what might be inside her—*Might be! Maybe! Maybe not!*—and then banished the subject of baby names from her mind. She drank her cocktail, glad that Ann had made it on the stiff side.

Luigi was across from her, next to Papa, and there were several children on both sides of the benches before Guy and Ann, who were both within earshot. Sal was agreeably out of range, cornering Mama. Vera and Dee were next to Sandy, a buffer against Mama's maledictions and Sal's recitations from *Playboy's Party Jokes*. Marie closed her eyes for a moment and listened to the choral blur of Mario Lanza and kid noise: *Perfetto. No, bellissimo però.* Already Marie felt better, and, in the lenient evening breezes, the scents of garlic and grilled meat were sweet again. Hands began to grab at the food when Mama barked for order, and Papa said grace.

"*Benedici, Signore, noi e questi tuoi doni, che stiamo per ricevere . . .*"

The pasta was ladled out, the wine uncorked. Papa leaned down to pinch little Anthony's cheek. Dee's boy, who had just turned nine. He'd been making faces at his seven-year-old sister, Genevieve.

"What you gonna be, when you grow up, huh? Tell Nonno."

"I dunno."

"This is America, you can be anything. A doctor, a judge, maybe even a business tycoon."

The boy squinted in concentration, and then he beamed when the answer occurred to him. "I know—a dinosaur!"

Papa thought for a moment, making sure that he understood. When he was certain, he rendered his opinion. "Whadda you, stupid?"

Genevieve perked up at her brother's fall from grace. "How about me, Nonno? Can I be anything?"

He smiled and blew her a kiss. "You can be a good girl."

Papa ate with deliberation, dipping down to scoop up a bite or two at a time, before raising his head to survey the long table. Marie could picture what he saw, how he saw it: *These are my children, this is what I have made. On an ordinary day here, we have more food than we'd get at a wedding, back home.* She read the movement of his eyes as they took in the abundance of platters, of grandchildren, as if the pages of a book were turned slowly before him. He had sailed alone to America when he was twelve years old. His fifteen-year-old brother Gio met him at the dock with a horse and wagon. A fifty-pound block of ice wrapped in newspaper was in the back. On the way home to the tenement where they'd share a cot, Gio stopped at a building on Broadway and pointed to where Papa had to haul the ice to the fifth floor. *Welcome to America!*

When Papa smiled, Marie touched his cheek, as if he were the child, and his face was so aglow with emotion that she was afraid he'd cry. Papa stiffened then for a moment, and then he blinked. Marie watched him intently, alert to the possibility that he was afflicted by something more than sentiment. "*Cara mia* . . ."

No, he was fine. Marie listened to Ann tell Guy about problems they were having with the ventilation at "the new building," as she called UN Headquarters on 49th Street. She'd begun when they were in Long Island. Luigi told Gaetano, Vera's eldest, that young Joe DiMaggio always ate his vegetables. Papa drained his wineglass, but when he reached for a refill, the bottle was empty. Luigi rose, but Marie told him to sit down. She wanted to get up and move around a little.

When she returned with two bottles of store-bought chianti, she set one beside Papa and took the other to the far end of the table. Sandy had an air of disquiet, while Mama appeared satisfied to a degree that was not entirely explained by the fine food and company. Marie stroked Sandy's hair. "What is it, baby?"

"Nothing."

"You sure?" Marie turned to her mother. "Ma? What's up?"

"*Le ho raccontato la storia di Sant'Antonio.*"

"A story about St. Anthony? It upset you, Sandy?"

"A little."

"I've told you St. Anthony stories before, he's a very holy man, the patron saint of lost things. Go ahead, tell me the story."

"There was a boy named Leonardo, who was very bad," Sandy began uncertainly. "He kicked his mother. But then he felt bad, he went to St. Anthony and confessed. St. Anthony says, anybody who kicks his own mommy, his foot should be cut off. So Leonardo runs away crying and cuts off his own foot."

Marie asked, "And then?"

"And then?" Sandy shrugged. "I guess he bled a lot. Did he die?"

"Ma, come on! Why did you tell her such a terrible story?"

"*Come può essere una storia terribile, se era un uomo santo?*"

"For one, it's a terrible story for a little girl. For another, you didn't finish it. What happened next, Sandy, was when St. Anthony heard about what Leonardo did, he went and got the foot and put it back on him. He cured him, he healed the foot."

"*Sì, è come finisce. Un miracolo, tanti miracoli.*"

"And it'll be a miracle if Sandy isn't up all night with nightmares. Come on, Mama, she's only a kid!"

Mama shrugged. Marie made a face at Vera for not stopping the story, or at least finishing it, but she knew that she shouldn't try to shift the blame. When Sal lunged across the table for the wine bottle, toppling his glass, Marie found a suitable target for her ire. "Can I pass you the wine, Sal?"

"Nah, I got it. You know who's a saint?" he said, indifferent to her sarcasm, righting the glass and filling it to the rim. When no one responded, he went on. "My Annie, that's who. That's why I don't have to be good, to get into heaven. She'll let me in the back door."

Sal looked at Mama, who laughed and playfully slapped his hand. Marie wanted to slap him, too. "Not such a bad plan," Marie said. "But what if you die first?"

Sal's smile faded, and the line of his mouth straightened, then twisted. Mama gripped his wrist, as if to keep the Angel of Death from taking him away. She sputtered in clear English: "How you say such a terrible thing to Salvatore!"

"It's a practical question," said Marie sweetly. "Now that you're in insurance, Sal, you know that better than anybody. Anything could happen."

Marie thoroughly enjoyed the rest of the meal. She was about to clear her plate when she noticed the change in Papa. Tears brimmed in his eyes, and then one spilled, and another. "God is good to me. That's no lie. Still, if only he was here, my son, my lost boy . . ."

"It's okay, Papa. It's okay."

Marie stood up and kissed him. She couldn't stay for this, not tonight. He didn't slip into these moods at every family party; when he did, they didn't last long. Maybe five minutes of soft moans and stifled cries, as his watery eyes searched for some vanishingly far point on the horizon. Mostly, Marie pitied him for his grief, even envied him for how he could love someone who never was, forty years after they never met. Tonight, Marie couldn't bear to listen. She picked up her plate, then his, and left for the kitchen. Ann rose as well, clearing dishes. Luigi tried to join them in their jailbreak, but Papa raised a hand—this was women's work—and he reluctantly returned to his seat.

Marie scraped the scraps into the garbage and put the plates in the sink. The kitchen warmth was cozy now, and she was content to stay. Ann put her hands on her shoulders. "Have a seat, you. Don't make me get rough," she said, pushing Marie into a chair. "You know how he is. It doesn't mean he doesn't love us any less. But I guess you just can't hear that right now. To hear him talk about losing a baby, when you . . . You are pregnant, aren't you, babe? You can tell me, I won't tell anybody. I already know. I know you."

For a moment, Marie thought she might begin to bawl again. She'd labored to contain all the emotional roil and broil about Sid, the toll the birth had taken on her last time. But when she opened her mouth, only empty breath left her, a weary sigh. "I don't know for sure, but I think I am. With Papa, I don't—"

"Don't let it get to you. Papa's too much sometimes. I wanted to say there was a phone call for you, or to set something on fire, just to get you away."

Marie laughed. Ann was like Doctor Levine, uncanny in what she picked up, astonishing in what she missed. No matter what goodwill Marie felt, taking in the limitless sympathy in her sister's eyes, she knew she couldn't confide in Ann. It was a sin, abortion. A crime. Professional suicide. Sometimes, actual death. And it would have been inhumanly cruel for Marie to say she wanted nothing more than to be rid of what Ann wanted most. "Thanks, sweetie."

"Don't mention it. And I wanted to tell you . . . I shouldn't. It's a secret, but I don't know why you shouldn't know, especially now. Are you taking vitamins?"

Marie was intrigued, even as she felt a twinge of anxiety about Ann's ability to keep her mouth shut. "Let's hear it."

"I don't know why Mama didn't tell anybody but me, why Papa never told anybody at all. It's not something to be ashamed about."

"Ann, please—"

"Not that I don't know that they didn't tell you, too. Did they?"

"Out with it."

"You really don't know, do you?"

"Ann—"

"Do you remember when Mama was pregnant with Vera?"

"Yeah."

"You remember how she was?"

"Sick."

"That's right. Sick as a dog through the whole thing. In bed, most of the time. Barely gained any weight, until the end. I remember it better than you. I remember when Mama was pregnant with Dee, too, but not as well. Still, it was the same."

"I know, she had a hard time carrying all of us," Marie recalled. "She mentioned it a couple of hundred times. But she had four kids, so we know she was healthy enough. A lot of women miscarry, especially with the first pregnancy."

The notion almost cheered Marie. Ann looked furtively out the window. She was so flamboyant in her effort to be clandestine that Marie struggled not to giggle. Ann took a seat beside her, huddling in close as she whispered, "Mama didn't."

"What?"

Marie didn't care that she was shouting, until she saw how pale and spent her sister looked, as if the secret had taken all her strength. "Ann, what do you mean? Just tell me, without all—"

Ann clutched her hand, and Marie lowered her voice. "Please, just—"

"Mama was sick, skinny, like she always was when she was pregnant, but they didn't know, because it was the first time. The doctor, he told Papa she couldn't keep it, it would kill her. She was pretty far along. He didn't ask Papa—forget about asking Mama—he just said it had to be done. After, the doctor told him that it would have been a boy. Papa started breaking things in the office, he tried to choke the doctor. Other people were there, they had to pull him off him."

Marie wanted to run back outside to her father. She tried to imagine how it was for him, a young immigrant with a new wife dying from the child he put in her. He could haggle over the price of kerosene in three languages, but he couldn't say a thing about gynecology in any of them. Any woman was a foreign country to him. And who could question a doctor? Marie thought of Dr. Levine again, how he talked about how little they knew about pregnancy back then. Witchcraft, he'd called it. The doctor who took care of Mama thought he was saving her life. Maybe he had.

"My God, Ann. My God. I had no idea."

"I know. I feel better, having told you. I mean, I know why he's ashamed, but he shouldn't be. Poor Papa!"

"Poor Papa, I know. Different times, back then."

"I can't even imagine. Do you think I should tell Dee and Vera?"

"Absolutely, Ann. But let's me and you go through it first, beginning to end. As much as you remember. By any chance, do you remember the doctor's name?"

12 YOU'VE HEARD THIS SONG BEFORE

When a felon's not engaged in his employment
Or maturing his felonious little plans
His capacity for innocent enjoyment
Is just as great as any honest man's.

Our feelings we with difficulty smother
When constabulary duty's to be done.
Ah, take one consideration with another
A policeman's lot is not a happy one.

—"The Policeman's Song"
W. S. Gilbert and Arthur Sullivan

APRIL 25, 1963
1645 HOURS

Marie never learned the old doctor's name. She found it maddening that she was so inept at finding another one, given her experience in the field. Had she spent the last three years handling bank robberies, she'd know how to rob a bank. And she'd know how not to get caught—what to do and not-do with guards and alarms and getaways—to remain a masked man instead of a face on a wanted poster. But AB cases weren't whodunits—the girls had the names and telephone numbers of the perpetrators. Some even had receipts. The investigations could be demanding, but they weren't difficult. *A child could . . .* Marie didn't want to think about children. Not the one she didn't want, by a husband she couldn't stand, which would lock her into marriage she hated and keep her from the job she loved. At the very least, she had to ask Mrs. M. for reassignment. Whatever happened, Marie didn't want to think about pregnancy during every waking moment.

Marie struggled against taking out her impatience on Sandy, but she'd told her, time and again, how to take telephone messages. To say only that "some lady called yesterday" was worse than no message at all, since it inspired a period of fraught and profitless speculation as to whether she'd missed a late notice for a court appearance, or if Carmen hadn't taken her death threats to heart.

Katie delivered the same cryptic message the next day, and the day after that. She then followed a revised protocol, instructing the caller on the second day that Marie would be home on the third, at five in the afternoon, should she care to make her intentions plain. Marie suspected it was Carmen, or a friend enlisted to call on her behalf, especially when Sid appeared at home, at a quarter-to-five. "Hey, honey! You got a minute to talk?"

"No, wait—I have to—"

Marie didn't know whether it was morning sickness again, or the twenty-four-hour-a-day revulsion she'd felt for him since he'd raped her, but she had to run to the bathroom when she saw him, and she didn't rush back. She rinsed her mouth, but she hoped that her breath still smelled of bile when she returned. "Yes?"

Sid's smile put her on guard. It was one she didn't recognize from his repertoire. She knew the contrite Sid, boyishly abashed; the brash, leading-man grin he wore among other men; the cavalier smirk with which he favored waitresses. This one had aspects of all three. It was softly pushy but withholding, as if he were a salesman who hadn't decided if she had any money. "Honey, you and me ought to get away for the weekend. Just the two of us. It's been a little rough between us lately. I know I've been a bit of a heel, but you haven't been your old self, either. And I wanna make it right. Whaddaya say? The Catskills? Or we hop on a plane to Miami. Why not? I know a guy, can get us a rate at the Fontainebleau. We can lay out by the pool. Or—Hey! We charter a boat for the day, go fishing. Nobody but you and me."

Marie hadn't expected the offer any more than she'd expected the smile. She wasn't sure if the just-us exclusivity referred to Sandy and Katie, or to Carmen.

"You know you're stuck with me," he went on, shifting back to contrition, biting his lower lip. Marie was glad she had nothing left in her stomach. Had he really just suggested a boat trip, in another jurisdiction? Where the happy couple would be alone together, miles from shore? *Till death do us part*—Sid had already won a medal for rescuing someone from drowning. Who could blame him, if his batting average dropped to .500? "Um—I don't know, I really don't think—"

"Baby, come on, we have to go away somewhere—"

"Catskills. Definitely, the Catskills."

Before Marie could consider the risks of going to the mountains, the phone rang, and she ran to get it. "Household Marie, how can I reference you?"

There was a pause on the line, and then there was laughter. "Poor kid! You sound worse than I feel! Don't tell me you're still stuck in the same rut, too, after all these years?"

The voice was familiar, but Marie was still too rattled to recognize it. "Who may I ask is calling?"

"I'm your favorite manicurist. We both had fiancés on the USS *Abraham Lincoln*. They were on a secret mission, you said. That's why they couldn't write home. Just calling to check in to see if your ship ever came in."

Now, Marie knew who it was. She was very glad to hear from Charlie, even if boating remained the topic of conversation. Her voice was lower, huskier than she remembered. There must have been a lot of cigarettes in the intervening years, a lot of shouting. "No, it's still at sea. Me, too. How about you?"

"I'm about to cast off. Finally! But I have something for you that's gonna put Gino away. Can you come over?"

Marie would have liked nothing more than to jump in the car, but she held back. She wanted to escape Sid, but she'd been down this road before. And the sound of Charlie's voice brought back all the other songs in that jukebox, including Paulie's endless serenades on informants: "If you need something from them, it has to happen now. If they want something, you stall, make 'em give you more."

"I don't know, Charlie. I have a lot of stuff going on here, and I don't know if I can leave. It's great to hear from you, and we can talk if you want sometime, but—"

"Come on, Marie. I know I deserve the runaround, but I need to see you, right away. What I have on Gino, it's pretty big."

"I'm listening, Charlie. Tell me what you got."

"How much time could he get for three ounces of heroin?"

"I don't want to make up any numbers. It depends on his record. Not as much as he deserves."

"How about a pound of heroin?"

"Is that what you have?"

"Well—"

"Well nothing, Charlie. We're not starting from scratch here, you and me. Calling in a hot tip about Gino selling dope? I'm not taking bets on last week's race. That horse is already in the glue factory."

Marie feared that Charlie would hang up. Had she been too harsh? She doubted Charlie had much to offer, but she still wanted to talk. Marie missed their desultory days in diners and beauty parlors, chatting about nothing and everything. And there was no one else she could even consider confiding in regarding her . . . situation. There were times when a bad friend was a true gift from God.

"Would you listen to yourself, Marie! You're not the same sweet young girl I once knew. I hate to hear it. Not that I have a right to complain. But time goes by, doesn't it? You don't notice what it takes until it's too late. And it goes a little faster for girls like me and you."

"What's 'me and you'? If you're trying to say—"

Charlie cut her off. "Stop! No, sweetie! Stop! Would you listen? You're a cop, and I'm . . . I'm a lost cause. Time's not on our side. Neither of us are gonna be as pretty as we used to be before we know it."

Marie closed her eyes and lowered the phone. She couldn't stand the self-pity, and she hadn't heard anything useful. "Come on, Charlie, what are you—thirty? Quit crying. If you have something real for me, we can maybe meet sometime, but—"

"Marie! That's the meanest thing I've ever heard! I just turned twenty-six last week, and I can't believe—"

Marie would have apologized, but Sid seized the receiver from her hand. "What the hell is this? Who's this Charlie guy you're so buddy-buddy with?"

Marie didn't reply. Sid barked into the phone, "Listen, you son of a bitch, this is Sid Carrara, Marie's husband, and I'm a cop. That's not gonna keep me from hunting you down, and shooting you on sight. Tell me where you are, right now, and I'll—"

Sid seemed confused at the response. "Eighty-eighth, between Second and Third. Fine. Second floor."

Marie liked where this was going. Sid's bewilderment deepened. "No, we're not gonna arm-wrestle for her. What I'm gonna do to you—"

She owed Charlie one, she supposed.

"What? 'Dinner after'? Are you out of—"

Finally, Sid caught on. Marie had enjoyed the exchange until she saw him shift to his third smile, the one he used for waitresses. "So, Charlie— what's it short for, Charlene?"

Marie took the phone from him. Sid lingered for a moment, waiting to see if his goofball exit from the conversation meant more than his thuggish entrance. When Marie turned her back on him, she heard him walk away, muttering. Now she wouldn't have to pack for the weekend, either for the mountains or the beach. "So Charlie, you were saying?"

"Jeez, Marie, he sounds like a barrel of laughs. How you can put up with—would you listen to me? Other people's problems are a cinch to fix, aren't they? I'd give your husband hell if he even looked at me crooked, and you'd have kicked Gino to the curb a long time ago. Should we both run away together? All us girls—I know you got a full house there. I got your kid on the line one day. Who's the other one, who talks like *My Fair Lady*?"

"Oh, that's Katie, the babysitter. I wouldn't know what I'd do without her."

"Fine, bring her along. The more, the merrier. And I like what she brings to the party. Very classy sounding. Tea at four, every day."

"Little cucumber sandwiches."

"Sherry, too. And champagne, of course."

"Why not?"

"We'll be very proper. I was gonna to say we should head to Miami, but with the gang we have, maybe Palm Beach is a better fit."

Marie might have gone along with the gag a little longer, but the mention of Miami brought the daydream to an end. She had no time to waste. She needed to tunnel out of prison, but Charlie was just digging holes. "Ah well, Charlie. It's good to hear from you. Really, it's been good to talk. Really."

"Really-really-really, Marie? Is this old home week? Am I asking you to be on the decoration committee for the dance? Are you going to hang up, without even hearing what I have to say?"

Marie was chastened by the obviousness of the brush-off. She'd let too much slip, like Patten's triple tells of thank you and possible, feasible, and necessary. "Tell me, Charlie. I'm listening."

"So all the dope Gino has, maybe pounds of it . . . it doesn't matter to you?"

"Not really. Don't get me wrong, it would be a great to lock him up. But he'd have to have it on him, and I couldn't do it on my own. I'd have to call Paulie. And he's not your biggest fan after the first go. Do you remember how long that took?"

"Every goddamned minute."

"Are you saying you have it? Or that he has it now?"

"No."

"No?"

"No."

Charlie sounded more confident than she should have. Marie took the bait. "So what do you have for me?"

"You remember how you told me to keep a diary? About every date, every drop? All the license plates? I did more than that. I wrote down everything Gino ever said about those guys. About how this Frankie is skimming money from that Frankie, and how the other Frankie's wife is cheating on him with Nunzi."

"Really? Which Nunzi?"

"Nunzi Farts."

"No!"

Marie was fascinated. What kind of woman could fall for a man called Farts? But she was as unimpressed as Paulie had been, years before, with the scarcity of facts a cop could act on, let alone what a court would allow. "To put that diary into evidence, you'd have to testify. It's called corroboration. You'd have to swear in court that the diary is yours."

"I can swear to you right now."

"Come on, Charlie, you know it doesn't work that way. Besides, if there's no drugs, there's nothing to corroborate. Gino couldn't get arrested because of a story in a diary, let alone prosecuted. I mean, I'd love to have it, or somebody would. I'd sit down with you, and go through it. It could be helpful, down the line."

"Not now? Just down the line?"

"Yeah."

"And how much time would he get?"

"I don't know, Charlie."

"Are you still with Narcotics, Marie?"

"No. I'm back in the Policewomen's Bureau."

"Oh." That painfully deflated vowel cost Charlie all the goodwill she'd just earned for making Sid look like an idiot. "I'm so sorry about that. Is it my fault? Are you still wearing that awful outfit, like you had on when we first met?"

"No."

"What are you doing? You're not back guarding perfume counters, are you? I'm so sorry, Marie, if—"

"Listen, Charlie, I'm not getting into that with you right now. It's pretty confidential stuff. But I deal with homicides, with bureau chiefs in DA offices, all over the city."

"Oh, Marie! That sounds so dangerous, so wonderful! I'm so relieved I didn't ruin your career. I'm so proud of you! I was wondering how I could make it up to you, after how we left it. But you've gone so far already. You're in Homicide now?"

"Yes."

"So, if, say, I had big-time evidence on Gino being involved in a murder?"

Marie wouldn't bite on this one. If Charlie couldn't come up with a dime bag of heroin, she was unlikely to produce a corpse with Gino's name on it. Marie didn't have vast experience with informants—it was deep, but narrow—but she tended to believe that the subject of murder usually arose earlier in these conversations. She hadn't lied about working in homicide, even if it felt like it, but she saw no reason to reopen the books with Charlie, as a source or as a friend. "Did he kill somebody, Charlie? Did you see it? Did he tell you?"

The delay did no favors for Charlie's credibility, nor did her eventual reply: "It's a little hard to explain, Marie. I don't want to get into it with you over the phone. And I don't want to bicker about what the lawyers would say. Can't me and you just talk? Can you come over?"

"When?"

"Now?"

"No."

That was what Paulie would have said, but nothing rebelled in her conscience. She felt bad for Charlie, but she wasn't sorry for refusing her. Charlie had been right about her toughening up since their last talk.

"Remember the Hawaii Kai, Marie?"

That just sounded sad, but Marie didn't have an extra cent of sentiment in her pocket to spare. "Like it was yesterday. I remember what happened after. Paulie and Paddy—Remember them? I had to fight to keep them from locking you up."

"Did you? Oh, honey, I never knew. I never understood why they didn't come for Gino. I didn't drive the packages with him for a while after that, but he never got pinched. And then I figured, why not? What happened?"

"I don't know. Maybe they found something bigger, maybe something easier. I got kicked out of Narcotics after. We didn't stay in touch."

"I'm sorry, Marie, I really am. I spent so many nights wondering why I never got the call from jail."

Marie couldn't keep the bitterness from her laughter. "You're something else, Charlie! Every other fretful female stuck with a bad guy, she's scared to death that call's gonna come. But you? You're waiting by the phone, fingers crossed it's the bail bondsman. You're one of a kind, honey. Unbelievable."

No rebuke that Charlie could ever deliver would have made Marie as ashamed as she was of herself just then. She'd picked up so many lines from so many people over the years, but she'd never used one of Sid's. She wanted to wash her mouth out with soap. When Charlie seemed to take no offense, Marie's gratitude was profound. Who was that patron saint of Not Getting the Joke? Whoever it was, she'd answered her prayer.

"Oh, Marie, you got me there! I really miss talking to you. But I told you from the first how I hated long bus rides. I'm not tough, not like you. I needed you guys to get rid of Gino for me, and I let you down. But I think I can do it, finally. When I brought up the Hawaii Kai, it wasn't because I want to go back for the spare ribs. They were good, though, weren't they? It was because me and you, we figured it out together, right there on the spot. Remember?"

"Yeah, but also, there were those pills—"

"Come on, we got it done. Nobody asked how it happened. You found out what Nunzi was up to, and that was it. Let's get the ball rolling, and you can tell me about the rules later."

"All right, Charlie, but I can't run down there right away. It's after five now. Seven-thirty is the earliest I'll get there."

"Make it eight, sharp. Don't be late."

Charlie hung up so abruptly that Marie considered not going. Who did Charlie think she was, giving orders like that? As if punctuality had ever been her strong suit. Almost three hours, she wanted. More than she needed to put herself together for an evening out. Was that what she had in mind? That wouldn't be too terrible, Marie supposed. It might be just what she needed.

After sitting down for a light and distracted supper with Sandy and Katie—Sid was dining elsewhere, it seemed—she picked out a silvery shift from the upper register of her of evening casuals, and a black cashmere sweater. She called the switchboard at Narcotics to leave word for Paulie about her appointment. She was inclined to leave a more detailed message but then decided against it. No matter what panned out with heroin or homicides, Marie very much looked forward to talking to Charlie. A glass of champagne would be lovely. Maybe more than one, since she was drinking for two. And Charlie was the kind of girl who might know someone who could help her change that.

On the drive down to the city, Marie didn't think much about Charlie. She tried not to get too far ahead of herself with what Sid had said about the weekend in Miami. If he really planned to kill her, the fishing trip should have been an offhand inspiration, once they were already there. Of course, that was how Marie would have played it, had she been plotting to kill him. Unlike her husband, she'd had some experience with the Homicide Bureau. And she knew how to swim. But what he'd said was disturbing nonetheless. He'd revealed more than he knew, proposing that the place to resolve their marital discord was far from shore. It showed the map of his mind, when it was wandering.

As Marie parked her car, the satisfaction she'd taken with her discernment vanished. No feats of map reading or mind reading were necessary—Sid had put up color coded traffic signs in abundance. *Stop! Road closed!* He'd said that she was stuck with him. He'd told her that if she left, he'd be the last thing she'd see. She could stay and die, or leave and live, or leave and die, or stay. Marie might be in need of something stronger than champagne. It was ten minutes before eight, but she was used to being kept waiting with Charlie. Marie walked up to the second floor and prepared to knock.

And then she heard a noise from inside. A thudding sound, as if a piece of furniture had been knocked over. The door muted the volume. One of the club chairs? No shouts or yelling, she noted. Was Charlie having a fit, or a fight? Marie waited, but she didn't hear anything else. Her gun was in her handbag. The bag was over her shoulder on a strap, at an awkward midpoint of her torso. She opened and closed the clasp, making sure it wouldn't stick. She opened it again, feeling for the gun, and then she closed it again. She tried the door, and it was unlocked. Gently, gently, she eased it open, inch by inch, and she peeked inside.

There it was, the club chair on the floor. The coffee table toppled over beside it. In the other chair, facing the door, Gino sat, doubled over. His head was in his hands, and his body heaved with silent sobbing. When he looked up at her, his eyes were red, and his cheeks glistened with tears. "She's gone."

Gino put his face back into his hands. There was only grief in his voice. No anger, or shame, or fear, or even any surprise at seeing Marie. *Gone.* Marie didn't believe Charlie had left town, but Gino spoke as if no one had done anything, only that something had happened. It was as if the two of them were at a hospital, summoned by an urgent call about a long-ailing loved one who'd taken a turn for the worse. *We're sorry, we did everything we could.*

Marie took a few steps inside and unclasped her purse. Not knowing what had happened made it impossible to decide what to do, what to say. She wanted to rush into the bedroom, to see if Charlie could still be saved; she knew that she couldn't let Gino leave. She wanted to demand answers, to order him to put his hands up. She needed to call the precinct, for reinforcements. Instead, she said nothing, did nothing. Gino sat up and lay back in the chair. His hair was mussed, and his necktie was loose, and he looked as if he'd slept in his suit. "It's good to see you, Marie." He didn't open his eyes. "She made me do it. She finally made me do it."

Now, Marie didn't have to go into the bedroom. Not just yet.

"She told me she was working with the cops," he went on. "Had been, almost the whole time we was together. She already told 'em everything."

Not quite everything. It appeared that there remained one last bit of news for Marie to break. He wasn't thinking clearly, to be sure, but he wouldn't confess to her if he knew she was a cop, too. That was to her advantage, she supposed. Was that the only one she had? Gino rolled his shoulders, forward and back, as if he were rousing himself from bed. When she saw the gun tucked in his waistband, a vain and vagrant notion crossed her mind about the danger of waking up sleepwalkers. It was followed by a more concrete conclusion regarding her advantages: gun-wise, they were even, but his was more readily at hand.

"You look good," Gino observed, with a punch-drunk smile. He rubbed his eyes and took in her form, up and down. "Did it work out for you? I guess it did."

Marie had no trouble mimicking the same addled tone. "Did what, Gino?"

"That was one part I never got," he went on, shaking his head. He reached into his shirt pocket and took out a cigarette, and then he patted himself for a match. One hand touched his pants leg as the other touched his coat, and then the hands reversed. And then they reversed again, a hand up, a hand down. What was the wind-up toy he looked like? A bear that played the drum. "I never got why you needed me, Marie."

Marie didn't interrupt him as he took the unlit cigarette from his mouth and replaced it with another. "I tried, I really gave it my best with you. And it seemed to go so good, didn't it? At first? At first, I said to myself, 'Kid, you really outdid yourself.' I really did." It seemed Gino had found the matches, because he was smoking. "But it all worked out for you in the end. I knew it would. I can see that. I got eyes in my head, don't I? Tell, me, are you happy?"

Marie was at a loss. When he talked about how she needed him, how he'd tried so hard with her, her best bad guess was that he'd snapped, that he believed she was Charlie. Again, she thought of sleepwalkers. "I don't know. How do you mean, 'happy,' Gino?"

"With your husband, dummy."

Again, his words couldn't be clearer, his meaning more obscure, until he wiggled the fingers on his left hand. "I noticed the ring."

"Oh," she replied. The rationality of his last point made his larger conversation no more reasonable. "We have our ups and downs, I guess."

"Same as everybody, huh?" Gino mused, his voice amiably drowsy. "Still, I really figured you and Nunzi for a couple of Romeos. That was some night, wasn't it? Perfect, until the end. Like me and Charlie . . . Anyway, Nunzi, he's getting out soon. Next month? Tell me if I'm outta line here—far be it from me, to get involved in your business—but if you want to maybe get a cup of coffee with him, for old time's sake, I could set that up, no problem. I could see him turning up his nose at a married broad, but who's he kidding? He's an ex-con, he can't be too picky."

At last, she took in what Gino meant. He was a romantic at heart, as Charlie had said. Love was on his mind, even now. What was on hers, she couldn't say, because she didn't react as she should have when Gino stood. She was the one who'd been sleepwalking. She reached into her purse, but he was on her at once. He knocked the purse from her grasp and held her around the waist so tightly she couldn't get any air. The gun was pressed against her side.

"What the hell am I talking about? Marie, have I lost my goddamned mind?"

"Can't . . . breathe . . ."

When he relaxed his grip, just slightly, she sucked in a lungful of air and looked up at him as he contended with himself. His teary eyes were bright with menace, but his face was the picture of need, trembling with tics; one hand held the gun, while the other rubbed her lower back, as if they were dancing to a slow waltz. There were cold patches on his shirt where the sweat had cooled, and warm ones where the sweat was fresh. "I can't leave you here, Marie. I'm so sorry, so sorry you had to be here. I hate . . . to even think . . . of hurting . . . Put yourself in my position."

Marie didn't know if he was asking for her permission, or her help. She imagined this was how it ended for Charlie, with words of magnanimous regret: *Let's just say this was nobody's choice, and nobody's fault, but here we are, and what has to be, has to be.* Maybe not. Maybe it was completely different. It had to end differently, she knew.

"I just can't see any other way."

Marie rested her head against his chest. It was an instinct more than an idea, as was her next move, extending a hand behind him to stroke his shoulders. The pistol dug in against her ribs and then withdrew, slightly. Despite the gravity and gross intimacy of the moment, she found herself slipping into a frame of mind much like Gino's; she felt impassive, at an impersonal remove. What next? She couldn't fight him. He was stronger, and he had a gun. She couldn't reason with him, exactly, and it would be a waste of breath to promise not to tell. Something would come to her, she was sure. Or it wouldn't. One way or another, this would be over soon.

"I'm sorry, Marie."

"I'm sorry, too."

She felt Gino's chin dip against her neck, and his left arm loosened from her waist. His left hand took hold of her right, and he stepped back, pulling her to the side. The move reminded her of dancing again, pivoting for a twirl, until she realized that he was turning her away, so he wouldn't have to see her face. Gently, she resisted. Gently, gently, she caught his eyes and smiled, with a gentle sadness, as she heard the hammer click on the gun. "You were right about Nunzi, Gino. I really fell in love with him that night. You're pretty amazing, honey, putting us together the way you did.

You've got a sixth sense. It would have worked out between us, I really believe. But not now."

Gino couldn't let her die without hearing the end of the story. "Why not?"

"You didn't notice? You're pulling my leg, aren't you?"

"What?

"You don't miss a thing, Gino. You're just trying to flatter me."

"What is it?"

"I'm having a baby."

That was the last thing Marie remembered before everything went dark. She didn't see anything, or hear anything, or even feel anything. She didn't know how much time had passed before she became aware of the dunning pain in her head. An apprehension of light followed, punishing beyond her shuttered eyes, and then she felt the roughness of the rug against her cheek. She was still here. And that was all that mattered, for now. She had scant reason to be proud of herself, and none to be thankful to Gino, but both fleeting beliefs made her head hurt less. She'd been right, at least, in expecting to spend more time on girl talk than cop talk when she got here. She closed her eyes and lay quiet for a while, smiling.

When she recalled that she had aspirin in her handbag, she began to stir, and then she rose with a jerk, once she realized what else it contained. She crawled across the floor and dumped out the purse, rejoicing when she saw the gun and shield bounce on the floor. She popped a few aspirin in her parched mouth and staggered into the kitchen, downing glass after glass of water. As the tap ran colder, she splashed her face. She wasn't herself, just yet, but it was time to get to work.

There was one thing she had to do before she called the precinct. At the bedroom door, she paused, as if she should knock, as once was her habit. The lipsticks and mascaras and bottles of scent were still upright. There hadn't been a struggle, at least not here. Marie couldn't quite bring herself to look at the bed, where a pale blue silk sheet covered the body. Gino wouldn't let a woman watch him when he shot her. That much she knew.

As Marie drew back the sheet, the loose tresses of red hair on the pillow had a tossed-back, windblown look; the eyes were closed, and the expression was untroubled; the makeup was perfect, as always, with subtle touches of color bringing out the lines and planes of her God-given face. Marie was about to mutter the old biddy-at-a-wake line—*So peaceful, she could be sleeping*—when she lowered the sheet farther, and it stuck, slightly, at a tacky spot on the chest. The bullet hole over the heart left a mark barely larger than if she'd been poked with a finger, and there wasn't much blood; what stood out was the dress Charlie wore. Marie hadn't seen it before, and it was stunning, rich black satin with a plunging neckline. Her first thought was that she'd have felt underdressed, had they gone out for cocktails together; her second was that Charlie had chosen it for her funeral.

Marie went back to the kitchen and called the precinct. In the living room, she resisted the temptation to straighten up, although the only straightening needed was with the coffee table and chair that Gino had kicked over. There hadn't been a fight here, either. When she sat down on the couch, she wondered how much of the pain in her head was from the butt of the gun. No fight in the living room, no fight in the bedroom. Charlie's last words to her were "Make it eight, sharp. Don't be late." After insisting she could pin a murder on Gino. Don't worry about rules and lawyers, she'd said. Just show up and we'll take it from there. *Eight, sharp.* Marie had been early, but Gino was always on time.

The sound of sirens liberated her from the gauntlet of revelations. Patrolmen arrived, and then bosses and precinct detectives—Ralph Marino among them—and then Paulie and Paddy. She repeated her account in expanding detail for each successive wave, but she couldn't have told a tenth of what had happened, even if she tried. This was the gist: Charlie had called with information about Gino; he had just killed her when Marie came in; after a struggle, he knocked her out and left. The bosses were content with the outline, satisfied that the case would be brought to a rapid conclusion. They asked only if she'd fired her gun, or if she needed medical attention. Ralph and the other detectives wanted particulars on time lines and statements. Paulie and Paddy said nothing. From the patrolmen, she overheard mumblings of praise for her moxie and dismay at her risk taking. There was an outpouring of concern for her safety, and a suggestion or two that it would have ended very differently had a real cop been here.

Marie retreated to the kitchen for more water, and Paulie and Ralph followed to continue the interview in privacy. Ralph exemplified the moxie-praising contingent; Paulie, the dismay.

"You're sure you're okay, Marie?" Ralph asked. "It doesn't look like you're bleeding. Don't get down on yourself about anything—if you couldn't save Charlie, nobody could. What a shame, I'm sorry. She was a real firecracker. And if you don't mind my saying, I never saw a prettier stiff. Like Sleeping Beauty."

Paulie shook his head. "These people are degenerates, one way or another. But this one? This one makes me sick. You know she set you up, right?"

Marie grieved to hear him, but she couldn't disagree. Hadn't Charlie said that the only way she was sure she could leave Gino was to put him in prison? Now, he was facing life. Hadn't she said that it would be better to be killed by someone who loved you, instead of a stranger on the street? Still, Marie didn't hate her, even now, and she knew she never would. "Yeah. What I don't know is, if she expected me to collar him or kill him. 'Whatever it takes,' remember?"

Ralph hadn't gotten that far ahead, apparently, and his protest was explosive: "Did she? My God, Marie! That's the worst. Not that I knew her, but I never woulda guessed she'd throw you under the bus like that."

The next contributor to the conversation was less welcome. "That's because you don't got a woman's intuition. We tore up the place pretty good, but we didn't find any diary. Who knows if there really is one? We did find this, though. Here you go, bright eyes, I think you deserve the souvenir."

When Marie turned to face Paddy, she saw that he held the little dog. She recalled his trick with the toothpick, years before, and her jaw tightened. It seemed to recognize her, barking and leaping up to lick her face. She didn't want to take anything from Paddy, even this, but Ralph urged her to bring it home. "Otherwise, it goes to the pound. They'll put it down, unless we find next of kin."

Marie wanted to leave almost as much as she had the last time she was here. The second-to-last time, when Giaconda had visited, and Gino asked Marie to come into the bedroom with them. Her head hurt. The only thing that held her was a reluctance to depart without some kind of comeback for Paddy. Was it just that? No, there was more. When Charlie had called earlier, she'd done the old soft-shoe when pressed for specifics about heroin, and the murder evidence she claimed to possess was— umm, premature?—but she'd been matter-of-fact about the diary. It had to be here somewhere. Charlie wouldn't have left it on the nightstand for Gino to take.

Marie rolled the little dog in the crook of her arm to rub its belly and didn't look up as she offered her thoughts. "Well, Paddy, you missed this little cutie, the first time you looked. Once, I couldn't find the entrance ramp to the George Washington Bridge, but I didn't go home and tell everybody there's no such thing as New Jersey. And Paulie, far be it from me to suggest that you—or anybody you might know—might be in the habit of talking out of turn to the press, but why don't we say we found it? And what it said that one of the boys was was cheating the boss with dope, one with—"

Marie never understood how Charlie's reason to live had become a reason to die. Her leaving Gino, Gino leaving her; what was the difference? Going or staying, that was the real quandary. But even on the ride home, Marie had already begun to take a cold consolation from the episode. Charlie never doubted that Marie was more than a match for whoever set himself against her. That the lesson was a little neat, and that she hadn't really learned it, were thoughts for another day.

The following morning, this was the headline of the early edition:

MOBSTER'S GAL PAL HAS THE LAST WORD
The underworld is abuzz with rumors that the murdered mistress of a Mafia drug kingpin kept a diary of their most sensational secrets. Worse still, according to confidential sources, are details of hoodlums' double-dealings with each other, and not just with money, but in affairs of the heart . . .

This time, Marie didn't mind that her name was left out of the story. Marino called to let her know that the diary had turned up in the apartment, as predicted, but he found the handwriting difficult to decipher. Narcotics had it now, and they would make of it what they could. Gino's body had been found as well. It wasn't pretty, Marino told her, and she didn't ask for details. Had she known it would end like this? She hadn't thought that far ahead, but she supposed that she'd have guessed as much. It was either his friends or the electric chair, though it sounded as if the chair would have been kinder. She took Gino's death with the same flat detachment as he'd taken Charlie's: he was gone, and that was that. Who had time for recriminations? Charlie had been right not to fret about the rules of evidence. If a judge wouldn't allow twelve men to hear her, she'd make her case to the millions. Charlie had said what she needed to say, and no one could shut her up, even now.

13 YOU DO WHAT YOU HAVE TO DO

I will ask you to consider the probabilities in this case.
And I'm going to ask you that, when the proof is all in,
to see if you don't say to yourself that this is a tragic case
of mistaken identity.

—Frank D. O'Connor
Alfred Hitchcock's *The Wrong Man*

MAY 1, 1963
0900 HOURS

M arie had been waiting for a sign, but this was not it. On the Bronx River Parkway, a milk truck had jammed itself into a picturesque stone overpass, halting all southbound cars for half a mile. What was the message, that she was stuck? She knew that already. Stuck: that was the word of the day. There was so much inside of her—in her body, on her mind—that she wanted to get out. Bits of both had managed to escape lately. She didn't know whether she was gaining courage or losing control. Sid had taken his weekend getaway without her. When he returned, she was tempted to tell him she was pregnant, if only to make him as miserable as she was, but she held back. Soon, it wouldn't be possible to avoid the subject. Maybe she'd feel better, once she let it out. Hadn't it done her a world of good when she told Gino? It had saved her life. She bellowed through the car window, "Make way! Lady with a baby here! Make way!"

Nope. Still stuck. This morning, Sandy had a fit because the blouse she wanted to wear to school was in the laundry. The unexpected gift of the pet had bought a week of beatific behavior from her; that, too, was apparently at an end. And the stupid little dog had pissed all over the kitchen

241

this morning. Looking at the gas gauge, she saw the tank was perilously low. As other drivers began to press on their horns, Marie turned up the volume on the radio as the announcer began the lead story of the hour, his voice mellow and crisp.

"An appalling discovery was made in Queens when pieces of a girl's body were found clogging the waste disposal drain leading from a residence and doctor's office. The area has been roped off, and there is frantic activity as attempts are made to retrieve the bits of bone and flesh. The victim is believed to be a nineteen-year-old girl from Westchester, missing since Sunday, when she went to the doctor's home for an abortion. An alarm has been issued for Dr. Harvey Lothringer of 185-01 Union Turnpike—"

Marie didn't hear the rest, and not just because of the blare of horns. She looked at the stalled line of cars ahead of her. She looked to her left, where the Bronx River lolled past, a wide brown ripple flanked by verdant lawn. On the far side, a woman held her daughter's hand at the bank, as the child threw bread to Canada geese. Marie wanted to abandon her car and wade across to join them.

Marie wouldn't have gone to Lothringer. She hadn't decided what she would do. By not-deciding long enough, the decision would be made for her, she knew. But she couldn't think of a doctor she'd investigated she'd trust to operate on her. Even when she was only pretending to be a patient, she'd found something repellent in each of them—a lecherous glance, breath fragrant with gin. With Lothringer, his cold manner and secretive maneuvers were disturbing enough; and then there was his dog. *His dog!* Marie would have given anything to make this go away. She would have cut off her hair and braided it into a frame around a picture of St. Anthony, like Mama had. But Marie couldn't pray for what she wanted. St. Anthony was the patron saint of lost things, not things you wanted to lose. *Tony, Tony, don't turn around* . . . She turned the radio back on.

"The extent of Lothringer's operations was indicated by District Attorney Frank D. O'Connor: 'My men moved in to pick Lothringer up on Monday in connection with two other abortions. We were just a day too late. His home had been under surveillance for weeks. He was part of a full-blown abortion ring, with steerers and referrers, operating citywide and throughout the state. Because of the present confusion over the legality of wiretaps, we did not wiretap the house. If we had used wiretaps, this poor girl would be alive today.'

"In the Bronx, the Yankees lost, after a late-inning rally—"

Marie turned off the radio. She felt cold, confused. She'd never heard O'Connor speak before. Could it really be him, telling such lies? Her imagination had been stretched beyond its ordinary contours lately, and the muscle tone might have become a little slack. What the hell had O'Connor said? *We were just a day too late.*

When Marie touched her forehead, her hand was wet with perspiration. *Because of the present confusion over the legality of wiretaps, we did not wiretap the house. If we had used wiretaps, this poor girl would be alive today.*

How could the man stand to live with himself? O'Connor didn't have to wiretap his office to find out how many wiretaps he had going. He had dozens of them. This game was as fixed as any game show had been. There was no mystery to these mystery boxes, and no prize hidden in any of them. She wasn't sure if she was angrier at Lothringer, or O'Connor, or the driver of the milk truck who trapped her on the road. O'Connor: he had shut down her case, and now he'd closed off her options. Queens wasn't safe territory for someone to approach somebody, to talk about whether it might be possible, even to consider—

Nope, this had to stop. And she had to go. Hadn't she been waiting for a sign? Marie wouldn't let this morning last any longer than it had to. She needed to move, to feel the free air on her face. She looked at the right side of the road, at the apron of grass that dipped down into a ditch and rose up to a row of hedges at the edge of the street. There seemed to be a gap at the top. What did the traffic rules matter, after the stone tablets of the commandments had been shattered? She pressed her elbow into her horn, cut the wheel hard, and stepped on the gas. As she bounced down the green incline and then back up, her car skidded, tearing up the turf, but managed the summit. A chorus of horns blasted their denunciations. She flattened the hedge as she vaulted through and made a rough landing on the asphalt. She was moving. Now, she could get to work, but she was irate and bedraggled, unfit for company.

After finding a gas station, Marie went to the ladies' room to make herself presentable. She was starting to feel a little better now, shadowboxing before she had to start throwing real punches. She'd make Lothringer pay, and she'd hold O'Connor to account. What did she have to lose? When she arrived downtown, she was in a mood of grim readiness.

As Marie marched into the office, the policewomen on clerical duty gathered in the vicinity regarded her in quiet horror, before letting loose a volley of questions.

"Marie, did you hear?"

"It's all over the news—"

"You can't believe the phone calls—"

"It's bad, Marie, the phone hasn't stopped ringing—"

Marie was annoyed by their henhouse noise. Didn't they have anything better to do? She raised her hands and nodded—*Yes, I know*—as if to brush them away. Emma led her in to the director. Mrs. M. was on the phone.

"I agree completely. Not at all, she's right here . . . No, on the contrary, I'm quite certain there is no need for you to speak with her. I am her supervisor, and what needs to be said and done will be said and done by me."

Mrs. M. shook her head when she spoke. Her eyes shut, and her mouth narrowed, and one of her hands opened and shut, as if squeezing juice from an unripe fruit. Marie was gladdened that they seemed to be just as angry, in exactly the same way. "Yes, we should speak this afternoon. Goodbye."

When Mrs. M. hung up the phone, she missed the receiver. For a woman of her poise, the slightest loss of control made her look epileptic. "That was Mr. O'Connor," said Mrs. M., closing her eyes again. "You can imagine his concerns. He finds himself in an awkward position. And he intends to ascertain, rather rudely, whether we will make it more so, or less. I don't care for his tone."

Marie gripped the arms of her chair. Rude? That man, to this woman? It was more than Marie could bear. "Let's hang him out to dry! If he'd done his job, that little girl would be alive today. Does he think he's gonna be mayor? If you let me—"

"Possibly," interjected Mrs. M., with a welcome recovery of equilibrium. "And perhaps not. The human tragedy remains, of course, but there may be advantages for us, in how this is resolved."

The musing and detached tone, so quickly regained, made Marie more uneasy than the brief lapse in composure. Mrs. M. continued, "Your request for a wiretap application was denied some six weeks ago. Many of these cases go on far longer, as you are well aware, and I recall that your interest in Dr. Lothringer was inspired, in part, by the ingenuity of his defenses. This could have occurred under our watch. We're fortunate, in a sense. This circumstance could provide an opportunity."

Marie supposed that she agreed, but when she nodded, she felt like a coward. There were politics to everything, and the vast majority of the men in the department understood the word *policewoman* to be a contradiction in terms. Still, the last comment reminded Marie of an undertaker measuring a body to calculate the markup on the coffin.

"And let's not forget," the inspector went on, wearily and with less warmth, "that the girl—with her mother accompanying her, God help us— was hardly blameless. The only true innocent was the child. I wonder what they will say to each other, when they meet before St. Peter?"

Marie could not envision divine judgment so specifically, with the mother and unborn child arraigned like bar brawlers on the last docket of night court. Marie hadn't really thought about the girl as a person, let alone as a perpetrator. She didn't even know her name. Whoever the father was, he couldn't be worse than Sid. Would Mrs. M. judge Marie so harshly, if she died in the same way? Would Mrs. M. even show up at her funeral? Maybe if she told Mrs. M. what it was like to be married to Sid, how the years of hurt made the life inside her feel like a death sentence—No, she couldn't. Mrs. M. shook her head, as if she'd read Marie's mind. "What were these people thinking? The woman was at least five months pregnant. It is one thing to solicit a murder, another to expect a miracle. There is blood on all of their hands."

No, Marie wouldn't say a word. Everything was at risk with her pregnancy; everything was at risk if she tried to end it. She wished she were still stuck in traffic on the Bronx River Parkway. The inspector looked into the distance for a while, indifferently squinting, as if at a billboard that she couldn't quite read. And then she sighed, scanning her desk for a manila file with newspaper edging beyond the borders. She handed it to Marie.

"I need you to prepare a dossier for them. A summary of your investigation. This is coverage of the incident. You may be able to provide insight, with your familiarity with his modus operandi. Is there anything else you might require?"

"No."

"Any suggestions or comments?"

"I might as well get to it."

As Marie took the folder, Mrs. M. gave her one of her probing looks. "Forgive me, my dear. I anticipated a debate with you, and I am grateful for its brevity. I know you feel deeply about your work, which is why I so value you. A false distinction, don't you think—personal and professional? No professional is ever that, unless she cares, very personally. I've had an office cleared for the next several hours, so that you may work without interruption."

Emma escorted Marie down the hall, dismissing with a severe look a lanky geriatric who departed with surly reluctance from his niche. Aside from a typewriter, the surface of his desk was empty, as if a wind had swept it clean, and Marie saw its contents in a cardboard box on the floor. She glanced at the topmost pages and saw correspondence with a horse-shoe factory in Pennsylvania; other equestrian matters were beneath. The department had a Mounted Division, she knew, and she supposed that someone had to be responsible for its administrative particulars. She wasn't offended that the policewomen were stabled near the horses, so to speak, but this alcove depressed Marie. The old clerk Marie had displaced may have first read with horror about Model Ts while sitting at this desk—*Horseless carriages!*—and wondered for the last half century when he'd be given his final notice.

Marie sat down and opened the folder, scanning each of the articles in the main papers. It was interesting to see the shifts in tone, which paper tended toward sanctimony, sentimentality, violence, or sex. The *Daily News* had the longest version.

Parts of a young woman's body were found choking the sewer line leading from the $85,000 brick ranch home and office of a well-to-do physician in the fashionable Jamaica Estates North section of Queens.

On Monday morning, Mr. & Mrs. L—had showed up at the Queens DA's office to make an official complaint that their daughter was missing. Somewhat reluctantly they told the story.

On Thursday, Barbara had come to them with the news that she was pregnant. L—, who was a pharmacist, had through a friend's intercession made arrangements to meet Dr. Lothringer at 2 a.m. in Grand Central Terminal.

There, on schedule, the girl and her parents were met by the doctor and a female friend. The price of the operation, set in advance, was $1,000. Mrs. L—paid the money and accompanied her daughter to the doctor's home and office, but Mr. L—was sent home.

The mother sat in the waiting room for hours. At 7:30, Monday morning, he came and told her that everything would be all right. "You can go home and come back for her later in the day." When she returned, the house was locked and dark and there was no answer to her many phone calls.

On Tuesday the doctor called a friend and asked him to have a sewer service clean out the traps in his house. He obtained the key from Lothringer's parents who lived nearby and let the sewer cleaner into the house.

As the work was being done, pieces of human flesh and other organs began coming out of the choked sewer lines. The cleaner called the police.

Marie closed the folder and began to compare the new case to the one she'd brought. There was the meeting at Grand Central Station, as with Helen and Benny; the female accomplice was present at the house, rather than just being a voice on the phone. And the price had doubled, to a thousand dollars. Did the family seem especially desperate, or especially wealthy? Given that the procedure usually took less than twenty minutes, Barbara probably died shortly after her arrival. Her mother sat waiting for hours, not knowing. How murderous it all seemed! And yet it wasn't that, Marie had no doubt. At worst, there was some medical error, but even if it rose to the level of malpractice, Dr. Lothringer surely intended for Barbara to walk out of his office. Some complication—an allergic reaction, a heart problem—was far more likely. He was a professional man, after all. In an eighty-five-thousand-dollar house. Marie hated to agree with ADA Patten on his distinction between the professionals and the hacks and quacks, but it mattered to the girls. Maybe not to Barbara, she supposed.

Marie found she'd had been staring at the wall for some time. Her report was due soon. *Ticktock, ticktock.* How many seconds were there in nine months? Sixty to a minute, and sixty minutes to an hour made for thirty-six hundred, times twenty-four, made for . . . Her notebook was soon covered with scratched-out sums. She had eighteen million seconds, give or take. All the time in the world.

Why did Lothringer wait until morning to tell Mrs. L. to leave? She must have sat there for hours. *Ticktock.* Marie imagined how the woman felt at seven-thirty in the morning, when the doctor told her to go home, that Barbara was fine, just resting. Marie couldn't believe she believed him. Surely, Mrs. L. must have balked at walking away, straining against some deep maternal coil that bound her there. And then her abjection on her return, finding the door locked, the house dark. Double-checking the street signs, desperate to convince herself that she'd made a simple little mix-up with the address, instead of a much bigger mistake. No, that was enough for Marie to imagine. She wouldn't try to see herself in anyone's place, mother or daughter, expecting or otherwise.

Marie began to type. She never used the word *I*, but the abbreviation *u/s* for *undersigned*, the police term used in lieu of the personal pronoun: "The u/s received information through a lawfully authorized telephonic intercept of an individual alleged to be in violation of New York State Penal Law Article . . ." The egoless term aided her immersion in her assignment. She summarized the accounts of Benny and Helen, annotated her sketches, listed observations on reports on the death of Barbara L. Marie lost herself in her work and was content to stay lost.

Sometime later, there was a knock at the door. It was Emma, telling her that it was one o'clock and that the director would see her now. What Marie had was sufficient, she supposed. No sense in being a perfectionist about a lie she didn't want to tell. As Marie gathered the papers, the sense of lulled focus that she'd just enjoyed left her. Her head filled again with static, the crossed signals telling her she had to do something, and that she didn't dare. And then her mind quieted. There was little comfort in the silence, but a chilly lucidity, a cold calm.

Marie couldn't go through with it. She couldn't try to find a doctor, in Queens or anywhere else. She was stuck. Stuck with this pregnancy for the next seven-plus months, stuck with Sid for the next six after. Stuck at home for a year. It didn't matter if she was more frightened of getting caught than of getting killed, or if she feared Mrs. M. more than the wrath of God. She didn't know what kind of movie her life was turning into, but it wouldn't be one of those tawdry women-in-prison pictures. Who knew if they wouldn't change the rules about locking up the girls if a policewoman was caught getting an abortion. A particular policewoman, who had sent so many abortionists to jail. And who had embarrassed a district attorney. Exceptions could always be made.

Marie sucked in her stomach and held her breath, for practice. She could hold it for five seconds, fifteen, twenty. Eighteen million seconds left, minus twenty. She had time to figure out the next step. *A false distinction, don't you think—personal and professional?* Motherhood had turned out much better than it had first seemed; marriage, far worse. But even the prospect of becoming a cop had changed her, and one day—not soon, but the day would surely come—it would allow her to become an ex-wife. If she had to keep the baby for no other reason than to keep her job, it was reason enough. So many good days it had given her, even if today was not one of them. It was time for a change of assignment, ASAP for the u/s. The pregnancy beat wasn't for her anymore.

Again, the boss was on the phone, her face the picture of strained patience, beckoning with an articulate flick of her hand for Marie to take a chair and surrender the documents. "As it happens, I am somewhat short-handed. I have what you requested. If you could send someone over, it would be most convenient."

When Mrs. M. smiled, it looked like the corners of her mouth were lifted by fishhooks. The sarcasm was gone now; this was hostility, barely concealed. Marie wasn't certain whether she was witnessing a skillful exertion of influence or a sad show of its absence. The only obvious fact was that Mrs. M. felt it necessary to shield Marie from an important man who was angry at both of them.

"By then, of course, I would expect the notification . . . Of course, your word is sufficient for me, as I hope mine is for you . . . There has never, ever been a question about her, either in the quality of her work or the quality of her character. Both are sterling. Good afternoon."

Mrs. M. hung up the phone. She took out a tissue and blotted her temples, damped her upper lip. The emptiness in Marie's stomach started to feel acidic. She needed to eat, but she had no appetite. The inspector stared down at her desk and then surveyed the broader expanse of her office. "Will I miss this?"

Was Mrs. M. thinking about retiring, or was it something worse? The room was painfully still, but Marie didn't break the silence. The question hadn't been asked for her to answer.

"Not this part," Mrs. M. said, after a while. "Forgive me if I seem unfeeling, but my husband and I have not been blessed with children." She plucked another tissue from the box. Marie wanted to take hold of her hand. She knew little of Mrs. M.'s private life and hadn't guessed its sorrows. She knew there was a Mr. Melchionne, but she had never met him. She didn't know his first name. The inspector picked up Marie's report and began to read it carefully, making notes on a yellow legal pad. The sound of the fountain pen on the pad was soft and secretive, like the worried tread of mice behind walls. She was dismayed by so many things—the death of the girl, the dishonesty of the DA, the escape of the doctor. Her own wretched circumstance, marital and maternal. She squirmed like a schoolgirl in her chair.

Finally, the inspector put down her pen. She rubbed her hands, as if to keep them warm. Marie was horrified to catch herself thinking she could use that, the next time she did the old lady disguise.

"I'm so sorry to keep you waiting, Marie. I should have told you earlier, but I have been reassigned from the Policewomen's Bureau. Just when I finished my graduate degree on the subject. Perfect timing, some might say. My new command will be with the Juvenile Division. 'Women and children.' Although I have been assured that it is not a demotion—repeatedly—it was not my decision. We must learn to make the best of things. You will, too, in time."

The phone rang twice, and then a third time, before Mrs. M. picked it up. "Yes, Emma? Who? Have him call back. No, I'll call him, in an hour. He's here? How rude. No, he can't come in. I'm speaking with Marie, and he should learn to make an appointment. I'll go out."

Mrs. M. hung up the phone. "Someone from the Youth Board. My appointment isn't official yet. Can't anyone keep a secret? Excuse me, dear."

Marie made no remark when Mrs. M. left her. The news hit her harder than this morning's story had in her car, but she couldn't turn off the radio, or change the station. She felt even more stupid, even more stuck, never having considered that more was at stake than her own position. The last time she'd sat where she was, in a like state, she was fretting over her transfer to Narcotics. Mrs. M. had surprised her by arranging for Sid's promotion to a gambling squad. The time before that, Marie had matron duty, so that she could attend Sid's medal ceremony. What prize was in store for him today? If there was one demand Marie would make of Mrs. M., aside from a getting out of ABs, it was—

No, Marie would make no demands. Mrs. M. couldn't do anything for her anymore. That was what Marie had to resign herself to, as much as her pregnancy. The loss of her protector, her adviser. Her friend, she almost dared to say. She wouldn't lose her job, not altogether. There were protections for civil servants, even for policewomen who had provoked powerful men. Thank God there had been a newspaper strike when she'd told off a bureau chief! But there might be no need to ask for a change of assignment. She dreaded the idea of returning to matron duty. After all she'd done, she'd be as much a prisoner as the prisoners she'd watch. Marie could try to get steady midnight tours, she supposed. That would be the responsible choice. At least she could see Sandy for breakfast every day, and dinner, though the rest of her life would be physically exhausting and professionally useless.

She tried not to look at her watch as five minutes became ten, and twelve minutes became fourteen. That was all? *Really?* She wasn't sure if she could manage fifteen years of eight-hour days in a staring contest with the clock. Her stomach sank further when she realized that she could, if she had to, if her house and child depended on it. Children, she'd have children then. It would be a fight to leave Sid, and money would be a part of it. Could she depend on him to pay for child support? Even if he managed to avoid indictment. Could she afford to keep Katie? Marie broke down and looked at her watch. God no, it couldn't be—was it back to eight minutes? No, time couldn't have gone backward, not even here. Her eyes must be wet. She lowered her head and feigned a sneeze, as if there were someone still here to pretend for. When the phone on the desk rang, no one answered. The sight of the inspector's empty chair made Marie nearly ill.

As Mrs. M. strode back into the room, Marie became hazily aware that Emma wouldn't have put the call through, unless the boss was returning. Marie watched intently as Mrs. M. lifted the receiver and spoke, wringing every syllable like a wet towel for all possible drops of meaning. It was a thrill to see Mrs. M. as her old self again, agile and assured. "Good afternoon. Oh, hello, Fred, yes . . . Mmm, that's not quite the case, but I see how he might have put it that way . . . yes, that's exactly it. No, I don't trust him, and there's no need for him to do it tomorrow, if he can do it today. Now, in fact. Yes. I have your word, yes? Thank you, your saying so is like having a United States Savings Bond. Yes, that's what I hear, too. Who knows?"

When Mrs. M. hung up the phone, her face resumed its mask of pensive melancholy. Marie struggled to remember the vivacity that that had moved through it like an electric current, seconds before. Now, she seemed as plain and plaintive as a widow in her weeds. "Marie, my dear, you will be missed. I am sorry about that. And whoever succeeds me in this position will feel the same way, I am sure."

"What?"

Marie was paralyzed. Could they fire her? They couldn't just fire her. No—

"It can't be helped," the inspector went on. "It isn't all you deserve, but—"

"What?"

"But you were made for the Detective Division. You're already better than most of the men there."

"What?"

Although Mrs. M. laughed at her stumped, repeated query, her voice was forlorn as she reached across the desk to take Marie's hand. "Forgive me. I'm so accustomed to having you in my confidence, but I couldn't tell you until I was certain. District Attorney O'Connor has strongly recommended you for the Detective Division, and I have secured the guarantee of the chief inspector, Fred Lussen, that the transfer has occurred. You will report tomorrow to Manhattan South Burglary."

"What? Why?"

"Fear, of course. Of me, of you. Isn't it wonderful?"

Now, Mrs. M. smiled in unmediated pleasure. "Why do you think Mr. O'Connor took such trouble with this? There are murders every day, and DAs don't call press conferences to say how hard they tried to prevent them. He could have simply assured the public that the matter would be pursued to the full extent of the law. That may have been the wisest course. But he was afraid that someone—you or I, to be precise—would contact one of the reporters who have covered our exploits with enthusiasm and alert him to the fact that Mr. O'Connor had refused to take action in what was, in the end, a matter of life or death."

There was much for Marie to take in. The day had been so full of awful shocks that she was unwilling—unable, really—to hear the glad tidings. And it seemed so shameful to celebrate, though she could have jumped up out of her seat and screamed with relief. Not fired. Promoted. She tried to find a more intelligent expression of her confusion, but she failed. "What he . . . I just don't—"

"To say nothing would likely have been preferable. One can't know, of course. These stories have a way of taking on lives of their own. Mr. O'Connor is an honorable man, in his fashion, and this foray into mendacity shows a lack of practice. Which is noteworthy, for a politician. Which reminds me—did you really threaten to put his bureau chief in the back of a station wagon, with a dog?"

"No, Mrs. M., I'd never—"

Mrs. M. laughed, and all was so well in the world that Marie wanted to cry. "I almost wish you had. Ah, well. Still, calling that press conference did force a reckoning. He wouldn't have to worry about waking up one morning to read of his malfeasance, weeks from now. Had he been willing to work with the Policewomen's Bureau, he would have known that I am not in the habit of disclosing our . . . missteps to the public. 'Dirty laundry' is an expression I don't care for. Nor do I think of this transaction as a kind of blackmail. It is a dangerous enterprise to make men of influence look foolish. Their reactions can't be predicted."

Marie knew the wisdom of that observation. She wondered where Mrs. M. had learned it. There wasn't any trepidation in the inspector's voice until she turned her head from the window to Marie, her eyes wide, then quivering with misgiving. She looked down at her desk and opened one of the side drawers, taking out another manila folder, thicker than the first she'd given her. Mrs. M. slid it across the desk, her voice a whisper. "Don't misunderstand me. To be respected as equals is what I want for us, and I believe that day will come. In the meantime, there can be an advantage in being overlooked, underestimated, insulting though it is. There are forgotten chapters of history, and the future is full of blank pages. Can I trust you with this?"

Please don't, Marie thought, her horror of complication outweighing any curiosity. The mention of blackmail unnerved her. What was she being offered? Love letters from the mayor to a showgirl? The encrypted missives of atomic spies? Marie couldn't refuse anything the boss asked on any day, let alone this one, her last in the Policewomen's Bureau. "Of course, Mrs. M."

"Be careful."

"I will."

"Keep it safe."

"Of course."

"I know you didn't ask for this, but . . ."

Marie nodded. "No one will ever know."

"I'm not sure what you mean by that," said Mrs. M. She seemed confused, at first, and then slightly cross. "In fact, I hope you are entirely mistaken. It's my master's thesis, and I only have one other copy. A history of policewomen in New York City. I assume it will be of interest. Haven't I always said that our story must be told? It doesn't always pay to persevere, Marie, but there is certainty in the alternative. Go home now, that's enough for one day, more than enough. I wish I could have done more for you— you'll retain your rank as policewoman for the time being, but I'm sure they will come to appreciate you as I do, and you'll get your gold shield as soon as one becomes available. I do so enjoy your company, and I am so grateful for your work. Please come see me when you can."

Marie rose from her seat, as if called to attention, and she had to fight her hand to keep it from a salute. She wasn't in uniform. *And now she wouldn't be, every midnight for the next fifteen years!* So awful, so wonderful, the whole day had been. She couldn't decide whether, she couldn't . . . No. She wouldn't think. She wouldn't think about how the death of a pregnant girl had brought her such good fortune. She wouldn't think about how her success with so many difficult cases had gained her nothing, but that doing nothing, saying nothing, had won her a chance to be a detective. She wouldn't think about telling Mrs. M. that she was pregnant, or how it happened, or how she felt about it, or what she'd thought about trying to do. There would be days ahead when she had to think, but today wasn't one of them. She began to blubber, softly, and she rushed around the desk to embrace Mrs. M., indifferent to decorum. Some sentiment would be indulged, just this once. When they let go, Marie turned quickly, snatched a tissue, and waved without looking back. She had almost recovered her composure, but she knew she'd lose it again if she saw the inspector's face. "Thank you, Mrs. M.!"

"Thank you, Marie!"

As Marie marched out, she touched Emma on the shoulder, but she didn't stop. She made for the exit as quickly as she could, swiping at her watery eyes. She didn't want to talk to anyone. She didn't work here anymore. The last thought made her blub again. As she left, one of the girls said, "I'm glad she left by the door. I was afraid she'd go out the window."

NO ONE WAS at home when Marie returned. No, not no one. The little dog capered and barked. It didn't even have a name yet, but it didn't seem to mind. Marie set Mrs. M.'s manila folder on the kitchen table, desperate to tell someone her good news. It hurt near to bursting to keep it to herself. She almost wished Sid were home. He would know what the transfer meant to her, what it would have meant to any cop. Would he be proud of her, as he had been, once upon a time? She couldn't wait to tell Dee and hoped the moment wouldn't be spoiled by any jealousy. What had Dee told her, in her kitchen? *You don't even know your own strength. You can get through anything.*

All the grave decisions of this morning had been made. Shut up; speak up. Keep it; don't. Stay, go. Now, all she had to do was have a baby and start a new job. Piece of cake. She turned on the radio, so the house wouldn't seem so empty, so still. She didn't have any demons to keep her company anymore. "Another reported organized crime figure has been found dead, in what authorities fear is a mob war—"

Marie turned it off before she could learn if it was another Nunzi. These things sometimes took on a life of their own, didn't they? She decided to walk around the corner to Vera's, to spare herself the agitation of passing the time alone. When the phone rang, she ran to answer. Who wanted to talk now? Her mother and sisters only called in the evening. Was it some kind of salesman, or one of the contractors she'd asked for an estimate on roof repairs? Did Katie have a beau? Whoever it was, they were going to hear that Marie was going to the Manhattan South Burglary Squad. She cleared her throat before picking up the phone, her voice mellifluous. "Good afternoon. This is the Carrara household. How can I help you?"

There was a pause before an answer. "Hello?"

"Good afternoon to you, too," came the response, still hesitant. A woman with an accent. What was the accent? "Marie. I . . . This is . . ."

Now, Marie knew. "Carmen."

"Carmen," Marie repeated. Her expression flattened, as if she were seconding a motion in a boardroom. "How can I help you today?"

"Oh, Marie, it's me who can help. I want to help you. Sid told me about what happened, how you are going to have a baby that neither of you want. I can help, I can stop it."

"Can you?"

"Yes, I can, Marie. I knew you would listen. As a woman, you know. I have helped other girls like you. You must, you must . . ."

"Yes?"

To be told of her obligations by this creature was beyond lunacy. If the little dog at her feet had begun to talk, she'd have paid greater heed to its advice.

"You must trust me. Sid, he'd never let you be hurt. He sent your brother to me, and I helped him."

Her brother? So, Marie had a brother, and he had been pregnant. That news would certainly liven up the next family dinner. Would Papa be pleased? "Go on."

"It only takes a few minutes. It's a kind of enema, with bleach."

That would do the trick, she supposed. It might do less damage than a small explosive charge in the uterus, but probably not by much. It saddened and sickened Marie to think that she might have almost considered it, had the offer not come from such a compromised party. But she was less interested in Carmen's technique than her service to her family. Excepting, obviously, what she'd done for her husband.

"No, I mean my brother. How did you help him?"

"Sal, his girlfriend, she was—"

Marie let go of the phone. It dropped almost to the floor before the cord reached its limit, and then it dangled and bounced, twisting. She walked over to the kitchen table and sat down. That Sal had cheated on Ann was not a surprise. That Ann was the infertile party in the marriage was also known to the sisters. When Sal had bragged about his *brazziole*, Marie's objections were not medical in nature. What made her nearly weep was knowing that Ann would have been glad to have any child, even the bastard of her bastard husband. Marie picked up a paper napkin and wiped her eyes. She didn't want to think about the poor idiot Sal had knocked up, after Carmen's chemistry experiment. No more baby-worries for her, after a bleached womb. And then Marie began to feel queasy.

How did Carmen know about her condition? Through Sid, of course, but it was too soon for him to have figured it out on his own. It had to have started from Ann. Ann to Sal, Sal to Sid. Keeping secrets about pregnancy wasn't Ann's strong suit. Sid wasn't stupid, but he wasn't . . . he wasn't a detective. Not like Marie.

And then she made a series of rapid deductions: Sid had beaten Carmen for calling the house the last time; he had likely shared the news of the pregnancy as the latest reason why he couldn't leave the marriage. He must have known that if he pressured Marie for an abortion, she would have resisted, out of reflex or spite. He'd taken too much from her already. He'd ruined too many days, too many years. He'd had too much to say in the story of her life. For the first time, Marie felt defensive, protective of the child she was carrying. She didn't want it just yet, but she wouldn't have it taken from her—not by Sid, and never by that absurd woman. Of course, now that Marie had decided against ending her pregnancy, she was getting offers for abortions over the phone.

What was Carmen thinking? Sid must have put her up to the call, betting on the chance that the hysterical women might bond, when there would be no chance if he made the offer, or the demand. Marie supposed she should be grateful he hadn't tried to push her down the stairs. Maybe that was Plan B. She'd have to be careful for the next few months, moving between floors. Sid could be with Carmen now, listening in. Marie ought to take advantage of the situation. Today was the day for that, wasn't it?

Marie stood up from the table and picked up the phone. She heard Carmen talking as the receiver rotated and recoiled. Her absence hadn't been noticed: "And the worst thing, for a child, is not to be loved, and I know—"

"Shut up for a second."

"And the worst-worst, is . . . what?"

"Shut up, Carmen."

"I . . . Marie, I don't want—"

"Shut up, Carmen. I won't tell you again. I'm not interested in anything you have to say. But I've had a great day, and I'm gonna start looking at the bright side of things. I got promoted to the Detective Division. It's a big deal."

"Oh, Marie, you—"

"Shut up, Carmen. Not that I don't think you have some use. For example, whenever I think I'm the biggest idiot in the world, I can always picture you and figure I'm not so bad off. At least I know the mistakes I made—the *big* mistake, marrying Sid—were mistakes. I got dealt a losing hand, and I want to get out of the game. You keep losing, and you keep doubling your bets. Do you play cards?"

"I play—"

"Shut up, Carmen. I don't care what you play, or who you play with. I'm gonna have a beautiful baby, and if Sid wants nothing to do with any of us, we'll be all the happier. But if I hear from you again, I will go to the district attorney to tell him about your bleach trick. I do these cases, these abortion cases. We have so many wiretaps running now, I can't count them all. Your phone, this conversation, the cops might already be listening in, recording it."

Marie didn't need to tell Carmen to shut up again. She didn't have much more to add, she supposed, but she was curious to find out what she'd say next. She felt dangerous, and she liked it. So many things had changed today. Why shouldn't she change, too? Now, she was ready to finish the conversation. She didn't care who might overhear, or what might happen later. *Whatever it takes.* "And Sid, if you never come home again, it's fine by me, but if you do, we need a couple of bags of mulch for the garden. And if you have a friend at the precinct who can give us a better deal on the roof, he better speak up soon, because I'm going to pick someone for the job, Monday latest.

"By the way, I do feel a little different, this time around. I think it could be twins, maybe triplets. Who knows? Anyway, I have to run. Call again, Carmen, and I'll kill you. Good riddance, goodbye, whatever."

Marie hung up the phone. For all she knew, Carmen had fainted, or Sid had knocked her out cold for failing at her assignment. Marie wasn't certain Sid was listening in. Maybe he'd told Carmen that she'd better fix things—*Or else!*—while he was with his backup mistress. Why not? The notion of triplets must have brought it to mind. Why just have two women, when there could be multiples, younger and younger, like Russian dolls? Marie laughed at the idea. She could conceive of so many possibilities with Sid and his captives, his deceits and their delusions, fiendishly elaborate or savagely simple. A detective's imagination wasn't a pretty place, but it was never dull.

Marie would have to shop for clothes, once she found out the dress code at the new squad. She'd have to pick out maternity things, as well. Could she really be having twins? She hoped not, but it would be nice if at least one were a boy. Looking out the kitchen window into the garden, she saw the azaleas in the afternoon sun. They'd come in like the blazes this year, but she really did need to pick up some mulch. There would be time for that, later on. Plenty of time. Marie wanted to see Vera, to tell her what had happened. Some of what had happened, anyway. Yes, she'd head over there, like she'd intended. Why not have part of the day go as planned? Marie picked up the ridiculous little dog, whatever its name was, and walked out the back door.

FOUR

IN A FAMILY WAY

14 YOU GET DOWN TO BUSINESS

The aforesaid events may give rise to another thought: the hand that rocks the cradle may rule the world; but if it is to mold public policy, that hand had better learn the ways of governmental process.

—Theresa M. Melchionne
Policewomen: Their Introduction into the Police Department of the City of New York. A Study of Organizational Response to Innovation.

JULY 8, 1963
0900 HOURS

Marie knew better than to believe that real detective work was the stuff of B movies and dime novels. She wouldn't be solving murder mysteries with a magnifying glass and a sly question. She kept telling herself that it wouldn't be glamorous, that the change wouldn't be profound. But how was she supposed to believe that, when she found herself hunting jewel thieves in luxury hotels, and hobnobbing with movie stars? It was too much fun. No episode of *Decoy* came close. The new job wasn't a dime novel—it was a fairy tale. She felt like Cinderella with a gun.

What she loved most was that she could talk about work after work, and everyone wanted to hear. When she was with the Degenerate Squad, the Abortion Squad, and most of the others, if anyone asked how her day had gone, her usual answer was, "Umm . . . fine." The hotel detail was a gas while it lasted, and it lasted a month.

At first, most of the thefts had been kept out of the papers. The hotels didn't want their clientele to fear their valuables might check out before they did; the cops didn't want the hoi polloi to think they were stumble-bums. The victims might not want it known which parts of their collections were priceless, and which were paste, or that they happened to be in a suite at the Stanhope on a particular date, let alone with whom. Still, there weren't many reputations worth more than the twenty-carat diamond ring that was taken from Mrs. Irene Mayer Selznick at the Hotel Pierre.

A dozen men had been assigned to the hotel detail from burglary squads all over the city, and more were added with each passing week, which made Marie's newness less noticeable. Almost everyone had been friendly, respectful, even grateful for her presence. She could linger in lounges or lobbies without anyone thinking she was a cop; she could pair with a male counterpart and mask his flatfoot spoor with her perfume. Even if some of the men had worked in Manhattan for a while, they didn't exactly fade into the background at the Waldorf. They were the salt of the earth, but some were saltier than others. One night's surveillance was ruined when a detective broke out into hysterical laughter at the sight of an elderly man in a top hat, white tie, and monocle: "Hey buddy! Go make a break for it before they put you back in the Monopoly box!"

But Marie didn't stare, didn't stutter when she was sent to interview the big shots. Most of the victims were women, and the bosses thought they'd find her reassuring. Week by week, her task shifted—one Monday, she'd be hauling a slop bucket, pretending to be a chambermaid; the next, she'd be kibitzing with the stars. Doris Day had warmed to Marie immediately, drawing her aside to tell her how her skin kept its honeyed glow: "Once a week, I smear Vaseline all over and sleep in footy pajamas." Dolores del Río confided that she managed to maintain the same complexion, even though she had a good fifteen years on Doris, by bathing in milk. The results of the interviews were duly noted.

Marie thought it beyond brilliant when one of the captains hatched a plan to anticipate the thieves. They'd reach out to likely marks and warn them, to prevent new cases from adding to the mounting pile of open ones; they'd stake out their rooms, and maybe grab a burglar in the act. She met Henry Fonda after they'd set up a tripwire under a mat that set off an alarm next door, where she waited with two other detectives. At the tail end of one festive evening, Fonda returned to his room and forgot about the alarm. When the cops sprang out, guns at the ready, he thought it so marvelous that he repeated his mat-stepping dance through what was, for him, a long and merry night. And Judy Garland, who answered the door in a silk kerchief and sunglasses like hubcaps and seemed as lonely as anyone Marie had ever met. If Judy—yes, "Call me Judy," she'd insisted— hadn't moved her arms, Marie would have guessed that she was wearing a couture straightjacket. She offered to sit with Marie and the men for the duration of the shift. When the team politely declined, she ordered a feast sent up for them from room service. Marie hoped someone nice would try to rob Judy, just to keep her company for a while.

And then there was Cary Grant. When he didn't leave his digs at the Plaza for a troubling length of time—he hadn't gone out for dinner, or ordered room service—they checked in on him. When he answered the door in a navy silk dressing gown, he was a little thicker than Marie remembered from the last time she'd seen him—*North by Northwest?*—his hair more salt than pepper, but he was as debonair as ever, his expression droll, his accent not exactly English but English-ish, from somewhere finer, more fun, than wherever you were from. "Are you from the welcoming committee?"

The men with Marie were dumbstruck, as they hadn't been for Garland or Fonda, as the sadness of one, the silliness of the other, were so remote from their images. But the Cary Grant before them was Cary Grant, unmistakably, no matter if he lacked overhead lights or makeup. It fell to Marie to make introductions. "Mr. Grant, we're from the police. I just wanted to make sure you know why we're here, and what's been happening."

"Yes, I've heard about it. Do come in."

Yaasss, he said, drawing out the sound. *Do* plinked like a violin string. The other detectives' eyes bulged as they took in the splendid expanse of the suite, with its gilt and velvet, its French furniture and Persian carpets. And the hot plate on a table in the corner, which held bubbling cans of Heinz baked beans and corned beef hash. The contrast of a hobo dinner with the regal room made it hard to concentrate.

"I'd ask you to stay for supper," he began, "But . . ."

"Thank you," Marie interjected, fearful her colleagues might have heard only an invitation. "I just want to let you know, we'll be right next door. I guess you've been told, headquarters had this idea to get the jump on these crooks by reaching out to . . . potential targets, and—"

"Very clever. I was in it already."

"Excuse me?"

"I was in the movie already. *To Catch a Thief.* Did you see it? It's the same plot. I play a retired cat burglar on the French Riviera who has to trap the real bandit to clear his name. The only thing different in your production, my dear, is that you have my part, and I have Grace Kelly's. Hmm, I wonder if I could write off my salary, as a sort of public service. I'll have to run that by my accountant."

That troubled Marie, maybe more than it should have. She hadn't considered that her new adventure could have been an old story. But the next day, one of the captains called just before she was about to head into work. "Say, Marie, do you have . . . whaddaya call 'em? Nightclothes?"

"Do you mean pajamas, Captain?"

"No, I mean a fancy dress."

"An evening gown? Yeah, I do."

"Good. Get yourself and it to the Waldorf forthwith."

And that was how Marie had met President Kennedy, at his forty-sixth birthday party, when he graciously insisted on meeting his security detail. No, Marie couldn't complain about her first few weeks at work, even if little was accomplished. Pilfered Hollywood plots didn't break the case in the end, but dull, old-fashioned diligence did. They stuck to the mutts who'd done hotel jobs before, and they grabbed them when they did them again. It wasn't exactly a fairy-tale ending, but it was a happy one nonetheless.

WHEN SHE REPORTED to Lieutenant Macken in his office the Monday morning after the arrests were made, he was in a benign and philosophical cast of mind, leaning back in his chair and savoring a toothpick as if it were a handmade cigar. He was a smallish, softish man, and Marie was unused to seeing him at ease or in command. Captains and inspectors had run the investigation, and he tended to recede behind the largest piece of furniture he could find when they haggled over strategy. The only thing distinctive about him was the toothpick. It never left his mouth, and it gave his round red mug the look of an unappealing sort of canape, like a little ball of pungent cheese. He had finished his bacon-egg-on-a-roll and coffee—light, three sugars, he'd made plain, should he ask for another—and three newspapers were spread across his desk. All the headlines told of the arrest of the Baby-Faced Bandit. He had reason to be proud, too, she supposed.

"So anyways, like I always say," Lt. Macken intoned, "It's wonderful how much can be accomplished when nobody worries about who gets the credit."

"Yes, sir."

Marie had read the papers, too. Her name hadn't been mentioned, which didn't surprise her. She'd played a secondary role, working the tails and joining in the interrogations. What the lieutenant had done to earn multiple quotes and a photo in the *Herald Tribune* escaped her, but he was her boss now. There was no sense in comparing him to Inspector Melchionne, but she wished she could look at him without wondering whether his mother had never corrected his posture, or if there was an actual hunch to his back.

And she found his remark peculiar, as it was the issue of credit that had broken the case. There hadn't been one arrest, but two, of onetime partners. The first, who defiantly claimed to be "the best Negro burglar on the East Coast," had felt slighted, as he was obliged to undertake elaborate masquerades—a turbaned foreign dignitary, or a tuxedoed member of the band—just to gain entry to the hotel lobbies. He could jimmy a window, leaving the barest of marks, and he could pick all the old warded locks and most of the new pin ones. He'd taught the rudiments of the trade to a cherubic blond twenty-one-year-old, who needed only a shoeshine, an off-the-rack suit, and his "dopey white baby-face smile" to win the unchallenged liberty of the upper floors. Baby Face could manage only the most basic technique—popping the spring lock on an unbolted door, with the celluloid "Do Not Disturb" signs conveniently provided by the hotels—but that was all he needed to collect a million dollars in jewelry in the past year, including the Selznick job. The old-timer hadn't done too bad, either, but he was peeved by the underworld scuttlebutt about how the new kid put him to shame. When he was arrested on another burglary, he gave up Baby Face.

"So, Marie, here we are, back to real life."

"Here we are."

"How's it going so far?"

"Great, just great. I'm really looking forward to working here."

During the detail, she'd been so caught up in the case that she hadn't thought about what would happen after it ended. She hadn't worried about finding a partner. In the Policewomen's Bureau, she'd worked alone more often than not. Only the Broadway Squad was a steady two-hander, patrolling the movie houses for pickpockets and perverts, but all the girls there were game and able. They switched up whenever and wherever, do-si-doing like square dancers instead of pairing off, cheek-to-cheek.

"So, who do I work with?"

"Well, usually, I'll stick the new man with a team until he gets his head above water. By then, he gets to know the other guys in the office, and things just sort themselves out."

"Oh, all right," she said. "What lucky devils are you going to put me with?"

"Whoa!" he sputtered. "I couldn't do that! They'd raise holy hell, if I put you with guys who didn't want you there."

"Well, I wouldn't want to go where I wasn't wanted . . ." That wasn't entirely true. She had no interest in spending eight hours a day with men who resented her, but she wasn't going to allow them to veto her chance at advancement. Though she cared for the lieutenant less with each passing moment, she realized that she could use his indecision to her advantage. "I don't want any special treatment. Tell you what, give me till the end of the day. See if I can't come up with somebody."

The lieutenant agreed, and Marie left the office. Eight hours were seven more than she should need. She'd have been pleased to work with any number of the men, and she assumed, maybe cavalierly, that the reverse was equally true. But her fallback plan had always been Ralph Marino. It wasn't even asking for a favor from him; it was collecting one. He'd sworn to her, years before, "Trust me, I won't forget. What you did for me, I will never forget. I owe you, Marie."

The favor for Marino had been Marie's first, as a cop, and it had the sentimental meaning of a first kiss. Ralph was in Manhattan South Burglary now, though hadn't worked the hotel detail—even by the end, less than half of the citywide burglary folks had been conscripted—but the warmth of his endorsement had helped pave the way for her ready acceptance. Marie liked his steady partner, Arthur, a tall, affable pipe-smoking Irishman. But when Marie took Ralph aside for a quiet word, the conversation was brief. "I'm sorry, Marie, I can't."

"What? Why?"

Marino had changed little since they first met. He was somewhat stouter, but his round brown eyes were still lively, his expression a constant, shifting battle between exasperation and amusement. He still favored a porkpie hat, though it was now in his hand, as if he were begging for change. He shook his head and lowered his eyes. "I asked my wife. I mean, I said you were working with us, since she was so grateful for what you did. She sent something after. Candy, flowers? Did you get it?"

Marie had gotten back thousands of swindled dollars for the Marinos, which didn't seem right to mention at the moment. "I don't know—probably. Ralph, it was years ago. Yes, I'm sure I got the candy. Thank you, thank her. What's wrong?"

"This started weeks ago, when you first showed up. She starts yapping about how terrific you are, how she can't imagine how you conned your way in with the old Gypsy broad, when she was such a con herself. Talked about you, asked about you, every week. Last night, I say you're coming back to regular work at the squad, and you're gonna need a partner. She drops the question real sly, casual-like. 'Oh that Marie, I worry for her out there on the street, fighting with those animals. Is she a big girl?' And I say, 'No, she's a little slip of a thing, but she can handle herself. When I first met her, she lumped up a guy twice her size.' And then she says, 'Well, if she gets into scrapes like that, she must look busted-up like a prizefighter by now.' I shoulda known she was setting me up. I say, 'No, some lady cops get a hard look to them, but Marie, she's a pretty Italian girl, with a helluva figure, and—'"

"Oh, Ralph, you poor sap."

"I know. Am I an idiot, or what?"

"You're an idiot."

For this, Marie had risked Gypsy curses? Marino had kept his word, in the strictest sense: He hadn't forgotten the favor she had done him. He remembered as if it were yesterday. He just wouldn't return it. "Yeah, I feel like such a *stroonz*," he continued, his remorse painfully plain. "All night, she was at me. 'If you think for one goddam minute you're gonna partner up with some Svengali with a *helluva* figure—'"

"Poor Ralph!"

"I couldn't live like that, Marie, God help me. Fighting all the time, suspicion. If your home, your family, isn't right, nothing is."

"Ain't that the truth."

Marie couldn't stay angry with him. She couldn't fault him for the importance he placed on domestic peace, though she was hardly acquainted with it herself.

By way of contrition, he confiscated a desk for her—their squad occupied two rooms upstairs at the 54th Street precinct—and, more important, he discreetly reviewed the roll call with her, scratching off the names of more than half of the men: *Goofball . . . Ass-grabber . . . Drinks three or four scotches at lunch . . . Never stops whistling the same song, a week at a time . . .* It was good to know. By the time she'd organized her desk and gathered office supplies, two hours had passed. Who would she pounce on next?

Bowen and Baxter were younger men, in their late twenties, businesslike in the better sense of being plainspoken, and the worse sense, too—they could be a little dull. When she spotted them, she had a passing reservation about how they might wear on her. There was a stuffiness to them, something rigid and dour. How quickly they set her mind at ease! When Marie made her offer, they looked at each other, then the ceiling, then the floor, and then each other again. She wondered how their necks could be so stiff, after such exercises. And then they giggled like schoolboys. "A woman on the team?"

"Hey, why not?"

"Every team should have one!"

"What's the French word? *Ménage à . . .?*"

"Whatever it is. Damn it, Marie, you should have said something when we were on the detail. What a waste."

"How many hours did we have to pass in hotel rooms, doing crosswords, playing cards?"

"Better late than never. Let's go to Gallagher's for lunch, we'll have champagne."

"I don't like champagne, Hal. Maybe Marie doesn't like champagne, either."

Marie raised her hands and backed away. "Oh, look," she said, laughing forcibly, hoping to inspire them to do the same. "Our first fight! And we haven't even started yet. Maybe it wasn't meant to be. I couldn't come between you boys. Besides, my husband's the old-fashioned type, he doesn't want me to be with two strange men at a time. Have fun at lunch."

Marie turned away quickly. There wasn't an expression they could have on their faces—hurt, hungry, haughty—that wouldn't make her want to smack them.

What to do? Delay wouldn't work in her favor. The last bit of wisdom Mrs. M. had offered was that Marie shouldn't type too quickly, in public, until she settled in. Someone would ask her to type something, and she'd oblige, just to be helpful, and then someone else would ask, because she'd done such a good job. Before long, the lieutenant would declare that she was essential to the office in that capacity. But she worked through the list of sober, nongrabby, nonwhistlers without even getting an "I'll think about it." Two offered the same apologetic refusal as Marino, alluding to jealous wives. If she approached one more man to offer the pleasure of her company, she was afraid she'd be arrested for solicitation.

It was after four when she noticed Macken staring at her. Better to make the first move, she thought. She went inside his office and shut the door behind her. "Hey, boss."

"Uh, well, I've been thinking. It can be hard enough breaking in a new man. With a girl, I can't even guess what . . . The thing is, I think you might have gotten the wrong idea about what we do here. We mix it up with some rough customers. The last month, it was all playing dress-up in fancy hotels. But the party's over. And now it's my responsibility to make sure you make it home safe every night."

Marie barely nodded as he went on, determined to let it be known that she understood him, not that she agreed with anything he'd said.

"Anyway, Frankie is out of the office today, but I could run it by him, looking out for you, and maybe he'd be willing to show you the ropes."

Marie wanted to race downtown to the Policewomen's Bureau and beg to be taken back. Frankie was known as "the Farmer," because he looked like he'd been bred to pull a plow, and he often dressed the part as well. He'd been kicked off the hotel detail four days after Marie's arrival by a particularly dapper captain, who noted that the Farmer's shirt was never unstained with ketchup, mustard, or gravy, at the beginning of the day as well as the end. What cut it for the captain was when the Farmer came in with a three-inch tear in the seat of his trousers, through which his undershorts were plainly visible. "What the hell is wrong with you? Do you have a wife at home? Does she walk around with dark glasses and a cane? Did she break all the mirrors? Nobody wants to see your ass!"

"Sorry, I thought my jacket would cover it."

"Then why aren't you wearing it?"

"I was hot."

The captain turned on Macken in cold spite. "Did this guy save your life during the war? Get him the hell out of here! I don't want to see him again."

When the Farmer had winked at Marie the first time—it had been a daily occurrence for the days he was tolerated—his face contorted so painfully she mistook it for a twitch. And as if the package wasn't already irresistible, he was also known as the office stool pigeon. He and the lieutenant lived near each other, in Rockland County, and the Farmer picked up the boss most mornings to drive him in. On duty and off, no chore was too demeaning for him, whether fetching the lieutenant's dry cleaning, or helping to build the back deck to his house on weekends. Now, Macken wanted to give Marie, like a pet, to his own pet.

Marie faked a cough and turned around. When she did so, she saw another man walk into the office. Who was he? It didn't matter. She had a fire in her belly—and a baby, too—and she didn't have time to waste. She jumped up from her seat. "Thanks, boss, but I got it all squared away. Appreciate you looking out for me!"

Marie fled and took the stranger by the arm. He was a stick of a man, tall, with a thick brush of black hair, and the pronounced features and tan-in-January skin that got actors with names like Rizzo and Rodriguez movie credits as varied as the Maharajah, Running Deer, or Comanche Brave. "Do me a favor, walk outside with me."

Startled, he complied. The suit he had on looked like he'd last worn it for his First Communion. Still, it was clean, and the man who wore it wasn't the Farmer. Did he even work here? Marie extended a hand and prayed that he wasn't an insurance salesman. "Detective, I'm Marie Carrara, I'm new here, and—"

"Al O'Callahan, nice to meet you."

Marie would not have cast him as an O'Callahan. Still, Aloysius O'Callahan's name was one that hadn't been crossed off Marino's list. "You need a partner, Marie?"

"Yeah."

"Do you mind driving?"

"No."

"Always?"

"Not at all."

"See you tomorrow."

THE MANHATTAN SOUTH Burglary Squad was misleadingly named. Burglary was stealing from a place—trespass plus theft—and it was rampant all over the city. But Al and Marie didn't spend their days taking fingerprints, or writing down serial numbers of stolen TVs. Their job wasn't to investigate old crimes but to prevent new ones, and any thief was fair game. Marie didn't care what they called the squad. She liked the open-endedness, and she liked how it was going with Al. One day, he spotted the broken window of a hot car as it screeched around a corner; another, the airborne shadow she saw in an alley proved to be a junkie with a crowbar, dangling from a fire escape. Arrests piled up.

What troubled her was that she couldn't call him her partner, at least not yet. Al's regular partner, Ed Lennon, was home convalescing from an ulcer, but he was due back in a week or so. Real partners were nearly matrimonial in their attachment, and a cop who didn't have a partner in his wedding party or as a pallbearer at his funeral either had a very large family or small talent for friendship. Working with Al was a tryout, less of an engagement than one long first date. Marie hated to think of the time she spent with Al as courtship, but the idea couldn't be avoided, even as they paid the office wisecracks little heed—*Would you look at the lovebirds!* He'd arrived in the squad only a few months before Marie, and he was as determined to make his name as she was. To find someone with her drive, undistracted by her gender, was romance enough.

As it was, their conversations were brief: "How about him?" "You see that?" "Let's take a look." When Marie made a joke about the ten-cent cigars he smoked, he smiled, but the closest either came to venturing a personal opinion was about lunch, and they always went to the Automat. Beyond the barest biographical facts—a Mrs. O'Callahan and several little O'Callahans awaited Al nightly in Queens—there was no chitchat about their lives, their families. They didn't bicker or banter. Nor did she raise the issue of what would happen when his old partner returned. It was Marino who told her about Ed Lennon's celebrated career: he helped catch the "Mad Bomber," whose mostly dud explosives terrified the city for years, and the man who blinded Victor Riesel, the labor columnist who fought with such fervor against Communists and gangsters that Albert Anastasia ordered a bucket of acid thrown in his face.

Marie was more than pleased, and less than surprised, on the Monday morning when Al said they had to drive out to Long Island, to Levittown. There was no need to explain their errand.

Lennon was pale as a potato, of middling height, gaunt except for a paunch, with half a head of buzz-cut silver hair. It seemed to recede before her eyes, like breath on a windowpane. Even allowing for his recent ill health, Lennon didn't just look awful, he looked odd. He had a shuffling gait and wore a baggy and hard-worn moss-colored corduroy suit. Amid the cheery uniformity of the mass-produced ranch houses, he could have passed for a lawn ornament. He regarded Marie with blue eyes that had a distinct gleam as he took the seat beside her. Apparently, her driving duties would continue uninterrupted.

"They turned me into a dishrag," he groaned. "Three weeks on nothing but milk and Maalox. I've lost twenty pounds. But don't worry, I'm coming back strong. They won't turn a spade over me, just yet. Are you ready to get to work?"

Marie hesitated. She was in no position to air doubts or set conditions, even though the legend she'd anticipated looked more like a liability. But everything had been so tentative and temporary, from the hotel rotations to her tryout with Al, that she didn't want to go on with any false assumptions. She kept her foot on the brake. "I'm ready. You don't have a problem working with a woman, do you?"

"As a matter of fact, I do," he said evenly. "I don't want to work with a woman. I want to work with a cop. And from what I hear, that's what you are."

Marie turned away, fearful that her eyes would well up, as she began to drive back to the city. "Let me know if you want to take the wheel any time, Ed. I'm good either way, but Al here likes to take in the scenery."

Ed turned around to the back seat. "You didn't tell her, lad?"

"Nah, not yet."

Ed shook his head. "You should have told her. Let's keep the surprises to a minimum, at least among the three of us."

Al grunted, and Marie was intrigued. Ed went on, "You didn't think Al was perfect, did you? We're all a bit damaged, on top of being second-class citizens. Me, I'm an old man with a stomach like Swiss cheese."

"Plus, you're going to hell," offered Al helpfully. "You're a left-footed traitor to your race. I already told her that. She took it in stride."

Marie had been told of Ed's handicap. He was a member of the Emerald Society, the fraternal organization for Irish cops, but not the Holy Name Society, which was for Catholics. Ed's religion wasn't a secret—he was president of the St. George Association, for Protestant cops—though most of his fellow Irishman thought it a true and needless shame. After all, a Jew would always be a Jew, a Negro a Negro, but all Ed had to do to join the majority, body and soul, was to sign on the dotted line. It had not been an asset to his career. Just to be safe, Marie was a dues-paying member of the Columbia Association, for Italian cops, and the Holy Name Society as well, but she only expended effort with the Policewomen's Endowment Association. The major tribes were represented in the "line organizations," as they were called, but their clout was more proportionate to their numbers on the Job, rather than the city at large. There was Pulaski for Poles, Steuben for Germans, Shomrim for Jews, the Guardians for Negroes, Vikings for Scandinavians, St. Paul's for Greeks. Was that all of them? The Hispanic Society was for Puerto Ricans, and maybe some stray Cubans or Argentinians. The Emerald Society was one of the newer ones, founded long after Columbia and Shomrim. No one had seen any need for it, since the department was an Irish clubhouse. And if you didn't like it, you could complain to anyone you wanted, from Commissioner Murphy to District Attorney Hogan to President Kennedy.

Ed went on, "Now, Marie, you've been with young Al for a couple of weeks now, and you're a trained observer. You tell me, what's wrong with him?"

She glanced in the rearview mirror to see the reaction from the back seat. Al didn't seem distressed, but he wasn't smiling, either. He and Ed could roughhouse in a way that she couldn't join in, just yet. "He could spring for a twenty-cent cigar now and then," she offered.

"I'm from the right country, but the wrong religion," Ed went on, teasingly. "Marie's from the wrong country, and she's the wrong sex, and I don't think there's any cure for either. On paper, Al's Irish Catholic, but I'd bet fifteen out of sixteen great-grandparents knew the words to "La Borinqueña" and not "Danny Boy." You ask him, all's he gonna say is he's American, and that's fine by me. The thing is, Al is, Al has . . . the way I'd put it—"

Marie didn't like Ed's sudden stammer, after his bracing bluntness. Al leaned forward. "I have epilepsy, Marie. I'm epileptic. The department, they'd have never hired me, if they knew. I'm a good detective, I think you know that. But I have seizures now and then. Not often, but they can happen. That's why I don't drive."

Ed leaned over, his voice dropping deeper. "Al trusts you, Marie. I do, too, even though we've only known each other for about ninety seconds. He said this would work out, and I believe him. Three's a lucky number. We're three defective detectives. Anything else wrong with you, honey, that me and Al should know? We're laying it all out here."

The impulse to confess took hold of her, as if she'd been caught in the pull of a riptide. But she couldn't talk, not about her marriage or her pregnancy. Not yet, not now, though at least one of those subjects wouldn't remain a secret for long. She replied haltingly: "I'm good, guys. And I think you're right, Ed. This could be pretty good, this thing."

Ed nodded and extended a hand. "I don't think I have to mention that Al's situation, it stays between us. Agreed?"

As Marie clasped Ed's clammy hand, Al leaned forward, sticking his head between them. "You promise? They'd fire me for this, if they knew. I got kids—"

"I promise, Al."

"You swear?"

"I swear to God, on my heart."

Al reached out, and she took his hand. It felt almost feverish in comparison to Ed's. "Shake on it?"

"Yeah."

Marie felt a sudden spasm in his grasp, and Al began to thrash in the back seat, his legs kicking, and Ed screamed, "Get a spoon! He'll swallow his tongue!"

Marie almost crashed into oncoming traffic, but she turned off to the right, and—*Thank God!*—there was a spot to swerve into before they wrecked. Turning around, she saw the rhythm of Al's fit was slowing, easing. She breathed in deeply and reached out to touch his forehead, uselessly, as if he were a child having a nightmare. And then she saw that Ed's spasms were picking up where Al's had left off, rapid and jerky. Would they both die on her first day with them? When tears began to roll down Ed's flushed face, she became suspicious, and when Al covered his own with a handkerchief, she knew. Both of them were bastards.

"I should shake both of you sons of bitches! It would serve you right, Al, if you had a real fit, and I thought you were joking. And as for you, you goddam Protestant, you could have three strokes, and I'd sit here doing my nails before I'd call an ambulance." She stamped on the gas pedal, throwing them both against their seats.

Once Ed recovered, he dried his eyes with his sleeve. He turned to Al and said, "It's true what they say. Women really don't have a sense of humor."

They'd resolved to make an arrest that day, to mark Lennon's return and to start the new partnership off right. None anticipated any difficulty. As most break-ins were committed by addicts, drug collars were encouraged. Some arrests were better than others, of course—the schlemiel who made his monthly quota by dragging in whatever puking dope fiend he could waylay on the 30th wouldn't last long, unless he was the Farmer. But a number was still a number, and one beat zero, every time.

They cruised for hours through Gramercy, where there had been a recent spree by a bogus door-to-door radio repairman whose sales pitch was a ploy to find unguarded apartments. *"Why would I spend ten bucks to fix a five-dollar radio?"*

—*Sorry, Ma'am. Maybe your neighbors . . .*

"Don't bother. Everyone on the floor is at work, except Mrs. Abrams, in #2C, and the Hausers, in 2D, who don't have two nickels to rub together . . ."

—*Thank you, Ma'am.*

It was an hour before quitting time when they took a break at the Chock Full o'Nuts in Times Square to reconnoiter over coffee. Their spirits were low.

"Maybe tomorrow," O'Callahan began, "we can—"

"Bite your tongue."

Lennon was at least half-serious, but the younger man rolled his eyes and sipped his coffee, unperturbed by the rebuke. Marie wasn't ready to call it a day, either. Whatever their problem was, it wasn't that they looked like cops. O'Callahan wore his standard baggy undershirt and dungarees, and passers-by took no more notice of him than they would have a pigeon. Lennon was also unlikely to be taken for a government official, in his dill-pickle corduroy. Sweat trickled from his forehead, leaving dark little slashes on his lapels. When he proposed they take a stroll west toward Eighth Avenue, she was afraid he'd get heatstroke. She pinched the fabric of his coat. It was heavy as a horse blanket. "You know what you should try, Ed? One of those Spanish shirts, the loose kind you don't tuck in."

"Already, with the fashion advice?"

As he leaned over to take in her attire, which was admittedly more *Farmers' Almanac* than *Harper's Bazaar*, she was reminded that her attempts to match O'Callahan's pumpboy plainness strained her wardrobe as much as her chic evenings in the hotel bars. She only had so many clothes she'd wear for gardening, and some looked more gardened-in than others. Again, she found it hard to measure his precise level of semiseriousness. "Not that green isn't your color, Ed, but with the other shirt, you could lose the jacket, and your gun wouldn't show."

"You want to play dress-up? Sure, on one condition."

"Name it."

"I get to pick out clothes for you, too."

"You're on. Benny's Thrift is right around the corner."

"You know they sell wigs, don't you?"

"Be careful what you wish for, Lennon."

Twenty minutes later, Ed and Marie were slumped on the stoop of a side street in the West 40s. Marie was in a threadbare red blouse and wig of bright copper curls, Ed in a black toupee and stained cream-colored guayabera shirt. They could have been starring in a Skid Row version of *I Love Lucy*—one look and you'd change the channel. But they aimed to be unwatchable, at least to the junkies who'd begun to gather down the block like crows around a carcass.

Hell's Kitchen was far from the worst neighborhood in the city. There were plenty of jobs nearby that paid decent wages. Men worked on the waterfront, in freight cargo and the luxury steamship trade, and the rail yards, where the New York Central, Erie, and Pennsylvania lines converged. Hell's Kitchen supplied Broadway with many of its stagehands, bartenders, and waiters and it had given the city any number of cops and firemen, priests and nuns. On the other hand, it had also produced her husband. If it were a decent neighborhood, she and Ed would have been run off their stoop.

Marie settled in to observe, as Ed seemingly—she hoped—dozed against the rail. The bray of traffic from Eighth and Ninth Avenues was audible but muted, and cooking smells from open windows mostly improved the fumes of incinerators and diesel exhaust. A few skinny ginkgoes cast narrow, patchy shadows as the afternoon sun warmed the sandstone and brick tenements. Marie made out a water tower on one roof, a pigeon coop on another. Laundry lines spiderwebbed between the buildings. Many of the fire escapes had been repurposed as yards, with lawn chairs and potted plants providing refuge from the heat. She watched two bony girls jump rope on the sidewalk, maybe ten years old, both in pigtails. A fourth-floor window opened above them for a housewife to beat a carpet, and the girls screeched as the cinders and dust descended. One looked up and howled, "You crazy old bat, you did that on purpose! You watch, your dog's gonna wind up poisoned!"

"Sorry! Sorry, dears. Here's for your trouble—"

A stout white arm in a sleeveless housedress dropped something from the window. A note? A dollar? One of the girls picked it up, and the other huddled close. What was it? The other girl struck a match on the curb with a practiced hand. Cigarettes. Marie shook her head and looked away. *Gesu, aiutami . . . Santissima Vergine benedicami.* They were Sandy's age. They sat together on the stoop and made no effort to conceal what they were doing. *You've come a long way, baby.* A skinny Puerto Rican boy walked by and gently wagged a finger, slowing down but not stopping. One of the girls spat. The other barked, "Mind your own damn business, dope fiend."

Marie sat up a little straighter. *Was he a dope fiend?* She hadn't made him for one. He didn't look more than twenty, and his reaction to the nicotine twins showed a decency that made his habit an even greater shame. And yet he joined the other lowlifes down the block, hovering by an alley. She supposed the girls had a point about his advice on healthy living.

"Yeah, the Puerto Rican kid is in the mix," she said. Ed had told her to announce the action as if it were a ball game on the radio, as it would help her keep track of the players. "Twenty years old, white T-shirt, blue jeans. He talked to the kid in the striped shirt, it's like a sailor shirt, I think French sailors have them. He's the maître d', I think. He—the stripe guy—"

"Frenchy, let's call him Frenchy," Ed muttered, without looking up. Sometimes he kept so still she was afraid he was napping.

And so they settled in for the better part of an hour, waiting with the junkies, and waiting like them, too, with mounting frustration. More addicts gathered, wastrel solitaries and hungry-eyed pairs, and none of the original retinue departed. Few stood still for long; when they did, they made it look like an exertion, as if they were treading water. Marie had little to tell Ed, whose breathing was growing more somnolent. She hated to think of herself as having less self-control than the addicts, but her behind was getting numb from being stuck to the stoop. When a young boy ran up to Frenchy, whispered a few words, and dashed away again, the addicts crowded in for the news.

"Okay, this is make-or-break time," Marie said. Frenchy raised his hands, and most of the junkies walked away. *Sorry kids.* One or two stayed, as if there might be something to argue about. There would be no dope for them today, not here. There would be nothing for any of them, cops or junkies. Marie felt mournful. Their first day together had brought them nothing.

"What a waste of time," Marie groused. "If I can unpeel my keister from the concrete, I have to drag it into a ladies' room somewhere."

She started to rise, but Ed held her arm. "Hang tight for a minute. Let's wait for them to clear out before we do, so it doesn't look like we were watching."

Marie groaned and settled back down. How long had it been since she'd chatted with Doris Day about beauty secrets? *Tell me, Doris, how do you deal with chronic stoop-butt?* Ed didn't have to feign any stiffness when he stood, and neither did Marie. She was about to stretch her legs when Al approached from Eighth Avenue. He dipped down beside them to tie his shoe. "Mickey Burns is around the corner, heading uptown. I saw him try a couple of car door handles."

Ed asked, "What's he wearing?"

"Black-and-blue checkered shirt, fedora. He's taking his time, but he's on the hunt. I'm gonna high-tail it up Ninth and cut back across, so he comes to me."

They separated without further words. Ed led Marie east, toward Eighth. She was thrilled by the news. "Who's Mickey Burns?"

"Mickey's a regular, but I haven't seen him in a while."

"Tall? Short? Thick? Thin? Black? White?"

"White, medium height, on the chunky side. Maybe thirty years old."

"So what's his story?"

"Doper, as usual, and a flat burglar," Ed went on, meaning a house-breaker. "A nasty bit of business. He'll run, and he'll fight. And he may have a little crowbar on him, or a blade. I hope you didn't wear heels today."

"Can't you catch Mickey the Chunky Junkie in those slippers I bought you?"

At Benny's, Marie had been delighted to find a pair of pointy-toed patent leathers in Ed's size. It wouldn't have been sporting for him to refuse them.

"Age before beauty, my dear," he said.

"One day, I'll wise up and see through your empty flattery."

"One day, maybe."

Arm in arm, they strolled to the corner and headed north. Ed was on the outside, and he watched the east side of Eighth. Marie peeked in the windows of bars and luncheonettes, scanning inside for a fedora, a checkered shirt. They walked slowly, stopping at corners to scan the cross streets. After three blocks, they picked him up at a pay phone where he'd stopped to fish for stray coins. They plodded past him and waited at the light. Ed twisted his head around as if he were trying to unscrew it, producing all manner of awful crackles and clicks that she felt as much as she heard. "You need some oil in those old joints, Tin Man."

"You're not in Kansas anymore, Dorothy. Look yonder, across the way. That was a signal to young Al, on the far side of the street."

Marie saw Al, barely visible behind a pretzel cart. He pulled on his ear in reply to Ed's neck-crack. She was impressed. "You still need some oil."

The light changed, and they faltered across the street, settling down on another stoop just west of the corner. Al took up residence at another phone booth. Mickey slouched against a parked car and tried the door handle. Marie tensed, and she could feel Ed tense, too: Mickey was a fish who was ready to bite. There was a lot of foot traffic on the avenue, and it was a bold move to break into a car there. Was Mickey that slick, or did he think no one cared? He drifted westbound, touching each car handle, as if for luck. Toward the end of the block, he ducked into an apartment building, catching the front door as a tenant walked out, before it could shut and lock. He was in. Ed asked, "Are you ready, young lady?"

Mickey was their last chance for a perfect first day. The three met in front of the building. Ed tried the door, which was locked. Al said, "Let me go in the alley, check the back. I'll come to the front and let you in, if I can."

"Good," said Ed. "By the size of this joint, it has to have at least two stairwells. Me and Marie can each take one, work our way up. If we get in before you, stay in the lobby. Remember, Mickey's a tough customer, and a man in need. Al, if you hear a lady scream, run to beat the devil to get there, because it'll probably be me."

It was as if they'd worked together for ages. Al disappeared down the alley. Ed and Marie weren't there for fifteen seconds before an old Italian woman in widow's weeds doddered through the lobby, head down. She opened the door before she noticed the awful redhead and the old slob. She tried to pull the door shut, but Marie had a better grip, and she stuck her foot inside to block it. Marie didn't want to be rough with the *nonna*, but if they took too much time for explanations, Mickey Burns could be working his crowbar at another *nonna's* door. Ed pushed past to take the stair to the right, and Marie deflected a series of slaps from the widow as she threatened to call the cops: "*Esci! Chiamo la polizia!*"

Marie lifted her wig and showed her badge, though neither gesture succeeded as reassurance, together or apart. She started to laugh at the next insult, which she hadn't heard in ages—"*Masca femina!*"—and felt a gob of spit on her cheek as she rushed past to take the stairs on the left. When she had time, she'd be disgusted. She ran up each flight on the buckled linoleum, stopping at every floor to peek out and listen. She tried to move quietly even as she maintained her speed and found Mickey on the fifth-floor landing, pie-eyed, with a needle in his arm. She was on the floor below. She felt as if she'd barged in on him in the bathroom.

"Hi," he said, with a length of rubber tube in his mouth, the other end of which was tied around his arm. Marie opened the door to the fourth-floor hall and bellowed, "Here we are, boys!"

Mickey began to chuckle, but he took his time to complete his injection. Cops or robbers, he'd get his fix. Marie took out her badge and her gun. She felt ridiculous in her wig, but taking it off right now would be too confusing. "Police. Easy now. Put your hands up."

Mickey stood up, and the hypodermic dangled for a moment from the crook of his elbow. He hesitated, bent, and took it out from his flesh. He smiled a wild smile as he held the hypo and waved it at her. It seemed less like a weapon than a little flag in the hand of a child, watching a parade. "Easy now," she said. "Put that away."

Instead, he ran into the fifth-floor hallway. Marie yelled, "Coming back your way, Ed!" and took off up the stairs. He was lighter on his feet than he looked, and she was still stiff from sitting, slightly out of breath. She should have cut over, intercepting him on the way down. As soon as she made the fifth floor, she heard Ed on the landing below her. She yelled, "Go back! He's on the other side!"

Ed disappeared, and Marie raced across the hall to descend the stairs at a gallop. She couldn't see Burns, but she'd just reached the second floor when she heard his tread shift from heel-heavy, four-stairs-at-time stomps to the slip-and-slide sprint across old linoleum. He was in the lobby then, and then she heard him shout, "Outta my way!"

And then she heard a muffled thud, the clatter of something metal rattling on the floor—*The knife? The crowbar?*—and she doubled her pace, hoping Burns had collided with Al. Instead, she saw the old *nonna* sprawled on her back, her cane a few feet away from her. Marie was tempted to stop and help when the woman reached for her cane. She hissed in *inglese*: "He runs from you, you witch!"

That was true, Marie supposed. She barreled through the door into the street and spotted Burns heading west. He hadn't lost much ground after knocking down *nonna*, and Marie didn't have much more wind. She nearly ran into a car when she crossed the street and made a final dash to close the gap. When he stumbled for a moment on broken pavement, she took her gun from her holster, and fired into the air. "Mickey Burns! The next one's going in your back!"

Whether it was the sound of the gun or his name, Mickey stopped and held his hands up. Marie didn't give any more orders. She didn't want him to hear the exhaustion in her voice. She walked up to him slowly, recovering her strength. The street hadn't been crowded, but people began to stop, and heads popped out of windows. It was time to move. She came up behind him and put the barrel of the gun against his back, directing him to put his hands on the wall. Ed came huffing along, and he cuffed Burns as Marie made a gingerly search of his pockets, plucking out a hypodermic needle, a switchblade, and a dirty handkerchief, which she returned unexamined, for now, to his pocket. Ed seized a handful of Burns's hair and banged his head against the tenement wall. "That's for the old lady. You'd hurt a lot more if she wasn't such a bitch."

They took his arms and marched him into the street, blocking the path of a taxi. Ed took his shield out to show the driver and ordered him to take them to the precinct. As they pulled away, Al ran out from the lobby, and Ed called out the window. "We got him! Meet us back at the house! And look for a crowbar somewhere inside!"

Al gave a thumbs-up and returned to the building, while the taxi went the few blocks to the station. Marie was warm from the chase. She yanked her wig off and tucked it inside her purse. When she nodded at Ed to follow suit with his toupee, he did so with some reluctance, she thought. Still, they were met skeptically at the precinct. Though their office was upstairs, the lieutenant asked to see their ID cards as well as their shields.

The reception was warmer upstairs at the detective squad, where they would process the arrest. One of the men, a tubercular-looking character in a shadowy corner, croaked a kind of welcome from behind an ashtray the size of a dinner plate, piled so high with butts that its silhouette looked alpine. "Is that you, Lennon?"

"Moriarty?"

"I heard you died, Eddie. Is it true?"

"Nah, Joe, I heard those rumors, too, and I believed them myself for a while. But there's life yet in these bones. You're the picture of health, as ever. Did you just come from a blood drive? How much did they give you?"

"A pint of O Negative now and then is all I need, Eddie. Now, I recognize the gent in your bracelets, the well-known man-about-town Mickey Burns, but the young lady is unfamiliar to me. Is she employed by the police department, or have you hired a traveling nurse? Or is it Mrs. Lennon, chaperoning you on your appointed rounds? I tell you, Eddie, you married well. But I hope you haven't come up here with some two-bit junk collar."

Marie felt Burns stiffen, and he turned to her, addled with opiates but genuinely offended. "Are you really his wife? You can't arrest me, you got no right!"

Marie slapped the hat off his head and pushed him into the holding cell, where Ed followed to search him again. "Shut up, you jackass," she said.

Moriarty tipped his cadaverous head back and let loose a high, rasping cackle that devolved into another cough. He hacked up what must have been half a teacup of phlegm and spat it in the corner. Marie waited as Ed searched Burns, patting pockets down before turning them inside out, and she picked up the hat from the floor. She felt along the inner band and plucked out two packets of heroin. Ed found three engagement rings sewn into the cuffs of Burns's trousers. He dropped them on Moriarty's desk. They were engraved, "To Peg from Mike," "To Kate from Joe," "A Odilia de Juan." Forever, Love, *Te Adoro*. Marie placed the switchblade, the heroin, and the hypo in a line on one side of them. And Al, who arrived then, added the crowbar to the sequence. The arrangement of objects made them read like a story in hieroglyphics, telling of the ruin of addiction. Moriarty laughed again.

"Now I know you're not dead yet, Eddie. Good catch." He opened his desk drawer to take out a notepad and a jeweler's loupe, which he snugged into the socket of his eye. Picking up one ring, then another, he began to write down the inscriptions. "I'll close cases with these, Eddie. Thanks. One day, you'll have to introduce me to your wife and son."

Marie found a typewriter, while Al scratched out the handwritten reports. The back-and-forth bitch-and-blather between Lennon and Moriarty kept them entertained until the phone rang. Moriarty looked at it resentfully and drew deeply on his last inch of cigarette, dropping it on his desk when it burnt his finger. "Shit. Moriarty here. What is it?"

His eyes bulged, and he began to cough as if there were a rat in his lung. He stuck the receiver of the phone under his armpit, until he recovered. "Sorry, Lieutenant. Tell me about this so-called kidnapping . . ."

Marie clacked out TWO GLASSINES OF WHITE POWDER on the voucher. Al had sweet-talked the knocked-down *nonna* into telling him what happened, and even though she wouldn't show up for court, they could charge Mickey with assault. It would make it harder for a judge to throw the case away. Marie began to put the paperwork together, thinking of what they'd done, what they needed, how they could make it better, when she heard

Lennon ask Moriarty, "Are you kidding? A kidnapping, in daylight, in midtown? How many calls did you get?"

Moriarty shook his head and rose with labor from his desk. "You know how it always happens, when you're ready to go home in half an hour? The other guys are out on a liquor store stickup. I ought to cover this myself."

Ed asked, "What's the story, Joe?"

"Like I said, it's crap. Somebody sees a young guy running down the street, a couple of odd characters in pursuit. There's a shot fired, and then the guy is dragged into a cab by a redhead and some other geezer. 'White slave trade' is the thought of the lieutenant downstairs. He lacks imagination, or maybe he has too much of it. Who hails a cab for a kidnapping? Still, we got other calls on the gunshot. People in this neighborhood know it when they hear it. I gotta go through the motions, at least."

Moriarty put on his suit coat and tightened his necktie. "Well, Eddie, it's been swell. I suppose you know where the coffee and spittoons can be found."

"Joe, settle yourself," Ed said soothingly, laying a hand on Moriarty's bony shoulder. "You'll be home on time today."

Marie didn't need the cue for her part. She donned her wig as Ed pulled his toupee from his pocket and dropped it on his pate. They linked arms and took a theatrical bow, doffing their hairpieces. "Does this match your description?"

Moriarty clapped and clapped, and then he whistled until another coughing fit overtook him. Marie rushed over to him with a cup of water. When his breath came back, he smiled and looked at his watch. "By my clock, you guys solved a kidnapping in ten seconds. A record, I think. You just might have a future in this business."

15 YOU CAN'T BELIEVE HOW SWEET IT CAN BE

The more maladjusted policemen, as measured by the Rorschach test . . . tended to be more satisfied with their work than the less maladjusted.

—Solis L. Cates
"Rorschach Responses, Strong Blank Scales,
and Job Satisfaction among Policemen."
Journal of Applied Psychology, 1950.

SEPTEMBER 6, 1963
1430 HOURS

Talk of the police department as family had never meant much to Marie, given that such sentiments were usually voiced by blowhard bosses at funerals, or by the boys after the fifth beer. That there was a fraternity among the men was undeniable, and Marie felt a distinctly daughterly devotion to Mrs. M., but the only policewoman who was like a sister was her sister Dee. If Sid had partners who were like brothers to him, they were strangers to her, and she was in no rush to acquire any in-laws. Did she have to put a name to what she had with Lennon and O'Callahan? All of them knew that they were more than the sum of their parts, working and otherwise. Ed had a regimen of pills to take throughout the day—one kind twenty minutes before meals, another just after—and he gobbled all manner of antacids. Marie had a mental map of every clean toilet south of 65th Street, and she visited them incessantly, out of precaution if not need. And with Al, so far so good, touch wood. It didn't really matter what she called them, she supposed, because she knew they'd come whenever she called. Other cops grabbed her ass much less often now, which was also nice.

Week after week, they ranked number one, two, and three in arrests for the squad by ever-larger measures, even though they had to whack up the credit by an extra share. Several detectives were dismissive—the has-been, the mute maybe-half-breed, and the girl—as if there weren't something real or right about them. The naysayers and backbiters spurred them to make a bolder show, and the notion of themselves as underdogs remained even as they consistently led the pack. This double-minded sense of grievance and superiority made them work all the harder. And they loved working, more than they were willing to admit, even to one another.

Work was better play than any childhood game. What kid was ever told, "Go out and look for trouble, and don't come home till you find it"? They had half of Manhattan as their playground. They could have shown their badges at the Empire State Building and swung like King Kong from the spire. They covered the Garment District, the Flower District, the Diamond District, and all the lesser intersections where coffee roasters or furriers or sheet-music sellers plied their trades. There were neighborhoods that they could have found blindfolded. Passing east on Fulton Street, you'd be hit with a wall of fish-reek from the market; walking north, the fishiness was overpowered by the acrid odor of the tanneries; farther north still, you were awash with the scent of cinnamon and cloves from spice warehouses. They could have Peking duck for lunch on Mott Street, *pasta e fagioli* on Mulberry, pierogies on Second Avenue, knishes on Orchard. Mammoth glass-and-steel towers rose all over midtown, but no matter how the wrecking balls swung, you didn't have to walk far to find the past. On Tenth Avenue in the forties, you could smell straw and manure and hear horses being shod; two miles down, in the slaughterhouse district, the gutters ran red with blood. On the Lower East Side, Hasidic Jews looked as if they'd stepped out from the Middle Ages; all over the city, you could see nuns in flowing habits and veils, brown and blue, white and black, that testified to devotions dating back a thousand years and more.

But the heart of their territory, and the heart of the city—if there was such a thing—was Times Square, where Broadway broke from the rigid city grid like a runaway train. Everything was there, high and low, bright and dark, beckoning you to buy, to bet, to join, from barking sergeants at the Army recruiting station to the brigades of whispering pimps. There were local sharpies in black leather jackets, sailors on leave in their swindle-me whites. If you wanted to go to a nightclub, there was the Peppermint Lounge for rock and roll, Birdland for jazz, the Palladium for Latin. The movie joints, like the Rivoli and the Capitol, were of palatial size and appointment, while the real theaters were on the side streets. *Barefoot in the Park* at the Biltmore and *Oliver!* at the Imperial were hits, but the season had been full of flops that shouted of flopdom—the marquees for *A Rainy Day in Newark* and *The Irregular Verb to Love* made Marie wonder if they were spelling tests for apprentice stagehands.

As for the show on the streets, it was never dull, and it never closed. Soapbox screamers proclaimed the true black nature of Israel; they denounced the Communist puppeteers who secretly controlled J. Edgar Hoover; they wailed in warning of the end of the world. Masses of people stood and gaped at the dazzle of lights, the twinkle and blaze of distractions—*Canadian Club! Camel Cigarettes! Live Girls! Happy Hour! Fortunes Told!*—that always delighted, even when they glinted with doomsday fire.

There were so many strangers with secrets they were eager to share: *Psst!* "You need a watch? How about one for your girl? You need a girl?" *Psst, c'mere!* "I'm in a situation. I found a thousand-dollar bill, and the bank isn't open yet." *Psst!*

More than a million people a day staggered through, most of them goggle-eyed. They could catch matinees of *Wild Gals of the Naked West* or *Blood Feast* on the sticky seats of the grind joints, play Pokerino or pinball at the arcades, gawk at the flea circus or the bearded lady at Hubert's Dime Museum. They could buy Hypno-Discs or X-ray Specs or plastic vomit at the Funny Store. If the taxi dancers at Honeymoon Lane looked as if they might have been foxtrotting since that sailor kissed that nurse on V-J Day, wasn't that part of the fun?

The new trio from the Manhattan South Burglary Squad was wholly at home among the hustlers. One day, Marie was a major in the Salvation Army, with a blue suit and a bell; the next, a go-go dancer. Ed was a tourist, a telephone repairman, an uptown swell on a tear, searching for the 52nd Street jazz joints that had closed ten years before. Al had neither the inclination nor the need for disguises, though once he went blind, so to speak, with dark glasses, a cane, and tin cup. He made a couple of bucks in change. Ed and Marie were flattered by the furious threat of one of their collars—a sixty-year-old pressman for the *Times* with a thriving lunchtime cocaine sideline—who bellowed at them, "You two are done here! You're finished! When I get out, everyone's gonna know to watch out for the blond chick, and the red-faced Irishman with the Santa Claus beard!"

They would drift, stroll, dawdle, watching how the shadier characters did the same, reading their moods, their maneuvers. What they did, and how they did it, was largely up to them. Not every thief was a junkie, but every junkie would steal. Yes, there were a few rich dopers who could draw on trust funds, and more than a few pretty ones who could sell themselves, but neither money nor beauty lasted long. There were addicts with fifty-dollar-a-day habits, more than most stockbrokers could afford. Eighteen thousand dollars a year! It was an astonishing figure, almost three times Marie's salary. And there were armies of addicts in the city, tens of thousands of them, their numbers ever growing even as they died like flies. Whatever else it was, it wasn't dull.

Ed and Marie paired together most often as Al ambled around on his own. In the car or on foot, Ed and Marie looked like a couple, instead of a couple of cops. Still, they worked in various combinations—two could still go out hunting, when the third was tied up in court with an arrest. They buddied up to court officers and clerks with coffee and pastries to get their cases called early as not to miss out on the fun. Marie was envious when Ed and Al came in with anything impressive or interesting when she wasn't there. Couldn't they have waited for her? They picked up the man who'd been doing the "radio repair" bit, making him from a vivid description—left-handed, prominent Adam's apple, red Esso jacket with one sleeve rolled up—supplied by a commercial artist who worked from home. There was the oaf who fell through the skylight when they chased him, and the stuporous goon who was so dirty they wouldn't have bothered with him, except that he kept on hacking away at a pay telephone with a screwdriver when they told him to take a hike. It turned out that he was wanted for two rapes in Baltimore.

Marie kidded them about saving the good collars for themselves. She hoped they didn't hear the note of desperation in her voice, the dread of a drunk who hears "Last call!" at the bar. Her quarrel was with the calendar, not her partners, as Labor Day would mark the end of her labors. Her chances for achievement, for adventure, dwindled with the days. The only thing that didn't dwindle was Marie. She'd read in *Reader's Digest* about the Trapp family singers, who had inspired the Broadway musical *The Sound of Music*. They had arrived from Austria just before the war, penniless, with the mother pregnant. Knowing that her condition would cost the troupe bookings, Mama bought ever-larger brassieres as she advanced, stuffing the cups so she remained somewhat proportionate even as she expanded.

The last Trapp family singer was practically delivered on stage. Marie copied the trick. She'd been strict about her diet, gaining only nine pounds, and wore looser and looser clothes. But just the other day, the Farmer made the first joke: "Hey Marie, maybe you ought to lay off the pasta fazoo!" That clod was never the first to notice anything. A midget would know it was raining before he did.

On her way into work one morning, Marie stopped at a light two blocks from the precinct. Her eyes were drawn to a scruffy-looking character on the uptown side of the street, doing his junk-hungry jitterbug—feet tapping, neck swiveling, on the lookout for a hot stove to steal. On the downtown side, a housewife walked up the steps to a building, her arms full of groceries, when another woman called out from a second-floor window. "You got any milk, Muriel?"

"No, sorry, and I don't got any at home."

The action proceeded with the clarity of a diagram: a dotted line for Milkless Mom as she left the building to walk to the store; another, bold and unbroken, as Jitterbug hotfooted it across the street, where no one was home in the second-floor apartment, left corner, facing the front. He must have been thinking, as Marie was, how sweet it could be when everything came together, just like that.

Ten minutes later, Marie marched one Rodney Shepherd into the precinct. Despite the fact that he'd ransacked an apartment with two infants inside, pocketed the family's rent money as well as a gold charm bracelet inherited from a beloved aunt, and pulled a switchblade on Marie, Shep quickly became a favorite of hers. Even more so than the Baby-Faced Bandit, though his ravaged, pockmarked visage would never have inspired any dashing nicknames. But he'd popped out like a rabbit from a hat, and he made her feel like a magician.

And he opened up to her, almost instantly. Male perps often did. Non-junkies sometimes tried to hit on her, but the addicts, whose sex drive always came second in their lives, usually saw her as a motherly figure. He told her he'd have sold the bracelet to a fence named Three-Finger Jack who paid thirty cents on the dollar, the best rate in town. With a sixty-five-dollar-a-day habit, Shep paid keen attention to what the middlemen had to offer. Marie did the math on a scrap of paper and told him that if he saved the money, he could buy a brand-new Plymouth Fury in thirty-nine days. He laughed and then began to whimper, "You don't know what it's like."

"You're right," she agreed.

"When I saw you today, I didn't believe you were a cop."

"I know. That's why I had to point a gun at your head."

"I thought . . . I thought you were gonna kill me."

"Well, Shep, I didn't want to then, and I don't want to now. But you were giving some thought to the idea of stabbing me. I'm an understanding person, but I have my limits."

"Yeah, sorry about that."

"No hard feelings. Promise me you won't carry the knife when you rob a place, next time. A little problem could turn into a big one."

"I swear! I thought I was gonna die today. I think I'm gonna have dreams about you shooting me."

"Live a better life, and you'll dream better dreams."

"From your lips, to God's ears."

When Marie went to the burglary office, Ed pretended to look at his watch, shaking his head. "We're never gonna catch bad guys if we don't get up before them."

"You can go back to bed. I got one already."

NOT EVERY DAY ended in applause. Not any day in their own squad, where Lt. Macken regarded them as troublemakers, lacking in deference and respect. He wasn't wrong about what they thought of him.

"Don't you worry about Macken, kids," said Ed as they sat down for lunch at a spaghetti joint in the Village. It was the last week of August, and Al was taking vacation the week after. Marie decided to postpone her maternity leave until he came back. Now was as good a time as any to tell them about it, but Ed was on a roll, and it would have been rude to interrupt.

"He's not our friend," he went on. "We all know that. Think of it this way, though. Every time you look at his pig-ignorant face, and see how he looks at us like we're Gypsies or communists or whatever else, remember that without his kind of stupidity, we'd be finished. So what if they stop us at half the precincts to ask if we know the Pledge of Allegiance? It's the same reason we're there almost every day, coming in with collars. Half the guys in the office look so much like cops, you might as well paint 'em blue. Most of 'em, they're not exactly contributing to the problem of overcrowded jails. Then, there are guys like the Farmer. Even though he looks more like a police horse than a policeman, the boss has to keep feeding him easy ones."

"Like yesterday," Al said, "When the call came in from the lady who said her ex-boyfriend pushed into her place and took her fur coat."

"Or last week, when nobody wanted to take the collar for the kids in the stolen car," Marie recalled. "Because the Garden sent over all those free tickets for the fights. The guy's basically on welfare."

"There you go." Ed paused to pop an antacid. "We don't need hand-outs. When Macken stops waving hello to us with his middle finger, that's when we worry."

It was an inspirational speech, and Marie almost believed him. Not for the first time, not for the last, she tried not to think about her old boss—it was masochistic to contrast Melchionne with Macken. This gig was all she'd hoped for, aside from the lieutenant; in her last days at the Police-women's Bureau, the inspector was the only part of work she could bear. What to make of a man who couldn't stand them for how good they were making him look? As it was, they were of a mind to make a statement. They had a week left in their first full month together as a team. Al wanted them to run up the score, so they'd have twice as many arrests as the next closest contender. Marie wasn't opposed, but then she remembered what Shep had told her about Three-Finger Jack. "I don't mind putting away one bad guy after another. But what if we hurt a lot of 'em, all at once?"

And so they took a break from their regular hustle of pickup collars and half-day tails, devoting the week to seeing how the master worked. Jack made regular rounds of Automats in the area. The mechanical caf-eterias seemed as futuristic as Flash Gordon when Marie was a kid. The food was in glass compartments in vending machines, and you'd drop your nickel into the slot for your dishes of Hungarian goulash, Harvard beets, Boston cream pie. The girls at the front had plastic thimbles on their fingers because they had to make so much change. Now, amid the steely geometry of midtown, the brass filigree and swiveling trays of condiments at the Automats were as old and hokey as . . . Flash Gordon. Still, the fare was fresh and cheap, and the coffee that flowed from the dolphin-head spigots was the best in the city. Hour by hour, day by day, Automat by Automat, they figured out that Jack used a system of runners and apprais-ers. It was a crackerjack system they were determined to crack.

It was after five on Friday afternoon in Times Square, and Jack was calling it a day. Marie and Ed were in position behind him, finishing their coffee and picking at a plate of peach melba. After leaving the res-taurant, they found Al slouching beside the statue of George M. Cohan.

They exchanged notes, muttering in frustration, when they saw Jack leave with an older man in a bespoke black gabardine suit who looked trim and nippy as a terrier. Gabardine shook an admonitory fist, and Jack's eight fingers gestured in apology. They hadn't seen Jack seem to be sorry about anything before.

There was no need to discuss the development. All week they'd thought of Jack as the biggest fish they'd ever hoped to catch. What kind of whale was Gabardine? The two perps headed west on 46th, and the three cops split in pursuit, with Al jogging down to 45th, to parallel them, and Ed and Marie taking opposite sides of 46th, at staggered lengths, behind Jack and Gabardine. When they halted, Marie continued past, slowly.

"How can I get that?" Jack protested. "Tell me how I can get it, and I'll get it. You know who I deal with."

"How you get it, I don't care. What I care about, is you get it."

"You gotta be reasonable. You gotta tell these people—"

"These people don't get told. They tell."

"You gotta be reasonable—"

"Shut up! Cops could be anywhere! And not just cops!"

What was going on here? Who was Gabardine to scold uncatchable Jack for carelessness? It pained Marie to keep walking, but she had no choice. She couldn't pretend to tie her slip-on shoes. If only she were in her old lady getup! She'd be burnt if she tried to rejoin the tail.

Marie stood beside a pay phone on the corner, pretending to fish for change. When she felt a tap on her shoulder, she knew that it was him. Turning around, she instinctively began to reach for her gun. Up close, Gabardine was an affable old stranger offering a dime for her phone call. When she stayed her hand and forced a smile, he stared at her, as if rereading a story he didn't want to believe: her hand moving to her, the lie in her eyes. He knew at once that she was neither a stranger nor a friend. Whatever kind of bad guy he was, he was very good at it. Marie's heart broke to see him walk away.

Gabardine didn't stop at the curb, didn't look up at the traffic or the light, and when he walked into the street, the taxi hit him so hard that his shoes remained where he took his last steps. Black broughams, freshly shined.

The next day, they learned that he had been identified as a suspect in at least a dozen gangland murders, going back to the days of Prohibition. He was wearing a watch that belonged to a witness to one of them, who had vanished without a trace in 1937. Marie hadn't caught him, but he hadn't gotten away.

SOMETHING WONDERFUL WAS going on that summer, something almost eerie. A stroke of luck became a streak, and then something else. Even their wrong turns went right. If it had happened to anyone else, Marie would have suspected a fix instead of a miracle. She didn't understand it, and she didn't think she had to just yet. She didn't want the summer to end. And she wasn't going to be the killjoy who said that it was over.

Beyond their immediate chain of command, their labors had not gone unnoticed or unappreciated. It always annoyed Lt. Macken to have to call them into his office with a request from another squad or the FBI to help locate or identify a suspect. Though he took few pains to conceal his distaste, he was in no position to refuse when a captain from the Homicide Division asked for Marie to be temporarily assigned to him when Al was on vacation. She was able to arrange for Ed join her. The murder was of an elderly woman named Adelaide Jenkins, who had lived in one of the doorman buildings near University Avenue in the Village. Adelaide was a lifelong resident of the neighborhood, doggedly independent. She had fine things in her home, friends nearby, and she had been determined to maintain her life as it was, as long as she could. One day, when she'd returned from the greengrocer's, she'd seen that her apartment door was open. Inside, she'd surprised a burglar who stabbed her with a carving fork. It was sticking upright in her chest when she was found.

An informant had come up with a nickname—"Shep"—as a suspect, and a search of the alias files had produced, among others, one Rodney Shepherd, male white, twenty-seven years old, five-foot eleven, one hundred and forty-five pounds, acne-scarred, who had last been arrested for another flat burglary by one Policewoman Marie Carrara. Marie wished she were surprised that he was out on bail. And she wondered—if Shep had in fact killed her—why he hadn't used the switchblade? Had he kept his promise to stop carrying one? The carving fork had been identified as the victim's property. There was no need for this murder, no cause for it, even by corkscrew junkie logic. She was eighty-five years old and weighed ninety-five pounds. He could have knocked her over with his bad breath. Marie didn't want to kill Shep, but she hoped to appear in his dreams, waking and otherwise.

Shep moved around: he'd racked up collars in the Bronx, Brooklyn, and Queens, and he usually gave a Bowery flophouse as his address, though no one there recognized his picture. They didn't know where he laid his head at night, or where he'd hit next. But he'd told Marie who his favorite fence was, and his sixty-five-dollar-a-day habit would likely soon reunite him with Three-Finger Jack. The week spent tailing the fence hadn't been wasted, after all.

They knew Jack's routines, his preferred tables—toward the middle, facing the front—which allowed them to arrive before he did. Jack was alert to surveillance, but it didn't occur to him that his watchers would be waiting for him, instead of trailing behind. During their earlier days with him, they'd learned to eat as little as possible, or they'd be stuffed and stupefied by midday, and there was only so much coffee they could drink without springing leaks. They promised each other that, if either of them died of clogged arteries, the other would try to have it designated a death in the line of duty. How did the old jingle go? *Oh, how I love the Automat, the place where all the food is at!*

Four days into their feeding frenzy, they observed Jack at one of his tables beside the gleaming chrome-and-glass machines at the Times Square store, receiving visitors like a ward boss. He was stout, middle-aged, sallow, always dressed in in a cheap but respectable suit of blue or gray pinstripe. He tended to keep his left hand, with the missing pinkie and ring fingers, under the table, and he shielded it to conceal his lost digits when he needed both hands. When a young patrolman walked in through the revolving door, Jack noticed but didn't appear to be perturbed, sipping his coffee and sending a runner on an errand. When the cop passed Ed and Marie, he didn't give them a second glance. Marie was taken by how young he was, how new he seemed. He was built like a linebacker, but he was so fresh-faced that he looked like he didn't need to shave.

And then she saw Shep outside on the sidewalk, pacing, then stopping to press his face against the glass. Marie gave Ed an elbow and rose. She was a beatnik today, with a wig of straight brown hair that descended to her waist, tortoise-shell spectacles of clear glass, one of Sid's silk dress shirts loosely bound with a belt. Ed was professorial, with a tweed coat, baggy brown chinos, and an eye patch. They walked to the front, and when Shep had stepped into the revolving door, traversing the circuit from two o'clock to four, Ed put his foot down to stop it, trapping Shep in the glass. Shep was confused, at first, pushing forward, then back; he glared at Ed and then began to berate him. And then Shep saw Marie, her hand reaching for the gun holstered on her hip, covered by the loose shirttails. Hadn't he dreamt it would end like this? He raised his hands and nodded. Marie went forward in the door, so she would be out in the street to meet Shep there, and Ed made sure that Shep didn't get off the merry-go-round until he was delivered outside to his partner.

That was easy, she thought. Shep popped out from behind the glass for them like a dish of Jell-O, and they didn't even have to spend a nickel. He shook like Jell-O, too, as they walked him down the block, each cop with a junkie arm. The streets were mobbed today, even more than usual, and they had to pummel and bump their way through the crowds to find a quiet spot to search and cuff him. Not everyone on the street would be helpful, even if they knew that they were cops.

"All right, Shep," Marie said. "It's all over now, you can relax. Where's the switchblade?"

"I don't, I haven't carried it, not since . . . not since we talked."

"Good, Shep. Anything else? You got a hypo? A razor? Anything?"

"A hypo, in my pants pocket, in the metal cigar tube."

"Glad you told me," Marie said. "I'm gonna take it out of your pocket."

Ed was quick to add, "You know we're gonna have to lock you up for it, for possession of narcotics paraphernalia."

Shep nodded, and Marie admired Ed's improvisation. She'd never locked up anyone for murder before. It hadn't occurred to her that Shep didn't know what they knew, and there was no need to bring up Adelaide Jenkins until they were safely in the precinct. Once they found a lobby or an alley, they'd stop. Marie could feel Shep shiver, and she smelled the sour sweat pumping from his pores. She kept her hand on her gun. Not far to go, and they would be done.

And then she heard the blow as much as she felt it, the *Pock!* of some kind of pipe or club as it struck against her hip. The blow caught her gun, mostly, but it also hit her hand, and her arm flailed away from her body like a ship's cable snapping loose. She felt someone behind her, seizing her by the hair. She stood, stunned and weak-kneed, as Shep dropped to the sidewalk beside her. The next second stretched out like elastic. *What was this?* Maybe Three-Finger Jack made her from this surveillance, or the last one, and he'd hit her with a bat, shivving Shep to shut him up forever. *No?* She lurched forward, leaving her wig behind. *No.* She couldn't feel her hand, or feel her gun. *What was this?*

Marie turned as she lurched forward. She felt like she was back in the revolving door. She saw the blue uniform, one hand holding a yard of auburn hair, the other with a nightstick raised to strike again, and then she heard Ed's voice tear through the air: "Put that club down, you goddamned rookie! We're with Homicide! If you've hurt either my partner or my perp, you're walking a beat in Staten Island tomorrow! And not the nice part of Staten Island, wherever that is!"

"Sorry, Detective! I coulda sworn I stopped a kidnapping . . ."

The three of them stood there for a moment. The young patrolman had a look of frozen confusion, and Marie guessed she wore one as well. He prodded Shep with the toe of his shoe, but he didn't respond. Now that Marie knew Shep hadn't been shanked, she supposed he'd fainted, mistaking the crack of the club for the bullet he thought she was saving for him. She regarded the prone form with more pity, maybe, than was warranted. Shep, at least, had no doubts that she was a cop.

"I didn't even lay a finger on him," the patrolman said, looking skyward in bafflement. "Maybe something dropped from a plane? A Russian Sputnik? If it was one of those space gadgets, I hope it was one of ours."

16   YOU'LL KNOW WHEN I NEED YOU TO KNOW

Use your gun as you would your lipstick. Use it only when
you need it, and use it intelligently. Don't overdo either one.

—Mayor Fiorello LaGuardia
Address to policewomen, 1943

OCTOBER 24, 1963
0830 HOURS

Once Marie realized that the only person who truly loved her was
the one she'd made, the idea of having a new baby became less
ominous, less oppressive. Now, there would be two of them. Still,
she resisted the reckoning every day she could. She had resolved to tell Ed
and Al about the pregnancy every Friday for the last seven weeks. Seven
stolen weeks of stakeouts and chases, the camaraderie of inside jokes and
outdoor adventure. Seven weeks of paychecks.

Shep had confessed to the murder. Her hand swelled up badly after
being hit by the nightstick, but she didn't report the injury to the Medical
Division, as the department surgeon might see through her bra stuffing.
When she asked Ed why the cop clubbed her instead of him, he deliber-
ated a while before replying, "Try to think of it as a blow for equality."
The young patrolman's last words—*I hope it was one of ours*—became Ed's
catchphrase for weeks. He said it when they heard a car backfire, when a
waiter dropped a tray of glasses, and when a pigeon unloaded a ribbon of
excrement on Al's shoulder. Marie wondered when the joke would get old,
but it hadn't, not yet.

Today, she would tell them. She swore she would. As she stood in the
kitchen, finishing the breakfast dishes, she realized that she hadn't had
a weekday dinner at home in weeks. She worked during the day, mostly,

297

as did most burglars, hitting apartments while the tenants were at work. TV and TV dinners had reduced the opportunities for evening break-ins, as bachelors and career girls opted increasingly for Dick Van Dyke and Mary Tyler Moore as dining companions. Marie took some comfort in the idea that her late start would make her last day last a little longer. She took off her rubber gloves and looked down at her stomach. "Hurry up, kid. If you're out by Christmas, you get an extra year of presents."

Sometime after New Year's was a better bet. She had to stay home for one hundred and eighty days after the birth, which put her back to work in June. Marie looked out the window at the trees. All the crimson and ginger of the early turning was gone; the leaves that still clung to the branches were the wan brown of lunch bags. She wished a wind would blow them away. She went upstairs and dressed. Dee had given her a few outfits from her maternity collection, roomy and designed to distract from the abdomen with padded shoulders and the like. Marie chose a black suit, as befit her mood of mourning. She decided to offset it with her favorite hat, the fedora with a leopard-skin print.

It was nine-thirty, and Marie was making a cup of coffee when she heard the car pull into the back. She was surprised. Katie had taken the car for a dental appointment, and she wasn't due back for a while. And Sid was surprised when he walked in and saw his wife in the kitchen. The absence of her car might have led him to make assumptions, too. Could it be that both of them scanned the driveway with the same anxiety when they returned home? They were like the hoboes who looked for scratched signs on fence posts, warning of farmers with shotguns, dogs that bite. Marie felt the muscles of her jaw tighten.

"Hey, honey," he said with a winsomely naughty grin, as if they'd woken up together after an evening of too many cocktails. "I didn't expect to see you here."

His tie was loose, and he tossed his fedora on the table beside hers. He was unshaven, and his shirt, his suit, looked like they'd spent the night in a pile on the floor. He was a looker still, all shoulders and smile, as long as you didn't look too close. She'd neither forgiven him nor forgotten what he'd done. But she was stuck with him until next June, at least, and she'd do what she could to keep the peace until the real battle began. She took a breath and forced her jaw to relax. "I'm heading out in a little while. You want coffee?"

"Sure. Let me take a quick shower first, I gotta head right back out."

As Marie added water to the coffeepot, Sid gave her a kiss on the cheek. He was in a better mood than she'd seen in some time. She wondered if she could somehow take advantage of it, or simply enjoy his unaccustomed goodwill. He went upstairs and returned when the coffee was ready, shaven and in a clean suit. "Thanks, honey, this hits the spot. They had us running around all night, taking down horse rooms."

Marie believed him. He didn't talk about work with her and neither of them thought it wise to discuss where he'd slept the night before. He sipped and glanced at her, up and down, when she stood to put the cream back in the refrigerator. "You look great. I mean, you're due kinda soon, right? It doesn't really show."

Marie laughed. It was something a neighbor would say. Not even a next-door neighbor, but someone she'd run into now and then at the supermarket. "Yeah, well, I still got 'em fooled at the squad, but it won't last much longer," she replied, deciding to keep things vague about her last day. "And then . . . well, it's not the most important thing, but we will have to economize a little, tighten up the budget."

Sid looked up from his coffee. "Why?"

"Because they don't pay me when I'm out on maternity. Once I go out, and then for six months after the birth."

"What? They don't pay you? That's lousy!" Sid sputtered. "You'd think with all you do, with all the money this city has . . . This job is one raw deal after another!"

This time, Marie didn't laugh. The image of her husband as champion of equality in the workplace was too beautiful to ruin by thinking about it. Sid took a last slug of coffee and stood up. He reached into his jacket pocket and pulled out his wallet, extracting two, three, four . . . Hesitating for a moment, he took out a fifth hundred-dollar bill and set it on the table. "There, that should hold you a while. Get yourself something nice, too. You deserve it."

Sid gave her a kiss and walked out of the kitchen. Marie stared at the money. She shook her head and said aloud, "I'm in the wrong line of work."

A tough night at the office, Sid had told her. Locking up gamblers, he'd said. And now he had a wallet full of hundred-dollar bills. As far as she knew, cops weren't supposed to take tips. She pocketed the cash, accounting it as alimony in advance. A time would come when his debts might not be settled with such dispatch. Still, Marie couldn't help but be affected by his largesse. She was ashamed she could be bought off so cheaply, but she didn't care. She had so few happy memories with her husband. If she fooled herself for an hour, a day, believing that he wasn't so bad, it brought her an hour, a day, closer to when she'd be back at work, and free to act.

Marie looked out the window into the backyard, smiling and waving as so many housewives did when their husbands left for the office. Sid didn't look back, and his pace was brisk. As he opened the driver's side door, she saw that there was a passenger in the car. His partner? No, she thought, not when she saw Sid lean over for a kiss. Was it Carmen? Marie couldn't tell. She wasn't sure if it mattered. She wasn't smiling anymore, but even as the car pulled out of the driveway, she kept on waving goodbye.

Three hours later, Marie was with Ed and Al at a restaurant in Chinatown. She'd insisted on it, as moo goo gai pan was hard to come by in the suburbs. At first, she entertained some fatuous hope that she might find an opportunity to work the subject of pregnancy into the conversation, so they wouldn't make a big fuss about it. As they sipped their egg drop soup, there was a possibility, she thought, when Ed and Al discussed the weight gain of a sergeant they knew. "He got fat."

"Not really. He used to be really skinny, though."

"Not fat-fat, but built like the one from last week, the one we caught taking the shoes off the Swedish tourist who fainted."

"Portly," Marie offered.

"Portly. Just the word."

Marie decided to pass. So too when Al beckoned the waiter. "What is this stuff about Year of the Rabbit? What does it mean?"

"Chinese Zodiac. 1963, Year of the Rabbit."

"Yeah, but—"

"Chinese Zodiac."

That would have to do for Al, and it wouldn't do for Marie. Besides, they didn't use rabbits any more for pregnancy tests. Maybe she should just come out with it. And then Ed pointed out an article in the paper about how a fugitive American had just been arrested in France. "Lothringer, comma, Harvey. Abortionist who cut up a girl who died on his table, stuffed the parts in the drain. Didn't you work this case, Marie?"

"That I did," she replied. "What does it say?"

"Let's see. He was living with his girlfriend under the names Mr. and Mrs. Victor Rey, in a tiny country called 'Andorra,' in between France and Spain. Population six thousand, four hundred. How about that!"

Al muttered dubiously, his mouth full of chow mein, "Six thousand people in a country? Can't be. There's more people than that in the Queensbridge Houses."

"Shush, Al, and chew your food. Go on, Ed."

"Well, they think they're a country," Ed related. "And they don't have an extradition treaty with us. French police grabbed them when they went over the border. 'The doctor said that the girl was five months pregnant, and he tried to talk her parents out of it by doubling the price, to a thousand dollars.' And then, he says, the parents 'crossed me up' when they agreed to pay. Died of an air bubble in her bloodstream, early in the operation. Crazy that a woman would risk that."

Al shook his head. "Disgusting."

Marie shook her head, unwilling to ask which one he was talking about. She'd wait for the subject to change from Harvey Lothringer before she broke the news of her baby. "Yeah, he was a beauty," she said, glancing casually over at the paper, as if Lothringer were just another case. "I went to the Queens DA to get a wiretap on him. They told me they don't do taps on doctors. When the girl died, they did backflips to say how hard they tried to get him. Next thing I know, I'm out of the Women's Bureau and in the Detective Division."

"Whoever said two wrongs don't make a right never worked in the police department," Ed reflected.

They finished the entrées without talking. Marie wondered if the fortune cookies might give her an opportunity and ordered coffee. Ed popped an antacid and wore an expression of worn patience. "As long as you hit the can before you go, Marie. I thought maybe we'd take a walk along the Bowery today, to look for someone I know who used to broker a lot of scrap metal, mostly copper. The jakes at the flophouses might not pass muster with you and your hoity-toity tastes."

"Funny you should mention the waterworks," Marie began, hesitantly. This wasn't the ideal segue, but if she delayed any further, she'd wind up delivering the baby on a stoop during a surveillance. "After today, think I can guarantee that's not gonna be such a big deal anymore. That's the good news. The bad news is, you guys are going to make do without any feminine intuition for a while. Mama Marie is taking a little time off, to be a mama again."

Both of the men were stunned for a moment, and then Ed jumped up and hugged her, and Al followed suit. "Sweet Jesus," Ed cried out. "I hope it's one of ours!"

Marie slapped his shoulder, trying to look angry. "My God, though, you're right. This one's gonna keep the office gossips busy for a while."

"You didn't tell Macken yet, did you?" Al asked. "He's gonna act like you should have asked his permission first."

"No, boys," she reassured them. "You're the first to know. But he ought to be next. By the end of the day. Don't worry, I'll be back in the spring, like the swallows at Capistrano. And we have time to walk around the Bowery, Ed, if you want, but I'll use the ladies' room here."

"If you think we're going to hit Skid Row, you're nuts." Ed said. "We'll take a nice slow drive back to the office, and then you can tell Macken. We won't wait till the end of the day, because you might need to explain the facts of life to him first."

When they returned to the car, Marie took the wheel, as she had the first day, and most others. Despite Ed's protest, she drove up the Bowery first, and then cut west, to the Village, just because she felt like it. The weather was warm for the season, and Ed and Al dozed after the heavy meal. She was so fond of them that she could have chucked their chins. So she'd be stuck at home for a while. She'd be able to take Sandy out trick-or-treating next week, and they could spend days making her Halloween costume. That would be nice. Then Thanksgiving, and then Christmas, and then the baby. She tried to cheer herself up by thinking that it would be almost summer when she came back. Anno Domini 1964, the Year of the Dragon. Marie took a meandering and roundabout route, in no hurry to see the day end.

West 10th Street was a handsome block of old brownstone townhouses and fine old elms, their leaves gilt and bronze. No one was out except for two men, at the head and foot of a flight of stone steps in front of one of the houses. The one at the top—the taller one, with a rolled-up newspaper under his arm—turned away from the door, shaking his head, and the one at the bottom eyeballed the street, back and forth, back and forth. Given the stillness of the street, they practically vibrated. They were Puerto Ricans on the darker side, or Negroes on the lighter side, and Marie insisted to herself that race prejudice didn't shape her perception as much as their hungry, jumpy looks and the dirty undershirts that hung on their bony arms. She didn't slow down when she passed them. Circling the block, she found them in the same position at another townhouse, three doors down. "Naptime's over, boys."

Marie pulled over once she rounded the corner and shook Al awake in the back seat. "You got a couple of daytime flat burglars, midblock, south side."

Al rubbed his eyes and made a face. "I was having the most beautiful dream. If you weren't a lady, I could tell you about it."

When Al slammed the door behind him, Ed stirred and cracked his neck. He looked over to her and frowned. "I won't let you take crazy chances, Marie. And it's crazy to take any. Let's go in."

Marie should have been less sharp in her reply. "Come on, old man, if I'm not bellyaching about my belly, you can't, either. Let's take care of business."

Ed's lips tightened. "I should handcuff you to the wheel. You better not get out of the car. Promise me you won't."

Marie didn't answer, and the hint of discord lingered in the air. A gust of wind lifted scraps of newspaper off the sidewalk to eddy at eye level. Ed was right, she knew. It was foolish to risk getting slugged or kicked, let alone being bitten, or stuck with a needle. But she was so resistant to being told what to do, whether by her body or her employer—*Almost a year without pay!*—that she pushed back, no matter how wise and well-meaning the advice.

Al returned and rapped on the window: "They're on the move. They hit one house, and somebody calls out a window, 'Who you looking for?' One of them says, 'Is this the Fleishman residence?' And the guy says, 'No, they're two doors down, closer to Fifth. They should be home.' So guess what they do?"

"They don't go to the Fleischman's," Ed replied.

"Every house but. They're moving uptown on Fourth. They haven't made me, I'm going back after them."

Marie headed south for two blocks, cut east, and went back uptown. The street grid constrained their movements painfully. She ground her teeth as her foot jumped between the gas and the brake. Ed glimpsed Al and whistled. Marie eased into a bus stop for an update. "They're went west on 11th," Al said.

"Damn all these one-way streets," Ed fumed. "You follow them, Al, we'll go up to 14th, then back down Broadway. We'll find a spot to wait above 13th."

They drove up again, over again, and down again on Broadway, where Ed chased a taxi from a hydrant, shattering the driver's dream of three minutes of peace with his pretzel. Marie scanned the far side of the street. "You see anyone?"

"Yeah, I make Al at the phone booth, northeast corner, and he's staring across the street at the truck right ahead of us. So the other two have to be . . ."

Marie saw a white box truck double-parked a few car lengths ahead of them. The back door was padlocked. And then she saw the taller of the pair walk past, approach the truck from behind, and pull out a foot-long crowbar from his rolled-up newspaper. Ed elbowed her. "You see this guy? Would you look at this knucklehead!"

Marie was about to say, "Too easy!" but she knew she'd jinx the grab. "I see."

The man stuck the crowbar in the lock and began to yank it around. Midday, on Broadway! But whether the teamster had a guardian angel or the thief did, someone shouted—*Hey! Watch it!*—and the tall man slipped his crowbar back into his newspaper and hustled back uptown. He passed their car without looking up. The teamster emerged from the cab of the truck to check the padlock and drove down Broadway. Marie watched Al wander north and circled the block again. They'd go to the park.

Union Square Park was sad and seedy, three blocks long, one block wide, bordered by old loft buildings and lower-end department stores— Klein's, Ohrbach's. Inside were statues of Washington and Lincoln and the Marquis de Lafayette, and dozens of hopheads and winos who didn't move much more than the statues. The thieves could cop here and shoot up in plain sight on a park bench—the mother-with-stroller crowd didn't favor the place—but these were men with empty pockets. Marie found a spot on 14th and watched Al move counterclockwise at a sleepwalker's pace around the park. Marie was starting to get impatient. It wasn't late— not even two-thirty—but she didn't want to miss the lieutenant, in case he left early. What was with these junkies? *Steal something already, wouldja!* She couldn't believe there was much opportunity in the park, unless they planned to rip off the dealers, and they didn't seem the roughneck type. She decided to drive ahead, to scout out the prospects, and see what might catch their eye before they did. All of their guardian angels could wrestle to see who'd have the lucky day. She looked at Ed, pale and fretful. Just this once, she wished he wasn't a Protestant.

Just off Union Square West, she saw a shiny new silver Pontiac Catalina pull up short and double-park. A woman got out from the passenger side, slamming the door—"If you think I'm gonna go with you now!"—and marched across the street. And then an actual, legit parking space opened up in front of Marie. She moved in to watch the man from the Catalina get out to follow—"Honey, would you listen to reason!"—and leave the door open. A new car, the engine running.

Too easy? No, she shouldn't even think it. Too late: the driver raced back, snatched the car keys, and shut the door before resuming his pursuit of his lady friend. Too easy, indeed. But the Catalina wasn't locked. What was inside? It wouldn't hurt to look, would it? Marie popped out before Ed could react. "Marie, where the hell are you—"

"Gimme ten seconds, I just gotta check."

And no more than half a minute passed before she was back, preempting Ed's protest by slapping his shoulder. "Don't even start! I won't run after anybody, I won't fight anybody, I won't do anything, okay? But the car's unlocked, with a back seat full of suitcases and a fur coat. This is the last stop for these two characters, believe me. And if I'm wrong, we'll call it a day. We'll head back to the office. Okay?"

Ed didn't answer, and Marie was afraid to look at him. They'd never even disagreed over where to eat lunch before. Another whirlwind of leaves and newspapers ascended in the sky. She didn't know how much longer she could avoid talking to Ed. How much longer before she had to go to the bathroom? Luchow's was nearby. Was she hungry enough for a potato pancake, so soon after lunch? Maybe she was.

And then she saw the thieves saunter up to the Catalina, and her faith in their criminal abilities was restored. One pushed in a back vent window, while the other tested the driver's door, but they were both inside at the same time. They left seconds later, suitcases in hand. The small one had a fur coat over his shoulder.

"Don't move a muscle," Ed growled, sounding so much like a stickup man that Marie expected to feel the barrel of his gun against her ribs. He left the car to limp across the street, and she saw Al move from where he lurked behind a statue. Marie saw the point where they'd all meet—Ed from behind the thieves, Al from the side—and the two feeble semi-invalids would collide against two determined professionals. Or vice versa. When Ed came from behind the taller one, he whirled around and flung the coat on Ed's head, covering it like a sack, and punched and punched away. Ed collapsed, and the man kicked him in the head. The other swung the suitcase at Al—a small, hard plastic valise—knocking the gun out of his hand. Al lurched to the side and seemed to shiver and buckle, as if having a fit, but then he snapped back up like a car antenna and lunged at his perp. They fell to the ground, thrashing and grappling. Ed didn't move at all.

The fur coat covered his face like a shroud. Marie sprinted into the park. Al pinned his perp and looked up at her, jerking his head toward the path where the other one jackrabbited. "Get him!"

Marie ran back to the car without checking on Ed. He lay so still that her heart misgave her. Al was there, and there was only one thing Marie could do for him, alive or dead—she'd make the perp pay. The car was still there, thank God, its door open, keys dangling in the ignition. She stiff-armed the horn and stamped on the gas pedal, cutting across the street to mount the curb onto the sidewalk. She didn't bother to yell, "Police!" No one would have believed her, even if they heard.

The perp had made for the parking lot in the north end of the park, and in seconds Marie was within fifty yards of him, forty. She steered with her left hand and held her gun in her right, looking for her shot. When she was almost on top of him—thirty yards, twenty—he doubled back, using the row of parked cars as a barrier. She sped fifty yards in reverse and stopped the car short. This was it. She raised her revolver and gripped it with both hands. She breathed in and out, to steady herself, and aligned her target in the sights. She aimed for the space between cars where the perp would pass her, in a second, for less than a second. She'd have him, she could— *No.* The space was too small, the time too short. *What then?* She got out of the car, pointed the gun in the air, and fired a warning shot.

The perp skidded to a halt, staggering, unsure where to run, if he could run, if he'd been hit. He was in the space where Marie knew he'd pass, and he stayed there. She saw his knees shake and his rib cage heave, desperate for air. He looked at her, watching the gun in her hand descend to aim at him. She saw his face then. His hair was just long enough to show the softness of the curl, and his moustache was trimmed, two dashes above his lip. With his high, wide cheeks and long, aquiline nose, he was darkly glamorous, like a Sheik of Araby. He looked at her with heartbreak in his eyes. And then Marie saw his leg dip, to push off the pavement to run. If a felon ran, a cop could shoot. Marie shot at him. She shot again.

The windshield of a Buick Rivera shattered behind him, but he was gone, cutting east, and Marie jumped back in the car, gunning it in reverse to block his exit into the street. Now he ran west, in a low, loping crouch, head down. Again, she almost had him when he darted between cars and bolted onto Broadway, running uptown, against traffic. Waving her gun out the window, she managed to clear a lane of oncoming cars, provoking a resounding cacophony of horns and screams.

"Wrong way!"

"She's got a gun!"

"Wrong way, you crazy lady!"

"You're going the goddamn wrong way, you stupid b—"

When she saw him turn on 18th, against traffic again, she forced her way into the intersection. The sight that met her was so unexpected, so welcome, that she almost cried: an empty street. No cars were coming! All the angry noises faded from her ears, and her mind became still as a chapel. The man hid behind a parked truck, and then he dashed along the building line. Marie floored it to speed past him, bouncing up onto the sidewalk and cutting him off with three thousand pounds of battered steel. He stumbled over the hood and tried to scramble over it, but his sweat-slicked hands found no purchase on the hot metal. Marie jumped out, seized a fistful of his shirt, and began to pound on his head with the butt of her gun: *Thuk! Thuk! Thuk!* The fabric began to tear, but she could feel the strength leave his body with each blow. When he collapsed on the hood of the car, holding his hands up, she stopped hitting him. "Move and I'll put one in you."

His head shook. It could have been a nod. After Marie cuffed him, she could barely stand. She hopped up on the hood and sat beside him as he lay prone, panting.

"I think you already did," he said, his voice weak but level.

"What?"

"You shot me."

"Where?"

"On the arm, the shoulder."

Marie looked down at his right side, the nearer one. She didn't see any blood, aside from where she'd wiped off her gun. "Get out of here. You're fine."

"No, the other side," he persisted. For the first time, there was the slightest note of complaint in his tone. Marie didn't get up to check. It couldn't have been too bad. It hadn't slowed him down. "What's your name?"

"Oliver. Theodore Oliver. What's yours?"

"Marie."

That was enough small talk for now. She closed her eyes for a moment— just for a moment—and thought about Ed. It saddened her that her last words with him might have been quarrelsome. It sickened her that they might have been last words. She heard sirens in the distance. Would she have to tell his wife? Marie had never met Mrs. Lennon. She and Al should tell her together, she supposed. She kept her eyes shut, just for a moment more.

When she opened them, she saw Ed staggering toward her. Sweat streamed down his pallid face, and he seemed to have aged twenty years in the last twenty minutes. Had it been twenty minutes or two since she'd seen him? He opened his mouth, but he was out of breath. His face was too wasted for her to see any emotion, whether anger or relief. He climbed up on the hood of the car with her. Marie remembered Moriarty's jibe when they'd arrived at his squad room with Mickey Burns, on their first day: *I heard you were dead, Eddie. Is it true?* She was so happy it wasn't. One day, they'd joke about it. Not just yet, though. She fanned herself with her leopard-print fedora.

Sirens sounded all around, and patrol cars began to fill the block, from both directions. Ed unclipped his gold shield from his belt and held it up like a lantern, so that they'd know what he was, even if he still couldn't talk. When Marie didn't take out hers, Ed cocked his head at her—*Why don't you? You should!* Marie shrugged. *What's the point?*

She smiled at the notion that she and Ed still weren't talking. There was no need. They were good again. She felt an irritation in her chest and reached inside her dress to pull out a handkerchief from one bra cup, then the other. Ed watched her, shaking his head, and then he started to laugh. *What the—?* Sweat dripped from his brow. Marie offered him one of the handkerchiefs, and he mopped his forehead. This wasn't the time to explain the trick she'd learned from Frau von Trapp. One less secret to keep, anyway. She felt better already. *The hills are alive, with the sound of music . . .* Marie took out her shield and held it up. Ed took it from her hand and switched it with his, so he'd have the silver, and she'd have the gold.

FIVE

BREAKS IN THE ACTION

17 YOUR WORLD IS NOT THE WORLD

Tutto a posto, niente in ordine.

—Italian adage

JULY 18 1964
1430 HOURS

While Marie was confined to her home, from that last, lunatic day in October through the spring, it seemed as if an age had passed. The world had begun to seem unsafe, unsound, in ways she had never felt before.

The president had been murdered. Marie was so proud to have met him. To have shaken his hand, to have seen his green eyes. She was glad to have helped protect him, in some small way, for a few hours. It made her feel less futile, less alone. And there was comfort in how one-hearted the nation became, resolute throughout the ordeal. Young and old, black and white, were equal in grief. You could almost believe people would try to make sense of the senselessness by trying to put things right, to make the world fairer, safer. Maybe it was stupid to believe that, but it wasn't wrong to hope.

A few months later, in March, there was another murder, much closer to home, that seemed to put the lie to that hope. A twenty-eight-year-old girl named Kitty Genovese came home from her job managing a bar, late at night, to her apartment in Queens. The neighborhood was middle-class, the houses prettily built in English styles, safe and stable, even dull. After she parked her car, a hundred feet from her door, Kitty was set upon by a man named Winston Mosely, who chased her down the street and stabbed her in the back. She screamed, "Oh my God! He stabbed me! Please help me!" Mosely fled when a man in a seventh-story apartment yelled out the window, "Leave that girl alone!" She staggered toward home, but she

311

couldn't get inside the locked lobby door. Ten minutes later, Mosely found her where she had fallen. He stabbed her again—seventeen times in all—and raped her as she was dying. When Mosely was arrested, he confessed to other burglaries and rapes, and two more murders. He'd never been in trouble with the law before. He had a good job, a wife and two kids. When asked if he feared being seen by neighbors, he replied, "Oh, I knew they wouldn't do anything. People never do."

Marie couldn't remember reading a single bit of good news all those months when she was home. No one seemed to be in charge in the city, and it seemed to be a meaner place by the day, angrier, colder, more crowded. They tore down Penn Station, turning a palace of pink marble into a pile of rubble, but they couldn't fill a pothole. Crime was going up. Schools, subways, and just about everything else was breaking down. In the spring, no one cared about the World's Fair in Queens, aside from the civil rights protesters who blocked the entrance. There were five days of riots in Harlem after a white cop killed a black teenager who came at him with a knife. More and more people talked about leaving.

Still, Marie knew better than to believe everything in the papers. Her pursuit in Union Square was splashed in all of them. The *Daily News* had a page-one banner, LADY COP CLUBS DOWN LOOTER. MOM-TO-BE LEADS GUN CHASE. The photo showed her with Theodore Oliver in the precinct, standing behind him as he sat in a chair. She'd looked at it often—too often, maybe. She was glad she'd worn her fedora. The leopard pattern popped, even in the shadowy newsprint. Her dress was a bit dressier than her usual undercover attire, as she hadn't planned on getting her hands dirty. Her gun and holster had been shifted from her right hip to the left. The picture was staged, and a captain from headquarters told her to do what the photographers wanted. It was her face that perplexed her, its waxen blankness. Was it the image of intrepid resolve? More like a KO'd prizefighter, flat on his back after the bell rang, smelling salts shoved under his nose: *How'd I do, Coach? Did I win?*

Theodore Oliver was posed like a hunting trophy. There was no ambiguity to his expression—he seemed to be in agony, clutching his wounded shoulder, the left sleeve of his white T-shirt torn. But his suffering was just as phony as Marie's stoicism. The medics had cut the sleeve, and the wound was a scratch. Oliver had been arrested a dozen times before, and he knew the routine. He'd be in jail for a couple of months, at most. All the hubbub was a welcome distraction, and he was a better sport about sitting this way or that, making faces for the cameras, than she had been.

When she got home that night, Marie went into the living room and sat down heavily on the couch. She knew Mrs. M. would have been proud of her at the press conference: "Yes, I get scared sometimes, but I know the boys are always there to back me up." That was sticking to the script, wasn't it? No need to dance for detectives at the Hotel Astor to prove her real cop-real lady bona fides if she could pop out a baby after pistol-whipping a man. She was ready for a good long rest, but she worried she'd be forgotten by the time she got back to work. Until the papers came out, she wasn't sure she'd be the hero of the story. Maybe people would be angry she'd worked through her seventh month. Ed hadn't been happy with her. Maybe she'd be lucky if people forgot her.

Katie greeted her warily. "Is everything all right?"

Some time passed before Marie realized she hadn't answered. "Sorry, Katie. It's been a day."

"The radio said a lady police shot someone. I figured it was you."

"Yeah, that was me. Did I tell you I was pregnant, Katie?"

"No, but I overheard a few . . . conversations."

"Does Sandy know?"

"I don't think so."

"Do you think she'll be happy about it?"

"Of course! Nothing could make her happier."

"Today was my last day at work. I'll be home for the next eight months."

Katie nodded. "I don't know what's customary, Marie—"

"'Congratulations' is what people say here," Marie replied absently. "What do you say in England?"

"We say that if service has been satisfactory, two weeks' notice and references upon request are . . ."

Marie flinched. "What?"

"I'm sorry, Marie, but it's Friday, and I won't be able to contact an agency, or put a notice in the paper. It only seems fair—"

Katie began to sob, and Marie began to laugh, leaping up to hug her. How could she ever think she was being fired?

"Why would you ever—"

You say things—maybe to yourself, I never know—things like, 'We'll just have to make do with less.' And the other day, you said, 'Some big changes have to be made.'"

"I must have been talking to myself. Of course I want you to stay! I need you!"

Marie couldn't blame the papers for why Katie got this story wrong. This was what happened in a house full of half-secrets. The clamor drew Sandy downstairs. "What is it? What happened?"

Marie was laughing and crying when she looked up. "Come on down here, honey."

Sandy stopped, trembling. "Is somebody dead?"

Marie was so overwhelmed by the silliness and the seriousness of it all that she jumbled the answer badly. "No, honey, Mommy only shot him in the shoulder."

There followed a scream from the stairs. "It wasn't Daddy, was it?"

Poor everybody! After all the tears were dried, Marie sat Sandy down on the couch to explain that everything was fine. *Really, better than fine!* Mommy would be in a lot of newspapers tomorrow, and everything was wonderful. At the end, Marie had comforted herself as much as she had Sandy. And then Sid burst in, with roses and champagne.

"Honey! I heard about what happened. Are you okay?"

Sandy rushed to grab him, squealing with enthusiasm, and Marie met his look of bafflement with a smile and a stage-whispered *Tell-you-later.* She pointed to her stomach and mouthed, "They know." Katie giggled, and Sid smiled, and Marie felt a rush of warmth as she saw them all together, a real family. Better than a real family, a TV one, bumbling through conspiracies that were all the funnier when they failed. Sid took them out to a diner by the raceway. He snuck in the champagne and made everyone have a sip, even Sandy, because it was such a special night. And it was. They weren't pretending, and they weren't not-pretending. Marie could live like this for a while, she thought. And she did.

LIFE AT HOME was happier than ever. Could that be why she thought things were out of balance? Her pregnancy, her delivery had gone beautifully. She adored her little boy, and she wasn't sick or sad afterward. Why? She didn't know. Katie and Sandy were angels. Marie saw her life as something that was getting bigger instead of smaller. Harder, too, but she was up for the task. And Sid didn't get in the way. He didn't start a fight when she said that the boy would be named James. He didn't argue with her in the hospital, and he didn't stay long. He bought a color TV for the living room, even though most shows were still in black-and-white.

While Marie was on leave, Sid never hit her. She once supposed idly that she hadn't given him any reason. And then she realized how awful her thinking was—she had no more control over him than she did the weather. The truce wouldn't last; it never had. As the date approached for her return to work, she contemplated the adjustments she'd have to make. Pumping breast milk, plus periodic uppercuts and low blows. But she had no hesitation about rejoining the battle outside. The only real way home was out the front door.

The coming summer could never be as golden as the last, she knew, with the heady delight of her new partners, the ticktock urgency of her pregnancy. But the first month back was as dull as matron duty, and even more confined. They were up on a wiretap, listening to "Tommy the Mole" talk with Jewish Abie, Cockeyed Jimmy, Long Beach Frankie, and Fifi Gencarullo as the crew planned an armored-car robbery. The names were more interesting than their conversations.

"Hey!"

"Hey. Who's this?"

"It's me."

"Oh, yeah, sure. Sorry, the kids are making a racket. What's up?'

"The place we met before?"

"Yeah?"

"Meet me there again, same time."

"Yeah, all right."

The wiretap plant was in a storeroom of an apartment basement, five feet wide by six long, which barely fit the table with their equipment. The room backed up against an efficient new boiler, and the temperature in their sweatbox never dropped below a hundred degrees. Ed, Al, and Marie worked four-to twelve shifts, mixing up tape-listening and Mole-tailing duties with Ralph and Arthur. Another team had the days. More people should have been assigned, but the lieutenant was of two minds about the case. By rights, a hijacking should have gone to the Safe, Loft, and Truck Squad, but it had been Ed's informant who provided the lead. Macken was eager to seize the chance at glory, but he was unwilling to devote the time and manpower to do things right. What was the expression? *Tutto a posto, niente in ordine.* Everything was fine, and nothing was right.

Tommy the Mole didn't say much, or do much. On tails, they'd follow him to the barber, the bank, his girlfriend's, or his other girlfriend's. There was an inside man at the armored-car company, but only Tommy knew who he was. They could be so cagey on the phone that they wound up confusing the hell out of each other.

"I got a guy for the stuff we need."

"Good."

"You think we might need two, or three?"

"Maybe three is better."

"Okay. How much you wanna spend on each?"

"Couple, maybe three hundred apiece."

"Are you kidding? I can get Department of Sanitation uniforms for ten bucks!"

"Are you an idiot? I'm talking about machine guns."

"Shit, I get so shifty sometimes, I don't even know what I'm talking about."

"Nah, I know, it makes me crazy. My kid, he asks me about 'That thing we gotta do,' and it's five minutes before I know he's talking about his Little League game."

Though the surveillance teams were cross-eyed with boredom most days, no one doubted Tommy was worth watching, and there was furious protest when Macken announced he'd allow the wiretap to expire at the end of its thirty-day authorization. "What a waste of time! The hell if I'm gonna ask the DA for another thirty days. I can't have another month go by without arrests from half my squad."

He reversed himself after a captain paid a visit to commend him for his dedication to the case. Someone in the office had made a phone call to headquarters, it seemed. Marie struggled not to smile as the lieutenant summoned her to his office, glowering, and sent her to court to renew the wiretap. Did he think she'd break down and confess after five seconds of stink eye? *What a dope!* She was the last person to have gone over his head, much as she'd have liked. The detectives applauded the informer, but no one even offered any idle speculation about who dunnit. It was better not to know.

The next week, the case started to heat up, as Tommy the Mole's ingrained caution began to rub against the other men's need for money. Ralph Marino was in the plant on Monday when Jimmy Long Beach called to complain about his gambling debts. The interest cost him a hundred dollars every week. Tommy shut him up by telling him that there would be at least $750,000 in the armored car, "And if you want to go back to robbing candy stores, don't let me stop you."

Marie was on duty Tuesday when a new subject called. "Hey, it's Cheech."

"Who?"

"Fifi's brudder-in-law."

"Yeah, right. How long you been out?"

"Couple of months. Fifi, he's married to my sister, Mimi."

"Congratulations."

"Thanks. Anyway, you know how Fifi, how he always spits, how he hacks up a lot of phlegm?"

"The man eats cigarettes. Five packs a day. What do you want from me, a cough drop?"

"No, I just wanna tell you, we had dinner last night, at his house. Mimi made the cavatelli with the pork gravy, and—"

"No recipes, Cheech. You never know who's listening."

Marie smiled at Tommy's dry aside, but it slid right past Cheech. "Right, right. Anyway, Fifi pukes blood all over the table. I call the ambulance, they bring him to Beth Israel. They're doing all kinds of tests, but the doctors, they say it don't look good. Probably the Big C."

"No! Goddam it!"

Fifi was the wheelman, a cool head who could speed down an alley at sixty miles an hour with two inches on either side of the car. He wouldn't be easy to replace. Marie was as rattled as Tommy was by the news. Was the job over? Had the past six weeks been wasted?

Tommy went on the move. He'd been something of a homebody before—ducking out for a meet, a date, a meal, never out past ten—but now he ranged around the city in his Oldsmobile, fifteen hours a day, from diners to bars to social clubs, rarely staying long. The surveillance team should have had more people, more cars, walkie-talkies, but there was no point in asking Macken for anything. Old-school dirty tricks would have to do, like when Ed slashed a tire when the Mole was parked outside a discotheque. Ed thought they'd been made, and they needed time to bring Ralph in from home to switch up the tail—needless to say, Marie wasn't the one to make that call, in case Mrs. Marino answered the phone. And when the Mole joined another no-neck thug in a late-model Cadillac, Ed knocked out the left taillight, so Marie could follow with ease. Things were getting rushed on both sides; a misstep was inevitable.

On Friday night, an unidentified male called Tommy. "It's me. It's time we met. It's now or never. Monday night at seven. Hoboken, the park by the church."

Finally! That weekend, if Marie thought about police work at all, it was of the bricks and bottles raining from uptown rooftops—the Harlem riots had begun. She wasn't sorry to miss them. The temperature was in the nineties on Saturday afternoon. She was sweating in the backyard, elbow deep in zucchini, when Katie ran out, yelling, "Ed says you have to get to a park in Jersey, right away!"

Marie had on a tattered old dress, her hair up in curlers. She grabbed her gun and car keys, her shield and ID, before taking the phone. "Hoboken?"

"Hoboken, I'm already at Al's, picking him up."

"Half an hour."

"See you there."

There wasn't time to ask any of the dozen questions that buzzed in her head. She jumped in her car and flew into the city, nearly getting arrested as she sped through the Lincoln Tunnel. When she finally arrived, she was exhausted as if she'd run the whole way, and she sat down to collect herself on a park bench. She looked down at her legs and pulled her ragged dress over her dirty knees. There was no sign of Ed or Al. She didn't see Tommy the Mole, either, which was a relief. She stood and began to stroll around, wondering why the meeting was changed on such short notice. Would it happen tonight? She almost didn't care. She was back on the set, back in action.

The park was crowded. There were pairs and threesomes of mothers with baby carriages, dawdling until infant cries prompted them to push on; older solitaries sat enrapt by their Bibles or racing forms; a pack of boys were playing dice—kind of—chasing after each wild throw like cats after mice. There were a couple of wider, whiter men, in suits and ties, which Marie wouldn't have expected on a Saturday.

She spotted Tommy first, as he stood beside a tall, thin man in sunglasses and a tweed cap, the brim pulled low. He wore an oversized short-sleeved shirt, canary yellow. A bit showy, but the inside man wouldn't be a street guy, wouldn't know how to stay under the radar. He and Tommy walked a few paces and stopped to talk, and then walked and stopped again, looking around, watching to see if they were watched. She sat down on a bench before they passed her.

As she did so, she saw Al charge up the path, his arms flailing, making odd grunting noises. Marie froze, horrified. *What the hell was he doing?* She turned her head just enough to see if Tommy and Yellow Shirt noticed. Of course they had. What the hell was wrong with Al? Was he blind? Was he drunk? As far she knew, he wasn't much of a drinker. Was he—

And then she saw that Al was deaf. He'd sprinted to join a party of two men and two women in their twenties. When one had something to say, they'd stop to face one another, their hands dancing in the air, touching their mouths, their hearts, their foreheads. Al looked like a catcher giving pitch signals, or like he was playing an imaginary saxophone, not at all well. Mostly, he looked like an idiot. The four deaf people—had it been a double date that he'd barged into?—responded with vigorous countersigns before they realized he was harmless. They thought he was an idiot, too. Tommy and Yellow Shirt shrugged and walked on: *Just some dummies.* Al threw up his hands like a jilted boyfriend. He was a nonentity now, and he could sit and watch, wherever he wanted. Marie smothered her giggles. She was more than a little proud of him.

She stayed put for another few minutes, watching her suspects drift away, not quite out of eyesight. Her sense of relief faded. Someone had to stay on them. Where was Ed? There was no chance of overhearing anything. If only she could deputize the deaf couples and enlist them to lip-read. The best move was to tail Yellow Shirt to a car or an address, to make an ID. Even if they had to sit on him through the night, and then all day and night again Sunday, following him to work Monday morning. She wondered when she'd get a chance to wash and change. As she was, she stood out—harmlessly, clownishly, for now—but she couldn't be seen by them again.

And then she saw Ed. He was in a straw hat, Bermuda shorts, and a Hawaiian shirt, and his otherwise blindingly white legs also showing evidence of Saturday gardening. They rushed to embrace, and then they growled in each other's ears.

"What the hell is this, Ed? You just passed the Mole and the inside man."

Marie felt the tension in his body and stepped back when she heard the anger in his voice, barely contained. "Yellow shirt. Yeah, I saw."

She leaned in close, as if to remind him to keep his voice low. "What's going on? Why such short notice? What gives?"

"We're lucky we were called at all."

Ed explained how the random detective on the morning shift overheard an abrupt call to Tommy: *Monday's the day for the job, let's meet tonight.*

"Good for him," said Marie. "I'm glad he wasn't getting a coffee, or beer, when it came up on the wire. Or was he? Why the delay?"

"There was no delay," Ed shook his head. Words left him painfully, as if he were passing kidney stones. "He called the good lieutenant. Four hours ago."

Marie shook a little, trying to suppress a spasm of disgust. Ed took her arm, and they began to walk. She had a headache. "I don't want to ask . . ."

"It's worse than you think," he said. "Macken calls everybody except us, but Arthur heard later, and he called me. Macken's been here for hours, with a bunch of local cops. Why he thinks he needs an army is beyond me. The stickup won't be today. That man could screw up a one-car funeral."

"Ed, please don't tell me—"

"Let's move over, so you can see how he's deployed his forces."

Right away, Marie spotted an unmarked police car, a dark-blue Ford, with an extra radio antenna that stuck out like an oil derrick. Two wide, white men in white shirts and dark, narrow ties were inside. Farther down the street, she saw another dark Ford. She clutched Ed's arm as they walked ahead. "He really called out the cavalry, didn't he? And he didn't want to call us. Where's that idiot hiding?"

"Right around the corner," Ed muttered. "I ran into him, on the way. He's with the Farmer and one of the locals, in one of their cars. He kept touching the switches, like a kid with a new toy. The Jersey cop practically slapped his hand away. His opinion of big-city detectives must have gone right down the toilet."

They were within twenty yards of Tommy and Yellow Shirt when the two men began to stare at them. It was time to put on another little show. "Take me home!" Marie moaned, breaking away from Ed to collapse on a bench. "I don't know why I ever bother with you!"

"What's the matter now?"

"You were gonna take me out to dinner!"

"The way you look? Are you nuts? Keep it down, people are looking at ya!"

Tommy and Yellow Shirt shook their heads and resumed their conversation. Ed led Marie to a bench, where she sobbed on his shoulder. They were invisible, still in play. The bell of an ice cream truck sounded, and children raced toward it. Marie wouldn't have minded something cold and sweet. If the surveillance went on long enough—

Just then, she heard a siren, a rising wail that broke off sharply, and then a braying klaxon—*Oooh-ahh! Oooh-ahh! Oooh-ahh!*—as if warning of an air raid. They were finished. The sound of a police car was an ordinary noise, but it was close by, and there was no police car in sight. The itinerant men in white shirts wandering through the park halted in unison. The klaxon stopped, seconds later.

Tommy the Mole and Yellow Shirt didn't shake hands or wave goodbye as they broke apart. Ed and Marie waited until Yellow Shirt had some thirty yards on them and then followed. At the far end of the park, he went into the public lavatory. Marie sat down on a bench near the entrance, and Ed left his hat and Hawaiian shirt with her before taking a position near a bus stop. She was glad he'd worn an undershirt. She hoped Ed had nickels, in case Yellow Shirt took the bus. She settled in and waited, checking her watch. The case was blown, but there was still a chance of salvaging something. There wouldn't be any stickup on Monday, but Tommy might postpone the job instead of canceling it. Yellow Shirt was the key.

At the lavatory, there was a modest amount of traffic, with two or three men going in and out every minute. After five minutes, she figured Yellow Shirt had business that couldn't be finished standing up—maybe the sound of the siren had a laxative effect. Most of the men went in alone, aside from a father and a young boy entered together. Another man, another, a pair. The father and the boy walked out. Ten minutes. Was there something else going on? Was Yellow Shirt looking for a different kind of relief? She couldn't go inside, and she didn't want to summon Ed back from his observation point. Where was Al? Twelve minutes.

And then Al walked up to her, eyes wide, eager for news. She hissed at him, "Yellow Shirt's in the john. He must be constipated. Check it out."

As Al disappeared inside the lavatory, Ed began to drift back toward Marie. He lifted his hands, palms up—*What gives?*—and Marie raised one hand in response, palm out: *Halt, wait.* A moment later, Al emerged, holding a yellow shirt in one hand, a tweed cap in the other. That was it. The day was over, and the case was done. Marie had underestimated the inside man, his slickness and quickness. As for the competence of certain of her own colleagues, she tried not to dwell on it. After all, it was her day off, and it was a sunny weekend, and she could get back to her zucchini. Ed, Al, and Marie looked at one another for a moment, and then they walked away as wordlessly as Tommy and Yellow Shirt had, minutes before. They were finished, and there was nothing more to say.

18 YOU WIN FRIENDS AND INFLUENCE PEOPLE

Sentence first—verdict afterwards.

—Lewis Carroll
Alice's Adventures in Wonderland

JULY 20, 1964
1615 HOURS

Someone had to be punished, that much was clear. On Monday after-noon, Lt. Macken was terse and impassive as he informed them of their assignments: Marie and Al were confined to the office for the next two weeks to update the mug shot files. Ed would be assigned to a steady midnight shift at a Brooklyn hotel, guarding a witness to a homicide. The lieutenant left as soon as his instructions were complete. There were no questions or comments until Al stuck his head out the window to confirm the departure. When he saw Macken and the Farmer on the sidewalk below, he took a coffee mug from the nearest desk and made to hurl it at them, until Ed grabbed his hand.

"Son of a bitch!"

"Stop! And take it easy! That's my coffee mug!"

"Son of a bitch!"

"Stop," Ed said. "Don't worry, kids. I got friends downtown, and I talked to a lot of 'em today. They know Macken made a mess of it."

If they'd harbored any doubts the case was over, the wiretap laid them to rest hours before. Cheech called Tommy to tell him about Fifi, who had passed away over the weekend. Tommy responded, "The job is dead and buried, too. Pass on my condolences to the widow, because it's too hot for me to stop by the wake."

And they'd found out about what had happened in Hoboken, because

323

Ed had driven out to talk to the cops there. He was dressed in a navy blue pinstriped suit, his Emerald Society pin prominent on his lapel. He'd found the guy who'd been stuck with Macken, and, after the first, defensive reaction—"It wasn't me! It wasn't us who screwed up!"—Ed learned the story of the siren. When the ice cream truck pulled up to the park, it had blocked the lieutenant's view. Macken leaned out the window, screaming at the driver to move on, and drew an upraised middle finger in response. Inside the police car, there was a switch on the instrument panel that changed the horn to a siren. With the NYPD cars, there were two positions—up and down, for horn and siren—but with the new models Hoboken had just acquired, there were three, in a triangle, for horn, siren, and klaxon. Their case had been destroyed by the half-inch flick of an infinitely idiotic thumb.

"So take it easy," Ed concluded, gently removing the coffee mug from Al's hand. "The bosses know who handed Tommy his get-out-of-jail-free card. Take it from me—you're not gonna spend the next two weeks getting paper cuts, and I'm not gonna spend any nights in Brooklyn hotels."

As Ed walked out of the office, Al began to follow, hectoring him with questions, but he wouldn't answer. Marie and Al fretted for an hour until the order came over the teletype: *All personnel assigned to borough burglary squads are to report to the Safe, Loft, and Truck Squad at 0800 hours.*

As a title, "Safe, Loft, and Truck" had all the glamor of a label on a packing crate, but it was one of the most elite units on the Job. They didn't deal with amateurs: safes attracted safecrackers; lofts were commercial warehouses, and those that held furs or high-end electronics were well-defended; and trucks didn't stop unless men with guns stopped them. The heists were associated, more often than not, with one of the organized crime syndicates. That there had never been a corruption scandal at SLATS was a matter of deserved pride. The selection process was rigorous, and only men with exceptional arrest records and impeccable reputations were allowed in. To have a "rabbi"—cop slang for any kind of patron, whether police, political, or clerical—never hurt, but neither was it enough to win assignment. A man's record and reputation had to be of his own making.

Unlike the rest of the department, where somebody's rabbi might be an actual rabbi, SLATS had its own idea of kosher. Aside from a few stray Italians or Poles, the squad was overwhelmingly Irish and devoutly Catholic. A number of senior detectives served as a confidential squad for the Archdiocese, dealing with problem priests who risked scandal, either by arrest or blackmail. Membership in the Holy Name Society was assumed, and weekend retreats at one of the friaries or monasteries around the city, once or twice a year, were customary. There were no divorced men in the squad. Church and state were in unison there, and bad men feared them.

Marie did not expect to be welcomed aboard. Until yesterday, SLATS had been a proud island of the chosen hundred, where no one was admitted except after long quarantine; overnight, a fleet had run aground on its shores, depositing seventy-odd refugees with dubious papers. In a way, the men of SLATS were like a hundred trousered Melchionnes, except for the lack of vowels at the end of their names. And she was delighted to see Lt. Macken get a cold shoulder from their captain the next morning, when he strode up to shake his hand at the auditorium at headquarters.

The captain was military in bearing, tall and regular in his features, but when he addressed the group, his voice wasn't any louder than if he'd been chatting with friends in his kitchen. Few heard what he said beyond the first rows. Marie was close enough to catch enough: all of this was regrettably unexpected, and everyone was to continue working as before. There was a choral mutter of *What-what-whats?* in the cheap seats before he declaimed his last words, which filled the room. "That's all. Dismissed. However, all females, all policewomen should follow me over to the room to the left."

The captain walked away as the women rose from their seats, slowly and warily. There were eight in all. Marie knew three, no four, from the Policewomen's Endowment Association—none terribly well, but they were all workers, real cops. It felt as if some terrible test or ritual awaited them. One was a Negro, and another was Jewish. Marie reproached herself for taking comfort in the idea that they might be even more undesirable than she was. Would it matter? Eight would go into the room. How many would leave? It was said that you could tell a witch if she floated. Maybe the captain was leading them to a pool of water. Oy vey. Marie missed her old rabbi.

After the ladies filed in to the appointed chamber, the captain shut the door. He did not prolong the suspense. For what it was worth, none were singled out. And none had a problem hearing him. "I do not want women in my squad. I have never tolerated a woman here, and I do not intend to start now. I've only called you in to tell you that if you have any preferences as to where you'd like to be assigned, I would suggest that you make whatever telephone calls you can, because I intend to get you transferred forthwith."

The women stared at him, agape. They were finished before they'd begun, sent away as abruptly as yesterday's teletype had ordered them to come. They couldn't go back to their old squads; they didn't exist anymore. Where would they be tomorrow? What if they had no favors to call in?

The captain tempered his tone as he went on. He didn't intend to be cruel but fatherly, it seemed, as if he were telling his teenage daughter she would not be going to the movies on Friday, no matter how nice the boy seemed to be. "Otherwise, I wish you the very best. This is nothing personal. I don't want my men distracted. I have good men here, and I don't want them to get in trouble.

"I mean this without any disrespect. I'm going over right now to the Chief of Detectives to request that all of you are transferred out of my command. I am confident that he'll understand. I'll tell him that my men are just not equipped to work with women."

The shock had worn off, and the way the captain kept on yapping made Marie angry. What did he want from them, a thank-you card? If they weren't staying, she wasn't going to sit and listen. And she certainly didn't have to bother with making a good impression. "What kind of equipment do you think they'll need, Captain?"

The captain couldn't believe Marie had missed his point so completely. When he realized that she hadn't, his mouth tightened and he walked out. The other women looked at her, some admiring, others appalled. All were amazed that she'd mouthed off to a boss on their first day in the squad, even if it was also their last.

Back in the auditorium, Marie apprised her partners of the news, as did the other women with their respective teams. She was cheered when Ed pointed out that, until there was a formal order by the Chief of Detectives, the policewomen would remain assigned to SLATS, no matter who was unhappy about it. Her hopes rose for a moment, and then they fell again when a sergeant approached her.

"Carrara? You have to see the inspector."

The captain reported to the inspector. She wondered if her wisecrack about equipment had been wise; maybe she'd be the only policewomen who wouldn't remain. She trudged to the inspector's office grinding her teeth, resolved to keep her mouth shut.

The inspector's hair was white, his skin pale to the point of transparency, and his eyes were so barely blue that they looked like a drop of ink in a quart of milk. He didn't rise to meet her or shake her hand, and he looked at her only briefly before returning his attention to papers on his desk. "Sit down, sit. So, you're in one of my squads, eh? What did you say your name was?"

Marie was elated that he hadn't asked about the captain, but he cut her off before she finished saying her name. "What? Could you spell that? Hmm. What kind of name is that? Italian? I see. Are you married? Oh, all right, it's your husband's name. What church were you married in? Uh-huh. Are you there now? What parish are you in now?"

He badgered her with questions that had nothing to do with police work, and her replies seemed to baffle and irritate him. "How many children do you have? Two? That's all?

"What's your maiden name? Panza—what? I won't even try to spell that, it's even more Italian than the other one. What school do you send your daughter to? Public school? What's wrong with the parish school?"

Marie didn't want to talk to him anymore. They didn't want her here, and she wasn't exactly crazy about them, either. But it was better to play nice. The interview itself could be taken as a sign that the policewomen were staying put, at least for the time being. As the subject of family seemed to be of such abiding concern, Marie redirected the talk to the two photographs on his desk. One was of an older woman, the other of a young man. "Is that your son? What an attractive boy. You must be very proud of him."

"Yeah, that's him all right," the inspector replied, without the slightest trace of warmth. He lifted his eyes from his papers and stared at the picture. "I used to have great faith in him, but he let me down. He let me down terribly."

Marie felt pity for him and then grew anxious. Was the boy in prison? Was he dead? Did he run away to join the circus? Not for nothing, but if the kid was a disaster, why was his picture on the desk? Marie didn't believe the next thing she'd say would be any more apt than the last, but it was too painful to sit there in silence.

"I'm so sorry, Inspector. Maybe, maybe it was something he couldn't help?"

That was innocuous enough, wasn't it?

"Oh, he could help it, all right. No one forced him, no one made him do anything. Did everything to try and stop him, for my part."

"What did he do?"

She had to ask, didn't she? Maybe it would be for the best if the captain succeeded in his mission with the chief, and she was sent somewhere far away. The inspector's voice rose in anger as he repeated the question, "What did he do?" And then it trailed off in disgust. "What he did was marry a Guinea."

Marie heard what he said, but the words lodged in her ears without moving to her brain. She knew how daft it must have sounded when she suggested, "She must have been a lovely girl, for him to have picked her."

The inspector glared at the photograph as if it were a mug shot. "And now, to add insult to injury, they've got a half-breed son. I never even let one in my squad before. Now I got one in my own family!"

It may have been that when the second slur landed in her ears, it pushed the first one farther inside, and the neon malice lit up in her mind like Times Square. "That's your grandson you're talking about!"

The inspector seized the silver frame and shook it, yelling, "He's no grandson, he's a goddamn half-breed!"

Marie jumped up, toppling her chair, and shouted as she left the office, "That's the best blood your family ever had! *Ciao, gentilissimo Ispettore!*"

When she returned to the auditorium, Ed ran to greet her, his smile bright and wide. "Great news, Marie! The Chief of Ds told the captain to take a hike—you're staying!"

"Let's get some breakfast."

After she told Ed and Al about the second interview, neither offered any empty assurances that things would work out in the end. She wasn't wrong, but what she'd done just wasn't done. She'd be back on matron duty tomorrow, she guessed. Maybe even brought up on department charges, as her insubordination had risen from rank to rank. They decided to make the best of their last day together. They ate quickly and went to work, tight-lipped and resolute.

But in the postriot quiet, the Manhattan streets were anxious, hunkered down. They rolled from the Bowery to Hell's Kitchen without seeing anyone spit on the sidewalk. By midday, she insisted on driving back to her car to get her old leopard-skin fedora from the trunk. Any kind of luck was better than no luck at all. It was after four when they dropped by the Automat at Eighth Avenue for some iced tea. Their mood was grim.

Marie's saw the man filling his cup at the coffee spigot and paid him little mind. He looked like a working stiff, in a tan summer suit and straw boater. But when he noticed her, his glance was anything but casual. He was a light-skinned black man with a lean build, clean-shaven, in his late twenties, and he looked exceedingly pleased to see her. She didn't recognize him, but her guard was up, and she alerted Ed and Al when he approached. His demeanor was anything but hostile, but they didn't often run into old fans of their work. Marie studied his face, searching her memory. *Nope.*

"Hey, guys! I can't believe I ran into you," the man said, shaking his head, his voice almost bashful. "How are you doing?"

"Just fine," Ed replied cheerily, though his eyes never left the man's hands. "And yourself?"

"Better than fine," the man said. He looked at Marie and smiled. "Better than ever. How's the baby?"

Marie tried harder to concentrate, to recall. *Nada. Niente.* Who the hell was this guy? "The baby's fine, thanks."

"Was it a boy?"

"Yeah, it was a boy," she said, making an effort to smile. "He's a real tiger."

"I knew it! I just had a feeling."

This was killing her. Couldn't Al or Ed step up here and admit that they'd forgotten his name? She kicked Al under the table, and he flinchingly followed her lead. "Don't take this the wrong way, buddy," he said. "But I'm better with names than faces. Who are you?"

The man laughed. "None of you know, do you? After all we done together? Nah, I don't mind. I'm glad I look different, because I am."

There was no meanness in his voice, but there was nothing familiar about him. Bupkes. She asked, "Can you give me a hint?"

The man put his coffee down and paused to consider. His face was suddenly transfixed with pain, his eyes half-closed, mouth open, showing his teeth. Tilting his head to the left, he leaned right and brought up his right hand to the shoulder.

Marie shouted, "No!" and the patrons around them started. Now, she got it! Ed and Al reached for their guns. "Oliver!" she cried. "Theodore Oliver!"

Oliver had reenacted his pose from the front page of the *Daily News.* He put his hands up, as if to say, "You got me!" Or maybe it meant, "Don't shoot!"

Marie jumped up and hugged him. Maybe that was a little much; when she looked over at her partners, they weren't smiling. She didn't care. She was delighted to see Oliver. She wasn't ashamed she hadn't recognized him—the man who stood before her was truly not the man she'd chased down that afternoon. Had it been ten months before? "Look at you! You could be a movie star. Look at you!"

She stepped back to take him in. "You look great, you really do. Tell me, what's going on? How have you been since . . . since that day?"

"The day she shot you," Ed added helpfully.

"Yeah. Since then? Well, I cleaned up, that's the main thing," Oliver said, his effusive tone shifting to the contemplative. "I did six months. I'm not proud of what I did, who I was, but I gotta tell you, I was kind of famous in jail. Not everybody gets shot by a lady cop. A pregnant lady cop! But, believe me, they get the newspapers there, too, and there was guys who asked me for autographs. Anyway, I got clean. And I'm gonna stay clean. I'm working. My wife took me back. My kids thought I was in the Army. It's good. Yeah. It's all good now."

For a moment, Marie thought Oliver would break down as he counted his blessings, and that she might shed a few tears as well. He recovered, smiling again.

"And you?" he asked. "All good with you?"

Marie nodded.

"The baby's healthy? Good. I won't take up any more of your time. I was just coming by, and I saw that hat with the spots, and I couldn't believe it. I couldn't. I didn't think I'd ever get the chance to let you know. To say . . . thanks?"

"Thank me by staying as good as you are," Marie replied, clasping his hand. "Honest to God, you really made my day, Mr. Oliver. I'm so glad you came up and said something. Take care of your wife and kids."

"I will. God bless."

"God bless you, too." As Oliver walked away, Ed called out, "And stay away from pregnant ladies with guns!"

Oliver laughed and waved. Al didn't know what to say, and he got up from the table to call the office to check in. Ed waited a while before he offered any comment. "You know, I'm glad he found Jesus and all that, but he could have said he was sorry for trying to knock my head off with that suitcase."

Marie nodded.

"It's still could have been me who shot him," he went on. "But who gets the credit? Not the Irishman, not the first-grade detective. All the bosses, all the papers, they have to make it a big whoop-de-doo about the new Italian chickadee, just because she's got a bun in the oven. Is that fair? I ask you, is it?"

Marie shrugged.

"Aren't you glad that you shoot like a girl?"

Marie rolled her eyes. Ed stood up. "I'm going to get us a couple more ice teas."

Marie nodded. She didn't want to talk, just yet. What had just happened? She felt as if she'd never done a truly good thing before. How could that be? Maybe it was because what she'd done—what cops did—was always on the negative side: You stopped bad things, bad people. She'd stopped hundreds of them, at least for a while, from Mr. Todd to Mrs. Abbie, Nunzi and Gino, from Dr. D. and his nurse to thieves and killers like Shep. But the damage had already been done, sometimes beyond repair. The highest score in the game was zero. For Theodore Oliver to pop out of nowhere and say she'd saved his life—on today of all days, maybe her last as a real cop—made her so happy it hurt. She listened to the nickels drop into the chambers for plates of macaroni salad and cherry pie. Ed came back with the iced tea. He raised his glass for a toast.

"Here's looking at you, kid," he said. "I had an idea, and I want you to hear me out. The captain, the inspector, the rest of them at SLATS, what they said to you, what they think about us, it's stupid and ass-backwards. No two ways about it. But think about it, from their point of view. They were high society, they were the fanciest joint in the city—the Stork Club, or 21. And then somebody downtown gets a bright idea, decides overnight that they're the YMCA."

"I get it," Marie said, "I just—"

"Hear me out," he went on. "All over the city, they're knocking things down. Nice old things, that just worked just fine. Did you hear how they want to bulldoze through Greenwich Village to make an expressway? I don't know how they come up with this stuff. A place like SLATS, it took a long time to build. The detectives there are as good as any in the world. They're like the Yankees. Good men, too—the only money in their wallets is their own. I've been around longer than you, Marie, and I can tell you, a great detective and a good man, they're not the same. There are men on this Job, honest as the day is long, who couldn't catch a ground ball. Baseball, I'm still talking baseball. Some of the best players in the game, from Ty Cobb to Mickey Mantle, they were no choirboys. You follow me?"

"I follow, I get it. We're a bunch of rubes with the Alabama Mud Hens, who showed up at Yankee Stadium."

"Well, with you and Al, definitely. Me, it's a little different. Anyway, maybe it's better, you think of the place as the Mayo Clinic, and—"

"Stop! Yes, it's the best! Carnegie Hall! West Point! Nathan's Famous Hot Dogs! Super-duper, we have to prove ourselves, and so we'll work our little heinies off, and one day the captain who hates women, and the inspector who hates Italians, they'll wake up and want enough Italian broads to make a Fellini movie!"

"A what?"

Marie shook her head and covered her eyes. She felt a headache coming on. She wondered if they were having a fight, and then she wondered why. She was still a little dazed from the Oliver visitation. And she was aggravated by the lectures. Was he defending the bosses to her? Ed wasn't waiting for a teletype that would send him to the dark side of the moon. She took pains not to raise her voice. "What is it then? What should we do?"

"Do I have to spell it out?"

Now, she was angry, but she kept her mouth shut. Ed had a solemn look when he reached across the table and took her hand. "I think you should shoot them, Marie. The captain, first, and then the inspector. Not because I want them dead, but people who you shoot seem to like you, later on."

Marie took hold of one of Ed's fingers and began to bend it back. He smiled and said nothing, even as his old digits felt the well-deserved pain. She glared at him and then let him go before she might really hurt him. "Fine. Can I shoot Macken, too?"

"Absolutely," he said, shaking his fingers. "But that's a different job. With the other bosses, I just want you to wing them, so they have a change of heart after they convalesce. With Macken, you can aim straight between the eyes."

Marie shook her head and smiled. If this was to be their last day together, it was a fine way to say goodbye. She expected Al to return from the pay phone with bad news, but his expression told of something else altogether.

"Marie, you're on a new case tomorrow, with a couple of the old boy crew from SLATS. Some kind of hotel caper. Dress fancy."

Marie thought he was joking, at first, but it wasn't the kind of joke that Al made. He was smiling. Marie didn't want to look at Ed, just yet. They'd been struggling with the idea that she'd be the one left behind. Ed was speechless for a second, and then ten. He snatched the fedora from Marie's head and dropped it on his own. "I think I'll hold on to your lucky hat until we're back together again. Somehow, I think we'll need it more than you."

"I'll be back before you know it," she said, forcing a grin. She drank her tea. "Don't worry, boys, I'll wrap this one up quick, and we'll be together again in a jiff." Just to be safe, she touched the brim of her hat before they left.

THE NEXT AFTERNOON, Marie met the two detectives she'd work with on the case. She couldn't call them partners. It seemed adulterous to even think of them that way, while Ed and Al were wearing black armbands until her return. Vince Murtagh and Casper Duggan, as they introduced themselves. As Casper did, strictly speaking; Murtagh offered a polite handshake, but he said nothing. He could have been a G-man on TV, tall and imposing, with grim, square features and straight white teeth. Casper was slighter and fairer, jokey, almost dandyish. His camel-hair sport coat and bow tie would have been frowned on had he worn it to the office. Ed had found out that both were first-grade detectives, and favorites of the captain. Casper explained that they had arranged for a suite on the sixth floor of the St. Moritz, across the hall from where the people they were after would be staying. He and Marie would park themselves in the lobby until they arrived, while Murtagh took up his position inside the room.

Casper was affable, but he said little more than his partner had about the case. Marie didn't know who they were looking for, or why. She didn't know if they'd asked for her, or if someone in SLATS knew something about her. Dress up, they told her. *Shut up*, she'd told herself, though she didn't regret mouthing off to the bosses the day before. She was in a ladies-who-lunch outfit, a flowered silk dress and straw hat, white gloves, pearls. She'd stowed her suitcase with other wardrobe options upstairs in the suite.

At five in the afternoon, an hour after they'd settled in the lobby, Casper tapped her on the hand. Marie saw an elegant trio approach the front desk, a man with a woman on each arm, and a train of luggage in tow. Three porters with carts bore what must have been ten pieces altogether, including two steamer trunks. Whoever they were, they weren't taking pains to avoid attention. Casper rose and Marie followed, linking arms as they strolled past them. When she saw them up close, she wanted to whistle—one was prettier than the next.

"Yes, Mr. Borrato, we have you down for a suite on the sixth floor," said the clerk, scanning the ledger. "Room 600."

Mr. Borrato was in his midtwenties, tall and slim, with a loose suit of cream-colored linen, and a deep blue silk shirt, unbuttoned at the top. To his left was a swan of a blonde, her hair swept up in a bouffant, in a tight pink top and black toreador pants. On his right was a lanky brunette in a low-cut peasant blouse. All wore sunglasses, and all smoked cigarettes in silver holders. They could have been models or movie stars. Just passing them made Marie want to fix her makeup.

In the elevator, Casper released Marie's arm and shook his head. "If I saw this guy when I was eighteen, I think I'd'a given the life of crime some very serious consideration. And all that luggage! I think we might be here for the long haul."

Marie smiled but said nothing. She'd remain in good-girl mode, seen and not heard. As they arrived at their room on the sixth floor, she saw they had a problem. Why hadn't she noticed when she'd dropped off her suitcase? They were across the hall from Borrato & Co., but not directly—one door was five feet down from the other, and if the detectives looked through their peephole, they'd only have a view of the wallpaper. Marie was about to break her vow of silence when she saw the new hole in the door, freshly drilled from the inside, at an angle. There were still wood shavings around the perimeter. Casper brushed them off and stuck a lens into the peephole. "They're right behind us," said Casper, as Murtagh opened the door. "Did management make a fuss about your drilling?"

Murtagh grunted and walked away. Marie was impressed. Murtagh had an attaché case open on the coffee table with a few carpenter's tools beside it. He wouldn't be doing any tails, Marie guessed. He could be in polka-dotted pajamas and still look as stiff and official as an admiral of the fleet. Casper had a valise, and he took out a dark suit and two ties—one red, one blue—to hang in a closet. Marie had a much larger suitcase, and the men stared as she unpacked a dowdy blue gown, as if she were the mother of the groom; a dark suit, proper and professional; and a black dress and spangled jacket she might wear if she were going out cocktailing. There were two wigs, two hats, three purses, and a makeup kit with sufficient powders and paints to cover a chorus line. Now, the men were impressed. Casper asked, "Do you mind if I ask you a personal question, Marie?"

"Not at all."

"Does it take you a while, to get ready in the morning?"

"It all depends on what I'm getting ready for."

Casper nodded, and Murtagh took up his post by the peephole. There were two bedrooms in the suite, on either side of the sitting room, and Casper told Marie to take one. She hoped this wouldn't be an overnight job, but she'd warned Katie to prepare for the possibility. When she returned to the sitting room, she saw Casper with a deck of cards, setting up for a game of solitaire. Murtagh returned briefly from the door to give Casper the thumbs-up before resuming his position. Casper nodded, walked over to the house phone, and gave instructions to the hotel manager: "Let me know if they order room service or whatever. Don't let their dinner come at the same time as ours. Check their calls, too, ingoing and outgoing, every hour."

Half an hour later, the phone rang again. "I see," said Casper. "What did they order?" Hanging up, he called to Murtagh, "They're eating in, Vince. Lobster Thermidor for three, a bottle of champagne, a pot of coffee. Getting ready for a long night. So should we, don't you think? What'll it be, Vince, the usual? Three steak sandwiches, extra well-done, six baked potatoes, and ten bottles of Coca-Cola?"

"Fine," said Murtagh, walking over to collapse on the sofa. He didn't seem tired; it was as if he were shutting his body down to conserve energy. Casper picked up the room service menu and perused it before handing it over to Marie.

"No thanks," she said. She had a ten-dollar bill in her wallet and a few singles. "I brought a tuna sandwich from home. If you get a pot of coffee, though, I'm in."

Murtagh seemed to rise slightly from his seat, and Casper pressed the menu into her hands. "Don't worry, it's 'on the arm.'"

On the arm. Marie didn't know where the term came from, but it meant that the police weren't paying. There were cops who wouldn't have noticed if their uniforms didn't have pockets, for all the times they reached into them to pay for lunch. During her last hotel detail, room service was complimentary. The hotels were desperate to have the cops there, and they fell all over themselves to keep the men happy. As they weren't free to leave their rooms, Marie didn't feel bad about not paying, and she'd have a bowl of soup or a sandwich when her team put in an order. She always made sure the bellboy got a tip. Still, there were a few who made regular pigs of themselves, eating as if it were their last meal before the electric chair. Over the years, Marie had heard more than a few sneering jokes about freeloading cops. She wouldn't be one of them. Three sandwiches seemed a little excessive, even for a man the size of Murtagh.

"Well," said Casper, looking briefly over at his partner, "Unless you have a Thanksgiving turkey in that suitcase of yours—and it wouldn't surprise me—you should have more than a tuna sandwich. We'll only get food sent up once, and we may be here through tomorrow. I'm getting a hamburger now, and a roast chicken I can eat later."

Marie nodded. "I'll get the same. Medium rare, for the burger."

"Good. That's the way I like it," said Casper. He looked at Murtagh and shook his head. "Extra well-done! That should be against the Geneva Convention, burning a steak like that."

Marie ventured a smile, but Murtagh remained stone-faced as he rose and walked back to the door. Casper called in the order. "I don't know how long it takes to make Lobster Thermidor," he said, after he hung up. "I don't even know what it is. But I bet it takes more time than it does to burn a steak."

When dinner arrived, Casper directed Marie to one of the bedrooms. There was too much food arriving for three people; maybe it would look like Murtagh was setting up a card game. They ate quickly, without talking. Murtagh waited for Casper to eat before leaving the door, and Casper watched while Murtagh ate. Marie went back to her bedroom and tried on a black sweater over her flowered dress. The two girls with Borrato were too stylish not to notice what other women were wearing. Better to change, she thought. She checked her watch—just after seven—and decided on the dark suit.

When she came back out, she saw Casper had changed his tie, but he still wore the camel-hair jacket. Too distinctive, she thought, especially if they were a pair again, but she decided to keep her complaints to herself. They sat in silence for an hour, eyes half-closed, until Murtagh came back from the peephole. "He's out with the blonde."

"Did he go left or right?" Marie asked. The elevator banks were to the right, the fire stairs to the left.

"Left. My left. Left from where I stood," replied Murtagh.

Marie had guessed what the job was, but now she knew. "Whaddaya say we give them a minute to get where they're going. They went to the stairs, not the elevator, so they're not working the place from the top down. Let me go alone, at first; they won't make me. I'll cover a couple of floors, above and below, see if we can see what they're checking out."

Casper nodded and turned to Murtagh. "Works for me. We still have the second girl inside the room. I can tail her if she goes someplace."

Murtagh noted the time in a pad and returned his attention to the peephole. Marie darted back to her bathroom for a final check in the mirror. Murtagh opened the door for her to leave and quietly shut it behind her. Marie descended to the fifth floor and waited by the fire door, listening. When she heard nothing, she stepped out into the hall. Rounding the corner, she saw the blonde knock on a door. As Marie walked past, it opened on a man in late middle age, highball in hand, his tie loosened.

"Yes, Miss?"

"Oh, my God," the blonde cried. "I'm sorry! I'm here to meet my . . . uncle. Is this room 627?"

"No, honey," came the reply. "It's 527, but if you'd like to make yourself comfortable, I'd be happy to call your uncle. I'd be happy to be your uncle!"

"Oh, you!" she cooed, walking away. As Marie turned another corner, she saw Borrato leaning down to tie his shoe, a massive suitcase on the floor beside him. She went to the elevator and took it back up to six. Murtagh opened the door before she could knock. He followed to the sitting room, where Casper was untying his tie.

"That was quick," he said.

"They are, too," Marie said. "And they've got a good scheme. I saw blondie start on the fifth floor. Whoever answers the door, they're not sorry to see a beautiful girl. And if nobody's home, Borrato goes in and fills his suitcase. Most everybody's out now—at dinner, the theater, whatever. I bet they're on the go until eleven, switching up the blonde and the brunette, floor by floor. Maybe they sleep in the morning, do another round, when the 'Maid, please clean room' signs are up."

Murtagh almost smiled, and Casper laughed. "Good stuff, Marie. Great. I heard great things about you, and now I know why. I didn't bring the wardrobe you did, so I don't think I should move around that much. Maybe you can put on the dowager duchess dress, at ten or so, and cover a couple of floors. At midnight, I can splash some scotch in my face and stagger around with you in the little black number. That way, we got a better chance of running into 'em when they're hitting rooms. With all that luggage, they could walk away with half the hotel, down to the spoons and the doorknobs."

Marie nodded. It wasn't the worst idea. With her wigs, makeup, and costumes, she could make herself into someone ready to accept an Academy Award or a welfare check. She could pass by Borrato and his girls three or four times without being made. Still, there was a risk, and there was no reason to take it. Every time they opened their door, they could bump into one of their neighbors from across the hall. "Casper, that's a helluva plan," she replied, cautiously. "Pardon my French, but it is. And I know I'm the new kid here, but you know what's better than doing something?"

"What?"

"Nothing. Let them clean the place out. They're going to go room to room. We don't have to catch them in the act. We just can't let them leave the hotel. I can't believe they'll stick around tomorrow, once everybody starts noticing what's missing. All their swag, it's gonna be in the suitcases and steamer trunks. As long as we don't lose the lovebirds and the luggage, the less we do, the better. They parked a car here, in the garage?"

Murtagh answered, "1964 Cadillac El Dorado, gold with white interior, Florida plate number—"

"Glad to hear it," Marie said. "Whaddaya say, we wait until the nice people across the hall are finished for the night, and then one of you goes down to the garage and borrows the spark plugs from the El Dorado. Come the morning, I'll cover the lobby again, just to be safe."

When she saw Casper smile, Marie indulged herself in a moment of vanity. She'd just showed up a pair of first-grade detectives. "So, boys, what do you think?"

Murtagh picked up his second steak sandwich and returned without comment to the door. The high-handedness felt cold as a slap to Marie. Casper shook his head and scooped up his deck of cards. "How long you been on the Job, Marie?"

"Eight years."

"Really?"

"Going on eight. Just after seven."

"I find that hard to believe. And how long have you been a detective?"

"I'm still not."

"Really? I can't believe that, either. Don't mind Vince. What he just told to you was 'Great idea! That's the plan!' He's just got a funny way of saying it. Sweet dreams, Marie. I'll arrange for a wake-up call at five."

And so Marie went to bed early, mostly placated. When she called home, she chatted with Sandy for a while, and she was profuse in her apologies to Katie, but she had a better night's sleep than she'd had in months. She didn't need the wake-up call. She watched the first light break over Central Park. She put on her dark suit, did her hair and makeup, and had a few bites of her cold chicken. There was no sign that Casper had risen, but Murtagh still stood sentry at the door.

"Are they in?"

"Got in about midnight," he grunted. He didn't take his eye from the peephole until he opened the door for her to leave. Downstairs, she sat in the lobby, ordered coffee, and began to read the papers. It was six in the morning. At seven, one of the staff began to look at her warily. She beckoned him over, instructing him with regal brevity to bring more coffee and the manager. More coffee and pastries were delivered, and she was left alone until after nine. She'd worked through all the New York papers, *Look*, *Life*, and *Time* and was midway through *El Diario* when a clerk walked over to her with a look of confused apology. "Are you Marie?"

"Yes," she said, lowering her paper slightly.

"Casper says to say, 'Boo!'"

"Thank you," she said, resuming her reading. Minutes later, Casper and Murtagh arrived in the lobby, just before the guests and goods from room 600 made their procession to the front desk. After Mr. Borrato paid his bill, the clerk who relayed the ghostly message to Marie had the same look of contrition when he told Borrato that there was some trouble with the car. A mechanic had been summoned to the garage. Borrato said that he understood and asked where he might find the men's room. The two women began to trail away, too, but the three detectives intercepted the three thieves and escorted them out the back. Their exit was as stylish as their entrance had been, as the cops who hustled them into waiting cars looked like celebrity bodyguards, sparing them the press of paparazzi. The flashbulbs popped in plenty, later on at the precinct, where the luggage was sent. There was a department store's worth of furs inside—mink and chinchilla and sable—as well as jewelry, cash, and traveler's checks. The brunette began to cry, "I knew we shoulda got breakfast before we left!"

Casper called the manager at the St. Moritz, and trays of fresh fruit, smoked salmon, and eggs Benedict were spirited to the squad room. Admissions were shortly obtained regarding the contents of the thirty-nine rooms burglarized, which proved to be of great assistance to the hotel when it later settled claims, some of them wildly exaggerated. Marie later heard that the captain and the inspector were delighted by the results, but they didn't convey their appreciation in person. She was willing to give them time.

19 YOU'RE THE TALK OF THE TOWN

No one can make you feel inferior without your consent.

—Eleanor Roosevelt

DECEMBER 10, 1964
2220 HOURS

As the months passed, Ed, Al, and Marie went back and forth between SLATS cases—hijacks, high-end burglaries—and their old knockaround fun. Once Marie had earned the respect of Casper and Murtagh, any number of Kehoes and Callahans warmed to her. If she still got a cold shoulder now and then, she noted with pleasure that the Farmer and Macken—Irish and Catholic and men, at least on paper—were still treated with a Siberian deep freeze, with no signs of a thaw. In general, the shotgun marriage between SLATS and the burglary squads was not the happiest, even though they didn't share an office most of the time. The masterminds at headquarters who had envisioned all manners of efficiency and innovation hadn't bothered to acquire additional desks and typewriters. The coffeepot sat empty and cold amid a feud over who owed what with the dollar-a-month dues. More than once, shoving matches erupted when brown-bagged lunches went missing from the refrigerator. For Marie, life at home with Sid then was civil by comparison. She and her partners did their jobs and kept their distance. Their reputation rose steadily, collar by collar, like the balance of a bank account.

In October, they were dispatched to the Plaza Hotel, where guests had reported the loss of sixty thousand dollars' worth of jewelry over the past three months. There had been no break-ins, and only a piece or two had disappeared at a time. A maid was suspected, which meant that Marie, to her relief, wouldn't have to play one. Though it was a wonderful way

341

to operate—shuffling along the halls, beneath notice—she'd found herself cleaning toilets on more than one occasion in the past. She and Ed loved to play dress-up; Al did not. Marie took Ed to her brother-in-law Luigi's shop, where he reluctantly agreed to refrain from acquiring more greenery. Ed was so taken with a black mohair suit that he bought it, though Luigi would have gladly loaned it out for the week. Marie raided her sisters' closets for a variety of ensembles, from the daring to the demure. Al would have rather worn a straitjacket than a suit and tie, and he put in for a week's vacation. On the first day of the operation, he arranged to borrow a limousine for an hour, along with chauffeur's livery, to drop Ed and Marie at the hotel. When the doorman at the Plaza rushed out to welcome the party, Al waved him away with a white-gloved hand. Ed gave Al a dime as he led Marie away. "That will be all, Aloysius," he said.

"Go shit in your hat, mister," replied Al.

Once the luggage was retrieved, the limousine drove away. "Mr. and Mrs. Joseph Edwards" were taken up to their suite, and staff was alerted to their status as Important People, for whom Management was Particularly Concerned. Fresh flowers and champagne awaited them. The Plaza was on Central Park South, like the St. Moritz. They were on the sixth floor again, with a splendid view of the park. You could see the paths, the people, the horses and carriages, but it was high enough to take in some treetop perspective, to pretend there was a little wilderness in the heart of the city. The last time Marie had seen it from the sixth floor, the park had been misted over and green, before the dawn in high summer; now, it was late in the afternoon, late in the year, and the sun descended with red-gold light over dusky autumn leaves that fluttered away when the wind blew. She made Ed come over to the window when they opened the champagne.

Ed drained his glass, wrinkling his nose. "Not bad, this stuff, but I still don't know why people make such a big deal about it. Personally, I'd rather have a nice cold Schlitz. But we have to finish the bottle, we can't leave any behind."

"We could dump it down the sink."

"You sicken me, Mrs. Edwards. You really do, sometimes. When you say things like that, I really have to question why we stay together."

"Go shit in your hat, Mr. Edwards."

Ed refilled his glass and topped off Marie's. She sighed, and took another sip. She was in a powder blue knit suit, Italian, with royal blue piping, that she'd borrowed from Ann. Ed was in his new mohair, with a red silk tie. He didn't look bad at all. When they'd first met, he seemed half-dead. Now, he was primarily alive—no more than a quarter dead—which was a pretty terrific fraction for the old man. He leaned over and smiled wide enough for her to see his gold canine teeth. "Well then, shall we go to bed, Mrs. Edwards?"

"I thought you'd never ask."

Marie kicked off her heels and took off her jacket, and Ed took her by the hand. He downed his second glass of champagne and filled a third, offering the bottle for Marie. "No thanks, Mr. Edwards," she said. "I want to remember every moment."

"You don't mind that I knock back another?"

"Just take off your shoes before we get started. I am a lady, after all."

"That's—"

"Shut up."

Ed coughed and finished his wine. After he took off his shoes, they faced each other from either side of the bed with wary, hungry eyes. "Ready?"

"Why wait?"

And then they hopped up onto the bed and began to jump. They bounced and danced, shrieked and moaned. The pillows, the sheets, and the blankets were kicked to the side. After Marie began to sweat, she picked up a pillow and wiped her face with it. She left the bed and plopped down on a chair.

"That's enough, lover boy," she said, suddenly fearful of her partner's condition. She really did love the old fellow, which would have made his expiring in a hotel room with her too difficult to explain. "Ed! Easy! Let's get to it!"

Ed bounced a few more times, and then he also mopped himself with bedclothes. Their work was done for the night. The eight maids under suspicion had all been assigned to the 7 a.m. shift. Ed and Marie would have to be back by five-thirty to get their room ready. "See you tomorrow?"

"See you tomorrow."

They had thought of everything, it seemed, but both had gone to bed with notebooks, and they'd woken up writing in them, spelling out the details of their morning and evening routines. The next morning, Ed ordered breakfast sent up, and they went to work. Marie opened the toothpaste and squirted out a teaspoon or so into the sink. She wet two new toothbrushes with the tap and rubbed her thumbs on the bristles.

She emptied an inch of shampoo from the bottle into the tub and then ran the shower, hot, for half an hour, so the damp would stay. She rumpled up towels, dropped them into the tub, and hung them, dripping, from hooks. She took out a new pair of stockings, rinsed them in the sink, and tossed them over the shower curtain to dry. Ed brought the shirt he'd worn the night before to drape over a chair; he also brought a pair of pajamas to change into and did jumping jacks in them until they were damp in the armpits. Joining Marie in the bathroom, he opened two sticks of deodorant, wiping down the tips so they seemed worn.

When there was a knock at the door, Ed was unwrapping a cake of soap to leave under the hot water tap. Marie threw on a robe and shower cap and was dabbing cold cream on her cheeks when she answered. "One minute, just a minute!"

The young man delivered his trays on the cart and removed last night's champagne bottle, bucket, and glasses. Marie fished out a dollar from her purse. He accepted it without gratitude. Should she have been more extravagant? Rockefeller was supposed to have given dimes when he tipped at all. She checked the menu and saw the two "American breakfasts," with eggs, bacon, home fries, and toast, were three bucks apiece. *The hell with that guy!* Mrs. Edwards would give him a piece of her mind if he came back with the same attitude. Marie yelled to the bathroom, "Breakfast is ready! And you owe me fifty cents for the tip, honey pie."

"Only the vulgar speak of money so forthrightly, dearest."

They ate their eggs and bacon and scattered the crumbs from their toast. When they were finished, Marie took out a jewelry case, a pretty little box of carved teak that some moony foreign muckety-muck had given Ann. It had a double level of velvet-lined, chambered trays on brass hinges for display. She had brought in a selection of her better brooches, bracelets, and earrings and had borrowed a few other pieces. From what they'd been told, the maid-thief had a decent eye for quality, but not really a professional one. The same could be said for Marie.

Ed had worked cases in the Diamond District, however, and he'd been schooled in how to tell a real rock from a chip of glass. Out of curiosity, she slipped off her engagement ring and dropped it in the case. It had a small stone, less than half a carat, but Marie didn't doubt its quality. Not because she had any faith in Sid, but he cared too much about appearances to have his wife wear junk on her finger.

"What about this one?" she asked, pointing it out as Ed gave the contents a once-over. He'd write a detailed description of each item and its location in the box, so they wouldn't be like the victims, noticing a week later that something was missing. He picked up the ring, held it close for a moment, and dropped it. "I hope you bought it with a three-dollar bill," he said.

Marie was glad Ed's eyes were on the jewelry. Had Sid been swindled, too? She supposed it was better to have one less thing holding her back. Ed put on a pair of rubber gloves and took out a kit of battered metal, not much larger than the jewelry case. He unstoppered a glass vial of powder and extracted a long white feather from a plastic tube. After spilling some powder onto a sheet of paper, he dipped the feather into it like a paintbrush and dusted the jewelry, making sure no piece was untouched. Once he finished, he poured the remnant of the powder back in the vial and burnt the paper in the sink. He turned the gloves inside out, wrapped them in toilet paper, and stuck them in his pocket for disposal elsewhere.

As she headed to the door, he called to her, "Off so soon, Mrs. Edwards?"

"I'm afraid I'm leaving you, Mr. Edwards."

"Is our marriage over so quickly?"

"Only the honeymoon," she said.

Marie drove home to change again, packing yet another bag. She drove downtown to the office and had Ralph Marino drive her back to the Plaza. Though she'd arrived in grander style the day before, far more notice was paid when she registered again, as Miss Marie Sorell. She was in a black leather pantsuit, black boots, and a cascade of voluptuous black curls that itched slightly but was worth the sacrifice. When she looked at herself in the mirror, she thought she looked dangerous, the type who might slip a barbiturate into James Bond's martini while pretending to succumb to his rough charms. Others, she knew, would draw a less nuanced conclusion: *Hooker!* She couldn't go inside the SLATS office on Broome Street, as the captain or the inspector might see her. Instead, she called Ralph.

"Should we stop by your place? I'd love to meet your wife," she said, touching up her lipstick in the rearview mirror.

"It would be quicker if you just shot me now."

At the hotel, the bellboys broke into fistfights over who would carry her bag. She was pleased when the winner proved to be the young fellow who had delivered breakfast to Mrs. Edwards, hours before. He failed to recognize Miss Sorrell when he escorted her to #634, and he was thrilled by the same dollar tip that had left him so jaded earlier. It was nearly noon when she finished settling in. She called the desk and asked to be connected to #636. "Hello, I'm your new neighbor. Ready, Eddie?"

"I'll see if the coast is clear. I'll knock twice. You have to hustle, though."

"That's what I do."

At the signal, she slipped back into the other room. Ed whistled. "When I look at you and think about the old battle-ax I married—"

"You're not speaking of Mrs. Lennon, I trust."

"My name is Edwards. I don't know who you're talking about, but I'm sure that this Mrs. Lennon is the most wonderful woman in the world, and whoever is lucky enough to be her husband cherishes every moment he spends with her."

"That's what I thought. No bites on the jewelry, huh?"

There hadn't been. Ed had left just after Marie, and the room had been cleaned. The breakfast dishes had been cleared, and the elaborately wetted, dropped, and uncapped toiletries had been stacked neatly in the bathroom. Nothing had been taken from the jewelry box. It was disappointing, but not unexpected. They didn't know which objects might catch the thief's eye or which victims might, whether it was envy or disdain that prompted her to pocket something pretty or pricey-looking.

And that was why they constructed two very different characters as potential marks. Mrs. Edwards would be the society matron who felt entitled to every extravagance; Miss Sorrell would be the high-priced call girl who'd earned every cent the hard way. The Sorrell collection included some flashier pieces, and those, too, were dusted by Ed, and returned carefully by Marie to her room. She kept them in a closed box, unclasped, so that none of the maids who might have innocently admired a bracelet would have been chemically branded as a felon.

Ed and Marie had devised their scheme with great care, and they were meticulous in its execution. Meals or drinks were delivered to both rooms at least once a day, and the Sorrell linens required changing more often than that of the Edwardses, but not enough for it to appear that #634 was operating on a wartime footing, to meet the needs of the troops. Bottles of mouthwash were lowered daily, in quarter-inch increments. Ed would take a shower a day in his room, using both towels, while Marie would shower twice a day, next door. It wasn't exactly a demanding assignment. The only risks taken were when Marie traveled from one room to the next, a few feet down the hall. Both of them were home with their families for dinner every night, which didn't often happen. That they were on the go before dawn wasn't much of a burden in comparison.

Four days in—Thursday—they were dejected by the lack of results. The eight maids could only be rotated to their rooms so often without raising a red flag. After lunch, Ed barked at the manager when it was mentioned in passing—*Not that I'm complaining, of course*—that the rooms they occupied went for a hundred dollars a night. How did that compare with sixty thousand bucks in jewelry thefts? Still, when Marie spotted the manager as she left that afternoon, she averted her eyes and skipped out the door, as if she were dodging a bill collector.

It was more than frustration. They'd thought of themselves as hotshots, as the team to beat; they were hell-bent on proving that they were as good as any cops in the department, and they hadn't been wrong yet. But there was only so much they could do to catch an unpredictably crooked cleaning lady. Ed would go back to the office during the down time, and he reported that there was a heightened friction between the burg folks and the SLATS guys. There was a shortage of office supplies, and the coffeepot was gathering dust. Cars were being returned to the garage with an ounce of gas in the tank. Someone had stolen Murtagh's lunch. They didn't want to go back at all, let alone in defeat.

On Friday morning, after their baubles remained unmolested after breakfast, Mr. and Mrs. Edwards decided to take some time apart. Mrs. Edwards was in her blue knit suit again as she embraced her husband outside of their room. "Will you miss me?"

"I'll count the hours."

A bellman was summoned to collect her luggage, where it would be supposedly sent on to the *Queen Mary*. Marie slipped into Sorrell's room, #634. She unbuttoned her blouse to show a broad expanse of cleavage and rolled her skirt up above the knee. Wrapping a fur coat around her—Dee's silver fox—she appeared to be otherwise naked. She picked up an ice bucket and sashayed down the hall to the machine at the far end of the floor. One of the maids, an older woman, thin and stooped, glared at her as she went past. When Marie returned to #636, the woman spoke sharply to her. "Sorry, Ma'am, you must be confused. That's where Mr. Edwards is. You're next door."

Marie let loose a wicked-witch cackle as the door opened, and a bony arm yanked her in. Before the door slammed shut, she yelled back, "Mind your own business, lady!"

Once inside, Ed and Marie didn't talk much. Neither hotel nor police management was likely to allow them to go on much longer. They played hearts for an hour, and then Ed poked his head outside, where he saw the stooped woman down the hall. Marie danced out, giggling, seemingly nude but for her fur again, back to her room next door. Her purse remained on Ed's dresser, as if she'd forgotten it, with five twenty-dollar bills dusted with the chemical inside. In fifteen minutes, he left hurriedly, his hat pulled low. Maid service was requested with a sign on the doorknob. Marie had coffee sent up, and then she dressed and departed, also leaving the sign on the door. *Maid, Please Rob Room!*

After lunch, Marie was crestfallen when the Sorrell collection was untouched, but her heart leapt when she heard Ed pounding his fist on the wall. When she ran to his room, he crowed, "She bit on the cash!" They shouted with delight, again full of newlywed joy, and jumped on the bed. Ed called the manager and told him to gather the eight shady ladies in the kitchen. From the beginning of the case, Marie knew exactly what she'd say now, what she'd do. When the pots and pans stopped clanging, she could almost hear a director call "Action!"

"I am Policewoman Marie Carrara from the New York City Police Department, and this is my partner, Detective Lennon. You may wonder why you were all brought here."

As the maids stood in line, Marie walked slowly past and met their eyes, one after the other. She pictured the room going dark as she was about to name the suspect, a shot ringing out. Ed carried a portable fingerprint kit with him; Marie wished she'd brought a magnifying glass. She knew how silly it looked, how trite she sounded, but she didn't care. The cooks and busboys were spellbound, and waiters lingered at the door. Her career as a cop resembled a mystery movie about as much as her marriage did a romance. This was her Hollywood moment, and she was going to milk it for all it was worth. "One of you here is a thief," she went on. "And once you wash your hands, we will take your fingerprints. Whoever cleaned room #636 will be coming with us to the precinct to discuss the situation. It will be useless to deny that you were in the room. Follow me, please."

Marie went to the sink and turned on the tap. The ladies looked at each other nervously. A few tried to drift out of line, but Ed ushered them back in formation. As it was, all of them had left prints in the room over the past week. Marie just needed them to wet their hands; the chemical powder on the jewelry and cash reacted to water. She studied their reactions as they rinsed their hands, shaking them dry as instructed, but all were fretful, jittery. Last came the older woman who had glared at Marie. She glared again; apparently, she didn't like cops any more than she liked hookers. Marie would have bet a week's pay she was guilty when a cry went up from one of the others. Her hands were a deep orange-brown, as if she'd dipped them in iodine. "Poison! They poisoned me!"

Cut and print! The other women gasped, and the kitchen staff applauded, and the manager stammered his thanks, swearing he'd write a letter of appreciation to the police commissioner. The reviews were ecstatic: One paper told of "Mrs. Edwards, a well-heeled but wide-eyed housewife, who traipsed off innocently in her mink stole,"—they invented the mink for the story—"leaving her husband to the temptations of the fleshpots of the city. However, both housewife and harlot were one and the same . . ." After the maid was arrested, it emerged that she had convictions for prostitution, theft, and even a homicide for stabbing a john. She'd been told of Sorrell's visit to the Edwards room—the old glarer had gossiped but hadn't otherwise played a part—and judged that the straying husband wouldn't make a stink. She confessed to taking jewelry worth twice as much as the hotel had estimated and was hurt to learn she'd been robbed as well: pawnbroker receipts showed $175 for a ten-thousand-dollar watch, seventy-five dollars for a seven-thousand-dollar ring. Marie was tempted to recommend her to Three-Fingered Jack when she got out of prison.

Ed and Marie spent the night at the precinct, the morning in court. Ed had spelled her for a quick trip home for a shower and breakfast with Sandy, and she handled the arraignment. It was midday when she returned to the SLATS office, haggard but light of heart, where she was greeted by a ten-man shouting match that threatened to spill into a brawl. Another unmarked car had been left with an empty gas tank, and a borrowed typewriter had been returned with a stuck cylinder. Another sandwich had been stolen from the refrigerator. Steak, well-done, as it happened. Murtagh lumbered around the room, murder in his eyes. The inspector mustn't have been around, as the language would have made a saint's statue weep. She intended to stay out of the fracas and was chagrined to see the Farmer shared her instinct, cowering in the corner. When Ed had a quick word with him, the Farmer touched his face and went into the bathroom. The significance of the act escaped her, but she didn't have time to think about it. Ed strode up to Murtagh and bellowed, "Listen, you big stiff, I'm so goddamned sick of you! I've got more time on this Job than you, and more time on this earth, and if you think I'm gonna stand around and do nothing when you accuse—"

Repartee was never Murtagh's strength. He lifted Ed by the lapels and carried him to a window, as if to deposit him on the sidewalk, seven floors below. Men charged in to stop him, but a few threw a cheap elbow or two in the scrum. Marie was sick to see it, and she jumped in, shrieking, "What's the matter with you! Are you all a pack of kids?"

She slapped Murtagh, but she was just as angry with Ed for becoming embroiled in the foolishness. She grabbed him by the ear and dragged him away. Ed yelped, and Murtagh began to laugh until Marie turned to him, shaking a finger in his face. "Don't you go anywhere! I'll deal with you in a minute, you wooden Indian. Lay a hand on my partner again, and you'll be the one going out the window!"

For a moment, the room was silent. Ed removed his earlobe from Marie's grip. He was pale and damp with sweat, short of breath. He straightened his tie and made a dazed examination of his new suit, making sure it hadn't been torn. Looking around the room, his eyes moved in challenge from face to face, but there was no escaping his humiliation at the hands of a larger man and a smaller woman. It distressed Marie deeply, but she didn't know what else she could have done. None of it made any sense. It made no sense when Ed smiled, and even less when he turned to Murtagh, jabbing a thumb toward the entrance of the office. "Look, Vinnie. Have a look. Am I right, or am I right?"

Murtagh turned his head as directed. Though his lips curled up over his teeth, his expression didn't seem joyful. All turned to see the Farmer where he stood at the door. He had the same dimly squinting expression he customarily wore, and his skin had, for the most part, the same Spam-pink tint, but he was otherwise a different man. Around his mouth and on his hands, he was stained an intense coppery shade. There was a blotch over his eye, and both nostrils were rimmed in brown.

Murtagh grunted. Ed grinned. The Farmer looked down at his hands, and then he turned and ran. Murtagh extended a hand for Ed to shake before taking off in hot pursuit. Casper began to clap, and then the rest of the men joined in the applause. Marie grabbed Ed's earlobe again. "And you couldn't let me in on it? You son of a . . . But that chemical stuff, didn't they say at the lab that we have to be real careful? That it might cause cancer, if it gets inside you?"

"I know! I must have spilled half the bottle on that sandwich!"

All the men in the office roared and wept, and Marie nearly fell down laughing herself. She left her reports for the next day. At home, she wore rubber gloves as she cleaned the jewelry in alcohol and bleach, several times over. When she finished wiping down her engagement ring, she decided not to put it back on.

THERE HAD BEEN some interesting developments on the domestic front in recent months. When she told Sid she'd leave him unless they went to a marriage counselor, he didn't erupt or storm out. He seemed worried, almost, and said he didn't see the harm. Though he missed the appointment, even pretending to care was a change for him. When he agreed to see a psychiatrist, she was astonished, and then she was embarrassed for having believed him. She wouldn't go to the department chaplain. She'd heard of wives who sought counsel about unfaithful cop husbands, and he'd had the men fired. Cops could be fired for adultery, and a few were, every year. Marie couldn't think of many ways to make her marriage worse, but taking away Sid's paycheck was a good place to start. Still, she wanted to talk to a priest about it. Even if she were ignored or dismissed, or told to offer it up, she knew she had to try. And St. Anthony hadn't let her down yet.

On the last Sunday in November, when she went to church at Annunciation, Mass was said in English. It hadn't been a secret, but it was still a shock. With parents from Bari, Latin wasn't an altogether alien tongue, but she was still unready to hear the Word of God in a Bronx accent. Monsignor Drosnan had a thickset build, like an old boxer, and he was known for his decency. After Mass, she asked if she might meet with him. In the rectory, she'd barely worked her way through half of Sid's major felonies before he burst out, "Divorce him! Run from the bum! Listen, Marie, the Catholic Church has plenty of martyrs already. Your children need you alive. Besides, strictly speaking, we don't forbid divorce. You just can't get remarried."

Her faith remained firm when the captain called her in to his office the next day. It had only been four months since he'd tried to yank away the welcome mat before she set foot on it. Their interim conversations had been few and formal. He began awkwardly. "Sit down, Marie. I want to tell you that I've been watching you. I mean—well, you know what I mean. This is new to me. Do you understand?"

Marie thought she might, but there was no benefit to guessing. If the captain was going to apologize, he ought to come right out with it. To be a man about it, as the saying went. Of course, maybe he wasn't going to apologize, in which case she had no interest in making things easier for him. She didn't want to appear anxious, or indignant, or eager for approval, though she was all three. She nodded in reply.

"Well," he went on. "When we first met, you might recall that I told you that I would request the transfer of the policewomen assigned here."

Yes, she did remember that. The captain didn't want women here, the inspector didn't want Italians. She was still guilty on both counts.

"I still don't believe they belong here," he went on. "With one exception. I'm aware of the work you've done, and the men—my men—have spoken without exception of how highly they think of you. I misjudged you."

Marie tried not to fixate on the qualifier, "my men." Did it mean that chumps like Macken had tried to sabotage her? Or that the Farmer pointed one of his thick, brown-stained fingers in accusation? She allowed herself a smile. She couldn't have stopped herself. Was the captain still jabbering on about how wrong he was about her? How wonderful she was? Yes, that was it. *Please, Captain, do go on.*

"I would like you to stay here. The other women will move on to other assignments. Move on, or move back. I don't know and I don't care. Most of the burglary squads will go back to borough commands. Not your team. Lennon and O'Callahan will stay as well. Would you be kind enough to tell them for me?"

Even though Marie felt that the captain might have indulged her girlish glee, just then, and even though she felt it in abundance, she stood quickly and was brief in her response. "I will. Thank you, Captain."

"Thank you."

What a year, 1964! First church, then state—both were on her side. And even after the boys finally welcomed her aboard, the girls embraced her as one of their own. Mrs. M. suggested that Marie run for the board of the Policewomen's Endowment Association. She won, handily, against a first-grade detective from the Pickpocket and Confidence Squad named Marilyn Bering. Bering had a reputation as a party girl, always one of the last to leave a racket, singing "Mother Machree" at the bar with the tipsier bosses. She had an uncle who was a judge, and a brother who was a vice president in the electricians' union. Marie was happy to win, but Mrs.

M. was overjoyed, taking particular pride in informing her that the final vote count had been a landslide. Mrs. M. had played no part in Detective Bering's professional rise.

"Be patient, my dear. It will come."

Marie hadn't asked about her promotion, but Mrs. M. didn't need to hear the question. They were back at the Hotel Astor, at the Christmas party for the Detectives' Endowment Association. Marie wasn't dancing at the gala this year. She wouldn't have come at all, except that she was obliged to attend—the PEA board had to go to the DEA party, and vice versa, as did all of the department sects and factions in the round robin of social events. "You know, my sister Dee got her shield, earlier in the summer."

"I know, I sent her a note. The district attorney lobbied on her behalf."

There were over two thousand detectives in the department, but the gold shields allotted to women were few and fixed in number: thirty-seven for third grade detectives; nine for second grade, four for first. No woman would be promoted unless another retired, died, or was fired. A second-grader made sergeant's pay, a first-grader that of a lieutenant, but the prestige mattered more than the money. Marie had been in the Detective Division for a year and a half without promotion. Al O'Callahan got his shield after a few months. Ed had made second grade after three years, first grade after seven. A man in the Detective Division got his gold shield in short order, or he was sent packing.

"It's just . . . to read the list of promotions, month after month," Marie said. "Well, enough about that. What a wonderful night!" She stuck close to her old mentor as she was corralled into introduction after introduction, with boss after boss. It gratified her that all seemed to know her, but the recognition never seemed to translate into the true coin of respect. She felt like an aging orphan shopped around to childless couples in her last cute year.

"It's different for women," Sid offered, scooping Marie into his arms after sneaking up behind her. She flinched; he'd surprised her. As in past years, he'd been good to her in the weeks before the dance, and he'd be a charmer throughout the night. He kissed her and then stepped back, holding her hand. "Hello, Inspector. Merry Christmas," he said brightly. "But I'm sure you'll make it, honey. Now, you even got lady sergeants. Who'd have believed? Me, I'm all for it."

That was an overreach. He was referring to the recent court decision that allowed two policewomen to take the test for sergeant. Mrs. M. was polite to him, but not warm. Marie had never seen that before. Did Mrs. M. know something? The three stood in pained silence until Sid excused himself. Marie felt sorry for him when he left. Checking her watch, she saw that it was after ten, and she was tired. She bid goodnight to Mrs. M., and she was nearly at the coat check when she was intercepted by Casper, who was so cockeyed with holiday cheer that she felt half-sloshed at the sight of him. His pallid cheeks blazed, and he smiled like he'd just heard Santa's sleigh on the roof. "Merry Christmas, Marie! You look terrific! Isn't this always a great party, isn't this always the greatest night?"

Marie made a worried face and felt his forehead, as if for fever. "Are you okay, Casper? Try to cheer up, would you? It's Christmas!"

Casper was confused for a moment, and then he blushed, further enflaming his cheeks. He made as if to punch her, playfully, as he would if she were one of the boys, but he caught himself before he connected. "You got me, Marie. You really did! I'm so glad you're staying at SLATS. You are, right? The captain talked to you?"

"He did, and I am. Me, Ed, and Al."

"I talked to the captain, Marie. A bunch of us did. Even Vinnie Murtagh."

"I didn't know he could talk."

"Of course he—Hey, that's funny. He's a straight shooter, Vinnie. Everything's black-and-white with him. I shouldn't say, but . . . well, why not? You know what made him change his mind about you?"

Marie knew he intended a compliment, but he put her in mind of an airplane with its engine sputtering, the runway lights nowhere in sight. She braced herself for a rough landing. "What was it, Casper?"

"The tuna sandwich."

"What?"

"That you didn't want room service. You weren't looking for a free lunch, or dinner, or whatever."

Marie laughed. Here they were, safe on the ground, with nothing on fire. Murtagh was an honest cop, and now he believed Marie was, too. That was how it sounded, and she was relieved to hear it. Still, she might as well make sure nothing else was implied. She'd likely get more out of Casper now, in his whiskeyed magnanimity, than she ever would again. "Thanks, Casper. I appreciate you speaking up for me, and I can promise you, I won't let you down. And now your partner knows, not every Italian is in the Mafia."

Casper hiccupped, and Marie patted him on the back. He raised a hand, collecting his breath, and spoke quickly. "Oh, it isn't that. His wife is Italian."

That was a perfectly satisfactory reply. No prejudice for Murtagh, just a wariness about unproven partners. *Good*, she thought. Better than good. Not just not-bad, but careful, principled, correct. "What is it then?"

"He used to work in the Bronx. In the Four-Four. He knows your husband."

Marie didn't answer. Casper inhaled briefly and hiccupped again. "Sid."

Marie knew her husband's name. She said nothing.

"Yeah, Hollywood Sid," Casper went on. "Didn't like him in the Four-Four, wasn't surprised when he went to plainclothes, to Public Morals. Public Morals!"

Casper shook his head. Marie didn't want to hear any more, but she felt neither willing nor able to stop him from talking. The plane hadn't landed yet. She was still in free fall. Nothing to do except to say a prayer and hold on tight.

"And for him to get kicked out! Back to the Bronx. What kind of crook to you have to be to get kicked out of that pack of crooks?"

Casper hiccupped again and shook his head. His eyes shimmered with tender tears. "Anyway, Marie. You want a drink? No? Anyway. I just wanted you to know, how me and Vinnie thought the world of you, how you kept your hands clean, your head high. You're you. Nobody else. No matter how bad it looks, you being with such a . . . Anyway. Merry Christmas!"

Marie felt incredibly stupid she hadn't known what had happened. Was Sid an especially big crook, or an especially bad one? She felt worse when she realized she was the last to know. Mrs. M. read the Personnel Orders like a stockbroker checked the tickertape. Ed and Vinnie Murtagh had become thick as thieves after they'd poisoned the Farmer, and whatever Murtagh told Ed, Ed would have told Al. She'd been so vigilant in keeping secrets that she'd guaranteed she'd be kept in the dark as well. She never brought up Sid in conversation. Even Al talked about his wife now and then, though he was a man of few words. Marie didn't feel like an orphan anymore; she felt like an infant.

Though she'd only had a glass of wine, she drove like a drunk, drifting from her lane. When she made it home, she didn't fall asleep for a while.

The baby woke her at three. She was glad to get out of bed. She wanted to ask Sid what happened. She wanted to ask when it had happened—a week ago? Six months? It explained why her demand to fix their marriage had provoked a sad, shifty, time-buying fib, instead of an automatic smack from the back of his hand. Sid needed her, and his need was flattering. It did her no good for him to become a professional liability as well as a personal tragedy, but the adjustment was refreshing, in its way. She wouldn't kick him when he was down. She could live with this, at least for a while.

20 YOU LIVE IN INTERESTING TIMES

In the life of puppets, there is always a "but" that ruins everything.

—Carlo Collodi
The Adventures of Pinocchio

JANUARY 15, 1965
2215 HOURS

A ll of it was coming together, now that it had finally fallen apart. Marie had told her partners she'd moved out, days before, but the subject of her marriage had still not been discussed. Late on a Friday night, as the temperature dipped into the teens, they conducted a private surveillance outside the Great Northern Hotel. The man who'd made her homelife a nightmare was meeting the man who tried to derail all of their careers. Sid and Lt. Macken were in parlay, illuminated beneath a streetlight, their lying breath forming silver plumes in the frigid air.

"Jesus, Marie," said Al. "If they started fighting, which one would you root for?"

"Honest to God, Al, I can't really say."

"It must be like *Frankenstein versus the Wolfman* for you."

"Or the Hitler-Stalin pact," offered Ed, searching for a more solemn analogy.

"I wish I could hear them," she said. They were in an unmarked department car some thirty yards from their subjects. Marie had been driving, with Ed beside her, Al in the back. They cracked the windows so they wouldn't fog. "Scratch that. I don't care. Besides, I know what they're saying."

Marie hadn't seen Sid since Christmas, and she would never live with him again. The day before, she was promoted to detective. When

Commissioner Murphy handed her the gold shield, she was giddy, and she posed for photographs with her parents, her sisters, with Sandy and the baby. With Mrs. M., of course, and Ed and Al. Al had worn a suit for the occasion that almost fit. Sid had been there, too, and she heard him bellow her name when it was called—*Marriiieee!*—as if she'd stepped up to the plate at Yankee Stadium. He just had time for a quick picture with her before he had to rush back to work: "Got a big case we're working on, you know how it is, honey." When Marie kissed him goodbye, she said she hoped to see him later. She wasn't lying. She knew a good day when she saw one.

Christmas Eve was at Dee's. Each of the sisters made one of the dishes, and Mama made three, for the traditional repast of the Seven Fishes. Sid didn't appear that night, but he was at the house early the next morning with a carload of presents. Though his demotion to patrol must have come at some cost, his gifts admitted of no thrift. She and Sandy got matching Persian lamb jackets with mink collars, gold lockets, and bags of clothes and accessories from Fifth Avenue stores. Some of the clothes were too grown-up for Sandy, who was only twelve, but Marie resolved to go through the outfits with Katie and figure out what ought to go up to the attic for another year, or six. What was the rush to grow up? Packs of kiddie cousins visited to see who'd gotten the most loot, and Marie was relieved to see Sandy join in roughneck fun with Anthony, Genevieve, Little Mikey, and the rest. Marie took out her shield to examine it, over and over, and she found herself half-consciously covering her left hand with her right, to hide the missing engagement ring. It felt like she'd traded one for the other. Sid left after an early dinner. All in all, it was the most joyous holiday ever.

The next day wasn't as wonderful. The baby began to cry after midnight, and Marie was with him through dawn, downstairs on the couch, so he wouldn't wake the rest of the house. He felt a little feverish, but it was a Saturday; Marie was divided about calling the pediatrician, knowing she'd get an answering service. Katie had plans to go ice-skating with a beau, and though she offered to stay home, Marie wouldn't hear of it. She was exhausted and distracted as she began to make breakfast, dropping a bottle of milk as she took it from the refrigerator. She slipped when she tried to catch it and found herself plopped on the floor beside the broken glass, milk soaking into her robe. Pancakes and bacon were a Saturday-morning tradition, and Marie hoped that Sandy wouldn't make a stink when the menu was changed to bacon and eggs. Sandy was usually up by eight, but when Marie went to check on her, just after nine, she was greeted by a screech from the bathroom: "Privacy, *please*! I am coming! *God!* Would you please get off my back!"

Marie was in a foul temper already, and Sandy had never talked back like that before. Was this dreadful noise a kind of reveille, announcing adolescence? At first, Marie was too surprised to react; after, she knew that if she said what was on her mind, she'd regret it. And so when she was summoned back downstairs by the baby's screaming and the smell of burning toast, she retreated. The toast was dumped into the sink, the baby quieted, and the eggs went in one pan, the bacon another, when Marie heard footsteps clumping down the stairs. She took a breath. *Are we calm?* Yes. No shoes would be thrown. There would be a reasoned discussion of manners and respect. Good would come of this.

And she was taken by how pretty Sandy looked. She wore the red sweater and yellow corduroys Katie had bought her, instead of the chancier, fancier duds from Sid. Still, she looked oddly grown-up as she stood at the edge of the kitchen, shyly smiling. "Sorry I talked back, Mom. Breakfast smells good."

"Come here, you."

Marie rushed over to hug her, touched by the apology. "Merry day-after-Christmas, my dearest Sandy! Your brother wasn't feeling well last night, and so Mommy's a little cranky this morning, but—"

When Sandy peered up at her, Marie nearly choked. She wore powder, and lipstick, and eye shadow. "What the hell? What the hell is this crap all over your face? Get over here to the sink. Dammit, Sandy, I oughtta—"

She dragged her across the kitchen, indifferent to cries of protest. They'd talked more than once about Mommy's things, and what was off limits. With guns in the house, privacy had to be respected in absolute terms. They had played with cosmetics before, but the lightness of Sandy's touch—the pink on the lips, the subtlety of blush on the cheeks—was damning evidence of practice. Twelve years old! Why did her goddamned father buy her such goddamned grown-up clothes? It was effing breakfast, dammit!

"Mommy! Stop!"

Marie fought to control herself. When she realized she was failing, she let Sandy go. "Fine! But you're not going anywhere! You wash your face, right now."

Sandy began to blub, but she did as she was told. Once she finished washing, she tried to run away. Marie caught her, gently. This time, when Sandy looked up again, Marie felt her knees weaken. Her baby had a black eye, the blood vessels dark and broken. What kind of savage would punch a little girl in the face? Marie held her to keep from falling down. An electrical storm of agonized half-thoughts short-circuited her brain, and she struggled to make the words that left her mouth calm and clear. "What happened, honey?

Sandy whimpered and looked away. *If Sid did this, he'd better get his gun.* Marie went on, "Mommy won't be mad, I promise. No matter what."

She felt her daughter sob on her breast, and she strained not to sob with her. *Was Sid at work? Was he at Carmen's? What was her last name? Where did she live?*

"I'm sorry, Mommy, I just took the lipstick, and the foundation, I didn't—"

That asshole Sal, he'd know Carmen's address. Let's see how long he'll keep it secret when I stick a gun in his mouth. What was Sandy talking about?

"No, honey. Not about the makeup. I'm not mad about that. I mean, that's—First, tell me about your black eye. What happened? How did you get hurt?"

It pained her to leave the question open-ended, convinced as she was that she knew who was responsible. But she couldn't put words in the child's mouth. This was work now, and she knew not to lead a witness.

"It was Little Mikey, with his hockey stick, but it was an accident, Mommy. We were in the basement. He didn't mean it."

Sandy began to cry again, and Marie cried, too. She'd been so sure Sid had hurt her baby. She should have been relieved to learn that he was blameless. This should be banner-headline great news: *The Germans have surrendered! The Yankees won!* There was no crime here, no crisis. Just a couple of kids playing. Still, Marie began to wail, and she clutched Sandy so tightly she squirmed. Marie let her go. Sid wasn't responsible, not for this.

This was so much worse. He wasn't the one who showed Sandy how to smile and lie and cover the bruises with pretty paints. That's what Mommy had taught her. How to be a victim, how to hide the hurt.

"The bacon smells like it's ready, Mommy. Can I get it out of the pan?"

"Sure, honey."

Marie looked around the kitchen. All her things, all her efforts. She remembered putting up the wallpaper. Yellow with pink peonies. The wallpaper was what made her decide to plant peonies in the garden.

"I'll take the eggs off the fire, Mommy."

Marie had made the curtains, too. They were lacy and white. The toast popped up from the toaster, golden-brown. Even when Sandy put a plate of bacon on the table in front of her, Marie still smelled the Christmas tree from the other room. She didn't have to close her eyes to see the tinsel, the bright star on the top. She'd worked so hard to make this a real home.

"I'm glad you made eggs, Mommy. I don't know why, but I didn't feel like pancakes today. Maybe later, we can go to Aunt Vera's, so Little Mikey doesn't get in trouble? It was an accident, and he felt bad."

"That's a good idea, Sandy. We'll do that. After we eat, we'll go to Aunt Vera's. And I think we're gonna stay there a while."

After breakfast, she'd packed up her children and a few of her things. Her call to Vera was brief: "I'm leaving, this time for good." Vera knew she meant it, because Marie wasn't crying or bleeding when she arrived. Katie came later that afternoon, as soon as she found the note. Sid didn't come across the letter Marie left him for three days. When he showed up at Vera's that night, drunk and furious, he would have broken down the door if Guy hadn't answered, unmoved and unafraid.

"I'm here for my wife."

"She's under my roof now. You can't come in. She doesn't want to talk to you."

Three weeks had passed since Marie had seen Sid. They'd spoken on the phone a couple of times, but he refused to agree to a divorce, or even to leave the house: "You're the crazy one, if you expect me to see a shrink. Why do you want a divorce now, when everything's going so good? Out of nowhere, when nothing bad happened!"

From his point of view, what he said was simple as arithmetic and true as gospel. If only she'd tried to divorce him before, early and often, the marriage might have been worth saving. But since she wasn't fighting for herself—or not just for herself—she wouldn't lose her nerve. Sandy would learn no further lessons about how to lie when someone hurt her.

IT HELPED MARIE to see her enemies allied, Hollywood Sid and Macken, together in the dark. What a pair they made. The day would come when she wouldn't have to deal with either of them.

That night, Ed, Al, and Marie were out on a pattern of nighttime loft

362 THE POLICEWOMEN'S BUREAU

break-ins in the garment district. It was a Friday, and they were on duty until eleven. They had the weekend off, and no one was looking to make an arrest. When the call came over the radio—"Come in, Car 235. Are you on the air?"—Ed picked up the microphone to reply. "235, on the air."

"10-1."

"10-4."

Marie pulled over to a pay phone for Ed to check in with the office. Seconds later, he waved Marie over. It was Murtagh, who said Sid had called. "He didn't ask for you, Marie. He wanted to find out where Macken was. He didn't remember me, and I didn't remind him. Told him to call back in a few, after I raised the lieutenant on the radio. Macken's outside the Great Northern. Seems like he got a tip about something big there, and he wants his boy the Farmer to make the grab. Sid's meeting him there in fifteen minutes."

"Thanks, Vinnie. Keep this under your hat, would you?"

They spotted the lieutenant's unmarked car on the first pass down 58th Street and settled in across the street just before Sid arrived in his mint-green Falcon. Ed rustled in the seat beside her. "What do you think he's asking the idiot?

"Sid's making him an offer," said Marie. "He doesn't understand why I left him, finally. 'For no reason.' Called my babysitter last week and said he'd pay for a free trip to England if she had anything on me. I don't know what he thinks he could get."

"I do," said Al after a moment, uncomfortably. "He came to my house. Sorry, Marie, but I didn't want to upset you. Last Friday, I come home, and he's in the living room talking to my wife. Says he thinks you're running around on him with another guy, and he'll buy us a vacation to Puerto Rico, if I say who it is."

Marie turned to him, disbelieving. "And you wait this long? Damn it, Al, why didn't you tell me? Of all people—if there's anybody I depend on, it's you and Ed—"

Al glared at Ed, as if to demand that he intercede. The old Irishman patted her on the shoulder. He mumbled in preamble, "Well, the thing is—"

"Spit it out, Lennon."

"Listen, Marie, it was me who told young Al here not to bring it up, for the time being. You didn't tell us yourself until a couple of days ago. Tuesday?"

Al growled from the back. "Wednesday. Two days ago, right before we went home. No questions allowed. And yesterday, you were at court the whole day. Not for nothing, Marie, but I caught hell from my wife, wanting to know what the story was with the 'sex scandal' at work. She wanted to know what else I was hiding."

Marie was chagrined. She had no right to be angry. Al wasn't wrong about the abruptness of her announcement, or her refusal to entertain questions. How long had she imposed on them the same awful and absurd rules of not-seeing and not-saying that Sid imposed on her? "I'm sorry. I really am."

Marie had never met Al's wife. She wondered whether she should send her something—a card, candy? No, that would probably make it worse. Mrs. O'Callahan could start a club with Mrs. Marino, Police Wives Against Marie. The partners weren't much given to chatter about their families. At work, they talked about work, mostly because it consumed them, but also from some superstitious wish to keep a distance between home, sweet home, and the dirt and danger of the city streets. So too with Marie, though the streets were often sweeter for her. As it was, her private hell wasn't private anymore. She wasn't surprised Sid had approached Katie, though he had no chance of winning her over. Al was unexpected; it told of desperation. Did Sid really think he could enlist her partner in his cause? Why not Ed? When Marie looked at him, he turned away. "Son of a gun!" she shouted. "What did he offer you?"

"Easy! Easy there, Marie, you don't want them to hear you!"

They glanced outside, but Sid and the lieutenant hadn't noticed any commotion. "I'm not mad at you, Ed," she said, her voice low. "I'm mad at Sid. What was your offer? A visit to Ireland? He must have a new chippie in a travel agency."

"Actually, it was a new car. A Buick."

Now, Al was irate. He leaned forward from the back seat. "What? I get a lousy weekend in San Juan, and you get a new car?"

"I'm the senior man, and a first-grade detective."

Marie started to laugh, but then she caught herself. Was Al really angry?

"Well, I hope you insist on the latest model, with all the extras," she said. "Somehow, I don't think I'm going to be able to retire on what I get in alimony."

Al snarled from the back seat. "So, Ed, when do you pick up the car?"

"Next Friday, Al. Do you need a ride to the airport?"

Al replied brightly, "Would you mind? The flight's at six, and my wife, she always has so much luggage."

"That's no problem. The new Buicks, they have plenty of room in the trunk."

Marie shoved both of them, but she was relieved they hadn't thought her too much of an invalid to needle her. "I deserve that, I guess. But if you boys were really quick on your feet, you'd have told Sid I was having a mad, passionate affair with the lieutenant here. We wouldn't be watching them haggle. Sid would pull out his .38 and put a couple of slugs in his fat head. You could have solved all our problems."

That shut them up. For a wordless moment, they stared out the wind-shield, imagining the bloody wonder that Marie had conjured: *Pop-pop! Pop!* Instead, Sid and Macken shook hands and went back to their cars. Sid drive off. Ed sighed, and Al whistled. Maybe next time. It was almost eleven, time to go home. Marie started to pull out when the radio spoke again. "Car 235? You out there, 235?"

It was Macken. Marie looked at Ed and Al. Had Macken seen them? Of course not. He'd have confronted them if he noticed, and noticing had never been his strong suit. It was late enough for them to claim they were already back in the office and hadn't heard the radio. "What do you think?"

Al shook his head. "Don't answer. No news is good news, especially from him."

Ed disagreed. "Nah, he's been out here all night with the Farmer. Murtagh said he had a line on something good, something easy, and he wanted to keep it for himself."

Marie nodded. "And now he thinks it's gone cold. Or he's cold, and he's getting tired, and he wants to go home. This one's up to you two. I've caused enough grief for one day. We can call it a night and enjoy the week-end, or see what happens. You guys decide."

Al muttered from the back, "If those two dummies think the lead's cold, I bet it's red hot. What do you think, old man?"

"I already feel a little sunburn," said Ed, picking up the radio. "235, on the air."

"Yeah, meet me on Five-Seven, between Seven and Eight."

57th Street, between 7th and 8th Avenues. "10-4."

Macken and the Farmer stood on the sidewalk, smoking cigars and laughing. Ed put the microphone down and moaned. "What a lummox!

We're on 58th Street. Doesn't he even know where he is? Let's have a little fun."

They slipped out of the car and ducked down the block, crossing the street at the corner to double back. Al went ahead of Ed and Marie. As they approached their marks, she saw from the exhaust that Macken's car was running. Al was dressed in his usual hobo style, in a wool coat and cap. He went to the car twenty feet ahead of the lieutenant and tried the door handles—front, back, driver's side, passenger's—before he flamboyantly took out a coat hanger and made to pop the lock. When Macken and the Farmer jumped out to give chase—"Halt! Police!"—they moved like yoked oxen. Marie and Ed let them run half a block ahead. There was no chance they'd catch up to Al, but there was a risk they'd fire a shot. Ed raced ahead to steal their car, and Marie jumped in beside him as they sped down the block. They didn't slow down when they passed them, or otherwise offer any sign that they were, ostensibly, on the same side of the law. Instead, they took a leisurely lap around the block, making odd, yipping noises with the siren, as if kids had stolen it, taunting Macken to picture how he'd have to explain the theft of the cop car, keys included. The two oafs were back where they'd begun their chase when Ed and Marie found them, doubled over and winded. "Jeez, Lieutenant!" Ed yelled, as he jumped out of the stolen car. "Are you guys okay? What happened?"

Marie grabbed the Farmer by the shoulders. "Are you crazy? You left your car open, anybody could have stolen it!"

Ed went on, "Thank God we came when we did! Boy, there would have been hell to pay, if you guys had a department car stolen from you. They would have put you guys through the ringer. Some of the bosses, they got no sense, no decency."

Marie bit her lip. The Farmer gasped and spat. "Gun. He had a gun. He tried . . ."

Marie supposed that was true. Al did have a gun. The lieutenant coughed and slumped over the hood of a Cadillac as he added his testimony. "He tried to . . . tried to steal a car, right in front of us. He was fast. Looked Puerto Rican . . ."

"Well, you might as well catch your breath," said Ed, "I bet he's on the next flight back to San Juan. Cheap airfare these days, I hear. Can't beat the price. Which car? Was it one of the new Buicks? A beautiful set of wheels. Wish I had one."

Marie turned away, pretending to sneeze. She wanted to tell Ed not to push it so hard, but she couldn't. She hoped he'd take this right to the edge, and then over it.

"Thank God we got here in time!" she exclaimed.

"You know, Lieutenant, what Marie says goes double for me. That you guys are all right is the most important thing. Lucky we were in the area. Thank heaven, no harm was done. That Puerto Rican, he'll be back for another Buick, and you'll get that rascal next time. What was it you wanted us here for?"

Marie was glad it was dark, and the two buffoons were spent, mentally and physically. She kept her distance until she finished laughing. In time, the lieutenant managed to say that they had been watching a car with Florida plates that the FBI had told them about. "Those damned Feds got it wrong. They went on about big-time thieves and a big hotel job. White Cadillac with Florida plates. It's gonna happen tonight, they swore it. Some hotshots they turned out to be! They said to print the car, inside and out, if nothing happened by midnight. Call Crime Scene, they'll take care of it. You three wait here until they come."

Ed asked, "Is that the Cadillac you're leaning on now, Lieutenant?"

"Oh, yeah, well . . ."

They didn't point out that they'd need a warrant to take fingerprints from inside the car. Or that calling Crime Scene this late when no one had been murdered was a waste of a dime. Arguing with him would shift the last laugh to the wrong side of the table. Once Macken and the Farmer departed, Al strolled back to ask, "Did we kill 'em yet?"

Ed replied, "No, but the night is young."

Two hours later, a three-man crew of master thieves were in hand-cuffs. The agents hadn't been oversold the case: the Caddy's trunk was full of sample cases that salesmen at the National Retail Jewelers' Convention didn't even know were gone. A kit of burglar's tools that later went on display at the FBI Academy in Quantico was recovered, as was a collection of four hundred keys that opened every hotel room in New York City. By morning, there was a crowd of reporters at the precinct, and the stories about the collar ran on radio, TV, and in the papers. The three detectives were untouchable, beyond the reach of their doubters. To make it all the sweeter, Macken was screamed at by the captain, the inspector, and even the Chief of Detectives himself for not notifying them about the arrest.

At the end, Marie felt as if she were dreaming. For a moment she was, and she might not have opened her eyes again. By Saturday afternoon, she'd been awake for a day and a half. As the weak winter sun began to set and snow began to fall, she was driving on the Bronx River Parkway when she felt the car scrape the center median. She jerked the wheel and skidded onto the grass beside the river, making the geese scatter. She got out of the car and jumped up and down, but she still wasn't fully awake. She was almost home. Not home, but Vera's. Close enough. She took her shoes off and stepped out onto the cold ground. It hurt, but she had to keep her eyes open for the next five minutes. She pictured a newspaper story, "Lady Detective Dies in Crash," that wouldn't have merited more than a paragraph, far from the front page. That wasn't the way she wanted to go, and now wasn't the time. Her feet went numb as she danced on the frozen grass.

SIX

TONY, TONY, TURN AROUND

21 YOU'LL MISS ME WHEN I'M GONE

The Police Department does not persist with its heroes; there is not a gradual letting go. It is a quick thing, as quick as the event. One day your name is headlined, editorialized; your picture is on the front pages and on the television screens—and the next day you are on patrol. You are even, to some degree, suspect. Should you follow up a sensational arrest with another unusual incident, eyebrows are raised. . . . On the other hand, should your arrest record hit a slump, questions are raised as to whether or not you are resting on your laurels. Publicity marks you in the Department.

—Dorothy Uhnak
Policewoman

APRIL 20, 1965
0945 HOURS

"This is a new assignment for you," Lt. Horvath told Marie. "And it'll take some time for you to see how we work. For the first three months, you'll be with a veteran investigator. You won't be expected to make any arrests. You won't be allowed to, as a matter of fact. Some people here call it 'probation'—and it is—but it's also time for you to settle in and learn from your training officer."

Any other day, Marie would have laughed at him. She'd have made fun of his firm-but-fair, camp-counselor tone, as if she were a fat kid sent to the mountains for sit-ups and fresh vegetables. She'd have made fun of how he looked, but she couldn't see him, couldn't have picked him out of a lineup even as he spoke. She'd been thrown out of SLATS the day before. She'd cried when she read the teletype. And she was glad she was home when she held the paper in her shaking hands. Ed had driven to Yonkers

371

to tell her, to show her. She was so grateful to him for so many things, but that last act as partner sustained her in the days that followed. To bear bad news in person was what a partner did. When Ed arrived at her door, it felt as if he were informing her of her own death. Today, it didn't feel much different. Almost all of the Burglary Squad people—Macken included, but not Ed and Al—had been sent back to their commands. For Marie to rejoin Macken without her partners would have been more than she could have endured, but she was still in a daze when she showed up for work at the Pickpocket and Confidence Squad.

"All right, Sarge, but I've made dozens of pick collars—jostlers, seat tippers, moll buzzers. With con games, I've done Gypsy cases, pocketbook drops, Murphies, jewelry swaps. What else? Three months' probation is more than I need, but . . . well, I guess everybody has more to learn. So, who am I working with? What's his name?"

The lieutenant stopped to think, maybe. "It's no 'him.' Men don't work with ladies here. The teams are separate. But don't worry, you're assigned to Marilyn Bering. She's a first-grade detective. You really couldn't ask for any better teacher."

Marie hesitated. "You know, Sarge, I don't want to get off on the wrong foot, but last fall, there was an election with the Policewomen's Endowment Association, and I ran against her and won. I don't really know her, and I don't have anything against her, but maybe, you know, it isn't really the right match—"

"Huh, that's funny. But there can't be any hard feelings, cause she asked for you to be assigned to her. Insisted on it! I'm sure she's forgotten all about the election. Maybe if she says you're up to snuff, we can shave a little time off your probation. We'll see what she thinks."

Soon enough, it became clear that Marilyn was counting on making a slew of easy arrests for the next three months, with her partner doing all the labor. Marie suspected that her probation might be extended. The term "rented mule" occurred to her, although the pace of their labor was less than backbreaking—at least twice a week, Marilyn frequented steakhouses for lunch. She liked Sparks for the porterhouse, Keens for the mutton chop, and she always washed them down with a cocktail or three. While the check never came, and Marie never had anything stronger than ginger ale, the tip on a free meal was more than she'd spend on an honest plate of spaghetti. Finances had become a concern since the separation. She couldn't afford the cost of the high life, and she couldn't stand the company. After two weeks, she resolved to sit down with Lt. Horvath and tell him that she wouldn't work with Detective Bering another day.

It was Sid who came to her rescue, so to speak. He arranged for her transfer from Pickpocket, much as he had with Safe, Loft, and Truck, though by different means. At the beginning of February, he'd called to tell her that he was going to Florida on vacation for two weeks. She'd moved back home and changed the locks. February turned to March, and she'd dared to delude herself that the matter might be resolved in an adult manner. After all, if he thought she was cheating on him, why would he want her back? Instead, the shoe hadn't dropped because the tailor hadn't finished—Sid had promised Macken a custom-made suit to sabotage her career. If she ever ran into Macken again, Marie resolved to tell him— among other things—that he could have held out for a new car. While his opinion ordinarily carried no weight with the captain and the inspector, they'd paid attention when he told them of the separation and more. She was having affairs with any number of men, he'd said. She was even car- rying on with a young English girl who lived with her, pretending to be the nanny.

In a squad where divorce was scandalous, tales of foreign lesbian- ism would have made Ethel Rosenberg more welcome than Marie. Mrs. Rosenberg might have been a traitor, but she wasn't a tramp. The trans- fers back to the burglary squads, which had been awaiting signatures for months, went into immediate effect. Ed told her that the bosses didn't believe the stories, exactly, but they couldn't bear to think about them. She was driven out like an unclean spirit.

Marie had prepared for retaliation. She had been confiding in a police chaplain. Not a priest, but a Protestant, Reverend William Kaladjian, who had a pretty little church on Bainbridge Avenue, in the Bronx, that Katie had joined. Reverend Bill was a gruff, practical man who told Marie she should divorce Sid for her children's sake, if not her own. When Sid heard she'd been talking to Kaladjian, he demanded equal time, and he went to Bainbridge Avenue for a sit-down. Once he'd made his case to Reverend Bill, the chaplain called Marie. "You have to report this, dear. You have to protect yourself. You have to report this to the Medical Bureau. He needs psychiatric help."

"I'm sorry, Padre, I really am. I'm glad you saw through him, he's such a charmer, such a liar, that he's got everybody fooled. He—"

"No, Marie, he was pretty honest, I think. He told me that if you didn't take him back, he'd shoot you dead in the street like a dog."

Because she'd heard so many worse things, she wasn't as scared as she might have been. As she should have been. Until now, he'd kept his threats behind closed doors. For him to threaten to kill her in public, to a department chaplain, should have deafened her from all the ringing alarms. But false hopes and foolish excuses were part of her metabolism. She was like a coal miner who didn't understand why the cough didn't go away, even after quitting cigarettes.

It was Friday night when the cop from Sid's precinct called. She never caught his name. "Hey, uh, is this Marie?"

"Yes. How can I—"

"I work with Sid. He's on his way home. He's pretty heated. Said he's gonna rape you, then he's gonna break your legs. I couldn't have it on my conscience, if—"

"How long ago did he leave?"

"Maybe twenty minutes."

Marie hung up the phone. She would have thanked him, if there was time. Couldn't he have called a little sooner? What had set Sid off? Had his sergeant yelled at him for something, or did he have an argument with Carmen? It didn't matter.

There was no time to think. A parade of sorry possibilities passed through her mind. She could get her gun. She could run away. She could call the cops. She could tell Sandy and Katie to grab the baby and go out the back door. Instead, she walked around the first floor of the house and turned off the lights, except for one standing lamp beside the armchair, in the front room. She sat down and waited. Did she pray? Maybe. Not really. She didn't really pray any more than she thought about getting the gun, or calling the cops. She would stay where she was. Whatever was going to happen would happen. She couldn't win the fight by fighting, not against him. She was so tired she could have fallen asleep.

A key scratched in the door. When it didn't fit, there was a kick, and a kick, and another. And then one of the wooden panels at shoulder-level splintered, and a hand reached inside to turn the knob. Sid bellowed, "I'll kill you, you goddamn bitch!"

Marie leapt up from the chair. She was shocked, but not by the threat. There was fear in his voice; she could hear it even if he couldn't. She would never not fight back again. She was at the door before he was inside, and the standing lamp was in her hands. She smashed it over his head, and then she gouged his shoulder with the bronze prongs and broken glass. It didn't stop him, but it slowed him down. By the time the door was open, she'd picked up an end table and broken it against the side of his head. For a moment, he stood at the threshold, astonished and hurt. She read his thoughts: *How could she do this to me?* He picked a shard of glass from the shoulder of his suit. And then he looked at her as if he'd never really seen her before. He seemed impressed.

Marie was so afraid he'd smile that she spit in his face. She knew how he'd react. Every blow of his hit like a sledgehammer, and every one of hers landed like the slap of a wet rag. She didn't care. It hurt like hell.

Marie must have been screaming, but she couldn't hear herself. At some point, Katie and Sandy came down from the second floor. Sid hit her in the face, again and again. She heard the weirdly zippery sound of a handful of hair being torn from her head. The sirens came sooner than expected. Cops rushed in and pulled Sid away. When she leaned over and tried to get up, her hand slipped in the pooled blood. Something stuck in her cheek when her face hit the floor. It was like a thumbtack. When she sat up, she plucked it from her skin. Like a thorn, she thought, but it was April, too early for roses. When she wiped her eyes, she saw that it was a tooth.

A man touched her shoulder. He sounded nice enough. "Do you want to press charges, Miss?"

"No."

"Do you want to go to the hospital?"

"No."

"I think you really should, Miss."

"All right."

Marie had no reason to be anything but miserable, but she almost smiled in the ambulance. She would have, even with a mouth full of blood, until she traced the jagged edges of her broken teeth with her tongue. No, no smiling for a while. But she didn't feel as bad as she might have, as she should have, because she knew Sid would never touch her again. She wouldn't let Sandy or Katie go with her to the hospital. One of them had to stay with the baby, and they needed each other more than Marie needed them right now. She told them to call one of her sisters to meet her at St. Joseph's. Once she had her first injection for the pain, she passed the time guessing which one would be summoned. Dee? No, she was a cop. Best to keep the cops out of it, though Marie had been plenty happy to see the boys from Yonkers. Vera? No, she'd imposed on her enough already. Ann was the best choice, all around. When Ann arrived in the emergency room, Marie bawled until she got another injection.

Later on, Marie learned that Reverend Bill reported Sid to the Medical Division, which had done nothing. He'd also met with the police commissioner of Yonkers, which might have saved her life. Her home had been classified as a "sensitive location," as if it were the residence of the Israeli ambassador. The radio car responded within minutes. Sid was suspended for thirty days, and his guns were removed indefinitely, pending the results of psychiatric evaluation. Marie was given two weeks of medical leave, which she was happy to take, and then she was given another two. Once her teeth were fixed, she wasn't ashamed to go outside anymore. She wasn't in any rush to return to Marilyn, but she was starting to worry. The department surgeons were known for their ruthlessness in sending cops back to work. Even if the halt and the lame were unfit for patrol, they could always be parked somewhere to answer telephones. Their indulgence with her was troubling.

At the end of May, Marie was visited by two officers in plainclothes. Surprise visits from the Medical Division were standard practice to weed out malingerers, and the consequences for being caught—in good health, or out of the house without permission—were severe. It occurred to her that they had never come by before. Between maternity and various injuries, she'd been on leave for a year. Had they trusted her until now, or had they forgotten her? What made her suddenly special?

"Are you Policewoman Carrara?"

"I'm Detective Carrara. Who are you?"

"We're from Inspections. We need to take your gun."

"May I see the order? It would have to be from Operations, right? Or is it the First Deputy Commissioner?"

"I don't have it with me."

Marie shut the door. She didn't think they were lying, but there had to be a mistake. Even after she confirmed the order had been issued, she was sure there had been an error—someone must have mixed up "Carrara, M." with "Carrara, S."—but she had no choice but to comply. As she took the receipt, she told them, "If you were planning to stop back later on, let me save you the trouble. I'm going to be out of residence. I'm going to see your boss and find out what the hell is going on."

When Marie barged into the office of the chief surgeon, he informed her that the decision had been made for her own safety. He was long-faced and sallow, with an unlit pipe clenched in his teeth, like General MacArthur.

Marie wondered why he wore a white coat when he only examined papers. "How do you figure, Doctor?"

"Well, the man is still your husband, and he still has access to your residence."

"You've ordered him to stay away, haven't you? It's a condition of employment, isn't it?"

The department could order a police officer not to see his brother if he was a convicted felon; it could order him not to visit his mother, if the brother lived with her. It could order a man to divorce his wife if she became addicted to drugs. It generally avoided such intrusions, but it reserved every right to intrude. "Yes, of course. Regrettably, sometimes orders are disobeyed. What's to prevent him from coming back to take it, and using it on you? He has made threats, you know."

Marie had been told that Sid had continued in his previously uncommon candor with his psychiatrist: "Yep, I really will kill her, if I get the chance." If he wanted to get his hands on a gun, it wouldn't take him long. He didn't need hers. But by taking her gun, the department was making sure that the next fight would be even less fair than the past ones had been. Didn't she have a right to defend herself? Wasn't it her *job*? Marie planned to make just that point, when the doctor made another: "You can imagine how it would look for the department if he killed you with your own gun, after he threatened to do just that."

It was a good thing that Marie didn't have her gun then. *Just kidding!* No, she was fully in control when she replied, "It would be very embarrassing, I'm sure."

The department surgeon was so impressed that he actually looked at her. "Exactly! I'm glad you see the bigger picture."

"Of course. If the bullets didn't kill me, the embarrassment would."

Marie thought he'd bite off the end of his pipe. He closed her file. "To be honest, Mrs. Carrara, it's been my experience that when marriages go sour, both parties bear a certain amount of blame. I believe it's better for the department not to take sides in these matters."

Marie was readying a more politic rebuttal when the doctor surprised her again. "In a month or two, it wouldn't surprise me if you were back together, telling everyone it was all just a tempest in a teapot. After all, your husband, Serafino, his present residence is the home of your sister and her husband. Mr. and Mrs. Salvatore . . . whatever. I'm not going to look it up. I'm sure you know their names."

Marie nodded, as if what he'd said was old news. She couldn't react, knowing that her reaction would betray her. As her sister had. She felt sick. Marie doubted that Ann had volunteered to take Sid in, but she hadn't refused him, either. She hadn't taken a stand. Marie had failed to defend herself for years, but her cowardice was confined to her own cause. This was too much to swallow. She couldn't. She'd vomit all over this awful man's awful white coat, and then she might never be able to get back to work. No, now was the time to pretend that she knew, that it didn't matter. She'd talk about something else.

"Doctor, if you take my gun, you know they'll take my detective shield as well. I worked very hard to get it, and I've only had it a couple of months. To deprive me of the ability to work, to support my family, is unjust. Especially now. You can request my personnel records if you have any questions about me. I assume that the psychiatrist assigned to my husband has reviewed his. You're right that the breakup of a marriage is a tragedy for both sides, but the blame isn't equal. I worked very hard to fix my marriage, and I always kept my private life private. I'm ashamed to be here, but I have nothing to be ashamed of, as a wife or a cop."

When the doctor said he would abide by the determination of a psychiatrist as to her fitness for duty, she indulged herself in some cautious hope. Though it took several weeks to get an appointment, she was delighted when the man told her he'd recommend her restoration to full duty forthwith. A week after that, she started to get angry again. Two weeks later, when she went back to see the chief surgeon, she wasn't allowed in. She began to call him every day to demand to know what was happening. She made calls to everyone she knew—Mrs. M., the PEA and the DEA, the Columbia Association, Reverend Bill. Ed Lennon pushed every Protestant he knew, Irish and otherwise, and Casper and Murtagh pulled all the Irish and Catholic strings at their disposal. Three weeks later, she was told that she was being sent back to the psychiatrist for reevaluation. When Marie saw him, at the end of July, he was angrier than she was, and he allowed her to hear him shout on the telephone as he took out his red pen and wrote in block capitals: TO BE RESTORED TO FULL DUTY, FORTHWITH. It was lovely and touching how many people believed in her. It would have mattered so much if it mattered at all. August passed without any news.

Had Marie known she would have had the summer off, she might have been able to enjoy it. She finally asked her divorce lawyer to recommend a labor lawyer, who filed a notice of claim against the city just before

Labor Day. The next day, someone from the union called to ask where she wanted to go. Marie was ready with her answer. The Property Recovery Squad worked on identifying fences and other traffickers in high-end stolen goods, from specialized machine parts to fine art. Peg Disco, who followed Mrs. M. as head of the Policewomen's Bureau, had begun there as a third-grade detective and left as a first-grader. She told Marie that they let you alone there, that they let workers work. It would be perfect.

22 YOU ARE WHERE YOU ARE

We're here, because
We're here, because
We're here, because we're here!

> —Sung by British soldiers during the First World
> War to the tune of *Auld Lang Syne*

AUGUST 30, 1969
1930 HOURS

When Marie had been at the Missing Persons Bureau for three years, she thought of something funny. After four more years, could she be declared dead? Not that she was complaining. She complained as infrequently as she joked. She never understood why she wound up here. She'd heard she almost went to the Property Clerk, instead of Property Recovery, and whenever she was bored, she reminded herself she could be logging bags of evidence at a warehouse in Brooklyn. She'd heard that the boss at Property Recovery had blocked her arrival— "I already had a woman here! Let somebody else take a turn!" She heard that someone downtown thought he was doing her a favor, getting her a desk job. Accident or sabotage or act of God, it didn't matter. She'd long ago learned to be wary of department rumors. More than one person had asked her over the years, "Is it true you got into a shoot-out with your husband?"

This wasn't the way her career was supposed to end, she'd think, but then she'd realize that it hadn't ended. The thought neither troubled nor comforted her. Missing Persons wasn't the worst assignment. She was in the office at eight, and she was out by four. Three nights a week, she was a college student, studying poetry and sociology and art history. On balance, it wasn't the worst trade-off. She didn't love the Job anymore, and not just because it didn't love her back. She didn't need it as much as she used to, but she sometimes missed it like an old flame. *Maybe I should report it missing, ha!* Was half a life better than a double life? *Nope.* No jokes, no complaints. Those went with the old life, for worse and for better. Mostly, she was too busy for regrets.

All of them were plenty busy at Missing Persons. On average, a detective caught fifteen cases a day. Fifteen a day meant seventy-five per week, three hundred a month. They typed and typed, and they made phone calls, and then they typed more. It was unusual to go outside to look for someone. Runaway daughters and husbands usually returned home, and other wanderers could sometimes be found, leading new lives in Mexico or Miami or Greenwich Village. Other cases were closed with morgue IDs. Every morning, there was a daily tally of who had washed up on shore, or had turned up DOA in alleyways or in flophouses, or who had keeled over in movie theaters or on city buses. There were homicides, suicides, car wrecks, and ever-higher numbers of overdoses. Corpses were matched with cases, male and female, black, white, and brown, with approximate ages and weights, particularities like scars, birthmarks, or tattoos, or— *Jackpot!*—dental records, X-rays, fingerprints. The reports went into folders, and the folders went into filing cabinets, and most were never seen again.

Everyone who worked there was being taken care of, somehow. Many of the detectives were competent, but they needed the steady schedule to care for ailing wives or handicapped children; others were drinkers or bunglers who couldn't hack it in the wider cop world. There were rebels and malcontents who had stepped on someone's toes, deservedly or not, and though their abilities varied, their attitudes didn't. There were more women than in most investigative units. By and large, they weren't being punished, or put on a shelf; they were wives and mothers, drawn to the stability of the schedule. There was also a cohort of gal pals of chiefs and city councilmen who needed an assignment that entitled them to gold shields while keeping their evenings free. Marie wasn't really a cop anymore.

But she wasn't a wife, either. Life had gone on, which wasn't always such a sure bet. It was far better to be a divorcée in 1969 than it would have been ten years before. Women could get mortgages and credit cards without a man cosigning for them. The first two women sergeants, Gertrude Schimmel and Felicia Spritzer, were now Lt. Schimmel and Lt. Spritzer, and they were soon to be made captains. Not all the ladies at the DA's office were secretaries. One even prosecuted homicides, although DA Hogan asked her to obtain written permission from her husband to do so. As for Marie, she was mostly content with college and wholehearted Mama-dom. Sandy was sixteen now, Baby Jim five, and Marie cherished her time with them. She'd been sad to see Katie move on, but she'd stood in the mother-of-the-bride spot at the wedding at Reverend Bill's church on Bainbridge Avenue. Sandy was the flower girl, and Baby Jim carried the ring on a little pink pillow. Katie stayed in touch, even after she moved out west with her husband. Marie didn't hire another housekeeper. She and Sandy would look after the baby and each other. For the first time, she wasn't afraid in her own home, and she didn't have to lie about what happened there.

Marie didn't worry about Sandy. What terrified her was the world her daughter walked out into every day. The way New York was destroying itself, there could have been a Manhattan Project dedicated to the ruin of Manhattan. Mayor Lindsay had campaigned like he was the second coming of Kennedy, a bold visionary who would usher in new age. On his first day in office, a transit strike shut down the city for twelve days. "I still think it's a fun city," he said. A teachers' strike and a sanitation strike followed. In Brooklyn and the Bronx, a plague of arson left some blocks with more rubble-strewn lots and charred foundations than inhabited buildings. Corporation after corporation fled midtown for Houston, Stamford, Los Angeles. Who knew that all the new highways they built were for people to leave? There were plenty of jobs, but a million people were on welfare. Only fools ventured into parks after dark. Seven times as many robberies in four years! As he ran for reelection, Lindsay mostly talked about the war in Vietnam. He gave a city job to a man who'd gone to prison for plotting to blow up the Statue of Liberty. A onetime ally said of him that he gave good intentions a bad name.

Marie didn't understand police work anymore. The mayor didn't believe cops could do much about crime, and Commissioner Leary—an odd little man from Philadelphia who went home on weekends—didn't prove him wrong. The race issue was tied up in everything. The debate about crime seemed to be an endless shouting match between people who didn't use the word "Negro" in private and people who thought the cities deserved to burn. It was rumored that interrogations would soon be banned altogether. When a lunatic in Chicago slaughtered seven nurses, cops didn't ask the killer a single question, as they feared it would lead to his release. The Supreme Court didn't go that far when it reversed the conviction of a rapist in Arizona, but the Miranda decision still shocked the police. The rapist's confession hadn't been coerced; detectives had done what they were supposed to do, in the way they were supposed to do it. But the court decided that he should have been warned he didn't have to talk at all. The new rule only affected the by-the-book types, of course. Why a cop inclined to beat a confession out of a suspect couldn't beat him into signing a piece of paper escaped Marie. She wasn't always sorry to be on the sidelines.

The only time she was frustrated was when she was interviewed for promotion, after one of the second-grade shields became available. When the sergeant asked how many arrests she'd made in the past year, the answer wasn't difficult: none. She didn't get the promotion. That was expected. What wasn't expected was that another girl in the office got it, the mistress of a captain. Marie didn't dwell on it long. The message that life wasn't fair had come across the teletype before.

And Marie wasn't troubled by the news that a new boss would be arriving, though Lt. Stackett's reputation was grim. There was always anxiety with a change of management, but more than a few of her colleagues could use some toughening up. Whoever was used to coming in late would have to jump out of bed when they first heard the alarm; whoever favored a liquid lunch would be wise to take the pledge, for the time being. So what?

On the day before the lieutenant was due, Marie's phone rang. The voice on the other end of the line slurred, "You guys are getting Stackett, right?"

"Yeah, so I hear. Who's this?"

"Who am I? I won't say my name, but what I am, is the happiest cop on the Job. Except for everybody else who works with me. Stackett was our boss, and we're having a party."

Marie smiled. Callers to the Missing Persons Bureau were rarely this lighthearted. "Well, he's not here yet, so I don't know how I can tell him about the festivity, but—"

"Listen."

No message followed. Marie cleared her throat.

She suspected that the conversation wouldn't be as much fun from here on in. "Hmm . . . you sound nice," he said.

"Thanks, buddy. You sound nice, too. But I have to get back to work, so—"

"The party's not for him. It's against him. I mean, because he's gone. A more vicious son of a bitch, you've never met. He had two guys fired, for no reason. One of them killed himself. If there's anybody you can call to get out, call today. He's an asshole. He's an asshole's asshole. If there was a convention of assholes, you know what they'd do?"

"What?"

"They'd wait until he left the room and then they'd say, 'What's up with *him*?'"

Marie covered the mouthpiece so he wouldn't hear her laughing. The caller's sincerity was beyond dispute. "You remember Hitler? Adolf Hitler? The guy who—"

"The name rings a bell."

"Stackett is a million times worse."

Still, Marie wasn't unduly perturbed. She'd had experience with bad bosses. She doubted that the two cops who had been fired hadn't done anything at all. When the dread lieutenant landed, he looked harmless enough—he had a rabbity look, bucktoothed and jumpy-eyed. He was in his late fifties, thin and atrophied, as if his last time he broke a sweat was doing jumping jacks in the police academy in 1936. After she had worked for Stackett for a few months, she forgot about how terrible he was supposed to be. No one was happy to be called into his office, and more than a few left it, fighting tears. He wasn't fun to be around, but Marie saw no need to recall any jurors to Nuremberg, just yet. She didn't think about him much at work, and she didn't think about him at all after she left.

That changed after January of 1969, when she broke her neck. Not too badly—nothing in her life was too anything then—but a vertebra was fractured when a drunk sideswiped her car on her way into work. She wasn't in much pain, and she enjoyed the fuss the cops made—a caravan of cars escorted her to Bellevue, as if she were a fallen warrior. They strapped her down and doped her up, and when Ann appeared, Marie would have hugged her if she could. They had begun to speak again, but without much affection. Sal had told Ann that he'd throw her out if she had any complaints about Sid moving in. Marie knew what Ann must have gone through, but the hardness never wholly left her heart until that afternoon. She had changed her next-of-kin notification from Sid to Ann after the last hospital emergency, and she was glad that she'd forgotten to change it again. Sid had long since moved in with Carmen. Ann began to cry, and then Marie cried as well.

"Please, Marie, please forgive me."

"It's all right, honey. It's all right. I'm fine, I really am. I mean it."

"I'm just so sorry, I—"

"No, Ann, I'm sorry. What you did, I know . . . I know what it's like."

"Yeah."

They sat for a while, having said all they could manage. It was a comfortable silence, reassuring. Ann fussed with Marie's bedclothes, put flowers in a vase, and left the magazines she'd brought on the side table. Marie must have dozed off, though whether it was for two minutes or two hours, she didn't know. When she awoke, they talked about practicalities—Ann would stay over with Sandy and Jim. Marie didn't want the kids to visit. When Ann rose to put her coat on, Marie didn't want her to leave. "Stay if you want, Ann, I know I'm not the best company, but—"

"No, honey, I don't want to keep you all to myself. You have another visitor, and only one person's allowed in at a time."

"Really? Who's there?"

"Your boss. Lieutenant Stackett."

Once Ann withdrew, he poked his bunny face shyly in the door, as if a sudden noise might send him scampering off to the safety of the underbrush. Marie couldn't say he was a welcome sight, but she probably wasn't looking her best, either. He asked if she needed anything. She said that she didn't and thanked him for coming. He wished her a speedy recovery and quietly departed. Marie reproached herself for misjudging him.

During her months of recovery, she was obliged to revise her opinion of him again. He called every week, at first, and cards and notes began to arrive in the mail. When the phone rang, Marie would implore Sandy to answer, and to make excuses whenever she could. One afternoon, Sandy tried the Spanish accent she'd been cultivating for her school play—*West Side Story*, in which she played one of the Sharks' girlfriends. "*Alo?* Jes?"

"Uh, this is Lieutenant Stackett. Is this the Carrara household?"

"Jes."

"Ah, um, to whom am I speaking?"

"This is Consuela. I clean."

"I see. May I speak with Mrs. Carrara?"

"Ah, no, meester. The señora, she sleeping."

"I won't trouble her then. But you will let her know that I asked after her."

"*Sí*, meester. I tell Señora."

Though Consuela soon became an indispensable member of the household, Marie couldn't dodge every call. Junkies napped less than Marie was said to, and Delores Del Río spent less time in the bathtub. She was almost amused by the fuss he made; it was a distraction, a game. She hadn't noticed he'd taken to calling after three, when the kids were home, until she read this note:

Greetings and Salutations!
Your beloved daughter had some wonderful things to say about her outstanding mother. It seems to me that with the halo you are wearing there will be no need for artificial illumination once you return to the office.

Best of everything,
Joe Stackett

Subsequent missives let slip that he knew little Jim's favorite food was macaroni, and that his favorite TV program was *Kimba, the White Lion.* He commiserated with Marie over Sandy's C-plus in math and angled for an invitation to the Roosevelt High School premiere of *West Side Story,* which wasn't going to happen for several reasons. By April, when she was back at work, she recalled with nostalgia the days when she had a boss who couldn't stand the sight of her. None of the bums in the office believed her stories about his unwelcome attentions. One of the women said, "Lt. Stackett is a very religious man. I can't believe he'd do that." One of the men said, "I don't buy it. If you were a guy, I could see it. You? No."

That was aggravating. What was infuriating was the emerging consensus that Lt. Stackett wasn't as bad as all that. The same slack-jaws and seat-fillers who so dreaded the new sheriff in town were free with their pearls of craven wisdom. "I wouldn't be in such a hurry to pass judgment, Marie, if you know what I mean."

"You know what he said last week, when Smitty showed up in the morning, still cockeyed from the night before? He said, 'Let him without sin cast the first stone.' Old Joe Stackett, he ain't the worst."

"Far be it from me to tell tales out of school, Marie, but he only has nice things to say about you. I really don't think you should be badmouthing him like that."

Several of his recent decencies were meaningful. When one of the men's children was in the hospital, he was told to stay home as long as he needed; a woman whose husband died was given three weeks off. Marie was glad for the kindness, but she refused to bear the burden of his better nature alone, still less to go down the road he expected them to travel. She reminded herself that she didn't have friends in the office, let alone partners, and she'd never put much stock in their opinions. For what it was worth, it wasn't long before no one doubted Stackett's devotion to her. He made a show of taking her coat when she arrived each morning, and holding out her chair for her to sit at her desk. "You must rest, Marie! You must *husband* your strength."

The letters became more frequent. There was this one:

Det. Carrara,
Please!!! Continue to refuse the Hollywood and Broadway contracts. Our department would never recover from your loss—

And this:

Princess Marie Terese,
It is with great appreciation and a deep sense of humility we are privileged to apprise you that in recognition of your outstanding performance of duty in the Flynn case, you will be excused from all duty on Thursday, May 22, and Friday, May 23—

The letters might as well have been published in the *Daily News.* Each detective had a mailbox, an open slot in a stack of wooden shelves. Marie's was stuffed to capacity every day, and its contents became required reading. If there wasn't a mash note, there would be a coupon for twenty-five cents off a jar of Nescafé, or for a buy-one, get-one-free deal at Hamburger Heaven. There were comic strips Baby Jim might enjoy, or pages torn from magazines with pictures of fashion models or actresses, with notes disparaging their relative charms, or recommending an outfit that would be just perfect for her. *To Commissioner Marie T. Carrara, the World's Most Beautiful and Photogenic Officer.*

The office was full of lighthearted laughter, as it had never been before.

"What movie will your boyfriend take you to on Friday?"

"Is *Psycho* playing at any of the revival houses?"

"Have you met his mother yet, or is she still with the taxidermist?"

No jokes, no complaints. That was the pledge she had taken. The rest of the office hadn't signed on.

Marie couldn't get mad at Smitty when he took her aside, late one afternoon, so blotto with scotch that he was more likely to become a missing person than he ever was to find one. He was a sweet-natured, deeply damaged man, and bets were divided between whether he'd be fired in his last year before retirement, or he'd die the year after. "You know, Marie, I don't know how to say this. I don't know how to thank you, and I wouldn't, I couldn't ask . . . I never thought of us being on a team here, you know? We were all just a bunch of . . . whatevers. Now, it's good. Guys are happy, they help each other. Never saw that here before. Anyway, I know I have no right to ask, but do you think you might ever really go out with him? Because if he doesn't wind up screwing you, he's gonna screw us. He's gonna screw all of us, real bad."

Marie didn't hit him. She didn't say anything. She walked out the door and went home. It was only three o'clock. She hadn't signed out, or put in a slip for time off. Why should she? She was good old Joe's special favorite, and she couldn't get in trouble if she tried. What Smitty said saddened her. He was right about what would happen when the honeymoon was over.

Soon after, Lt. Stackett asked to take her and the children out to dinner. For a few weeks, she was able to stall him. Weeknights were out of the question because of evening classes, and then weekends were postponed because of parish events, family duties. She learned not to say that one of the kids was sick after he greeted her one morning with a bright smile and a lollipop.

"Please, give this to dear Jim. The little ones do suffer so when they're ill. Green is his favorite color, you know. I happened to be in the neighborhood yesterday—just by coincidence—and I stopped by your house. I thought maybe we could get coffee. You were out somewhere, sadly. But Jim looked fit as a fiddle, I'm delighted to say."

"Well, you know, with kids, they bounce right back."

At dinner that night, Marie warned her son about talking to strangers.

"I know, Mommy. Uncle Joe told me the same thing."

"'Uncle Joe?'"

"Who works with you. He gave me a lollipop. He's nice."

That was when Marie knew she had to put an end to it. For a moment, she thought about telling Sid, putting his crazy jealousy to use, for once. *Nope.* That was the worst idea she'd had in a while. She hadn't had any trouble from him since the divorce, but there was no guessing what would happen if she opened that door, even just a crack. Now that Marie was talking to Ann again, she knew what Sid told Sal: "Sure, I know I got screwed. Marie can be a nutty broad sometimes, but one day, she'll come to her senses, and she'll beg me to come back."

Marie sat down with the lieutenant in his office. She decided to play to his religiosity, maintaining that her divorce made any kind of relationship impossible. When he replied that he only had the noblest intentions, she was afraid she'd miscalculated. Did he only want long walks in the moonlight, holding hands, forever and ever and ever? She told him that his attentions were exposing her to ridicule, and she had to protect her reputation. He reacted angrily, demanding to know names and quotes. Marie refused to answer. His face clenched with indignation and then became ashen and still. He told her that she was dismissed for the remainder of the day. Marie took care to fill out a slip for the time off. As she left the office, Smitty stumbled in, his eyes bloodshot. He was suspended for being unfit for duty.

The lieutenant still sent Marie notes, but they were very different in nature.

Det. Carrara—
Please leave a written report on my desk listing by date and providing in detail your efforts to locate the parents, relatives, guardians, etc., of the four-year-old who is at the Children's Center. The time and date of the teletype message that was transmitted will be entered on the report.

In addition, I am interested in knowing what investigative leads you are pursuing and your plans for a solution to this case.

For your strict compliance.

Lt. Stackett,
Commanding Officer, MPB

Soon after, many of her cases were subject to similar scrutiny. Her evaluation was coming up, and her chances of promotion, however slim, would disappear altogether. She was sick at heart. Had it really come to this? It could be worse. It had been worse. And it was worse, now, for others she loved.

No jokes, no complaints. There was no complaining to Dee, at least. Marie hadn't been the only one in the family in the hospital over the winter.

Marie's broken neck was good news compared to Luigi's bone cancer. He'd dwindled to a wisp, and he was in such agony that Dee had forbidden visitors, as he was either weeping from pain or delirious from the painkillers. Marie hadn't seen him since February. Dee had arranged for the sale of the clothing store in April, when they couldn't find a second opinion, or a tenth, that offered any hope at all. The other sisters agreed that it was a mercy when poor, sweet Luigi died.

The wake would be that night, and the funeral fell on Marie's day off, so she'd be spared from having to ask the lieutenant for any favors. When she got home, she helped Sandy pick out a dress. Jim was left with a neighbor, in tears. He was too young to attend. The wake would be open casket. Marie wanted him to remember Luigi in his vitality, for all the time spent with him to soften a father's neglect. Jim was barely mollified when Marie gave him a lollipop. "Green's my favorite color," he said.

So Marie had been told. Jim wouldn't get a chance to say goodbye to either uncle he'd lost in recent days. At the funeral home, Dee set the tone of rigid dignity and controlled grief. Whenever someone sobbed, she shot them a look. If someone broke down, they were escorted to the lobby. Marie and Sandy signed the register, picked up prayer cards from the stack beside it, and took their places in line. Luigi had many friends. The room was crowded with flowers, thick with smoke. Mama and Papa were in black, as was Dee and her three children. Dee stood beside the coffin with the eldest boy, while Mama and Papa sat in the front row, beside the younger two. Vera and Ann were behind them.

When Marie and Sandy reached the coffin, they knelt and prayed, saying an Our Father and a Hail Mary. Marie drew in her breath at the sight of Luigi. His face more horrible than she'd imagined, emaciated and painted like a clown. She leaned down to kiss him goodbye. When she rose, Sandy looked frightened—*Mama, do I have to kiss him?* Marie shook her head. Sandy began to weep. Dee held her gently, briefly, and let her go. Sandy went to Mama and Papa to hug them before taking a seat beside Vera and Ann.

Marie hesitated as she offered condolences. Dee's face had changed, too. There was a coldness to her, a stillness, that made her seem more like Luigi than any of the mourners in the room. Her remove was such that Marie couldn't contain her own emotions. She embraced her and began to cry. "Sis, I'm so sorry. Luigi, he was so good. I don't, I can't . . ."

Marie could feel her sister's body recoil, but she couldn't let go. She knew that she should be offering support instead of asking for it, but she needed to hold her. Dee pushed her away gently. Her eyes were dry, and her voice was calm when she said, "Now I'm alone, like you."

Marie didn't understand. The words were clear enough, but the meaning was not. There no compliment in them, but there was no need to understand the insult right now. Marie offered a sad smile in response. "No, Dee, honey. Not like me. You have good memories. Luigi loved you, and you loved him. I was always alone."

Dee's expression didn't change. Marie touched her arm and took her seat with her daughter, her sisters, and her numberless confusions. What had Dee meant? Were they rivals in tragedy now? Maybe she'd ask, later on. Maybe not. Didn't Dee know that was how the game was played? Marie tried to keep her temper. Not for nothing, but if there was a game show called *Who's Life Is Worse?* Dee had a long way to go before she caught up. Dee was a second-grade detective, and she hadn't made any more arrests at the Brooklyn DA's Squad than Marie had at Missing Persons. She'd been accommodated and adored, at work and at home. And if you thought about it—

"Mom? How long do we have to stay?"

"Nine o'clock."

"Oh."

Marie held Sandy's hand until Ann called her over. "C'mere, Sandy, I want to ask you a couple of things. What do you think—"

When Mama turned around to shush them, Ann led Sandy out to the lobby. *Thank you, Ann!* Marie watched Dee as she met each mourner in line to accept fifteen seconds of commiseration. She could have been an usher taking tickets at the movies. Vera sidled over to Marie. "Are you okay?"

"I'm all right, Vera. Seeing Luigi, it was . . ."

"I know, I know."

Really, if you thought about it, that Dee only had seventeen beautiful years with Luigi was a sad thing. But Marie's marriage had been a disgrace, a nightmare, from the first night to the last. She coughed from the smoke. She needed fresh air.

"I have mints. Do you want one?"

"No thanks, Vera. I ought to go check on Sandy, to make sure—"

When Marie rose, Mama turned around again, and she sat back down. What an awful night this was. New grudges joined old griefs. Still, if Dee wanted to make this a fight, it would end in a knockout, not a decision.

And then Marie was ashamed of herself. Whatever bitter pills Dee needed to take or to hand out, she was entitled to them, at least for tonight. Maybe that stillness in her face was from Valium. Marie was the big sister, and she had to be better—not that it was a competition—

Vera nudged her. "Who's the lady? Isn't it your old boss? She's looking at you."

It was Mrs. M.! She nodded at Marie but remained in line, kneeling and praying before paying her respects. As she walked out, she waved for Marie to follow. Just before they reached the lobby, Mrs. M. gave her an elbow, tilting her head toward the coffin. Sid was in line, and he wasn't alone. Marie followed Mrs. M. outside. "I'm so sorry, my dear. I truly am. For your sister, but also for you. He was a wonderful man, Luigi."

"Thank you, Mrs. M. I appreciate it."

"How are you doing, Marie?"

The inquiry wasn't casual, and Marie knew better than to lie. "I've been better. I've been worse, too. For the last couple of months, I feel like I'm back at the Degenerate Squad, except the biggest degenerate is the guy in charge."

"Joe Stackett? Really?"

"Really, truly, Mrs. M. He shows up at my house. He calls my kids. Every day for months, he sent me love notes. I had to sit him down and set him straight."

"And then?"

"He's on the warpath. And he's after my scalp."

"Did you save the notes? Were they . . . graphic?"

"I have a bunch of them," Marie replied, considering. "And they're not really dirty. It's like he's a weird teenager writing in his diary. *To Miss Universe of 1969.*"

"Oh, my! Well, we have something to work with, then. What can I do?"

"Get me out."

"Where? When?"

"Anywhere. Yesterday."

"I can put you somewhere next week. It won't be what you deserve, but it will be familiar. I'll call Peg Disco. I can't say how long the Bureau will last, however."

"Oh."

"You understand me?"

"I do."

Marie would blackmail her way back to the Policewomen's Bureau, as she'd blackmailed her way out. It wasn't where she wanted to be, but she had to go somewhere. Whatever it takes, as they used to say. She kissed Mrs. M. goodbye and went back inside. The moment of elation passed. She wasn't surprised to see Sid. She wasn't afraid of him anymore. She supposed it would be nice for Sandy to see him, but she wished he hadn't brought a date. He wouldn't stay long, she knew. Marie wouldn't hide from him.

As she returned to her seat, she saw Sid leave the line to shake Papa's hand. Mama rose to embrace him. Marie wished she'd been spared the sight of that. Mama had wept bitterly at the news of the divorce. Papa had said nothing. And then the muffled hum of the mourners was broken by a wail, "My God, he was so young!"

It was Carmen, who had collapsed at the side of the casket. She was a woman of deep feeling, Marie knew well. As Sid tried to hoist her to her feet, Marie started to laugh so hard that she began to cough. She covered her mouth and turned away, knowing what she would see in each face: murder in Dee's eyes, tears in Sandy's, Ann and Vera overtaken by the same madhouse hilarity. Better to step outside, to breathe freer air. In the lobby, she drank a paper cup of water from the cooler.

Sid and Carmen appeared soon after. They held hands as they walked. When Carmen spied Marie, she dragged Sid behind like a tugboat pulling a barge. "I'm so sorry, Marie, I'm so sorry for your brother."

This wasn't the first time that Carmen had failed to apprehend the particularities of Marie's family tree, but it didn't bear correction. Marie had nothing to say to her when they were sharing Sid; now they had nothing in common at all. Carmen awaited a reply that never came. When she realized that it wouldn't, she pressed ahead. "I need you to let him go, Marie," she said solemnly.

Marie was confused. Had Sid told her they were still married? Did he expect Marie to play along, for old time's sake? She looked at Sid, who wore a sullen expression. Carmen didn't deserve a response, but Marie wanted to abbreviate this encounter rather than prolong it. "I have no idea what you are talking about. We have been divorced for years. I don't see him, and I don't want to."

"Oh, I know, and thank you. I thank you for finally giving in to the divorce. I know you are a very religious woman."

Marie glared at Sid. "It was nothing. *De nada.*"

"It's the money."

"What money?"

Sid didn't pay alimony, and she'd bought him out of his share of the house with a loan from Papa. That left the twenty-five dollars a week in child support. He wasn't always punctual, but he paid. An honest cop could afford it, so it shouldn't have been any problem for Sid. What was he telling this whore?

"For the boy, I don't think it's really right, when we're trying to start out—"

"Shut up, Carmen," Marie snapped. She knew that Carmen was about to tell her that Sid never wanted the baby, which was true, or maybe that Marie had tricked him into impregnating her. Fact or fantasy, Marie didn't care to hear it. And then she had an idea: "Sid, if you swear that you'll give up any claim you have on your son, forever, if you'll sign a statement, I have no problem with it. Let's go, let's write it up right here, right now."

Marie led him to the office of the funeral director. As it happened, the man was a notary. He offered a sheet of stationery for Marie to type out her paragraph, and then she paused. Her voice was calm when she made her proposal. "Listen, Sid, you know what the judge said about support payments. If you had one kid, you'd owe twenty bucks a month, not twelve-fifty. That's not a big difference. Think about this. You have to support Sandy for two more years, no matter what. Pay your share for her—all of it, up front, today—and we'll put an end to this. Let's call it an even two grand. You can still see Sandy, same as before. You won't have to pay another penny for my son."

Marie watched his face darken, his chest tighten. The corner of his lip rose. "That's nice of you. So, you'll still let me see her every month?"

"It's every other weekend, Sid," she replied, keeping all but the slightest hint of spite from her voice. "You just don't show up half the time."

"Unbelievable. I swear to God, Marie, I swear to God . . ."

Marie still didn't know what he meant. The funeral director took a step back. There was a letter opener on the desk, and she'd plunge it into his neck if he raised a hand to her. She guessed he couldn't fall into one of his rages while he was trying to do the math on the deal. She had done it already: a thousand dollars now, for the early buyout on Sandy, against a thousand a year, for thirteen years, for the sale of his son. It was too generous, she knew. Too good to pass up, she hoped. But if Sid signed, she'd finally be finished with him.

"I swear to God, Marie . . ."

Marie stopped typing and turned to face him. One hand remained by the letter opener. "Swear all you want. That's why we have the notary. But I'm not arguing, Sid. Take it or leave it. Do you have a check with you?"

Their eyes met one last time. Sid stared at her, waiting for her to flinch, to tremble. When she didn't, he spat on the floor and reached for his wallet. "Yeah, but wait until next Monday to cash it."

23 YOU PUT A NICKEL IN THE SLOT

"Would you tell me, please, which way I ought to go from here?"
"That depends a good deal on where you want to get to," said the
Cat.
"I don't much care where—" said Alice.
"Then it doesn't matter which way you go," said the Cat.
"—so long as I get *somewhere*," Alice added as an explanation.
"Oh, you're sure to do that," said the Cat, "if you only walk long
enough."

—Lewis Carroll
Alice's Adventures in Wonderland

SEPTEMBER 6, 1969
1115 HOURS

Marie was in her Salvation Army suit and gray wig, nursing her
third cup of coffee and growing testier by the minute. Her partner was late. Marie had been at the Automat since ten, and it
was after eleven. The new girl had made her feel ancient when they met
the day before, and Marie had decided to roll with the notions of wisdom
and arthritis in the character. Her hand still ached now and then from her
last visit here, when the rookie cop had whacked her with his nightstick
to foil a supposed kidnapping. For all she knew, he was a sergeant now, or
even a detective, God forbid. What was the world coming to? Marie was
getting old. North of forty, not that she'd admit it, not even if she was hit
with a nightstick. Outside, the crowds of Times Square thronged past, the
girls with long hair and short skirts, the men in suits without hats. She was
a different woman now, in a different city.

The Automats had become sadder, seedier in the intervening years.

For the lunch rush, they still had their share of taxpayers, but there was plenty of opportunity to make cases during the off-hours. The Depression-era policy of not rousting loiterers was as out of date as the decor: the seats once filled by able-bodied men who'd rush out on the rumor of a job now held hustlers and sad sacks killing time. Marie kept an eye out for Three-Finger Jack. She had called Ed Lennon the night before, and he'd told her that Jack remained faithful in his rounds, a pillar of constancy in a changing world. Marie and Ed hadn't talked in a while, but when they spoke, it was as if they'd just seen each other minutes before. They were on the phone for an hour.

"You sound good, Marie."

"I'm not bad, Eddie."

"Let's get together soon."

"Let's do that."

It had been years since she'd been out in the street, longer since she'd done an undercover caper. She didn't feel unready or unsteady, exactly, but she didn't feel right. If she were with Ed and Al, she'd be raring to jump back in. Her second preference would have been to work alone. *Where was the little idiot?* She shouldn't think that, she knew.

How long should Marie wait for Policewoman Millie Cooper? Until noon? Midnight? *Ticktock, ticktock.* Millie might have less time then she thought. Marie, too. As Mrs. M. had said, the days of the Policewomen's Bureau were numbered. Sooner or later—sooner, certainly—the courts or congress would end it. The opposition from the men to working in patrol cars with women was widespread and predictable, but the loudest protests came from cops' wives. If their husbands spent eight hours a day elbow to elbow with a female, the old joke about cops being closer to their partners than their spouses wouldn't be so funny anymore.

Jealousy raised the temperature, but the main claim had to do with safety. Even if a policewoman could handle herself, it was said, there were perps out there who'd see her as vulnerable, an opportunity to attack. And men would make mistakes that they wouldn't otherwise make. In a fight, some would be distracted, overprotective—chivalry wasn't dead alto-gether—while others would be tempted to show off, taking foolish risks. As assaults on city cops had soared in the last few years, Marie had some sympathy for the doubters.

For the most part, though, chivalry had nothing to do with it. In California, one chief claimed that monthly hormonal cycles made women unfit for street duty. In the Midwest, a male cop and his new female partner got into a gunfight over who would drive. Both were wounded, but both survived. The whole problem could have been avoided, Marie supposed, if the woman worked with Al O'Callahan. He'd have been delighted to have her take the wheel.

Much of the debate was old hat to Marie. She wasn't about to start pounding a beat at her age. She'd worked with Ed and Al for years without any issue. Sid didn't need a policewoman in his car to have a robust, extracurricular sex life. But she'd also heard an earful about what Ralph Marino's wife felt on the subject, and she shouldn't have been taken aback by the reaction. There were pickets outside of headquarters, with wives and kids carrying signs, when Marie rejoined the women's bureau. She remembered one: *Roses are Red, Violets are Blue, If your Daddy Wore Blue, You'd Worry, Too!* The poetry wasn't impressive, but the passion was real.

What was deflating was how many policewomen agreed with the wives. The department surveyed the three hundred-odd women about working with men on patrol. Eighteen expressed interest. Maybe Marie shouldn't have been surprised. Guarding female prisoners wasn't especially fulfilling, but most women didn't expect fulfillment from a city job. A paycheck and a pension would be just fine, thank you. Matrons worked steady shifts, with steady days off. Patrolmen rotated through days, four-to-twelves, and midnights. For women with families, it couldn't be managed. Some threatened to quit if the change came to pass. Most women worked for a living; they didn't live to work. Just like the men, mostly, as far as Marie had seen.

Marie didn't live to work anymore. The Job wasn't the refuge it once had been, but she was less in need of refuge. Still, she wanted to work like she used to, to come alive as she once had. She was good at this cop stuff, maybe better than good. She noticed things. She could read people. The costume party of undercover gigs never got old. But what she missed most were the moments when—how could she put it? She could be in hot pursuit, or watching a set, or running her mouth, but there were times when she was *doing* something, and she was what she did. She felt like her best self, and like someone else altogether.

Marie didn't say that when she met with Peg Disco. Peg had spent years undercover. In her spare time, Mrs. Disco raised five children and was a nationally ranked tennis champ. Well-rounded, you could say. But when Peg offered Marie an administrative job, she made it plain she wanted to be back in the game. The inspector was surprised, at first, and then she seemed pleased. "Anything you want, Marie. I thought I was doing you a favor, letting you put your feet up for a while."

"I appreciate it, but I did nothing but sit at Missing Persons. It's been too long. I was looking at the funny bracelets in my jewelry box the other day for the longest time, before I remembered they were handcuffs. I'd like to get back in the street."

"Good for you, Marie. And there's a new girl, who I think has a real future. I'd like you to take her out, show her how a real detective works."

"No problem, boss."

And so Marie was introduced to Millie Cooper. She seemed small, though they were more or less the same size. Pretty, with wide blue eyes and long, dark hair. She had to be at least twenty-one, didn't she? It was the wideness of the eyes, the mouth that hung slightly open, that made her seem so childish, needy, and confident that her needs would be met. She spoke in a breathy trill. "Oh, Marie, I'm so *happy* you picked *meee*, when you could have picked anyone in the office, and it was *meee*. I want to be just like you, I really do. Ohh, things are going to be *so, sooo* good!"

Millie took her by the hand as if they were about to go skipping down the street. Marie couldn't bear the Kewpie-doll act, and she was dismayed that Peg seemed to be charmed by it. Had Peg gone soft, or had Marie grown old and mean, hard of heart? Once they left Peg's office, Marie decided to be blunt. "Millie, do you really want to work with me?"

"Oh, my goodness, do I! My God, I really—"

"Then do me a favor, would you?"

"Anything! Just ask!"

"Cut the bullshit, all right?"

Millie closed her mouth. She said nothing for a moment, and her voice dropped half an octave. "Fine. But you don't have to be such a bitch about it."

Marie liked the idea that there was a toughness beneath the marsh-mallow exterior. She'd reserve judgment. How many cops had been quick to dismiss Marie as a lightweight, out of her league? Benefit of the doubt, and all that. Marie would do better by Millie, now that she had finally arrived in the Automat.

Millie wore a bright red silk kerchief tied around her hair, and large, square sunglasses of the type that Jackie Kennedy favored, but Millie seemed to be seeking the attention the First Lady sought to avoid. Still,

Marie was content that there was no mistaking her for a cop. She walked over to her and took her hand, as Millie had done to her, the day before. "Can you buy me a cup of coffee, Miss?"

Millie yanked her hand away. "Buzz off, Granny."

"That's no way to talk to your elders, Miss Cooper."

"What? Sorry, Marie, I didn't recognize you!"

"If you did, I'd buy the coffee. Now, it's on you. Let's sit down somewhere."

"My God, Marie, I'm amazed how you look, but the honest truth is, I wouldn't . . . I don't know how to say it—"

"Give it a try."

"I would never go out looking like that. Not for all the money in the world."

Marie decided to save that discussion for later. "Well, you're late, but so is Three-Finger Jack. Let's get something straight, Millie, I'm not your mother, I'm not your sister, I'm not your friend. I don't know you yet. But we're partners, so I have your back, and you have to have mine. We never worked together, so let's go slow and easy, and see what happens."

The cafeteria began to fill up for lunch. Marie drank coffee, and Millie chewed through a pack of gum. At Marie's direction, Millie didn't stick close by, but one or the other kept the spot Marie had chosen, near the front, to watch the foot traffic. Millie flirted with the manager, she insisted, to keep them from being evicted from their seats. That he was a fetching young man—an aspiring actor who'd come *this close* to a part in *Little Murders*—must have made it nicer for Millie, but she got the job done.

Marie was tired, though they hadn't really begun. She closed her eyes and didn't open them, even when she heard two men sit down beside her. One asked, "How much money do you got?"

The other responded, "I can't even count. Here, you look."

After a moment, the first announced the tally. "Nineteen. And I got a buck. So we're good for four nickels. We just gotta find a guy."

Marie opened her eyes to take a sidelong measure of the pair. Both were young and white, with curly dark hair in need of cutting. That was the extent of their likeness. The first was burly, ruddy-cheeked, six feet tall and over two hundred pounds, more muscle than fat. She'd never have made him as a doper, and she doubted he'd been using long. His eyes were too bright, his movements too sure and steady. He wore a plaid short-sleeved shirt, and there were no track marks on his arms. There was no mistaking the other as anything but. He was as tall as the first but weighed sixty pounds less. He wore a dirty brown sweater, and his coffee cup clicked against the saucer like castanets when he tried to lift it. She felt silly at how excited they made her—*Golly gee, junkies!*—but she was impatient to begin.

Once they left, Marie hustled to the door to check their direction—*Uptown on Broadway*—and collected Millie, disengaging her from conversation with the manager with some abruptness. "Did you see them, Millie? The two dopers, one obvious, the other healthy-looking, they're on the move—"

"No, sorry, I—"

"Listen, we got a couple of hot ones teamed up to score. Let's call the big guy in the plaid short sleeve 'Blue Shirt,' and the bag of bones in the brown sweater, he's 'Brown Sweater.' They'll stick together, probably, but in case they split up, I'll go with Blue Shirt because he has the money, and—"

Millie put a hand on Marie's shoulder. "I'm sorry, but I have no idea what you just said. Tell me what you want me to do, and I'll do it."

Marie took a breath. It was smart of the girl to interrupt. "Sorry. Good for you. Better to stop and ask. This is how we make the play . . ."

As Marie began to explain her plan, she saw Three-Finger Jack enter the restaurant. He could have been wearing the same mud-brown suit, the same sat-on-looking fedora as when she last saw him. He was heavier, and he hurried into the air-conditioning as if he were made of meat about to spoil. Last night, Ed told her he'd once rousted Jack on a lousy loitering charge, to check his ID and see what he had in his pockets. Five hundred dollars in his wallet, along with the business card of his lawyer, and voter registration. Independent, if he recalled correctly. Not a picture of a wife or kid, a dog or a goldfish. The address on the voter card was for a cheap hotel around the corner. No thief they'd ever collared had ever failed to find him, Sunday or Thanksgiving or New Year's. He must have been a millionaire. What did he do with his money? What did he want it for? His habit must have been as joyless as any junkie's.

Seeing him now, she almost felt sorry for him. Was it that? She remembered the endless hours on counter stools and in corner booths tailing him, trying not to eat too much, trying not to attract notice. No, she'd have gladly collared him, but she didn't want to waste her first day back waiting for him to make a mistake he'd never made before. Better to follow the fresh trail, the sure thing with the junkies. There was the new girl to consider. A pain in the neck, yes, but promising. Marie wondered if she'd be as critical if she were more at ease herself. She felt like a crotchety head-mistress handing out merits for a proper curtsy, demerits for daydreaming in class. Was she trying to improve Millie or to impress her?

Millie won a merit card for her follow-up question about how to follow the junkies. "Okay, I got you. How close should I get to them?"

"Not close. And I want you to drop back when I catch up. I'll tail them, and you tail me. Keep your distance, but keep me in sight. And take off your Red Riding Hood. It stands out."

"My what?"

"The kerchief."

"Got it."

As Millie made for the exit, Jack whistled at her, and she turned to him, smiling, before she left. *Double demerit!* Millie should be looking for perps, not compliments, least of all from the likes of him. Marie recalled how her old friend Shep sought Jack after sticking a fork in an old lady's chest. Maybe she'd stop by on her way out and have a word with him. What could be the harm? She was just an old woman, a shell of her old self. She shuffled over and smiled a cracked smile. She wasn't sure why she reached for the cuffs in her pocket. Was it superstition? Nostalgia? "Don't I know you from somewhere, young man?"

"Piss off, bitch."

What moved through her mind then couldn't be called a thought; it felt faraway and fleeting, like the passing shadow of a cloud. Her hand didn't feel like her hand as it gripped the cuffs in a fist and punched him in the jaw. The connection was solid, and Jack slumped over the side of his chair. She was about to make a scene, yelling about how he had pinched her, but no one seemed to notice or care. She walked outside. Had she really done that? Yes. Maybe later, she'd be ashamed. Now, she felt young again. The sun was warm on her face.

Marie saw Millie standing at the edge of Father Duffy Square. She hadn't taken off her red kerchief. *Demerit.* Had she lost them already? *Demerit.* Marie was about to bark at her—*Giddy up, girl!*—when she saw the junkies on a bench. *Withdrawn.* Marie took a seat behind them. For some twenty minutes, their conversation wandered no more widely than they did.

"Whaddaya think? Should we stay here? Is this good?"

"Yeah."

"How come nobody's out then?"

"I don't know. They don't check in with me."

"We might as well be in Salt Lake City for all the action going on."

"Why don't you write a letter to the mayor? I'll give you six cents for the stamp."

Marie had forgotten how dope fiends viewed the world. This was dullsville? She was sickened how Times Square had changed. The vagabond and seedy charms of the flea-circus-and-taxi-dance days had given way to an open sewer. The same forward-thinking judges who held that women could be captains of police also allowed them to be put on display rutting with strangers in mob-run hellholes. In front of her, a marquee announced, "The FILTHIEST Show in Town!" Marie had never been to Salt Lake, but she doubted it was so *SEXtacular! SEXciting!* and *SEXsational!* If she were back in the Degenerate Squad, she'd need a fleet of paddy wagons to haul off everyone she'd collar here. No, maybe not—Ed told her that the "bookstores" sold pornographic pictures of children, and there was nothing the cops could do about it. It wasn't against the law. Blue Shirt and Brown Sweater couldn't have cared less.

"Think it might be better, closer to Eighth?

"Why don't you go and have a look."

"No thanks, I'll stay right here by you, and my nineteen bucks. I wasn't born yesterday, you know."

"No kidding. New babies, they have all the blood and shit washed off them. When's the last time you did?"

Blue Shirt wasn't wrong about the stink. Marie plugged her nostrils with bits of tissue. She was glad Millie couldn't see her latest facial adornment from where she loitered at the top of the square, by the side of the statue. One man after another stopped to chat her up, and Marie laughed when three in a row did the same tap-the-wrist gesture—*My watch must have stopped, do you have the time?*

If Marie and Millie continued to work together, Marie resolved to school the girl on how to operate. The first lecture would be about being on time. But there was the business with the shorthand—Blue Shirt, Brown Sweater—that Ed had taught her, even if she wasn't talking to anyone else, because it made things easier to remember. She realized that she'd offered little more guidance that she'd been given, when she was new. There ought to be more to swimming lessons than being pushed into the pool. Still, there was something lightweight about the girl, something entitled. Was it her age, or the times?

As if to illustrate the point, three addicts meandered over to the two on the bench for a conference about local supply. Most of them bore a greater resemblance to Brown Sweater, and they didn't show much gumption, even by junkie standards. "Hey man, anything out here?"

"Nah, not that I seen. Where you been?"

"Here, waiting to see what turns up. You?"

"It's dry, man. Sahara."

"I hear there's this cat, he's always there, in a bar, 50th and Tenth."

"Come on, man, that's miles away. I dunno, you know?"

Kids these days, they wouldn't walk five blocks for their heroin. What was the matter with them? Did they expect old ladies to drop purses full of pension checks at their feet, and dealers to deliver like room service at the Plaza?

"There's gotta be something closer."

"There's gotta be."

Blue Shirt asked, "Hey, man, why you wearing that black armband?"

"Ho Chi Minh died, man."

"Get the hell out of here, you goddam Commie!"

God Bless America, Marie supposed. The three newcomers drifted off. The laziness of the two mutts behind her was rewarded, soon enough, when another young man stopped to talk. He could have been a brother of Blue Shirt—tall and well-fed, fair and wavy-haired. Had Marie seen him somewhere else, she would have pegged him as a sparring partner at Gleason's Gym instead of a gofer in the opium trade. *Gleason*. He was Gleason. "You looking?"

"Yeah."

"What you got?"

"Twenty."

"Let's see it. All right, come on."

When both men rose from the bench, Gleason objected, "What is this, a parade? One of you. Only one. You."

As Blue Shirt knew, the only reason to prefer Brown Sweater was that he couldn't put up a fight if the score turned into a scam. "Nope. If it's just one, it's me. You don't know me, and I don't know you. My pal here, he needs his rest."

There was a delay before the ruling, but Gleason was amenable. "Fine by me. Your friend looks like he's about to keel over, and I don't need the attention. The place is crawling with cops."

Marie glanced over at Millie, who was engrossed in conversation with another gent who had forgotten to wind his watch. Marie shook her head but turned back when Brown Sweater called out to the departing men, "Hurry up, Harvey, I don't feel so good."

"Don't worry, Mike."

Mike and Harvey, check. Healthy Harvey, Shaky Mike. Mike had just caught a break, although he wouldn't see it that way. Soon enough, he'd be shivering and puking through withdrawal, but he wouldn't be shivering and puking in jail. She'd go for the buyer-seller pair, Harvey and Gleason. Marie hung back as they walked uptown, right past Millie and her suitor—Marie made him as an account exec with a seven-year itch—and Gleason whistled as he passed. Millie laughed, and she held back the exec by his sleeve when he stepped up to defend her honor. Gleason spat on the sidewalk but kept moving. So far, so good.

Gleason led Harvey north on Broadway, cutting back and forth in slow diagonals, checking for surveillance. Marie looked up at the marquees: *Goodbye, Columbus* and *Sweden: Heaven and Hell.* She made her way through the toughs and the tourists, past the Brill Building and the Winter Garden, where *Mame* was playing. Gleason and Harvey stopped at 51st. She wasn't getting impatient, exactly, but she didn't know what was taking so long. Was this a dope deal or a date? And then she realized Gleason might have other concerns. A real junkie had scars to show by way of bona fides. Harvey was most likely still a skin-popper, shooting up in a thigh, a buttock, instead of mainlining a vein. He did look like a cop, in his way, as did Gleason. Would they wind up trying to arrest each other? She'd heard of collisions between undercovers on drug cases, with city cops bumping into federal cousins. At long last, Harvey and Gleason headed back downtown.

Once they reached Duffy Square again, Marie saw the red scarf. Millie hadn't taken it off. She was in the same place, gabbing away with the same man. Marie came to a halt. Millie wasn't playing stupid now; she was being stupid. Or careless, or lazy, or whatever. Marie wanted to knock her pretty teeth out. The most backward opinions of the most backward cops rang in her ears. *Why did they let these floozies on the Job?* If Peg Disco thought Marie was going to work with this useless chick again, she better think twice.

When Marie saw that another bag lady had taken her spot on the bench, she was only slightly mollified. They weren't twins; the other crone had glasses, and a battered old chapeau with a spray of violets. As Marie passed by again, she gave Millie a thump with a shoulder and hissed, "Watch where you're going, bright eyes!"

"You watch yourself, lady!"

Marie wasn't convinced Millie recognized her, but she couldn't stop to talk. Shaky Mike was within earshot, and Harvey and Gleason were almost out of sight. Marie followed them, muttering curses. On 45th Street, by Loew's State—*Bullitt, Bonnie and Clyde*—they cut left and stopped in front of a fleabag hotel. When Gleason called up, a man leaned out from a second-floor window and waved them east. Marie followed from the uptown side of the street. Just before they reached the corner, she saw Harvey hand Gleason the cash. They were at another Automat, on Sixth. Gleason went inside, and Harvey waited on the sidewalk, dancing with impatience. This was not convenient.

This Automat had always been Three-Finger Jack's next stop, after Times Square. Marie wasn't sure if following Gleason was the right play, but now she couldn't go inside. She had never done anything like slugging Jack—Was it forty minutes ago? An hour? She hadn't even been tempted. She could lose her job for what she did. Marie didn't feel guilty, exactly, even as she knew she'd done wrong. She could hardly lecture Millie about self-awareness, about self-control, if they ever spoke again. A cheap shot with a heavy hand was Sid's MO, not Marie's. Had he rubbed off on her? Two of a kind they were, or would be, a before-and-after pair, like Harvey and Mike. Like Marie and . . . Where was Millie? *Tony, Tony, turn around!* Marie was getting as edgy as Harvey, and she was just as relieved to see Gleason return.

They crossed the street and walked toward her as she sat on a drainpipe. Thoughts of Sid, Jack, and the rest of the rotten world fell away. She homed in on Harvey as closely as Harvey did on the dope. *Come to Mama.* And they did. Marie let them pass, maybe ten feet ahead. She hadn't seen the transaction yet, the exchange.

Harvey asked, "You got it? We good?"

They were good: Gleason tapped Harvey's wrist with a closed first and dropped the glassines into his open palm. Marie switched her cuffs from her right pocket to her left, so she could grab her gun. She pulled open her lapel, so her detective shield would show. She didn't look very official, but she was confident she'd make an impression. "Police!" she yelled. "Hands up, you're under arrest!"

Gleason and Harvey broke into a sprint, and Marie fired a warning shot into the pavement. They stopped short. When they turned around, their expressions were of curiosity as much as fear. *Who is this crazy lady?* If there were just one of them, Marie would have managed without any trouble. But there were two, each twice her size. Gleason looked confused, but Harvey's face twisted in fury, adrenalin flooding his bloodstream instead of heroin. He pulled out a knife and flipped it open. It had a long blade, six inches at least. "I'll take care of this bitch."

He lunged at her, and she dodged him like a matador. She shot him as he passed, and he went down on the sidewalk, spitting and shrieking, holding on to his thigh. Marie picked up the knife from the ground, and then she picked up the heroin. She leaned down, putting her knee on his back, and her gun to his head.

"You crazy bitch, you shot me!"

"Give me your hands, or I'll put another one in you."

Marie cuffed him and looked over at Gleason where he stood, stunned. She became aware of cabbies shouting, the crowds on the sidewalks, the suits and secretaries and laborers. Most ran away, but a few rushed over to see what was happening. And then Gleason ran, too, heading up Sixth. Two men, and then a third approached, and Marie yelled, "Police! Call it in! Say a policewoman's holding one, and to send an ambulance!"

"What are you—"

"What happened?"

"Why did—"

Marie didn't wait to explain. She followed Gleason uptown for two blocks and saw where he dodged inside a commercial building. It was a jewelry exchange, a maze of little shops like stalls in a bazaar. The light was dim, and Marie could barely make out the faces of the old men who poked their heads out from their stores. "Vat?"

"Vat, vat?"

"Police! I'm a policewoman! Where did he go, the man who came in here?"

Doors slammed shut as she passed each shop, gun in hand, and the shops went dark, as if a rolling blackout followed in her wake. Marie ran a lap around the first floor and then ascended to the second, where history repeated itself even as time seemed to fast-forward. Bad light; old heads; quizzical syllables in foreign accents: "Vat?"

"I'm a policewoman! Call the police! Where did he run?"

Marie didn't see who called out from one of the shops. The door was open, but the lights were off. A voice in the dark said, "He's in the toilet."

Marie didn't think the jeweler expected to be thanked. She jogged ahead until she found the restroom. "Police! Come on out, with your hands up!"

There was no response. The door opened inward. Marie wouldn't be knocked down if the man inside jumped out. She opened it, just a crack, and held it ajar with her foot, "Police! Come on out! Come out with your hands up, or I'll shoot you like I shot your friend!"

When she felt the door move, she stepped back, maintaining her aim, chest-level. "Easy now. Hands up, lemme see 'em."

Gleason had one hand up, the other on the door handle. He raised both when he was outside. He was wet with sweat, trembling, but she could see from his darting eyes that he was adding up his chances, making a plan. She had to break his concentration. She shouted, "Turn around! Against the wall! Hands against the wall!"

Marie kicked his feet apart so he was spread-eagled, off balance, and she slapped his raised hands back up when he began to lower them. She pressed her gun against his lower spine and gave him a quick pat-down. She'd check the bathroom later to see if he'd stashed anything there. Now, it didn't matter. She only cared if he had a gun, a blade on him. So far, so good. She wished she had another pair of handcuffs. A partner would have been helpful, too. *Stop*. Marie had a hand on his shoulder when she felt his muscles flex. She jammed the gun into his back.

"Don't be stupid. I know what you're thinking. You might be fast, but you're not faster than a bullet. Put your hands on your head. Walk forward."

Marie saw heads play peekaboo from the darkened shops as she marched Gleason down the hall. She felt relief at the sound of sirens outside, but she didn't relax. When they reached the heavy metal fire door at the top of the stairwell, she knew that Gleason was weighing his opportunities again. He could slam the door shut on her hand, her gun. The rhythm changed in the movement of his ribs as his breath slowed. He was getting ready to make his move.

"Stop." She grabbed his shirt and felt him recoil. It was time to make an impression on him again, to reintroduce herself. She nestled the barrel of the gun behind his right ear. "I told you to stop."

When she felt his weight shift, from one leg to the next, she kneed him at the back of his knee, knocking out the solid leg from beneath him. When he fell, she tossed her gun like a juggler, an inch in the air, and grabbed the barrel to smash him in the head with the butt. She'd never done that before. It must have looked like rodeo trick, but she wasn't showing off. It was the fastest way to change her grip. There was no anger in her when she struck him, no flicker of malice, as she'd felt with Jack. She was no more emotional than the bullets she'd just fired, and her path would be no less direct. Everything was simple. The only thing she had to do in her life was to move this man down a flight of stairs, and into the street. She flipped the gun again and put her finger on the trigger. Gleason was on the floor of the stair landing. It was better for him to stay down.

"Make your way downstairs." When he began to rise, she kicked him. "I didn't say to stand. Down on your belly."

"You can't . . . I can't go out like a snake!"

Now, it seemed as if he'd given in, given up. He sounded utterly humiliated. Marie didn't care. "Move. When we get out of the stairwell, you can get on your feet."

"I can't—"

Marie kicked him. "You can, or you'll never walk again."

Gleason half-slid, half-clambered down the stairs. When he reached the first floor, he began to stand, and Marie kicked him back down. There was another metal door, heavier than she was, and she wasn't going to be hit with it. She heard the sirens, closer now, but not close enough. If only she had another pair of handcuffs. Gleason began to cry. She didn't hear him, but she could see his chest heave, and his hands covered his face. She remembered how many times she'd lain on the ground like that, with Sid standing above her, one hand over her eyes, so she couldn't see, the other shoved in her mouth, so she wouldn't wake the baby. Not when the baby was two, not when she was twelve. Marie always tried not to cry aloud. Kids need their sleep. Marie didn't enjoy what she was doing. She had broken this man because he needed breaking.

"Please, Miss, don't make me go outside in front of everybody, crawling like an animal. Officer, Miss, please . . ."

Maybe Sid didn't enjoy what he'd done to Marie, either. Maybe he thought what he did was right and necessary—urgent, even, as if he were a doctor in the emergency room, pounding on a chest to revive a stalled heart. How much did she have to hurt Gleason? She didn't know. He lay on the floor below her, on the first and second stairs, covering his eyes like a child afraid of the dark. The woeful tone could be a con to make her lower her guard. For what it was worth, she could now rule out the possibility that Harvey and Gleason were cops. She nudged him with her foot. "What's your name?"

"Tommy."

"Tommy, take your hands from your face, and look at me. Tommy what?"

"Tommy O'Brien."

"All right, Tommy O'Brien. My name is Detective Carrara, and you're under arrest, in case you hadn't noticed."

"Yes, ma'am."

He sounded defeated, but she couldn't be sure. He might not be sure, either. She didn't want to shoot him. She hadn't wanted to shoot Harvey, but there wasn't time to talk when he came at her with a knife. She'd try to talk to Gleason—Tommy O'Brien, whoever he was. The little stairwell was crowded with aliases. Marie the old lady, the abused wife, the no-longer-young cop. Her mind was noisy with voices. She had to shut them up. "You're in a little trouble now, Tommy, I won't lie to you, but there's no need to make it any bigger than it is. So let's try and get you outside without any foolishness. I don't want to shoot you, but I will. Understand?"

"Yes, ma'am."

This was the last door before the exit. Marie didn't want to get stuck here. "Once we get out of here, you can stand up. But you're on your knees until we get into the lobby. Got it?"

Tommy O'Brien took his hands from his face, exposing the real tears that dripped sideways down his cheeks, the snot that spilled sideways from his nose. He nodded and wiped his face with his hands, his hands with his undershirt. He rose on an elbow, and then a knee, and then he was on all fours. One of his hands went up to the door, to reach for the knob. There wasn't any knob or handle; it pushed out. Marie was about to say that when he bucked and tried to mule-kick her with both feet. She jumped and shot at once. All instinct, she was all instinct, except—

Marie couldn't hear anything. When her arm was against the wall where she had landed, three steps up, she could feel all kinds of vibrations. The building hummed like a beehive. Shakes and rumbles, the slamming of doors and lowering of gates. She thought she could feel the sound of cop cars rolling down the block. She still couldn't hear. She should look down, she knew. Strands of gray matted her face, and she felt the sweat on her cheeks and brow when she brushed them away. When she looked down, she saw O'Brien motionless on the ground. This was sad. This was not how

Marie wanted this to end. She'd tried to talk to him, to avoid this. When his hand moved, she was overjoyed. And then it shoved the door open. She realized she didn't see any blood. She was glad, at first, and then he rose to his knees again, readying to break out. *Nope.* Marie jumped down on his lower back, stomping him back to the floor. She stepped onto his shoulders, flattening him. The deal was off. He would stay down until the cops came. She pushed open the door and saw everyone running. Black suits running outside, blue suits running in.

"Police! Policewoman! Here!"

Marie couldn't hear herself when she yelled. She put a foot down on O'Brien's shoulder. She holstered her gun and signaled with her right hand, holding out the shield on her lapel with her left. Could they see the gold, in this light? Two patrolmen saw her, and she waved them over— *Move faster!*—and yelled, "Cuff him up!" She couldn't hear what she said, or what they said. They looked at her, and then they looked at each other, and then one leaned down to put cuffs on O'Brien. When the perp stood, he spat at Marie, and she felt the spit catch on one of the loose tresses of her wig. That persuaded the cops that they'd arrested the right party. One of them punched O'Brien, and the other held him out, as if to offer Marie a turn, out of courtesy. She shook her head. She still couldn't hear them. It didn't really matter, she thought. This was over.

They made their way back to 45th Street, where half the cops in Manhattan seemed to have assembled. Cops and detectives and bosses, in uniforms and suits. Most seemed to be yelling, and she could feel their excited breaths buffet the air. She made out a dozen mouths shape the words, "What happened?" and "Are you okay?" When she nodded, only the first question was repeated. She pointed to her ears and shook her head. *Can't hear.* She made a trigger-pull motion with her hand and pointed to her ears again. She really was deaf, but she had to pretend muteness. She had no idea where Millie was, and she had no idea what to say about it.

Most of the men asking questions were in uniform. They were in white shirts instead of blue, with gold on their shoulders. Oak leaves, eagles, stars. Stars were the most important. Those were the questions she'd answer first, if she could hear them. And then she saw another man, a pale man in a green corduroy suit, push past the men with the stars. She tried not to smile when she saw him and pantomimed again how she couldn't hear. She took out the knife from her pocket, the four decks of heroin, and pointed to Harvey where he lay on the sidewalk, surrounded by paramedics. She handed the contraband to Lennon and said, "Buyer. Tried to stab me. Harvey. Shot him. Knife and drugs are from him. Exchange was observed, cash outside the Automat, drugs right here. Drugs from the seller, just brought out. Said his name is O'Brien."

That was all they needed to know right now. She didn't want to say anything else. No need to include the lesser characters in the cast, like Three-Finger Jack or Millie. She'd done wrong to one, and she'd been wronged by the other. Could they call it even? Ed turned to the nearest boss and translated her remarks. He seemed to be satisfied. Ed took her by the arm and led her away. She needed to sit down. She didn't even look up until she was at the door of the Automat. She didn't want to go in. Was Jack there? With all the cops around, he was likely more sensible about leaving than Marie had been about coming back. When she took her seat, she didn't see him, but she didn't look very hard.

Ed returned with several glasses of ginger ale, and she gulped them down. Her hearing was beginning to return. She tried not to shout when she told him about how Millie failed to follow her, twice. Had the nice man she'd met led her away, offering candy? Unless Millie had been run over by a taxi, there weren't many excuses Marie was willing to entertain. "Honest to God, Ed, I don't want to get anybody in trouble, but I don't care if she gets jammed up over this. She was useless. I would have been better off working alone. And—"

"Hold on, let's see what we can do. I can't think of anything she'd say that doesn't make her look bad, but we should try to get her side of the story. Let me try to get hold of her."

When Ed stepped back outside, she could see that reporters had gathered amid the throng of cops. This was a story the bosses would be eager to get out, and they'd push Marie in front of the microphones as soon as they could. The cameras, too, she realized. She pulled off the wig and dropped it on the table. It looked like an opossum, flattened on the side of the road. She supposed that she ought to fix herself up a bit. When she looked toward the restroom, she saw two young men walk out, side by side. One was ragged and pale, in a long-sleeved sweatshirt; the other was rough-looking, with a tank top and tattoos on both shoulders. The ragged man turned to the exit and said, "Thanks." Tattoo walked away and returned to the far side of the Automat. Marie shook her head. Hadn't they noticed all the cops outside? *Kids these days!* Why couldn't she have spotted this pair of junkies first? It wasn't as if she were looking for another collar, but she still had eyes in her head. Cop eyes, that didn't always see the best in people.

Marie picked up her wig and went to the restroom. She didn't have a change of clothes, but she could at least wash her face, touch up her makeup. Should she put the wig back on? It would be better for the story to model her masquerade. Maybe muggers would see tomorrow's papers and hesitate the next time they saw an old woman doddering down the street. These things mattered, they helped shape what people believed. As she combed the dead possum, she was doubly furious at Millie, knowing what could be made of the story, if it became known. Millie would become the poster girl for why women didn't belong in the police department. Marie finished with her repairs and turned away from the mirror, her stomach tight.

When she walked back out into the restaurant, she saw Ed, and they sat down again together to confer. He'd dispatched several detectives to find her erstwhile partner. He'd also bought time with the bosses. A paramedic had examined Marie's ears, he'd told them. She needed at least fifteen minutes for the ringing to subside, but that she'd soon be ready to make statements that would make them all proud. Ed and Marie nattered on about nothing in particular, as if nothing had happened this afternoon, and all the travails of the intervening years hadn't happened at all. Al had been at court that day, and Ed had been nearby, interviewing an informant. But they didn't talk about work, mostly, not nearly as much as they had in the past. "The kids, how are the they?"

"All good. Yours?"

"Can't complain. A nice summer, sad that it's over. Some great days on the boat. With the garden, I have more tomatoes than I know what to do with."

"That's because you're Irish. What kind of tomatoes, beefsteak or plum?"

"Both."

"I should come out there, show you how to make sauce, or soup, and you can freeze it, or put it in jars."

"Would you? That would be great. Saturday?"

Not long after, Millie was hauled into the Automat by two detectives. She wasn't in cuffs, but she hadn't been collected respectfully. Ed had told the men Millie had tried to impersonate a policewoman, and not to trust a thing that she said. Marie couldn't even look at her when she began her charade, lips aquiver in helpless protest: "Marie! Thank heaven you're all right! I didn't even notice when you left—"

Ed played the role of the inquisitor with unfeigned disdain. "Cut the shit. Thank heaven all you want. If Marie's all right, it's no thanks to you. Where the hell were you?"

Millie stuttered and dodged and even tried to attribute blame to Marie, because of her mastery of disguise. Marie looked at the detectives who had brought Millie in, but they'd turned away from the interrogation. It was too shameful to witness. "When she bumped into me, I didn't even recognize her! When I realized it must have been her, she was already gone. And the man I was talking to, he said he was new in town, and he didn't know how to get to the Statue of Liberty—"

"Stop," Ed said, flatly. "Don't embarrass yourself. The guy knew where he wanted to go, and so did you. As for asking directions, once all the radio cars in midtown were flying by, why didn't you try to find where they were going?"

"I didn't—"

"Why didn't you go to a call box and ask the switchboard at the precinct?"

"I couldn't—"

"Why don't you go down to Missing Persons, and file a report on yourself? Do you even know where you are, right now?"

Millie began to cry. Marie wished that her hearing hadn't come back yet. She stopped watching as Ed told Millie to get a grip on herself. "Knock off the waterworks! Nobody cares. Listen to what I tell you, if you don't want to get fired. You shouldn't say anything to anybody, but in case you have to, maybe you followed Marie as she tailed these two mutts down Broadway, then east on 45th . . ."

Marie didn't want to hear any more. She detested the thought that Millie's failings might become part of some larger argument. Millie didn't prove that females shouldn't be cops, any more than Sid, Macken, Stackett, or any number of other creeps and goons demonstrated why men shouldn't be. There were so many real-deal policewomen Marie had known—Olga Ford, Claire Faulhaber, Johanna MacFarland, Laurette Valente, Gloria O'Meara, Dorothy Uhnak. To say nothing of Peg Disco, or Mrs. M. But as Millie began to protest that it was all too much for her to remember, Marie decided to get out of earshot, before she started to have second thoughts on the subject.

Marie walked over to the vending machines. She hadn't had anything to eat for hours. What time was it now? Almost three, she saw. She fished out nickels from her purse, dropping them in slots for an egg salad sandwich, a slice of pound cake. She would have a long night ahead of her, and she was more than a little rusty on the paperwork. What did she need? Vouchers for the drugs and knife. A complaint report, for sale and possession, attempted felony assault, criminal possession of a weapon. Two arrest reports, for Harvey and Tommy. There might be other department forms that had been introduced over the years. Ed would stay to help her, she knew. There would likely be a few other familiar faces in the squad room. Maybe even Moriarty, behind the smoky mountain of cigarette butts in his ashtray. Did he still live and breathe, in spite of himself? Marie took a seat a few tables away from where Ed was schooling Millie. She'd save her indigestion for later.

Que sera, sera. The egg salad needed a little salt and pepper. A few shakes later, Marie thought the sandwich was the best thing she'd ever tasted. She was content, ready to collect herself and tell her story. And then Tattoo led another man in long sleeves toward the men's room. *Really?* Did they have to do this now, right in front of her, in front of all of them? She didn't have to do anything about it. Not long ago, her sole mission in life was to move a man down a flight of stairs; now, it was to eat an egg salad sandwich. She saw Tattoo and his customer scope out the Automat from one side of the room to the other, as if they were master spies. There were four detectives within fifteen feet, and a hundred cops outside. Marie threw a fork at the long-sleeved customer, and it hit him in the shoulder. The junkie didn't even turn around; he scratched his back, as if bitten by a flea. Marie would leave them alone. She finished her pound cake with her fingers.

Marie could picture tomorrow's headlines. And when tomorrow came, she knew she was shrewd to keep the opossum on her head. She was all over the front pages: LADY COP IN WIG SHOOTS DOPE ADDICT. *Showdown— when the little old lady pulled her gun on the dope peddlers.* TIMES SQUARE SHOOTING! *Police Tigress Shoots Dope Suspect.* Another medal, another ceremony at headquarters. Again, Marie was offered her choice of assignments. Fan mail arrived from all over the country. When she was given the *Daily News* "Hero of the Month" award, in front of a cheering crowd at Yankee Stadium, it was more than a little unreal. The half-seconds of half-catastrophe when she'd shot one man, and tried to shoot another, were recounted like a highlight from last week's game: "A great catch, that turned into a double play!" The applause sounded like surf breaking on the shore.

Marie knew the rekindled romance with the Job wouldn't last. She'd been through this before. And maybe that let her take all the more pleasure in the moment, the many moments, as they happened. She could see the stagecraft and still enjoy the show. The *Daily News* award came with a five-hundred-dollar check. Regulations forbade Marie from accepting money—at least for the picture—but Mama posed for the photos, as her proxy, and gave her the cash, later on. Marie had seen her cry before, but never from pride. Her own eyes—a cop's eyes still—stayed dry, but it warmed her heart to see Mama's old heart soften. People changed, sometimes. Later still, Marie heard that Millie had been badmouthing her, griping that the reward money hadn't been split: "Wasn't that the right thing to do? Weren't we partners? No wonder her husband left her! Did'ja hear they got in a shoot-out with each other?" Some people never changed, never learned.

But all that happened later on. Marie was finishing her pound cake when she saw the man in the pale blue summer suit amble through the revolving door. He was sweating and preoccupied, reading the *Times* folded in narrow quarters, as men did with broadsheets on crowded subways, their elbows tucked in like chicken wings. He didn't notice as two other men, slim and small of stature, took their positions, one in front of him, the other behind. Pickpockets, she made them instantly. What would they do—the Bump, Lift, and Toss? Marie wanted to take the newspaper, roll it up, and rap the mark on the nose with it. *Wake up! Pay attention!* The mark headed toward the vending machines without looking up, one hand reaching blindly into his pants pocket for nickels. Marie scanned the room for the third man, who would walk away with the wallet. There he was, on the move from the dessert section.

Seconds later, the first man stopped short, and then the mark stumbled into him—*Bump*—and the man behind crashed into him, as if he had no time to slam on the brakes. The mark turned around, his coat sweeping open as he did so—*Lift*—and then the man in front yelled at him, and then the man behind yelled, and then the third joined in—*Toss*—to yell at the first to watch where he was going. They fell into a noisy round of argument and apology, circling one another, hands in the air.

Marie closed her eyes. She didn't have time for this. But she was rested now, ready again. She'd eaten and drunk. She'd even done her hair. She began to rise from her seat before she'd decided what to do, as if her body had known before her mind. The last man to join the do-si-do was the first to break away, and he was stepping toward her. *Come to mama.* He'd have the wallet. It was as if he were asking her to dance. *Why, I'd be delighted!* It made her feel young again. Someone else could take the collar, maybe one of the pair who had scooped up Millie. It would be a little token of her thanks, these gift-wrapped pickpockets. It was too much, sometimes. Wasn't that better than too little?

There would be time to think about that, later on. Now, she had to move—

ACKNOWLEDGMENTS

The seed for this book was planted when my friend Bonnie Timmerman, a casting agent and producer, asked me about women police officers.

I owe a great deal to early readers, particularly Elizabeth Callender, Meg Burnie, Amanda Weil, and Lisa Micheli. John Lambros and Karen Duffy gave me a house to write in for weeks on end, as did Scott and Kristin Paton, and William Murray. Duff introduced me to my publisher, Jeannette Seaver, and Bill to my agent, David Granger. Thank you twice.

Amy Lippman inspired me to throw away the first fifty pages. She saved the book. Beth Canova made it much better.

My mother, Elizabeth Conlon, and Jane Driscoll provided generous explanations about what it was like to be a pregnant working mother in the 1960s. Mary Cahill was kind enough to relay obstetric information from her father, Dr. John Cahill.

And I am most grateful to Cindy and Jim Cirile for their patience as I tried to tell the story of their heroic mother, Marie.